T0364994

The Atema

THE ENLIGHTENED ONES

ROBYN ADAMS

BALBOA.PRESS

A DIVISION OF HAY HOUSE

Balboa Press books may be ordered through booksellers or by contacting:

Balboa Press
A Division of Hay House
1663 Liberty Drive
Bloomington, IN 47403
www.balboapress.com.au
AU TFN: 1 800 844 925 (Toll Free inside Australia)
AU Local: 0283 107 086 (+61 2 8310 7086 from outside Australia)

Print information available on the last page.

ISBN: 978-1-5043-2198-3 (sc)
ISBN: 978-1-5043-2201-0 (e)

Balboa Press rev. date: 10/14/2020

CONTENTS

LIST OF CHARACTERS

The Atema		Present day	
Aloma	the Princess		
Kaitewha	the Songmaster -	Judith	reincarnation of Aloma
	Aloma's consort	Philip	Judith's husband
Garlita	the High Priestess	Lynda	reincarnation of Garlita
Rahitan	the High Priest	Arthur	reincarnation of Rahitan
Morpheus	the Dream master	Veronica creator of Zuvuyaland	
Pausanin	the Master Brewer and	Vernon curator of Tauhara Centre	
	Herbalist		
Zenita	the Healer/ masseuse		
Thieron	the Scribe		
Erana	the Healer		
Annaraleah	daughter of Aloma and Kaitewha		
Haeata	son of Thieron and Erana		
Annibale	daughter of Annaraleah and Haeata		
Kelama	Aloma's grandmother		
Albinon	Chief of Matarau tribe		
Lonaki	Chief of Arakiki tribe		
Carilan	Chief of Akariri tribe		
Honehe	Chief of Gadami tribe		
Rakaheke	Chief of Waitaha tribe		
Ioannes	Chief of Levanti tribe		

This book is dedicated to the 144 Lightworkers who participated in the Time Shift Ceremony in Taupo in 1992, and to all Lightworkers who have awoken to their destiny, and all those yet to awaken.

We are travelers on a cosmic journey, stardust, swirling and dancing in the eddies and whirlpools of infinity. Life is eternal. We have stopped for a moment to encounter each other, to meet, to love, to share.
This is a precious moment. It is a little parenthesis in eternity.
Paulo Coelho

The journey between what you once were and who you are now becoming is where the dance of life really takes place.
Barbara De Angelis

PROLOGUE

Deep in the Kaimanawa Forest, 50 kilometres from Lake Taupo in the centre of the North Island of New Zealand, stands a wall. It is very ancient; made of granite cyclopean ignimbrite blocks, some with bevelled upper surfaces, and covered in moss and ferns. Above them stand other stones forming what appears to be a semicircular structure extending into the hill. It was discovered by men forging a road through the ancient forest in the 1930's. It is not a Maori site. The wall tells a great story.

A tall being of light approached the woman who sat above the wall. She was wearing a long flowing, feathery cloak. Her name she said was A-lo-ma, meaning love in their ancient language. This place was where the A-te-ma - the Enlightened Ones - came when they had completed their mundane life and were ready for the wisdom life. They were called on an inner, spiritual level, and came from many different tribes to meld as the A-te-ma to be responsible for the harmony and well-being of the land on the higher levels.

From Australia, an aboriginal Light Dreaming man who travelled with the woman who sat above the wall, introduced himself to A-lo-ma as Gudje-wa. Another tall, light being approached, who was introduced as Kai-te-wha, (the Song Master), and the spiritual partner of A-lo-ma. Gudje-wa told the couple that his mission was to travel many lands with the woman. Together they created a vortex of light to enable trapped spirit entities to ascend, so any of the A-te-ma who wished to leave this place had only to enter its spinning light. A-lo-ma said she recognised the woman as one of the A-te-ma of ancient times and welcomed her back to them.

Twenty-six thousand years before present time the immense forces of nature prevailed causing the enormous explosion that formed Lake Taupo, devastating the entire area. Everyone within a huge radius was physically killed but the A-te-ma in spirit bodies wandered disoriented for thousands of years, trying to find their home. Slowly the vegetation re-grew and they found a very small portion of their temple complex, on which we were now standing. On the hill behind and above and in the surrounding hills, the A-te-ma slowly regrouped but in a very diminished capacity. For aeons they lived thus, replaying the holograph of the time of their demise, until about four thousand years before present. Following a vibrational call, many of the original A-te-ma gathered once again in physical bodies, called to the area of their former home and temple complex which they rebuilt, although in a much lesser capacity.They lived in peace and harmony until a second eruption devastated the area of Lake Taupo nearly two thousand years ago and once again, they were annihilated, although with greater consciousness on how to survive the blast. Now as the Earth is about to undergo another transformation the A-te-ma are being called to gather once again to become the Enlightened Ones, remembering their sacred vows, until they are able to ascend, their work of assisting in the raising of consciousness on Earth completed.

Aloma sent a call out across the area for the A-te-ma to assemble and they were told what was to occur. No longer need they guard this place or be limited to the astral spirit plane but they could ascend to merge again with the universal light and the place from where they could incarnate in the physical again if that was their soul plan, or be free to merge with an already incarnate aspect of their soul group.

The vortex was activated and a long line of the A-te-ma entered to rise up. Some three hundred went, leaving A-lo-ma and Kai-te-wha and a few chosen assistants in the forest. Their choice was to travel around the North Island with the woman and her partner on a journey to assist in the awakening of all those who were to gather together again as the A-te-ma until it was time to ascend with the Earth to the universal light. The two light beings would then to remain at Zuvuyaland, for as long as they were needed to begin the process of creating a place for the Enlightened Ones, both in physical and spiritual form to come and live in peace and harmony after two thousand years.

After travelling around the North Island of New Zealand, assisting the woman in clearing thousands of trapped native spirits through the vortex, the two light beings came to the Sanctuary at the Tauhara Centre standing majestically on a hill above Lake Taupo in the centre of the North Island. In this chapel of silence and great beauty, A-lo-ma and Kai-te-wha met the Angel of Tauhara, who would instruct them in adapting to the 21st Century, to integrate and enable them to understand more fully the mindsets of those presently incarnated, and those who would be drawn to Zuvuyaland, a sacred area of land across the road from the Tauhara Centre in Taupo, so lovingly prepared by the custodian. Zuvuyaland was the place where, in July 1992, the great ceremony called Time Shift was held and 144 people from many nations participated. Thus A-lo-ma and Kai-te-wha would be able to communicate more easily with those whose destiny it was to heed the call to remember. Many people from all over the world are being called to New Zealand, Zuvuyaland and to the Wall.

This is their story........

ONE

Aloma

It came wafting on the sweet smelling spring air, hardly discernible, yet for those who were meant to hear the call, it was loud and clear. Aloma paused, lifted her head, and took a deep breath. A vibration entered her body, causing it to shake so hard she needed to sit down on a nearby log. At last, she had been chosen. The feeling was exactly as her grandmother, Kelama, had told her to expect. First the smell of perfume, followed by the vibration within the body. What had become of the expected sound? Aloma tensed as the first echoes of celestial music filled her ears. It was so enchanting yet poignant that she felt hot tears rushing to her eyes. The sound of divine remembrance entered her mind, causing her to cry with suppressed tears of longing for a more fulfilling life. For several moments she just sat, doing nothing but opening to the core of her ancient memory.

Teringa, her aging step-mother, found her lying in the clearing near the vegetable patch with a look of such bliss on her face, that the old woman shrieked. This brought the rest of the tribe running from all directions, thinking something serious had happened. Teringa, her straggly grey hair matted with mud, continued screaming like a mad woman, berating her step-daughter for wasting time and sleeping instead of working, until two old men pulled her from the scene, while two others ran to call the chief. By the time he arrived, Aloma had regained her composure. A bright light emanated from her eyes and her whole face had softened making her more radiant. She had always seemed a little different from the others in the tribe, even as a child, never playing the same games, happy to be on her own. Her step-mother, still wailing and cursing in the distance, had treated her with indifference, rarely showing love or kindness. Aloma's father Remira, had adored her, which made Teringa even more annoyed. Since her father's premature death in a hunting accident, Aloma had spent most of her time alone. Teringa had wished for a daughter she could be proud of, one who would do her bidding, and she had look after this day-dreamer who lived in her own world, communing with spirits and creatures no one else could see. Teringa, to her everlasting regret, had birthed no children of her own to Remira and she had become mean and embittered since his death. In spite of Teringa's best efforts, no husband had been found for the girl who was considered a poor match as she was not interested in the ways of ordinary women; bearing children, keeping house, and pleasing her man. Instead, Aloma spent many hours wandering in the forest, picking flowers which she wove into garlands, talking to the birds and animals, singing with the wind and lying in the sun, and dancing with the storms; her spirit free and joyous.

She was a beautiful child, with long blond hair and blue eyes, so clear that they seemed to take those who looked into them on a journey to the unknown part of their inner self. This had the most confusing effect on others of trying not to look at her, yet being magnetically drawn into her gaze. For whatever the reason, whether they felt comfortable with or afraid of this unusual girl, the people knew her to be a gift to their village, and each family took turns in caring for her, often to their benefit, as Teringa had relinquished that responsibility following the death of Remira when the girl was twelve years old. This was the time she should have been coming into womanhood, yet showed no indications of physically doing so. She already had the mind of one who knew the wisdom of the forest and its wild things. How or where she obtained this knowledge no one knew, but whenever an animal was sick, or crops began to fail, Aloma would be fetched. No one, not even the wise village healer, could match her skill or speed in healing.

During her late adolescent years, Aloma began to develop the body of a woman; tall, with well-formed breasts, smooth skin, and piercing eyes that flashed at untruth, unkindness or lack of love in others. Unable to help themselves, although their mothers strictly forbade it, many of the young men in the village wished to marry her, for she was exciting and different compared with the other girls her age. They knew she would always demand her freedom to be an individual, but that did not matter if life was full of laughter and love. But no man had the courage to step forward to claim her as his partner. The young women of the village were threatened by her presence, keeping their distance or being openly rude and cruel.

Her only friend had been her grandmother, Kelama, until she disappeared one day leaving Aloma, then aged eleven, heartbroken and alone. Teringa had roughly tried to explain that Kelama had the call, but could not elaborate. Kelama was the mother of Remira, who had partnered Teringa when Aloma was a baby, against his mother's wishes in the desire to give Aloma motherly guidance. The girl felt of her grandmother's blood but not her Teringa's. Kelama had explained one day that she was not of Teringa's womb, but was the daughter of Remira's first wife, a gentle woman with a great love of the natural world. Being of an open heart, when her son's wife died birthing her, Kelama had brought her up as her own until Remira had taken Teringa as his second wife. That was a relief and comfort to Aloma, who understood how certain energy and knowledge was passed through the line of blood.

No one could explain the call. It was something that drifted on the wind, being only known to those for whom it was destined. It usually arrived when a man or woman was around forty years of age. This was deemed the time when their ordinary village life was over, when their children were grown with partners and children of their own, when the cares of life were no longer the same as in the mundane days. Occasionally the call came earlier, to those like Aloma who were not interested in being partnered or bearing children. A tribe was usually pleased when the call came to one of their members. Now it had come to Aloma, although she was only twenty summers. This was considered by the elders to be exceptional as they gathered around the glowing young woman who both bewitched and frightened them, initially expressing their concern and giving their blessing. The signs were unmistakable. A trance-like state, the speaking in strange tongues, the rolling of the eyes through which light poured, the change in the energy field. Yes, her call had come. They would allow her to go to the place, unknown to those living on the ordinary level, where she would spend the rest of her days. All that was known or guessed at, was that it was a place of great teaching and harmony. It's location was a well kept secret, for none who entered the sacred area unbidden ever returned.

The villagers gave her a great leave taking ceremony and feasted far into the night. The next morning a party of warriors escorted her along the track to the edge of the forbidding forest in which lived the ones to whom Aloma had been called. Its name was Kaimanawa, the place where the heart is sustained by love. She was not sorry that she would never see the villagers again. Shouldering her few possessions in a woven grass bag, she waved and gaily set off down a faint track that led into the forest. She had only taken three steps when she disappeared entirely from the warriors' sight. They were afraid and preparing to run when she reappeared, laughing.

"Why are warriors so brave in battle so afraid of a little magic?" she said. "Does not one brave man have the courage to follow me to see where I walk? Nobility of spirit is a long way from your blood stained hearts."

As one they turned and fled back to the safety of the village and their known world. The last thing they heard was Aloma's tinkling laugh, mocking them. Soon she could be heard singing for the pure joy of being alive as she felt an invisible energy pulling her unerringly deeper into the forest.

TWO

The Big Bang

It was a day of great excitement in the Crystalline temple complex of the Atema. The day when *She* would come dawned clear and fresh. The central crystal had been vibrating more intensely each day since the last full moon and the sense of anticipation mounted. The older Enlightened Ones in the temple, those who had dwelt there for what appeared to be centuries, kept smiling and when asked what was happening, just nodded sagely saying, "Soon She will come, our long lost Princess".

Searching through the temple archives one day, a young scribe called Thieron, chanced upon a scroll of thinly beaten gold rolled around two rods of polished obsidian. It was wrapped in a soft tanned bird skin with the feathers still attached. Although the protective covering seemed very old, the contents were bright and clear. With trembling hands, Thieron eased the scroll from its hiding place which he found behind a carefully concealed loose stone block at the back of a storage shelf in a niche hidden in the stone wall of the ancient library. Scholars had used the library since ancient times but the scroll had kept its secret. As he gently unrolled it, Thieron fell into a trance and saw himself as a young scribe taking notes from an imposing looking man with a long white beard and piercing blue eyes that beamed love and compassion, but also wisdom and strength.

He recognised the man as Rahitan, his present Master. Rahitan was worried, the lines in his brow deeply creased.

"Thieron, my boy," he confided. "Something is afoot. The great mountain God Tane has been talking to me. He says the volcanic force can no longer be held in check and is set to explode very soon."

Thieron looked up from the sheet of woven flax on which he had been sketching. "What did you say? Explode?" he stuttered.

"Yes," murmured Rahitan. "I have kept quiet until now as I did not wish to alarm the others and especially those newly arrived, but now I must speak. Go to the High Priestess and ask that she assemble everyone in the temple courtyard. Then return to me."

Thieron ran from his Master's room to tell Garlita, the High Priestess of the Atema, to summon the people. Soon the temple bell, carved from a huge quartz crystal, began to send its melodious vibration reverberating around the complex. This was no ordinary bell with a clapper making a noise by striking the body of the bell, but rather, one activated by Garlita's mind. As High Priestess only she knew how to activate its penetrating sound. One initiation test of a High Priestess of the Atema was the ability to vibrate the bell. Failure to do so meant the candidate could never become a High Priestess. To over-stimulate the bell could shatter it. On the rare occasions that Garlita was required to vibrate the bell, she did so with trepidation as it was only used in the direst emergency as in this instance, or, pitched to a higher vibration to call those who were destined to join the Atema, the Enlightened Ones.

Thieron's dream continued as he saw people drop what they were doing and race to the courtyard, responding to the call of the bell. Rahitan appeared looking very solemn as a buzz of consternation flowed through those gathered. Mounting a three-stepped dais in the centre of the courtyard, he held up his hands for silence.

"My dear friends." He spoke slowly and distinctly. "I have some dreadful news. Tane, the great God of the Light and the Mountains has been talking to me for the past few days. He tells us to prepare for the end of our world as we know it. He says there will be a massive explosion not far from our temple that will blow our world into oblivion. He asks us to either flee to safety or to prepare ourselves for the eternal life."

Even though the crowd began to murmur it remained calm. Rahitan paused and looked with love and tears in his eyes at his friends. His voice faltered before saying, "We have work to do. Our world will end in three days. Those who want to leave and return to their village may do so. The rest of us will leave this world together. Tane says he has held the powers back for a long time but now can no longer do so."

Rahitan drew himself up to his full dignity, his long white beard sparkling with tear drops, and continued. "It has nothing to do with our lack of love or service towards him. It is just a fact of the natural and unstable forces of this land that will forever remould themselves to match the consciousness of its inhabitants. Unfortunately negative forces run rampant outside our hidden complex."

He gazed at the expectant faces below him saying, "As our own temple and village will be obliterated, we must leave signs for those who come after us in far off times. If any of us are incarnate again when the land reveals her secrets we will recognise the area and know where to search. We will prepare a new golden scroll, a statue, an etheric imprint into rocks, or a gift of projected love. What we deem most fitting to be found down through time when the energies of our world are once again of an appropriate vibration. Be creative and honour yourselves, my dear friends. We will meet here in on the morrow to prepare ourselves." Beckoning Thieron to follow, the holy man hurried down the steps and back to the library.

Golden scrolls were rarely used. Scribes had heard of their existence but few had seen or read one. They were part of the heritage of the eternal mystery that was whispered to have come from the stars, brought by the original inhabitants of Earth.

"Now, Thieron my boy, pay attention. This will be our greatest test in this life," said Rahitan.

The old mystic pulled aside a heavy linen curtain, woven from the flax plants which grew abundantly in the forest, to reveal several shelves stacked with very old books bound in a dull metallic substance. These were never to be touched by scribes, Thieron had once been informed emphatically by the head librarian. Reverently Rahitan placed them on the floor.

"Now watch," ordered Rahitan. Counting seven blocks up the wall, he stopped and rubbed a worn symbol of an encircled equal sided cross etched on a stone three times with a widdershins motion. A light whirring noise made Thieron jump back as the stone block shot out of its snug bed. Rahitan took a lamp made from a shining crystal globe from a niche in the wall and peered through the large hole that had been revealed.

"Ah!" He sighed with satisfaction. "Still there. Good. Look through the hole, my boy."

Thieron took the globe and put his face in the hole. The light reflected the glint of gold and shining colours. A slight musty odour tinged with the smell of kauri resin drifted from the cavern behind the library wall.

"What are they?" he whispered in awe.

"That, Thieron, is our story," beamed Rahitan.

Reaching through the hole towards his right, he felt for the knob he knew would open the hidden door into the chamber of records. Although unused for decades, the heavy stone door, built to look like apart of the wall, glided smoothly open.

"In you go," said Rahitan, barely able to conceal his joy. "Our destruction will be our liberation."

Rahitan touched a button on the low vaulted ceiling of the chamber of records and instantly a bright light filled the space, its fingers probing the long dark recesses, sliding under shelves and into cabinets, waking the room from its long sleep.

"Now, let's get to work," he said as he pushed another button. The stone door swung closed as Thieron anxiously looked around. "Don't want to be disturbed by nosy parkers now do we? Stand before me and look into my eyes." The command was unexpcted and the young scribe jumped in front of his Master. "This is the most important thing I will ever tell you, so listen well and let the words burn into your memory." So saying, Rahitan picked up a rod of pure gold with a lustrous golden pearl fixed to its tip and lightly touched his young acolyte on his forehead between his eyes. Instantly, a light exploded in his head knocking him over.

Suddenly the dream ended and the young man awoke in fright, clasping his arms and legs to find out if he was still in one piece. He was sure he had exploded in light. Relieved, he tried to re-enter his dream, to return to the dream time when he was previously called Thieron. It meant dispenser of Truth. He sensed the urgency of his Master and tried desperately to recall what he had been told. Had he ever known what the most important thing was? Try as he might, Thieron could not recall the message, so he rose from his pallet, pulled on his rough woollen russet gown, splashed cold water on his face to clear his heavy head, and went to find Morpheus, the dream master.

"Ah, Thieron, come in, I was expecting you," said a voice from deep in the darkened room.

Caught off guard, Thieron pushed a heavy curtain aside and entered in to the world of the interpreter of dreams who often interpreted the nightly dreams of the Atema.

"You have dreamed of the Master Rahitan, and you wish me to help you uncover his message from the dusty recesses of your small but growing mind. Is that not so? Mmm?" purred the dream master.

"How did you know?" gasped an astonished Thieron.

"Ah! my young friend, it is my job," was all Morpheus would say. "Now lie on that couch over there and close your eyes. I'll help you reclaim your memory."

Thieron did as he was told and lay down. Morpheus sat beside him on a small stool, took his hand, and began to sing softly. Thieron didn't recognise the words, for they were of the old language. He felt himself relaxing, falling, flying, then floating in a ball of bright light. Suddenly he was back in the secret room of the golden scrolls with Rahitan.

"Welcome back. You left rather suddenly. Now, sit at that desk and write what I dictate," he ordered.

Thieron saw a thin sheet of beaten gold lying neatly across the wooden desk He picked up a stylus of hard material, and breathed deeply, focussing his concentration. He felt strange, alive and tingling yet expanded in his body as though it was two sizes too small. Rahitan started pacing up and down the room with his hands clasped behind his back as a blue light began to emanate from him.

"Write," he commanded. Nervously Thieron held the stylus tightly and puckered his mouth, his tongue protruding slightly.

"In the third epoch of the 10th circuit of the heavens around the great central sun, I, Rahitan, the High Priest of the Atema, write the next chapter of our story. Soon our temple, our village, our people from many tribes who form the Atema, the Enlightened Ones, and a great area of our unique land as we now know it will cease to exist. Tane, the Great God of Light and of the Mountain, has held back this day for a long time, but can no longer be permitted to do so. The land around us will burst forth with great force and then subside, causing the largest conflagration ever known on this jewel of a planet since the human form gained its soul and began the great experiment now being played out through the ages. Many times humankind has risen and fallen. Earlier scrolls tell of reasons; sometimes through its own wrong doing or stellar mistakes beyond its control, and at other times, through the immense power of the natural forces also at play on this planet."

"Where our village now stands, a great and bottomless lake will appear. This will form part of a vast landscape temple to be built by those who know the Universal plan. The great and powerful forces whom we call Nature, and Papatuanuku, the Earth Mother, will assist these beings in shaping the features of the land. Mountains rise and fall, lakes appear and drain, seas cover land or reveal it, continents drift across the surface of the Earth. Great forces of the volcano Gods run rampant with none to stop their rapacious hunger. Even we, the Atema, whose sacred role it is to bring harmony and balance to all the tribes living in this stingray shaped island of plenty, beauty and peace, are powerless to prevent what is about to happen.

We can prepare ourselves by knowing it is not the end but only a ripple in time as our old and comfortable way of life on the physical plane ceases to exist. Soon I will go to prepare the Atema to stand firm, to survive the apocalypse, and tell them how to regather in our spiritual bodies. They will them have the choice of departing to a safe place or after the explosion, remaining as a member of the Atema in the higher dimensions of the many levels of reality, or rising to the level of reallocation to continue their soul destiny on Earth. Each

12

is free to choose. This scroll is to be added to those which tell our story since before we began to incarnate on Earth. We were called from many corners of the great universe by Io, the One Creator, to volunteer for a great work, as co-creators of The Light and The Love which binds all universes together. Our destiny is to keep that flame alive throughout the epochs until the end time."

As Rahitan was talking, his voice assumed great power that flowed into Thieron and into the words being inscribed. The luminous blue light intensified until it filled the room and surrounded the sheet of gold. The air felt electric as if a great burst of lightning was about to strike, and the hair on the young scribe's arms and head stood erect. Crackling noises could be heard from their clothes and the room seemed to be beyond time and the awful threat of destruction that loomed over them.

Rahitan stood still, then audibly breathed out, releasing the force that had overlighted him. The words were written in Thieron's neat script, set down for a future time. Shaking his head as if to clear his mind, the old Master looked deeply into his pupil's eyes and said, "I am with you always. You only have to remember and call."

Tears welled in Thieron's large brown eyes and he roughly brushed them away with the long sleeve of his russet coloured shirt. They left a dark, wet stain.

"I have something to show you, my boy," boomed Rahitan, quite back to his old self. "Roll up the gold scroll in the way I showed you. The obsidian rods have been prepared. They are on the ledge under the desk. That obsidian comes from the smoking island towards the rising sun. It is the result of sand being heated to great temperature by the fiery power of Nature."

Carefully, Thieron pulled out the two shafts and finding the slit running along the side, inserted one end of the thin gold sheet firmly in one, attaching it with golden pins inserted into tiny holes. He repeated the procedure with the second shaft and then rolled the sheet of gold neatly around one rod and secured the other with a plaited gold tie. He then took a softly tanned skin holding the feathers of a flightless bird sacred to the Atema, and wrapped it around the scroll.

Satisfied, Rahitan smiled, saying, "Now I have a gift for you. You will be allowed to hear our story. There are twelve large golden scrolls stored in this room, one for each of the circuits we traverse and twelve smaller ones depicting the epochs. Each has rods of a different coloured stone, denoting the circuit. The first one is of rose quartz for the gift of love bestowed by the Creator of all worlds on those who volunteered for this task on Earth. It tells where we came from, names each of us by our eternal name, not the one earthly given when we incarnate. The Creator knows and loves each of us dearly, although we often forget that love. Our eternal name is more of a vibration than a word and when we remember it we awaken once more to our divine role. Alas, in some of our earthly lives, we are under a total veil of forgetfulness for our entire life and never awaken to the glory of who we truly are.

There were one hundred and forty-four thousand souls from across the Universe who volunteered aeons ago for this great experiment on Earth, and in the epochs to come, as the great zodiac turns through the ages around the central sun, many of us will fall into a deep, deep slumber. In this scroll it is written that if that happens we have all been programmed to awaken to various stimuli. This happens at the end of this circuit as the Zodiac moves once again into the position we are now entering, the sign of Aquarius, the sign of universal peace and humanness, some twenty-five thousand years hence. Our galaxy is about to enter a band of light that will change the way we perceive life. For many, the awakening will be very painful, for others full of joy once they remember their heavenly role. But all one hundred and forty-four thousand, along with many millions more, must awaken to their true destiny for the end of this era to be completed to the cosmic plan specifications. At that time there will be vast hordes of humans on the Earth; and they will have reached plague proportions in some lands. In this land we now inhabit, the numbers will be kept to a manageable level although there will be vast numbers of an animal yet unknown to us. It will have a very small brain and be used by humans for meat and warm clothing and will have a round and woolly appearance.

The second scroll has rods of a very rare and precious metal that landed on Earth and was a gift from the stars in the form of a meteorite. It has many colours flowing through it, sometimes fixed, sometimes fluid, depending on the consciousness prevailing when it is being read."

Rahitan bent down to extract the second scroll from its metal case. "This case is time proof. What do you see, master scribe?" He held the scroll to the light and Thieron gasped in admiration. As the light played on the shafts they seemed to burst into rainbow colours that danced around the room like a fairy released from long imprisonment in a dungeon. Then suddenly, the light faded and went out. The colour drained from Rahitan's face and he whispered, "It is upon us. That is why we must make the transition."

Puzzled, Thieron said, "What could be so awful to make the lights die?"

"Consciousness, or lack of it in the world," croaked his Master. "I suspected this, but didn't wish to know how low it had sunk in our land of peace, or in the rest of the world. We, the Atema, are weakening and can no longer hold the world in balance. Now I know we are in for a long, long sleep. We will regroup again for four thousand years but the ninth scroll tells of a time when the Atema will once again be obliterated by a great explosion under the lake that formed during the conflagration about to occur, in the first epoch of the eleventh circuit at the beginning of the next age of Pisces, when world consciousness has reached an all time low. It tells of a great Master, a son of God, incarnated into this world to lift the veil of forgetfulness from humankind but who would be crucified on a wooden cross for his efforts. At that time he visited every land on earth in some form or other, even this island so far from the main centre of population. Those brown people who will one day inhabit this land will have a legend about that visit, while those with a white skin who come after them will not take much credence in their story, for in their sacred book, they will have their own version. They also have books called his-story, written by men who won wars or explored the forgotten worlds, claiming discovery."

Thieron's was totally captivated as Rahitan smiled, rolled up the scroll and placed it back in its container.

"When our distant ancestors came from the stars they also brought our story written on these scrolls, kept safe through the ages. In other lands, a tribe similar to ours exists, Enlightened Ones who have faithfully kept the knowledge inscribed on similar scrolls hidden in their temples. There are twelve tribes and each has a set of scrolls. Some sets are active, while some may be lost forever or for many epochs until the time is right for them to be found by those who can decipher them. If they are found by men of superstitious minds steeped in fanaticism, all the precious knowledge could be destroyed. However, that won't happen, as the scrolls tell us how to return to our home among the stars, where the stargates are hidden, and how to activate them. Personally, I think we will return in the manner we arrived; as pure consciousness, focussing our minds to create a vehicle of light that will transport us safely to our destination. We will then spend a circuit in the heart of the Creator having a well earned rest after so many, many epochs on the front line. At the end we will be very soul weary." Tears began to trickle down the grooved, time worn face of the old sage as he looked far in to the future of the land.

Thieron tried to comfort Rahitan as he lamented, "How will we sustain ourselves when the sustenance ceases?" This was an awful moment, to see his Master in such distress, but Rahitan composed himself and continued, "The other scrolls tell of ages of evolution, but there is no time to read them now. We have to ensure that they survive the immanent destruction of the temple. We can place a symbolic copy of each scroll in the etheric grid that encircles the planet which may be retrieved by any of the Atema who awaken in any circuit, to remind them not to lose faith and that all is going to plan. And what a plan it is. When we volunteered for this mission, we were not told that we would get amnesia and forget our source of light and love. Occasionally, we will awaken and be reminded of who we are. The Atema in this sector have been allotted with the task of keeping the plan consciously alive, although I don't know what will happen after the explosion. The scroll says we will sleep for a long time, nearly twenty thousand years, until we begin to awaken, only to be annihilated some four thousand years later for nearly another two thousand years. The scroll says we can not get too far ahead of the rest of humankind, so we have to mark time, hold the dream of the plan and be ready to disseminate it in a pure form at the beginning of the next Aquarian Age. Just as well time doesn't exist in the interdimensional world, eh, young man!"

Thieron mumbled under his breath, "My head is about to burst" which sounded to Rahitan like, "I have a great thirst," which he took to mean for knowledge.

"No more now. We have to make sure the story of this world survives so we will leave the scroll you have just written outside the room. This will lead whosoever finds it in future to the others that are hidden behind it and tell them how to open the door. Pray that some of our temple complex survives the eruption. However, just to be on the safe side, we will send another copy of the scrolls to the Northland, where the volcanic eruption won't destroy the land. I will give directions to those who volunteer for the task. Remember well, young Thieron, for it may very likely be up to you."

Back in Morpheus's room, Thieron slowly rubbed his eyes and sat up. It took some time for him to remember where he was. The dream master was smiling in a satisfied way. Thieron leapt up and tried to run from the room but the dream master restrained him. "Not so fast, young man. Soon we'll have to find the rest of the scrolls and warn the others that perhaps our world is once again about to be blown to smithereens. It was so inconvenient last time. I was just getting the hang of being in a human body again and then....poof; my physical and etheric bodies blown all over the land. Had a ghastly time trying to piece myself back together." Morpheus stood up and released the young scribe. "As Rahitan says, we will have to wait for the Princess to arrive. She should be here soon. I wonder if she has already remembered who she is?"

"The Princess?" questioned Thieron. "Who is the Princess?"

"Princess Aloma. Don't you remember her? Even though you tried to keep it a secret everyone knew how much you loved her and how brave she was just before our world was torn apart last time. Well, now she is coming among us again. She is truly a gift from Io and we have missed her greatly. Somehow her presence in the temple enhanced the life of even the most enlightened of us, so it's a shame that she won't have very long with us before our world explodes again. Do you want to see what occurred just prior to the big bang?"

Thieron relaxed back on the couch and closed his eyes. Morpheus touched him lightly on his forehead. He felt himself drifting back through time and saw the Earth changing; wars being fought, people loving each other, great volcanoes spewing forth the contents of the Earth's stomach and then being covered in ice. He saw trees where there was once ice and glaciers where once tall forests had majestically surveyed their domain. Great civilisations rose and fell, pyramids were built, mankind's destiny ebbed and flowed, reaching a very critical point when a war in heaven smashed the firmament protecting the Earth, causing the great floods that all but annihilated humankind. Great icy glaciers melted and rain fell in torrents from the skies, covering the land, until only the tops of the highest mountains were visible.

Thieron saw a large vessel come to rest near the summit of a partly submerged mountain a long way from his land at the end of the long white cloud. He witnessed a great continent sink beneath the waves of the central ocean and he knew it was in punishment for its inhabitants who had tried to become more powerful than their Creator. They had tried to control the natural forces of the earth with a series of great crystals. Compassionately, the Creator had prevented the ones with dark hearts from negatively influencing the hearts and minds of the rest of the population. Those who were forewarned by Io and told to flee their land, survived and were able to take their knowledge and the sacred scrolls to faraway lands. One of those groups had come to this island in the far southern ocean of the planet.

Thieron, in his light body, hovered over his temple home as it had been twenty-four thousand years ago, and then slowly descended. The buildings were far superior in style and construction and size to those presently standing. The temple housing a great earth keeper crystal shone in the morning sun, lighting up the entire area with rainbow lights. He saw a young man who looked very much like his reflection in the surface of the lake on a still day. The man was talking earnestly to an older man, and calling him Master. Thieron was shocked to recognise Rahitan as the man in his dream. Then that young man must be himself. That realisation caused bumps to crawl over the outline of his light body making him decidedly uncomfortable. Could they see him? He didn't think so. A thought struck him. "Do I have the power to change the future from the past?" Then he remembered. "Don't meddle," Morpheus had sternly instructed before putting him in this trance.

Thieron was so intent on the scene below him that he didn't notice a woman walking towards them. Then he saw her and his light body heart expanded with love and joy. How could he have forgotten his Princess? He attempted to turn a somersault but instead, his light body shot straight up high above the temple. From that vantage point he could make out the cyclopean walls surrounding the star shaped temple. Funny, he had never realised before that the temple was in the shape of a six pointed star. It looked like two enormous triangles inserted into each other, one blue and one white. The earth keeper crystal temple stood in the central courtyard located in the very centre of a complex maze. Fountains played and colourful flowers and trees grew in landscaped gardens outside the maze. He remembered the legend of the maze. Many tried to enter it to bathe in the fountain of immortality that played around the great crystal but it was said that only those whose love was true could enter. Many couples, convinced they truly loved each other also tried, but few found the concealed entrance. If the magic was right the entrance to the maze opened, and a huge iridescent butterfly led the ones who truly loved straight to the centre. True love was not always directed towards another being but often to Io, the One Creator of life after the earthly passions waned in the body. Those ones also easily found the centre of the maze.

From his vantage point, Thieron could see the pattern of the maze, the crystal and the Fountain of Immortality that flowed from the mouth of a huge sculptured dragon that looked so lifelike that it could breathe fire as well as water at any moment. Suddenly Thieron remembered that his Princess whom he had loved with all his heart had found the centre of the maze. It broke his heart when she chose Kaitewha as her partner to enter the maze. The moment they touched hands, and looked into each other's eyes, the maze opened and an enormous, brilliantly coloured butterfly emerged from a vibrant flower to lead them inside. Everyone rejoiced that their Princess had found her soul partner. All except for Thieron who crept into a store cupboard and wept tears of longing. His sensible mind told him how impossible the situation was, and that the Princess Aloma could never fall in love with a lowly scribe, even though he was of the Atema. Eventually his heart mended, but he had never looked at another woman and instead had thrown himself into a lifetime of study. Now she was below him talking to the one who used to be him and the Master Rahitan who was instructing her in what was to come. Her sparkling blue eyes and cornsilk hair shone in the bright sun. "Ah, Princess, I'm glad you've come," said the dignified older man. "I have told the people of our impending demise. What else do you suggest we do?"

To Thieron the voice of Princess Aloma sounded like celestial bells tinkling in the still air. "Master Rahitan, I'm going to suggest a party. A wild and wonderful party to make our last days as happy and carefree as we can. Why be immersed in gloom and doom? Can that help us through? No, only joy and laughter can lift the spirit." She paused and winked at Thieron. "Of course, we could all run away and save ourselves from being blown up, but somehow I don't think that is what destiny intended for us. What do you think, Thieron?"

Thieron blushed to the roots of his dark red curly hair and stammered, "A wonderful idea, my Princess." Then plucking up his courage added, "May I dance with you?"

"Of course," she laughed. "I'll even dance with Master Rahitan. I hear he used to be quite a dancer in his youth."

Rahitan smiled indulgently, his beard curled up and down three times and he spun around three times on his toes. Thieron's jaw dropped and the Princess laughed.

"Now we have work to do," said Aloma as she left them. Over her shoulder she called, "And so have you two."

As Thieron in his light body watched from his high place in a giant kauri tree, the Atema began to prepare themselves for their final three days in those particular bodies. The Princess's idea of a huge party was eagerly accepted and everyone joined in the preparations. Master Rahitan's request was discussed and groups formed to create an object of great beauty which would endure the epochs and the desecration of their land. The master sculptor and his apprentices began chiselling a huge block of green stone from which the form of Princess Aloma gracefully emerged. The Atema wondered at its power as the finished statue stood on the dais. Energy was absorbed from everyone who touched it, to empower and bless the Princess down the ages. A garland of yellow flowers was draped around the statue, whose eyes smiled through precious lapis lazuli brought from a land far away. Each of the Enlightened Ones poured their love into the statue of the Princess, imprinting it with power and love to be regained when next they found each other. No one contemplated leaving to save themselves, although it would have been easy for the whole village to move a day's walk away in any direction to safety. They knew they could not run from destiny. Six men and women volunteered to transport the copy of the golden scrolls to the tail of the great stingray in case the Kaimanawa forest was too devastated to ever recover. Standing around the central courtyard, with a scroll under each arm, they mind-merged and bi-located to a secluded cave in a cliff that would one day become the burial cave of Chiefs as they prepared to enter the underworld, only to reappear shortly afterwards, their journey completed. All the requests of the gifts to the future suggested by Rahitan were rolled into one in the statue. It glowed and pulsed with the love and life projected into it so powerfully that it disappeared into a higher dimension, to return, as they all knew, when the time was right.

Then the party began in earnest. As, soon after their arrival, each of the Atema had learned to live on the orgonic energy of light there was no need to prepare food, but the priests of herbal medicine made a brew of sacred herbs for them to drink. This would normally only be available to the seers and not permitted to be taken by anyone else, but now their world was about to change and they would go gladly, fortified by hallucinatory herbs. As Thieron continued to watch from his hiding place at a speeded up version of the last three days of his former life, he became aware of such of sense of joy pervading the temple, he succumbed to its allure.

The Princess was radiant. Everyone was touched by her aura of love and all the pain of parting eased as people embraced. At the final moment, they all joined hands around the dais where the statue of the Princess stood, and began to sing, under the influence of the herbal brew. Thieron felt a tug pulling him back to his body in the future and, unable to resist, surrendered to the pull. He left just as a rumble began deep in the earth below the temple complex. His memory of the final moments burst into consciousness and he saw the earth open up, the temple disintegrate in seconds, the Atema dissolve, as a vast tongue of fiery lava and ash shot into the air and settle over the area. Merged as one mind, their souls took flight and headed for a bright ball of light, high in the heavens. But most of them did not reach the source of light and comfort, for looking down, they saw a devastated land where no living thing could survive, and were pulled back towards the odorous sulphur gasses issuing from vents exposed like sores on the shattered landscape. Death came instantly to every living thing, animal, vegetable and mineral, for the rocks too changed their form in the process of birth and death.

Many souls in the surrounding area left the physical plane that day as several villages disappeared when the land collapsed under them. The flimsy straw huts and stronger wood and stone houses exploded into flames, and burnt in a flash leaving their occupants unaware of their transition. The Atema had sought to warn the chiefs of nearby villages of the coming conflagration, but those warnings fell on deaf ears. As the caldera spread, the great depression which was to become Lake Taupo formed, landscaping the area with the mighty hand of the Creator of landmasses and water. Where once the verdant forest stood tall and proud and alive with sustenance for all beings, pumice and rock fell like choking rain in a fiery storm that nothing could survive. Foul gas squeezed the breath from living things and a fine ash settled like a mantle over the landscape. The awesome power of Nature had called and the Earth had responded. The huge white cliffs along the western edge of the lake were formed by this collapse and the old land surface lay buried many hundreds of metres below the floor of Lake Taupo. When the earth ceased her orgasmic outburst, everything was still. Silence descended like a shroud and nothing moved. There was no room for sound, so loud was the silence. Darkness covered the land as the great columns of ash and debris spewed from the gaping wound, blotting out the sun's light. Death and desolation stalked claiming their rights. Shattered souls wailed in silent despair following the catastrophe but no one heard or responded. The sacrifice had been made and accepted. It was over.

Many of the Atema, even though they had prepared for the event, had no prior knowledge of the magnitude of the explosion which devastated their land. This left them shattered to the core of their souls, unable to find a focus for their despair. They felt betrayed by Tane, their God of Light and sank into oblivion for a long, long time. Even Enlightened Ones, the priests and seers were shocked to the core. They knew that Tane was not the supreme creator, they knew that the life of the soul was eternal and that each life was like a day in the life of the soul whose task it was to gather experience for Io, the Supreme Creator. The sacred herbs had dulled the pain of their physical bodies but failed to quench the deep sense of failure and betrayal caused by the sudden end of their physical world. Their belief in the fact that the central core within each being held the indefinable presence of the divine creative force had been shattered. This was the hardest blow of all. They thought themselves immortal. And so they wandered, stuck between the worlds, unable to go up or down, or back to the divine source or to incarnate on earth until they were released by their Princess Aloma, at a time far into the future, for she had escaped into the light with Rahitan, Garlita, Kaitewha, Morpheus and only a score of the Atema.

THREE

Follow the Song

Aloma felt no sense of loss or sadness when she saw the warrior escort fade as she stepped on to the path. Her heart sang with joy and an overwhelming sense of freedom flooded her being. A ripple of laughter rose from her body to float on the warm air. Birds and butterflies came to greet her and flowers brushed her sandalled feet. For the first time in her life, Aloma felt truly happy. A mantle of sorrow as a result of at being in an alien environment lifted and she began to sing, a strange song of words she did not understand. Her grandmother Kelama had taught it to her when she was very young, telling her never to sing it when anyone else could hear, especially her step-mother, Teringa. A pang of sadness flitted out of her heart for the loss of her beloved grandmother, but was soon replaced by an inner knowing that Aloma would meet her again. The song continued, rising unbidden from her throat, and it seemed as though the rocks, trees and flowers and the birds circling around her head all knew the song. The air vibrated with the melody and Aloma noticed the words began to make sense; words that were like a map guiding her through the forest, a sort of song map relating to features in the landscape. Here was the large guardian rock shaped like a lion. She knew it was a lion, but, until she saw the rock looming beside the path, she had no idea what a lion looked like; crouched as if to spring on the unwary and devour them. The song greeted the lion rock, whose features relaxed and joined in the song.

The young woman continued the song that led her beside a fast flowing river she knew she must cross, but not how. The song told her to go upstream until she came to a cataract of tumbled rocks, where she would be able to cross. The waters joined the song, reaching a crescendo as she neared the dancing spray of the cataract. A brilliant splash of blue made Aloma stop and laugh. A bird chasing insects darted amongst the white water. When he heard her song he opened his beak and vibrated his throat to blend with her. Aloma held up her hand and the brightly plumed bird landed on it to gaze intently into her deep blue eyes. *He seems to know me*, she thought.

Across the river the path became smoother, as if worn by the passing of many feet. In some of the damper sections, smooth flat stones had been placed to keep feet dry. Roughly hewn seats of dark timber had been placed along the path for travellers to rest and enjoy the display of flowers and shrubs that grew in profusion along the river bank. But Aloma would not stop to rest, as her sense of anticipation grew with every guided step. The song grew stronger as each landmark greeted her. An azure blue bird circled overhead, and was joined by red-tailed amokura, and other colourful birds with long tail feathers, each one singing its song. Butterflies galore flew along the path as if welcoming her. There was the giant tree of the song, its branches open like loving arms, the huge stone shaped like a woman's head with long hair, the arch through the rock, the narrow fern and moss covered pass and beyond a small crystal clear lake.

Soon the song would end. Where was it taking her? Aloma felt no fear, only a mounting sense of excitement. The final verse took her over a small hill. On the crest she stopped in amazement. Below her stretched a walled village with shining white buildings set in a neat circular design around a star shaped temple with a dome that gleamed in the sun. Aloma felt the excitement course through her body and her hands and feet tingle. A surge of recognition overwhelmed her and tears sprang unbidden in her eyes. She was home. How could she have forgotten this place? From somewhere deep inside her a note sprang forth, sounding loud and clear, to be carried by the breeze towards the village. She could see people in different coloured robes stop what they were doing and turn towards the hill. They heard her call and listened. From within the temple, a bell sounding more like a vibration rang out, calling the Atema to gather.

"She has come. Our Princess has returned to us at last," shouted a sprightly old woman, whom Aloma recognised as her grandmother Kelama. "My granddaughter has come."

The Atema crowded together along the path, hurrying towards Aloma who stood on the hill, tears flowing down her face, as the High Priestess Garlita dashed from the central temple to greet her. A golden light emanated from Aloma as the last notes of the song died on her lips. Kelama, her beloved grandmother was the first to reach the amazed young woman. They hugged until they were breathless. "Grandmother Kelama, I twas told you were dead. How wonderful to see you. You look wonderful, so full of life".

Garlita, followed closely by Thieron and Morpheus bowed before her, much to her embarrassment. "Princess Aloma, our Princess," they corussed. A tall thin man with piercing blue eyes and long white hair and beard, bowed deeply. "Welcome, welcome back to us. We have been expecting you. Do you remember us?"

Princess? Remember? Remember what? Aloma was overcome with emotion. Garlita stood in front of her and looked deeply into her shining blue eyes."Look at me," she commanded. From Garlita's intense gold-flecked, sea-grey eyes came a strong ray of energy which entered Aloma's heart. She felt something release and her heart burst open in a flood of love and recognition.

"Garlita, is it you? I had forgotten you. And the Master Rahitan and Morpheus. Where is my beloved Kaitewha? Is he here? How are my people? I have been asleep for such a long, long time," cried Aloma.

"Princess Aloma." Morpheus, the dream master, was overjoyed as he knelt before her. "I have dreamed of your return.Your people are prepared. Your rangatiratanga (kingdom) is restored."

Aloma felt shy, and very embarrassed. "Please get up, Morpheus. I am no longer a Princess but a refugee from my tribe. I heard a call and followed a song."

Thieron who was also on his knees, grasped her hand and kissed it. The touch of her cool skin sent shivers through his tense body as the remembrance of his longing and unrequited love flooded his senses. Whilst he fervently hoped that Kaitewha would not return, he had heard only yesterday, Morpheus tell Garlita that Kaitewha would come soon after Aloma. Soon many others would also find their way home, drawn by the vibration of the song that had been sent out from the crystal bell to call the Atema.

Aloma's face, wet from tears that glistened in the spring sunshine, became radiant, until she stood purified, as layers of the pain of separation peeled away from her subtle bodies. Her surrounding colours became clear and vibrant, awakening memories in those who watched her, memories of the time long past when their lives were intertwined.

"Welcome, Princess Aloma. Welcome." A great cry arose from the throats of the Atema.

Everyone tried to kiss her hand and hug her, while from the back of the crowd a voice was heard calling "Let us through," and four strong men appeared carrying a fur covered litter which they placed on the ground before their amazed Princess. Though shy, she smiled and she gracefully sat on the soft seat as the men carefully lifted the litter so as not to tilt her.

"Please," she whispered to Garlita, "don't let them make such a fuss. I do not deserve to be treated so regally."

"Nonsense," smiled the High Priestess, "your Highness must obey the wishes of her people. It is the strength of your memory that has enabled us to regroup. It has been the inspiration for us to rebuild the temple in the hope you would find us. Please indulge them until any changes you wish can be made. Your long sleep is over and we have much to do."

With a nod from Garlita, the men hoisted the litter on their shoulders and slowly began the procession to the temple to give thanks for the coming of the Princess and the power of the song which drew her back.

In their excitement no one noticed a tall, good looking, dark brown skinned young man standing quietly on the side of the hill. His black eyes shone with love and his long, dark hair reflected red rays from the sun. Camouflaged by his long flowing cloak adorned with shimmering green black feathers he gazed in adoration at his wife of so long ago, before the big bang, the woman soon to be restored to him. Aloma - so well named, the word for love. His heart raced but then froze. Would she remember him? His love convinced him she would.

FOUR

Kaitewha (The Songmaster)

The little boy lay as still as the tall reeds which concealed him at the edge of the lake. His small waka, lapped by the gentle rolling ripples, was also hidden. He was waiting for the whistling blue ducks that nested in the reeds to land on the lake and begin to feed. In one hand he clutched a long, hollow reed that, when the time came, would enable him to breathe under water. Soon he heard the familiar whistle as the ducks slid to a stop on the smooth surface of the lake and settled, ready to feed unaware of the boy or his intention. Very slowly, in the manner of one endowed with the skills of an experienced hunter, the boy slid into the water and allowed himself to sink beneath the surface. Placing the hollow reed between his lips, he breathed easily as he neared the dangling feet of the ducks. Choosing a large male, he slipped a plaited noose that he had tied around his leg and gently slid it over the webbed feet, then pulled down hard. The duck whistled in surprise as the others took off. It tried to follow but found itself firmly restrained by the noose that the boy held fast around its legs.

"Got you, my beauty," he laughed as he wound the length of plaited sisal around the duck's wings, trussing it into submission. The boy did not hold this duck underwater until it drowned or snap its neck as he would if it was destined for dinner. Instead, he pushed it along in front of him towards his waka and thrust it in.

"You are too fine a bird for my mother's cooking pot," the boy said as he stroked his catch. "How would you like to be my friend instead?"

The duck whistled loudly to its mate circling anxiously above in the clear blue sky.

"No, well you'll change in time. Perhaps I can catch your mate to keep us both company."

The boy picked up a small oar from the bottom of his waka and expertly began to paddle across the lake to a small village nestled near the foot of a high waterfall that tumbled its contents, green and clear, into the edge of the lake. Smoke from the cooking fires trailed lazily towards the sky and the sun was low on the horizon when he pulled his small waka up the beach. Gently lifting the duck, he sat with it cradled in his arms, watching the sun sink behind the distant mountain that was shaped like a woman large with child, lying on her back. Splashes of brilliant colour tinged the low lying clouds over the distant horizon and were reflected on the lake's calm surface. The boy sighed contentedly as he stroked the shiny wing feathers of the duck. It relaxed, sensing the peace within the boy's heart. closed its eyes and cradled its head on the boy's arm, feeling safe. Its mate still circled above, crying loudly while the captured duck surrendered to its fate, at least for the moment.

"You will need a name," whispered the boy into the duck's back. "Everything needs a name. You are no longer just a duck, but my special duck, so I will call you Whio, like the cry you make. Whio Whio."

"Tewha, Te-ee-wha." The boy jumped. His mother was calling in the voice she used when she was angry.

"What now?" he mumbled to Whio. "Why would she spoil a perfectly wonderful day."

Tucking the duck firmly under one arm, Tewha strolled up the beach to his home, a neat hut made from smooth rocks covered with mud and lined with raupo leaves. From a hole in the thatched roof, smoke drifted to merge with the sky. On a wooden seat outside the hut sat his father, Arukororia, (following glory) whittling a walking stick from a branch fof a rimu tree.

"Hello, son," he smiled. "What have you caught? Dinner? Your mother will be pleased."

"This is Whio," answered Tewha "Please don't tell mother. He is to be my friend. I could never eat my friend."

"Your friend, uh?" said Arukororia. "Why do you need a duck for a friend when you have so many sisters and brothers?"

Tewha became defensive. "They don't listen to me. They laugh at my ideas. They can't see the same things as I do. Not one of them can see the special colours around people, let alone read what's in their heart."

"Colours? You can see colours around people? Why didn't you tell me?" His father asked.

"You never asked me," was all Tewha said.

"That's a special gift, my son," his father told him. "I think we must tell our tohunga of this. Come, we will go now, before your mother calls us for our meal."

Carefully, Arukororia placed his sharp carving flints in a soft leather pouch, wrapped his partly finished stick in leaves and then stood. He was a tall man, solidly built but without any excess fat. His dark curly hair was cut very short and the hair on his face scraped smooth every morning, using a sharpened shell dipped in very hot water from a nearby pool that welled up from the steaming stream that ran into the lake not far from the village. His sons loved watching the ritual and began to emulate him as soon as down appeared on their faces. Their shells came from the sea and were traded for pumice stones that were washed up on the shores of the lake. The pumice was a legacy from the volcano gods of the land and came from deep within the earth. Tewha as yet showed no sign of facial hair. His voice was still high, not broken to the deeper tones of men.

Just then his mother, Ririmana, banged a stick on a hollow tube and called from the cooking area. "Come on, you lot, dinner's ready". Children of all ages suddenly appeared, yelling and laughing, ready to demolish the food.

Once, when his mother had been exceptionally hard to get along with, his father had told Tewha that her name meant angry bird, as that is what she looked like when she was born. A scrawny, angry bird, screaming constantly. He had thought to tame and gentle her through love, marriage and children. However, she had only become more angry and birdlike. Her hair was straight and severely tied back with a length of plaited flax. Her black eyes, rarely blinking, darted everywhere, missing nothing. A beaked nose and sharp chin completed the picture, making her look hard and cold. Most people felt afraid in her presence and avoided her company. Not Arukororia however. He loved her dearly and knew that occasionally, behind the angry facade his wife was a gentle and loving woman.

"I spend all day collecting and preparing food and it is gone in no time", Ririmana complained.

Arukororia winked at her. "Come now my dear, we are a healthy family so you must be doing something right."

"Aiee, and who would care if I ran away or drowned in the lake," she wailed

As soon as they had eaten, the children, not all of whom were Tewha's brothers and sisters, ran back to their games or work, leaving Ririmana to her misery.

"Come, son," said Arukororia taking Tewha by the hand, "Let's go and see the tohunga."

They found the wise spiritual leader of the village seated on a rock, watching the steam rise from the stream. Rongonui looked up at their approach, smiled and beckoned them to be seated on rocks beside him. "You have at last brought the boy," he said. "I feared you would find his secret too late for me to help him develop his gift."

"How did you know about my gift/" burst out Tewha.

"It is my job to recognise the gifts in our children and encourage them explore them," said the wise man. "But I also need the permission of the parents to teach them."

Looking directly at Tewha he continued, "I tried to tell your mother long ago that you were not an ordinary child, but she insisted that I leave you to grow through your boyhood before you were told. Now the time has come. Very soon you will leave your parents house and come to live with me in the House of Learning. Does that excite you?"

Tewha could hardly contain his joy. "Oh, yes," he replied. "Would tomorrow be too soon? I have hardly anything to bring. Only the fishing line my father made for me and my duck."

"Tomorrow is as good a day as any to begin your new life," smiled Rongonui. "The stars are auspicious and the moon is growing larger and will soon be full, if that suits you, Arukororia? I am very pleased to have him as my pupil."

"How are we going to tell your mother?" Arukororia asked as the they walked back towards their home. "Do we just come out with the truth or ask the tohunga to tell her?"

"I'll tell her, father. She will be glad to have one less mouth to cook for. She is always complaining about the work she has to do." Tewha danced around his father in a state of happiness he had never felt before, not even when he had caught Whio. "Why doesn't someone come to help her with the work. There are those who could."

Arukororia nodded sadly. "There is no one who has not felt the lashing of her sharp tongue. She is not liked by the people of the village so they avoid her. Have you not noticed that?"

When they returned home, Tewha rushed up to his mother and flung his arms around her. Even though her first response was to scowl, she allowed him to lead her in a dance of such joy that she was soon .relaxed. Something awoke inside her and with a shout, she began to dance wildly with him. Hands clasped, they spun around the house, out through the door and around the garden, singing loudly. Arukororia looked on in astonishment and laughed. He had a glimpse of the woman he had fallen in love with so long ago and his heart surged with love once again. Ririmana held out a hand to him and he joined the whirling pair. Soon the other children, attracted by the noise, were dancing, twirling around and around, until they all fell in a tumbled heap on the grass, breathless and laughing. Their neighbours, drawn by the commotion, shook their heads sadly, fearful that at last Ririmana had gone crazy. In a way this was true, for the cord of restraint and sadness that had previously bound her, had indeed cracked and she felt a warmth and release as the nervous tension flowed from her. Then she began to cry, but her crying was different from the wailing the children sometimes heard late at night. These tears came with laughter as her face lightened. She hugged each of her children and anyone else who was near and turned to Arukororia.

"It seems as if a spell has been broken, that I can feel again. What has happened?"

"We have just been to see the tohunga. He has requested that Tewha be allowed to live with him from tomorrow and begin special training. He also said you knew our son had special gifts but wanted him to grow through boyhood. Why didn't you tell me?"

"I tried to, many times," Ririmana said, "but the words would not come out. Forgive me."

Arukororia, amazed at those last two words, looked into her eyes. Never in her life had she apologised to anyone, least of all him. What had come over her? Was it a permanent change or would she soon revert to her unpleasant old ways? If permanent this would take some getting used to.

"Yes. Of course I forgive you, my love". He put his arms around her thin frame and hugged her. Unusally, she made no attempt to draw away from his embrace. She actually rested her head on his shoulder and relaxed. The children were quick to notice the change in their mother, but hung back, fearing that soon she would become the old witch they feared. Then she held her arms out and they all rushed into them, pushing and shoving to be the closest.

"Yes, the spell is broken", she laughed. "I was cursed by my mother's sister at birth. She was jealous that my mother had a child with the man she also loved, even though she was then too old to bear a child herself. She was a powerful kuia (old woman). My mother knew about the curse but neither she nor anyone else had the power to lift it."

Lovingly, Ririmana took Tewha in her arms. "The spell was to be broken when one of my children was accepted for training by a tohunga. What was considered impossible by my aunt has come to pass. Now I know it could have been broken earlier but the veil of ignorance was over me. Now I can really see. Sometimes there is much darkness in the hearts of others. Thank you and bless you, my son. I will help you gather your things in the morning. Then you can begin your real life."

Tewha spent his first ever sleepless night. He had untied the restraints from Whio's wings and held him tightly snuggled in his arms. The duck relaxed and slept. No thoughts or excitement coursed through its body as it did in the boys. At the crack of dawn, as fingers of light poked their way across the lake, and clouds made patterns and reflections of brilliant dawn colours, Tewha quietly roused himself and carefully picked his way through his still sleeping brothers and sisters towards the door. Once outside he ran with Whio tightly clutched in his arms, and felt a surge of energy course through his body, but as yet unfamiliar with the ways of the tohunga, he was unable to recognise it as the universal life force that can be activated in anyone who has the power to transform themselves.

For the next ten summers, Tewha and two other boys lived with Rongonui as he taught them the secret ways of the tohunga, the experts on many subjects. Only one of them would reach the exalted state of spiritual leader, but all were trained in case the chosen one met an untimely death. During the day they learned of the ways of nature, how the insects spread pollen from one plant to another, how the wild bees made honey, where the animals had their homes, which herbs could be used for healing or poisoning the body, to heal the sick and how to read the stars. Rongonui knew he had an outstanding pupil in Tewha and hoped that the boy some day would follow in his footsteps. He had heard of the Atema, the tribe living deep in the heart of the forest across the vast lake, and knew that one had to earn the right to be called to join them, but to this day he had not been contacted. Surely that call would come soon and he could leave this village in the care of his star pupil and retire to be with those of his own kind, for the life of one set apart was often a lonely one. He had never married for many of the young women were afraid of his powers and thought they would burn up if his seed entered them. Foolish women, not one with the power to match his. It never occurred to Rongonui that anyone in the village other than he would receive the call. So when Tewha began to show the unmistakable signs of one who had received a deep inner vision, he was visibly annoyed, even jealous.

"Nonsense, Tewha," he thundered, losing his composure which he rarely did, "you must be mistaken. I can't hear any music or smell any perfume. I would know if you had been called."

Tewha continued to stare at the sky, with a smile of such bliss on his face that his friends laughed, which made Rongonui even angrier.

"You boys, go" he yelled. "I need to deal with this. Don't come back until I call you." The two young men exchanged a knowing look, for this prestigious summons had been discussed occasionally around the night fire. The symptoms had been described in detail by Rongonui so that when his call came they would all know and allow him to leave without any fuss. The question was, why Tewha? Why not him, who had worked so long and hard for others?

Three years earlier, Tewha's beloved mother Ririmana had died suddenly during an intense cold spell in a long, icy winter. One year later Arukororia followed her to an easier life on the other side of death. Some said he died of a broken heart, and the loneliness of one whose beloved life partner has gone. Since her conversion, Ririmana and Arukororia had become like romantic sweethearts, never leaving each other's side, much to their children's amusement. When she died, Arukororia seemed to shrivel until he became a wizened little old man. So there was no one from whom Tewha needed to ask permission to leave, except Rongonui who was honour bound to release him, which he did with bad grace. The two young men in training with Tewha were sad to see him go. They all paddled across the great lake to accompany him to the entrance of the forbidden track that entered the sacred forest and watched until he very quickly disappeared from sight. The song he had heard Rongonui secretly singing late at night when he thought no one could hear, entered Tewha's head and he found himself recalling it, singing the strange words that he did not understand. Unerrimgly, the song led him through the forest, along barely discernible tracks, beside a river, past strangely shaped rocks, and over hills to a sight that made him gasp in astonishment.

Spread below him was a village complex, with its white dome shining in the afternoon sun. People, glowing with health and light, were gathered around a young woman with long flowing fair hair who seemed embarrassed by the attention and was indicating her reluctance to accept their praise. Something snapped open in his heart and a veil lifted from his vision. Below him was Aloma, his wife, his divine love, getting into a litter to be borne aloft by strong young men taking her towards the gates of the temple. He stood entranced as the people of different skin and hair colour filed through into the courtyard singing and dancing showing their joy towards the shy young woman, crying "She has returned, our Princess has returned to us." Then the large ornate gate closed, shutting him out. Tewha sat down on one of the large, egg shaped stones arranged beside the gate and relaxed, trying to regain his composure. Suddenly his consciousness was catapulted from his body to one of the stars in the group known as Matariki, the Seven Sisters. How he knew this he had no idea. Rongonui had told him their ancestors had come from Matariki so very long ago. Silvery light figures glided around him, encircling and singing to the bewildered young initiate who sat in silence. The tall glowing figure of an imposing woman shimmering with vibrant rainbow colours stood in front of him and gently touched his forehead with a golden rod tipped with a flame of light. His head felt as though it had exploded into fragments of light and colour that travelled across the zones of time and space. A voice penetrated Tewha's mind. "Kaitewha, welcome to Electra, your home star. I am called Seraleah, the chief librarian of this vast hall of records located here. Before you embark on the next phase of your life your must be aware of a few things. Look though your scroll and then tell me what you can understand."

Tewha stood as though paralysed, while wondering how he had been transported to the celestial library. The voice of Seraleah came again. "That rounded stone that you unwittingly sat on is directly connected to this place energetically. Somehow you managed to activate it by touching a certain place to trigger the magnetic force that enabled you to be sent here. Perhaps it was prepared by Rahitan, who knows many things."

Tewha knew himself to be in the ancient library that Rongonui had said contained records of the thoughts, deeds and history of each being, each spark of the Creator's light in the universe. He was to be guided by the priestess to find his own story. With trembling hands, he took the heavy gold-sheathed scroll Seraleah indicated from a neat row of scrolls. In his light body, Tewha carried his scroll to a large, ornately carved, gold plated table and drew up a chair and carefully began to remove the sheath. *Strange to be able to do this without my physical body*, he thought. On the front of the sheath was emblazoned a symbol that brought back a flood of memories. It was in the shape of an equal sided cross with each of its four arms divided into two, forming eight points and encircled by a ring of gold. A large ruby was set into the centre of the cross.

As the silvery being nodded in approval and glided away, Tewha began to read his story. For a long time he poured through his scroll, as the story of his existence was revealed in line after line of ornate script. He opened to the vastness of the universe as the symbols and inscribed words leapt clearly into his mind. In that short space of earth time he relived his entire existence. From his beginning as an expression of a Divine spark of light and love from the heart and mind of the Creator of all things, though his sojourns in unfamiliar bodies and forms on different planets and stars in several universes, to his present life. He experienced his births, lives and deaths over and over, but a thread ran through each incarnation. He knew he was being shown his scroll to remind him of his divine promise to the Creator. He was to live his truth and have as many experiences as possible so as to also enable the Creator to be part of each life. His thread, the continuity of his existence was based on truth and love and the upliftment of the Goddess in all things to prevent her essence from being defiled by ignorant savages on the planets where he had purposefully incarnated. He thought of the example of his mother and her awakening and smiled. Seraleah glided soundlessly along the corridor between rows and rows of scrolls, one for each spark of the Creator and merged with his mind.

"Kaitewha, Kaitewha", she called, for he was so immersed in his scroll he was unaware of her presence. "What have you learnt of your soul path?"

"What have I learned? Oh Seraleah, I will never remember it all. The main thing is my enduring love for Aloma who is my twin flame, and that I am a great musician who writes and sings songs of joy and blessing which touch the hearts and minds of those who hear them. I am a song-master, and will have to remember how to play that complicated instrument again," groaned Tewha. "But why do you call me Kaitewha?"

Seraleah smiled. "That is your whole name. It means Master of Songs. From this time forward you will be called Kaitewha. But now it is time for you to return to your body, sitting patiently and empty on the stone by the ornate gates of the village of the Atema. Put your scroll back on the shelf and prepare yourself. You may be a bit overwhelemed when you remember this time and the contents of your scroll. Ready?"

Seraleah touched him gently on the back of his neck, just under the hairline and when Tewha opened his eyes, he was back in his physical body sitting on the egg shaped rock. The vibration from behind the walls increased to a loud hum as, rather stunned, he sat looking at the imposing entrance gates set in the high cyclopean wall surrounding the buildings. They were made of an unfamiliar metal and emanated a dull blue light. As he walked towards them he felt an electric shock run though his body while lines of blue light flashed across the entrance. Had he forgotten something? He delved into the deep recesses of his mind, trying to recall the last words of the song. They came to him and he yelled, "Open to me, for I am Kaitewha who has been called." The blue lines disappeared, the gates swung smoothly open and there in the courtyard stood the people, dressed in white or coloured robes of differing styles, smiling in welcome. An imposing looking man with piercing blue eyes and a long white beard addressed him. "Kaitewha, welcome, we have been expecting you?" he boomed, his voice seeming to come from deep within his chest. "I am Rahitan. You may remember me. Follow me to the temple and I will introduce you to some of our people".

At first the young man was speechless, standing there with his mouth hanging open, feeling like a fool and a prince at the same time. Then he found his voice. "I have always been called Tewha, not Kaitewha. How do you know who I am? How did you know I was coming? Where am I?" After he'd recovered his composure, more questions tumbled from his lips for in his surprise he forgot the information so recently read in his scroll. "Where is Aloma, my wife?"

"All in good time, my boy, all in good time," was all the answer he received.

Rahitan, the High Priest of the Atema, introduced himself and turned, beckoning Kaitewha to follow him. Swiftly, he walked across the smoothly paved courtyard and up the wide steps that led into the great white, shining temple of the Atema. Ornate carvings of symbols, flowers and birds decorated the curved lintels over the large embossed gold covered doors. Lifelike statues of men and women, each smiling benevolently, stood in niches along the outer walls. Inside, when his eyes became accustomed to the diffused light that streamed through small holes along the wall, forming a pattern of flowers on the polished floor, Kaitewha could see a giant bell fashioned from one perfect crystal. A tall, imperious, dark haired woman, dressed in a long flowing white gown, was standing beside it, with a look of intense concentration on her serene face. Rahitan gestured to the young man to stop on a certain spot and to remain silent until the woman came out of her trance. Kaitewha held his breath, for he felt to breathe in such a holy place seemed like a sacrilege. His eyes roamed the surroundings in which he found himself, searching for Aloma.

The ceiling of the temple formed a high dome, adorned with vibrant paintings of angelic beings, flowers, starry patterns and rainbows. High up along the walls, intricate windows made of coloured glass impregnated with the healing spirit of the world added to the impression of a place not of the earth that he knew. The patterns on the floor kept changing as the sun moved across the heavens along its predestined course. The air hummed to the vibration of the crystal bell and then abruptly ceased. The priestess opened her dark grey gold flecked eyes and stared right into the heart of Kaitewha. Totally surprised he no time to protect himself. He felt her mind probing his, her eyes searching through his body, touching his imperfections, understanding his weaknesses, praising his strengths, and her heart merging with his. Then he was released by her smile.

"Welcome, Kaitewha," she said in a voice that sent shivers through his tense body. Shivers, not of lust but of something far higher, expectations of an opening to higher forces, hinted at but not yet experienced. "I am Garlita, the High Priestess of the Atema. This is the most holy area of the sanctuary that serves as the place of worship for the Atema. Your timing is perfect. To arrive on the same day as our Princess is a double blessing for us. Do you know who we are?"

"I have heard of you but never expected to be called," said Kaitewha truthfully, for he knew he could tell nothing but the truth in this place. "I know of you from my teacher Rongonui, who fully expected to be called and was upset when I instead was summonsed. As I sat on the egg-shaped rock just outside the entrance gates I had an experience of being lifted out of my body to a place where I was shown my past and my future. My head is still trying to the knowledge."

"Ah, yes. Rahitan hoped that might happen. We are called The Enlightened Ones, those whose task it is to keep the peace and harmony of this special land. It is a land truly beloved of the Creator of this universe," she said. "So now you remember who you are and your place with us. Now you can once again carry your ancient name - Kaitewha, songmaster, composer and singer of songs."

"I remember by beloved wife," he whispered. "Where is she? Can I see her?"

"Soon. Kaitewha, soon," answered Garlita. "She is being prepared for you and the rest of us as well. When her memory and yours fully return, then you will be together again."

Rahitan led him towards a man with a massive, curly beard and hair of striped orange and gold. He stood tall and straight, his deep-set blue eyes under bushy golden brows smiling at Kaitewha.

"Do you remember Morpheus, the Dream master, Kaitewha? He will further restore your memory of your previous time with us, and bring you up to date with the changes we have undergone since the big bang. Go with him. I will visit you later this day to take you to your dwelling place. Welcome back, lad."

Thus dismissed, Kaitewha followed the Dream master to a small, comfortably furnished room to one side of the temple.

FIVE

The Gathering

"Lie on this couch and relax your body, Kaitewha," commanded Morpheus. "Good, now breathe deeply...One...in....One... out... two... in...two...out...in...out. That's it, slowly, deeply. Relax your body. Listen to my voice. Feel yourself drifting into a peaceful space and know that you are safe. Concentrate on my voice. Breathe...in...out. Good."

The Dream master placed two fingers of his right hand on the young man's forehead, which caused a light to explode in his brain. This forced him to lift the haze that shrouded his vision. It felt like layers of fear and doubt, aeons of forgetfulness, years of aloneness melted from him. Morpheus then began to count from twenty backwards saying, "Listen to my voice. When I get to ten you will be very relaxed, your mind will begin to wander free from the constraints of fear and ignorance. Nine...eight...seven...six...Now you are going deeper and deeper in the state of relaxation and knowing that your true identity will open to you. Five...four...three...you are feeling relaxed but alert, your inner knowing is opening to you. What is hidden will emerge into your consciousness. .two..one...Now you are in a temple similar to the one you have just walked through. There are several people there. Do you recognise any of them?"

Kaitewha's memory emerged from deep within him as visions flashed onto the screen in the centre of his forehead, alternating with flashes of light like starbursts. He stopped breathing until Morpheus suggested he should continue to do so. Then, as though a button had been pushed, the visions began to present themselves in chronological order. Kaitewha lay on the couch and watched, fascinated, as this other world that he could not enter physically, unfolded. playing scenes he had read in his scroll.

Morpheus's voice came through from a great distance. "Kaitewha, tell me what you see."

Instead of Kaitewha's voice, another's emerged through Kaitewha's mouth,

"Greetings, my friends. I am Ashtaroth of the planet Sirius. At last I have been freed to communicate with you. For aeons I have been held in suspended animation, put there by the shock of the explosion which destroyed the heart of the land of the stingray at the time of the great annihilation. At that time I walked among you. Recently a vibration, a call came from the great Being who guides and overlights this planet, rekindling a memory amongst those who were called to regather and to awaken them to their next part of the planetary mission. This vibration also moved through all the universes. Once again, it is time for the Children of the Rainbow to regroup in this land in the far south of the earth and recommence their work for the advancement of the human race. The thread of light that was expressed at the beginning of time is connected to you always. It serves to encourage all who feel the call, to turn their conscious awareness to the light within, and the power of love that connects all structures in this Universe. Remember it, and turn within yourself to reconnect with that divine light that will activate vast experiences of love and joy, for that is the nature of the essence of the creator that sustains each and every one of you. For the more light you are able to flow through your body, the easier and more harmonious this awakening will be."

"Far away from this land, there is a dry, barren land through which a great river runs into a large inland sea, once inhabited by civilisations superior to ours. There, others are also being called to awaken, to remember their mission. It was once known by the ancients, as the centre of the earth. On a large plateau overlooking the sacred river Nile, sit three great pyramids erected by our ancient brothers and sisters. They fled from their highly advanced homeland just before it was inundated by a cataclysmic flood that destroyed their land. Deep within these pyramids, lie hidden clues to as their culture, which will be rediscovered far into your future, at the time of a millennium change. A great teacher called Thoth who presents himself with the body of a man and the head of an ibis, the sacred bird of that land called Khem, the black land because of its yearly inundation of silt from the flooding river Nile, is awakening those who volunteered for this important time in the history of earth. Your brothers and sisters of light who visit or live in that land which has already seen civilisations rise and fall, have a different job to undertake, as do those who are being stimulated to awaken in different areas of this jewel of a planet, so beloved of the Creator.

In a land far to the east, across the great ocean where the long tides run, two great continents are joined only by a narrow isthmus. Over the great calm ocean across which future warlike inhabitants of your land will sail, there is a land rich with gold and unfamiliar foods and animals, where others are being stirred into remembrance. In every land towering monuments and temples will be constructed to honour the true gods, the spiritual beings who oversee this world. It is not that the gods wish this to be done, but do not discourage it. What they wish to prevent is the re-emergence of the worship of false idols, symbols and substitutes for the true Godhead, which self-appointed priests use to empower themselves and control others through ritual and fear. That practice ultimately leads to the distortion of truth and an imbalance within the society they originally sought to serve."

Morpheus made a sign over Kaitewha's head. "Welcome, Lord Ashtaroth, it is a pleasure to talk to you once again. It is a long time since we spoke, not since Kaitewha was with us before the big bang. I have some questions for you."

"Ask away, O Master of Dreams," answered the voice coming out of Kaitewha's mouth.

"For some time I have been having my own dreams which I have never shared with anyone. I am the one who is supposed to know all the interpretations. However, there is one that has me mystified. Each time it is the same. I see a fleet of great canoes flying through the sky. They pulse with light and hum incessantly whilst manoeuvring at great speeds. They can change direction in an instant, disappear and reappear and are merged with the consciousness of the occupants. There are banks of glowing lights, strange machines, rooms where medical examinations are carried out, and large areas where many unusual looking people, dressed in colourful clothing, sit around a vast table to converse. I feel I am up there with them, but how can that be, for when I wake up in the morning, I am here in the temple."

"Ah, Morpheus, you remember the nightly conferences, the ships in the sky carrying those whose sacred task it is to guide the process of evolving humanity. You are very much a part of that process. It is considered by the evolved spiritual hierarchy that those whose task it is to incarnate into human form would find it too painful to remember the nightly journeys, taken by their soul while the body sleeps. Part of your mind knows this. Some go to areas of the universe which are so beautiful where they are surrounded by such love that they may not wish to return to their earthly body. It is a form of protection."

Morpheus sat still with tears in his eyes. Yes, it was better he didn't remember too often for the pain of remembering cut deep. A surge of longing coursed through his body and he gave into the emotion, entirely forgetting Kaitewha lying on the couch.

"Morpheus, Morpheus." The insistent sound of the voice roused him as he wiped the tears from his eyes. "It is not the way of the Master of Dreams to wallow so. If you can stand the power of knowledge, we will open your remembering so that you can constantly sustain the contact. Is that acceptable?"

"Oh, yes, my Lord Ashtaroth," whispered Morpheus.

"Now, let's see to our sleeping young prince. He hardly breathes. How am I to communicate with you if his body is not working, huh?" said the weakened voice through Kaitewha.

"Kaitewha, breathe deeply, in...out...in...out. That's it. Good," responded Morpheus quietly. "Now My Lord, can you stimulate a deeper response in Kaitewha's memory so that he can recall where the entrance to the chamber of the golden scrolls can be found. Rahitan says it is time to find the other scrolls, for the scroll that the young scribe found has jolted our memory. As there is no such thing as a co-incidence, I assume he was divinely guided?"

"The chamber still exists but now lies deep underground. A great deal of debris, from the cataclysmic explosion that formed the lake and buried the temple, will have to be dug out. With guidance from Master Rahitan and the thoughts I will stimulate in Kaitewha's mind, the chamber can be reached in five days, with a little luck and a lot of hard work. Something of great beauty may also be found that will astonish and delight you all."

The voice chuckled and continued, "Perhaps you can try some of those new mind techniques for moving rocks to help ease the work."

"How did you know that?" gasped Morpheus Then remembered he wasn't only talking to the young prince but to an omnipotent being who knew all things. "Yes, it may prove useful."

"Now, let me work on Kaitewha's mind," intoned the Lord Ashtaroth.

Morpheus sat very still. Rahitan had told him that it was nearly time for the scrolls to be read again and brought up to date, but confided he did not know where they were hidden. He remembered the time just before the explosion when he had dictated a scroll to Thieron. However, the landscape had changed so much that it was impossible to locate the entrance to the chamber. The fact that Thieron had chanced upon that one scroll indicated to him that the time was close.

"I am finished with his mind. Now I will take my leave. Call on me when you wish to talk again, or if you can't find the scroll chamber." The farewell was so abrupt it took Morpheus by surprise.

He began to count Kaitewha out of his hypnotic state, and with that, the young man stretched, yawned and opened his eyes and said, "What was all that about. I had a powerful vision of a being, dressed in a tight fitting suit of deep blue with a strange symbol pinned to his left shoulder, who used my body to speak to you. Tell me what he said."

"Well, Kaitewha, since Thieron found the golden scroll a few days ago, Master Rahitan, Garlita and I have been pondering on how to find the chamber containing the rest of the scrolls. They still exist, but after the great explosion that devastated the area so long ago, they were buried under layers of volcanic debris. Your mind has been reprogrammed by the Lord Ashtaroth to remember how to locate the chamber. Come, let's visit Rahitan."

Morpheus strode out of the room, leaving an astonished Kaitewha to unsteadily get to his feet and follow him. They found the High Priest deep in meditation in front of the crystal bell in the temple. When they turned to tiptoe out, he called to them in a deep voice, "Stay. You have something important to tell me."

"We have been contacted by Lord Ashtaroth who has implanted in Kaitewha's mind the memory of how to find the entrance to the scroll chamber," said Morpheus.

"Good, good," said the deep disembodied voice of Rahitan. "Now leave me, I will be with you shortly."

Quietly the two walked from the temple and sat on a bench in the sun to wait.

"Morpheus," ordered Rahitan, "go and find four of the youngest and strongest gardeners and ask them to come to me, and also ask someone to find Thieron, and tell him to come to the temple. We have work to do, or rather they will do the heavy work while we sit and watch, and direct them where to dig. Kaitewha, where do you think we should start?"

"Underneath the southern wall of the temple," replied the young man. "If we dig at an angle from outside, we won't disturb the foundations. We know that the ancient library was deeply buried for safe keeping."

"The work needs to be completed in five days." said Rahitan, "before the celebration of the Ceremony of Light. Perhaps the scrolls will reveal when the ceremony began and its significance. It is always a revelation to find out how a traditional ceremony came to be practiced. Often the real reason is forgotten and it's memory is distorted."

The young gardeners, whose normal role it was to maintain the temple complex, soon appeared. They were pushing a large tunnelling machine that they attached to a point of power inside the temple and switched it on. The power to drive machinery, provide light and generally make life more comfortable to the Atema came from a programmed crystal that quietly hummed in a specially constructed room under the temple. Few of the Atema had ever visited the room and had little idea how it all worked, but were glad of the comfort it provided in their homes.

Thieron came running along the path and stopped in astonishment at the sight of Kaitewha. "When did you arrive? I hoped you would not come so soon." Instantly he regretted his words, but they were spoken and couldn't be unsaid.

"Greetings, Thieron. Just a short time ago, not long after Aloma. I am so impatienct to see her and to hold her in my arms again. Oh! sorry Thieron. Was it because of your love for her that you wished I would not come?" Kaitewha playfully ruffled the young scribe's hair, causing him to cringe in embarrassment. How had Kaitewha remembered? Did everyone know?

"Now my young friends," interrupted Rahitan, "I am also impatient, but with the need to locate the scrolls, buried so long ago at the time of the big bang. With your help it should not take us long. Now concentrate, both of you, for you can guide the men and the tunnelling machine accordingly and with a minimum amount of damage to the old library. Aloma will have to await your presence a little longer. She has much to remember, and be told about our new existence. Perhaps we will also discover the green stone statue made in her image just before the big bang, if it has returned to the physical plane. Do any of you remember why it was made?"

Kaitewha looked blankly at Rahitan. "I have so much to remember," he signed, "But once I am in the arms of my beloved, I'm sure it will all come flooding back."

"Patience, young man." Rahitan gestured. "For protection from the explosion and the destructive forces of Nature, the statue was lifted on the vibration of love into a higher dimension where the convulsions of the earth could not shatter it. We need to concentrate and merge our minds to bring it back to our mortal sight. It is imbued with the knowledge, power and love of our previous existence. Now we are but a weak representation of what we were."

In the sacred hall of the temple, Aloma's eyes shone, and her heart danced with happiness. Under Garlita's hypnotic guidance, she began to recall her many former lives with the Atema. For thousands of years the tribe had incarnated many times, to hold the balance and harmony in their chosen and sacred land. Each life was long and happy once they had been summoned from their mundane life by the vibration of the crystal bell and found their way to the village of the Atema. Children were never actually born into that village, but incarnated through carefully chosen parents in other areas of the land. Once called and safely awakened to the special way of life of the Atema, they lived very long and productive lives. This was greatly enhanced by receiving instruction on how to be sustained by light and prana instead of needing to eat food. This created a high source of energy and life force to enhance the beauty and vibrational emanation of the body. Most of the women were past child-bearing age, although the few fertile women with partners drank Poroporo tea each morning to inhibit unplanned conception.

The Atema were not expected to be celibate and practised a sacred art of sensual pleasure. Some time after settling in to the life of the village, new arrivals were encouraged to find a partner with whom they resonated, even though they may have left a long time partner behind. Then couples would be instructed by initiates in the Temple of Sacred Love. Much of the instruction centred around a form of magnetisation called the Art of Connubial Love. The priesthood knew the power of sacredly directed sexual energy to heal and regenerate the body, and align with the higher forces of Creation.

Garlita spoke softly, bringing Aloma out of her reverie. "Kaitewha has found his way to us. He arrived just after you and is engaged in helping Rahitan and Morpheus to locate the ancient library, which, since the big bang, has been buried under a thick layer of ash. Strange priorities these old men have. They think using Kaitewha's knowledge to find the concealed entrance is far more important than reuniting two lovers."

"Kaitewha has arrived? When can I see him? Has his appearance changed?" questions poured from Aloma's lips. "Will I still love him? Will he still love me? I think we may need to spend some time in the Temple of Sacred Love getting re acquainted, for I have not yet been intimate with a man in this life."

"All in good time, my dear," smiled Garlita. "Now, whilst Kaitewha is directing the digging operations below the temple, how would you like the sublime and pleasurable experience of an aromatic bath in the healing waters of the Temple of Rejuvenation?"

"Wonderful," sighed Aloma. "It was a long walk from my old village and it will refresh me before I meet Kaitewha. How long do you think they will be? My body is beginning to remember and crave for his caress."

"Perhaps days," murmured Garlita. "The priorities of men are sometimes puzzling. Why search for the treasure beneath the ground when a far better treasure awaits right here? Even a High Priestess knows that some things should not wait, especially love. I'll see what I can do, my dear. I know that Kaitewha is just as impatient as you are to become reunited. You may not have too many times together, as Tane, the great God of Light, has told Rahitan that another explosion may be due soon, and that it like the big bang, can not be prevented. That is why it was so urgent to recall as many as possible."

"Oh Garlita," said Aloma with anguish, "How long do you think we have? I couldn't bear to have just found you and then lose you. After my bath, can we visit the people, tell them how happy I am to be back, and to share some love?"

"Of course, Princess Aloma. But now come, the bath is prepared," the older woman smiled and thought, *Still our Princess, thinking of the needs of others before herself.*

Garlita led Aloma through into a large building adorned by arched columns of red and white speckled marble. Peering through the doors, Aloma gasped at the sheer beauty of the place. A series of crystal clear pools were arranged around a large fountain that played jets of hot water into each pool, keeping them hot for those wallowing in the therapeutic waters. White robed women came forward smiling.

"Welcome, Princess Aloma," said one tall, muscular woman, who seemed to be in charge of the healing temple. "We have prepared you a special bath with all the herbs and flowers you used to love so much. We remember how you like the water temperature, not too hot, and that you loved to be massaged after your bath."

Tears of remembrance welled in Aloma's eyes, to run unchecked down her cheeks. Rushing forward she threw her arms around the tall woman.

"Angelica, how wonderful to see you here. And Marlette, Phoete and Erana. Have you been here long?" Excitedly, Aloma danced around the smiling women, singing a song that rushed into her head. "Joy, joy, joy, there is so much joy in the world, let me share some with you."

Angelica led Aloma to a cubicle to help her disrobe and to prepare for the herbal bath. When the younger woman stood naked in front of her, Angelica nodded in approval at Aloma's small, firm breasts, slender waist, rounded thighs and long shapely legs.

"As always, you have chosen a beautiful body. With your blond hair and blue eyes you seem more like the Princess I remember. When last we were together, your hair was brown and your eyes green. For most of your lives you have had fair hair and blue eyes and a sensitive, caring nature, a mark of the Pleiadian lineage. Let me wrap this warm towel around you and prepare for the luxury of the bath, my Princess. Now, come with me to the pool".

Letting the towel drop to the floor, Aloma slid into the steaming pool, letting out a sigh of contentment and inhaled deeply. Flowers of all colours floated on the surface, releasing their perfumes ino the steam.

"We had no such pool in our village, although the boiling water that bubbled up through holes in the ground was used for cooking," said Aloma. "I once suggested to the Chief that a pool could be dug and filled with water siphoned off from the boiling holes, but he did not understand how therapeutic this would be for tired bodies and refused my request. In spite of his refusal, some of the women then got together and under my instruction, dug a hole large enough for two to enter but as it was not sealed, the mud made it uncomfortable. But I knew that the mud did wonders for the health of the skin and body, so I used it often."

Aloma relaxed in the pool until Angelica returned to tell her that it was time for the massage, and stood holding the towel while Aloma wrapped herself in its warm folds.

The massage area was warmed by passing steam through large stone cylinders that lined the room. Each cylinder was decorated with brightly painted birds, flowers and symbols, while a bowl of perfumed oil pressed from plants sat warming in a small niche. Aloma climbed onto the massage table and relaxed completely. With expert hands, Angelica began to smooth away the tension in Aloma's body, finding tender areas and releasing knots in her muscles, caused by the long walk through the forest.

"Mmm, what utter bliss," murmured Aloma. "If I had remembered how good this felt, I would have arrived years ago."

"Have you spoken to Kaitewha yet, Princess?" asked Angelica. "I heard he was overwhelmed with impatience to be with you. How unfair it seems that he has to help Rahitan find the scrolls. You must be longing to reunite with him."

"I have not yet seen him. Is he still handsome? After so many aeons, what is another day or two? "Aloma relaxed even more, as the pampering to her limbs and torso continued. "I could lie here forever being massaged by you, Angelica."

Emerging from the Temple of Rejuvenation with a look of relaxed bliss on her face, and wearing a new long green gown enhancing the curves of her body, Aloma sought Garlita and together they walked slowly around the village, greeting the people from whom she had been so long parted. Her infectious laugh preceded her, so that the Atema came to greet and hug her. As they approached the main temple, Garlita stopped suddenly, as though she had walked into an invisible wall.

"Princess, we should go no further. The men are busy with the excavation but I have something that will please you," she said.

Just then, a great shout arose from the end of the tunnel being dug under the temple. Kaitewha, covered in ash and dirt, his white teeth gleaming though the grime, emerged holding a small shining object in his hand. He was about to place it in Rahitan's outstretched hand, when he looked up, straight into the eyes of Aloma. His heart missed a beat, as slowly he walked toward her and knelt, to instead offer her the object.

"My Love, how beautiful you are. You look so fresh and clean and I am covered with dirt. Do I dare to touch you?" He looked at the object glittering in the sun and then at Aloma. "My Princess, do you remember the statue we made in your likeness just before the big bang? We have found it. Here is the golden ball it's hand held. Somehow it has reappeared in this dimension; perhaps because you have come to us."

Just as Aloma stretched out her hand to take the ball, Rahitan grabbed it.

"No, I wish to hold it first. If the energetic memory is still intact, we should be able to play the scenes of its creation on the side of the temple wall. Stand aside."

Holding the golden ball gently in both hands he held it aloft, closed his eyes and began to hum softly. The ball started to glow with a soft yellow light which quickly became stronger. Rahitan then held it out in front of him and focused on the smooth white wall of the temple. Fascinated, the assembled group watched as moving colours and shapes became discernible. Kaitewha, still kneeling, glanced up at the radiant woman standing before him and took her hand.

"You are my breath, my life, my wife. I love you," he whispered.

Aloma blushed for in this life, she had little experience of a lover's words.

"Kaitewha, my love, how happy I am today. It is the first day of my, our, new life. The old one has vanished now that we have again found each other."

Kaitewha leapt to his feet to embrace her. Such was the power of their love, that as their energies merged, the golden ball began to vibrate with music and light, projecting strong images onto the wall. The lovers parted to watch in awe. They saw themselves nearly twenty-four thousand years earlier in a state of animation preparing for their demise at the wrath of the volcano gods. Figures they recognised dashed around a courtyard in front of a temple far grander than the one before which they now stood. Thieron gasped as he recognised the identical scenes he had been shown during his regression with Morpheus. A large block of green stone from the Canoe shaped island lying to the south of the great stingray, was placed on a plinth, and under the skilled hands of the master sculptor, began to assume the shape of the Princess. The maker of jewellery fashioned the eyes from lapis lazuli and agate and placed them lovingly in the sculpted sockets. The worker in gold approached, holding a shining golden ball which he placed in the completed statue's outstretched hand. Magically, the statue assumed a living essence as many of the Atema filed past it, pouring gifts of love, knowledge, wisdom, healing, crafts, joy and happiness into its form and into the golden ball. The onlookers saw and recalled the last days of their former existence, how they danced and sang under the influence of Pausanius' sacred herbal brew, how they embraced each other in preparation for their demise. They watched how, as a group, they had raised the vibration of the statue until it disappeared from their sight to be protected from the physical forces that would destroy their village. When the images stopped, they stood in silence, memory flooding through them, tears trickling down their cheeks. Even Rahitan was moved. Now they had regrouped for the last time before the next explosion. Memories of times and incarnations since their first regrouping after the big bang, nearly four thousand years earlier surfaced. Peaceful lives in which they left a succession of bodies worn out by advancing years, lives of learning, contentment, and love, continuously focussed on the sacred work of holding the harmonious balance in their land.

And now that the golden ball had been found, the green stone statue of Aloma must be just further along the blocked tunnel. Rahitan called to the gardeners, "Remove the tunnelling equipment and proceed by hand, and be very careful not to damage the statue. You have seen what a splendid work of art it is."

Turning to Garlita he continued, "I wonder why we did not find this statue a couple of thousand years ago. Perhaps we had to follow a different line of development. When we find the ancient library, one of the scrolls will should us. Unfortunately, my memory is still not completely intact."

The four young men struggled to pull the tunnelling equipment from the hole, and after bowing to Aloma, returned to the tunnel with hand spades and digging sticks. Many of the Atema were now gathered around the entrance, awaiting the re-emergence of the statue.

"What a momentous occasion," whispered Angelica to Garlita. "To find the living and the immortalised Princess on the same day."

A shout of elation came from the tunnel. "Shine more light down here. We have found her. I can feel the hand that held the golden ball."

The Atema crowded closer, all wanting a glimpse of the statue, for so long hidden, and now holding the key to their past and future and to the scrolls.

"Move back," yelled Rahitan. "Give the men room to breathe. We will all see her statue soon enough. In the meantime, let us cherish our living Princess who has found us on this day."

So saying, he called for carriers to bring the litter on which Aloma had entered the village. He bade her sit on it, and personally escorted her around the village, stopping to greet everyone for the second time. Aloma was overjoyed at her reception but relieved when she was finally returned to the courtyard. Standing on its three tiered plinth was the statue, cleaned and shining in the warm sun. It appeared to have suffered no ill effects from being entombed for centuries. Or perhaps, as Rahitan informed them, it had remained in another dimension until very recently. Aloma's return to the village of the Atema, prior to their next demise, seemed to coincide with its discovery.

"We have had enough excitement for one day. Let us retire to contemplate the importance of our discovery. We will resume digging for the scroll room tomorrow and also try out Morpheus's rock levitating technique."

Rahitan sighed and turned to Garlita. "Why do we have to experience another annihilation? So much work achieved only to be obliterated again. I am so tired of this earthly game."

"What do we do now, Rahitan?" asked Garlita. "We need time to retrieve the gifts we stored, and replace them with updated knowledge, before the Lord of the lake and mountain blows his top again."

"Ah, my dear," Rahitan spoke so softly that Garlita had to strain to hear him. "This bang will not be nearly as devastating as the first one, but nevertheless, it will be very unpleasant for us all. Once again we will make the transition, and then about 2000 years in the future will come a third explosion. After that, the land will be at rest until the end of time, as we experience it. But the world as we know it will be radically changed. Tane tells me that he can hold the forces from erupting for the moment so we may work our harmonic balancing act over the land now that most of us have returned. It is in sore need of some light and the forces of darkness are ever watchful for weakness. But eventually will come the devastation. Care to join me again for a third round?"

"I too am becoming rather weary of the constant replaying of the familiar story, my old friend," said Garlita, her sensitive face curling up in distaste. "I wonder if there is an alternative."

"The alternative is eternal life in the realms of other worlds, that part of us which always rests with the creator of our world. Ah, Garlita, would that things were different for you and I. But we have our destiny to follow. True intelligence is the capacity of the mind to honour the wisdom of the heart," replied Rahitan, gently stroking her cheek and looking deeply into her gold flecked eyes. "But first we must unearth the scroll room. However, that awaits until tomorrow, and I am so weary from the excitement of this day. Come, my Priestess, the sun sinks below the horizon and the shadows lengthen. Join me for a glass of the nectar of the Gods, whose colour resembles the golden flecks in your eyes. To see the ardour in the eyes of our young lovers has made me feel old. They need time to re-acquaint themselves with the bliss of love."

Turning to the workmen he called, "Leave the digging for the scroll room for tomorrow. You have done well today and with our Princess returned we are twice blessed. We will resume following the morning meditation." Tucking Garlita's hand into the crook of his elbow, he guided her towards his private quarters, a place she rarely visited.

"What has moved you to romance, Rahitan?" laughed Garlita, looking fondly into her old friends deep blue eyes. "I know the weight for the responsibility of the Temple hangs heavy at times, but would you exchange it for a lesser life?"

Rahitan stopped and turned towards her. "Yes, there are times when I would gladly choose love, but this time my life destiny has not chosen so. Perhaps on our next round we can come together as an ordinary couple. Come, my dear, let us drink to love."

"What of the celebration to welcome back our Princess and Kaitewha. Is now the right time for it to be arranged?" asked Garlita.

"No," replied Rahitan. "Let them have tonight to themselves in the Temple of Sacred Love. When the scrolls have been found and deciphered, and the information in the statue reanimated, we will hold a great ceremony at the next fullness of the moon. I know our people will understand. For tonight let us forget our public roles and enjoy each other's company."

SIX

The Golden Scrolls

As the golden light of dawn flowed across the land, the resounding melody of the great crystal bell, played by Garlita's mind, awoke the Atema to a new day. Birds joyfully joined in with their melodious calls to the new day as small animals searched for food. In the Temple of Sacred Love Kaitewha and Aloma sighed with total contentment.

"Was there ever such a wonder as the night we have just experienced?" murmured Kaitewha burying his face into the long sweet smelling hair of his twin flame. "Our hearts have merged as one, our minds and bodies remember the sweetness of all the times we have been together, and still you are the greatest mystery I have ever known. I love you, Aloma."

Aloma rolled a little stiffly onto her back and gazed into the eyes of her refound lover and murmured, "I now know why none of the young men in the village of my birth interested me. I was waiting for you. I think I shall burst with happiness. It may take a little while for my body to fully merge with yours, as we once used to, but I am willing to practice every night. The healing priestess gave me some herbs to take each day so I that would not conceive a child. One day we will bring a special soul into this world, one who will have a great destiny in the outer world. But not for some time yet. Can we practice again?"

"That, my beloved, is exactly what I had in mind," Kaitewha smiled. "We need to catch up on a lot of lost time."

Aloma closed her eyes and surrendered to love. Her heart merged with her soul essence to allow energy from the higher realms of herself to flow into her body, and through her energy centres into Kaitewha. Thus fused, they merged their energies to experience the bliss of two lovers totally united. As their breath mingled, an alchemical process of fusion completed their union.

Some time later, Kaitewha took a deep breath and reclaimed his essence. "Ah, my dearest love, I wish never to be separated from you for a moment. After the golden scrolls have been found and my assistance is no longer needed, we can spend as much time as we wish in the Temple of Sacred Love with the masters of the Art of Connubial Love so we can join on the highest levels of our being. I'm sure it won't take us long to remember how ecstatic that can be."

"I had forgotten how beautiful this Temple is even now, in its diminished state," said Aloma. "The original Temple that I was shown during the recalling with Garlita yesterday was far more splendid than this one, but look, the fountain still plays water in time with music, the rainbow colours glow and then fade, and the perfume is as sweet as ever."

"And these beds are as soft and supporting, although I wonder if the mechanism for swivelling them into different positions has been installed," added Kaitewha as he luxuriously stretched before getting to his feet. "Let's have a look."

Bending down, he opened a small flap set into the base of the wide bed and pressed a button marked "Spin." Immediately, the bed with Aloma stretched out on it began to rotate, slowly at first and then with increasing speed.

"Stop it, my love, I'm getting dizzy," she yelled.

"I can't reach the off button, and the bed is going too fast for me to catch it," Kaitewha answered, as he frantically searched the room for a master switch. "This must be a different design. Perhaps I should have read the instructions first. That's me. Press first, regret later. Ah, this looks like something." He pressed a large red button set into a niche behind the door, and immediately the bed stopped its wild spinning and sank into the floor, leaving Aloma feeling sick with fright. A soft whirring noise alerted Kaitewha to a panel sliding over the bed, and he pulled the dizzy young woman up, just before she was entombed.

"Are you all right? We must find out what that is really for and how to use it," suggested Kaitewha with a sigh of relief. "Can't be caught like that again, my love."

"Yes. It is a long time since I have felt the emotion of fear as strongly as that. I must ask Garlita what happened. But first, take me in your arms. I am still shaking." Aloma was soon enveloped in the strong arms of her lover and relaxed into his warm embrace. Strengthened, she looked towards the courtyard where she saw Rahitan and Garlita mount the three steps of the raised central platform to address the Atema, who had gathered to greet the rising sun. Rahitan raised both arms causing the long loose sleeves of his dark blue robe to slide down, revealing a tattoo on each arm. The mark of the High Priest of the Atema throughout time rippled around his forearms, writhing its serpent body; its head had glowing golden eyes implanted on the back of each hand, revealing small oval pieces of gold that were inserted under his skin. Reflecting rays of light from the sun arced into his outstretched fingers, along his arms to his body and out through his eyes to shine over those gathered. This caused each to feel vitalized and peaceful, prepared for this day that would bring revelations to the whole group. During this daily morning salute to the sun, the Atema absorbed sustenance to strengthen and sustain their physical bodies and the merging of their minds to strengthen their unity and spiritual power to hold the balance in the land.

Thinking themselves unnoticed, Kaitewha and Aloma quietly slipped in amongst the people, joining in the morning ritual. Then Garlita raised her arms, revealing a tattooed symbol, similar to Rahitan's, curling around her forearms. Instead of gold, the eyes of her serpents sparkled silver beams over those below, helping their minds to become focussed on the work they were about to undertake each day and to sustain their emotional bodies. Aloma remembered how important both the male and female instruments of the Creator were in all aspects of life, especially during rituals designed to balance the land and those who lived there.

I wonder when my jewels will be inserted, Aloma thought, before asking herself, *Why did I think that?*

After the ceremony of the salute to the sun for sustenance, Aloma asked Rahitan, "Master Rahitan, during the ceremony I noticed the design of blue serpents entwined around your arms and the golden eyes in its head at the back of your hand. Why do they not show during other times?"

The High Priest gazed deeply into her eyes for such a long time that Aloma felt quite uncomfortable, and lowered her head. Gently Rahitan placed one hand with the glowing golden eyes still shining, under her chin and lifted her head. "Princess, don't you remember your marks? Soon it will be time to replace your symbols. It will be done during the celebrations that will be held during the next full moon."

Aloma shut her eyes in thought. "Yes, I think so. I remember a spiral, the ancient symbol of the universe, with a diamond in its centre, was tattooed onto the back of each hand. When the diamond was activated by the sun's rays, refracted light displayed the image of the sacred rainbow over everything. Kaitewha also had a symbol, an eagle with its wings soaring up his forearms and bright blue stones set as eyes in its head on the back of his hands. When not being used in the power of ceremony, they faded from view."

"Well remembered," said Rahitan, then he winked at her. "Do you wish to keep the same symbol this time or choose another? We have a good range available."

"Perhaps this time she should have a diamond symbol tattoo, with an eye-shaped emerald in the centre," suggested Garlita. "Will that suit you, Aloma?"

Aloma laughed. "Whatever you say, my Priestess. I am just so happy to be here that I would even have the mark of the dragon tattooed on the back of my hand."

Garlita grabbed her arm and looked deeply into her eyes. "Never speak lightly of such things. There are some matters about which even you cannot jest, Princess."

Kaitewha slipped his arm around Aloma's waist. "My beloved, we have a lot to relearn." Turning to Rahitan he said, "When will we begin the search for the scroll room? I had some time to ponder on the whereabouts of the entrance last night, and my guidance tells me that we should dig no further below the statue's bed. Instead, we must look behind the library. Isn't that where Thieron found the scroll?"

Turning to the assembled and attentive crowd, Rahitan raised his voice. "My friends, today we embark on a journey of discovery. Why the time to rediscover the golden scrolls has only just opened to us I do not know, but perhaps we had other knowledge to find.

Now we can compare our discoveries of the last four thousand years with the ancient wisdom this will reveal, and see how far off the path we have wandered. Or even if both the old and the new are relevant. Times and ideals change. We cannot hold the ancient times bound in stone, never growing nor changing through the eras. That won't lead to an evolution of consciousness in the human species. Now let's get to work."

Kaitewha turned to Thieron who was standing as close to Aloma as he possible could without touching her, and asked "Where did you find the scroll, young scribe?"

Blushing as if caught out Thieron replied, "Perhaps I should show you. Follow me."

The library was built at the far end of the central courtyard and at its entrance Kaitewha stopped and then walked to the opposite side of the large stone building, and began to climb the hill behind it. From its summit he looked out over the whole star shaped temple complex, at the village built in circles around it and then closed his eyes. For some time he remained unmoving then said, "What we seek is under this hill and the entrance is behind those large head-shaped rocks. Morpheus, I am told you have developed a way of moving rocks and earth that doesn't involve hard physical labour. Would you care to share it so that we can all learn?"

The Master of Dreams laughed into his bushy orange beard glistening in the sunlight. "Of course, there are no secrets among us, you only have to ask. It may not work perfectly but with the power of group focus, I'm certain something will happen. Now if everyone will stand in two semi-circles behind me and close their eyes."

As instructed, the Atema formed two semi-circles, facing the monoliths with Morpheus in the middle. "Mind merge," instructed Morpheus. "Good, now concentrate on finding the entrance to the tunnel we wish to excavate.......... Now visualise the two great rocks blocking the entrance being separated, but remaining upright. They would make good guardians after we open the way."

Slowly the giant rocks began to move, earth and smaller rocks falling away, until they stood at a distance of four arm lengths apart, wide enough for a man to walk between. Kaitewha rushed through the opening and instantly disappeared from view.

A loud cry brought the others to the entrance. Kaitewha yelled, "Help! I need some light. I have fallen into a hole but I'm not hurt. Perhaps we should have visualised some stairs or asked the guardian spirits for permission to enter. Someone lower a light down using a long rope. I can tie it around my waist in case I fall again."

The rope and light were soon lowered with Thieron attached. "I'm coming with you."

Kaitewha untied the lantern and held it aloft. Shadows, released from their long sleep, danced around a great cave, and crept towards a tunnel at the far end. The two young men followed them.

"What do you make of this, Thieron?" asked Kaitewha. "This entrance is surrounded by hewn stone covered in symbols. Do you recognise any of them?

Thieron activated his own light for a closer look. "Yes," he replied becoming very excited. "Yes. This is in the same ancient script I saw when Rahitan showed me some of the scrolls during my regression with Morpheus; it looks like the same symbol as on the one Rahitan read to me just before the last big bang. Hold up your light so I can get a better look."

Another light flared and flickered as Rahitan and Morpheus were lowered down to the floor of the cave.

"We couldn't stand the suspense," confessed the High Priest. "What do the symbols over the entrance tell us, young scribe. I'll give you the honour of reading the first words."

Thieron became very still and muttered, "Beware, those who enter without permission."

"What was that? What did you say?" asked Morpheus.

"It says 'Beware, those who enter without permission,'" repeated Thieron more loudly.

"Haa. Of course," laughed Rahitan. "I remember I booby trapped the tunnel, long before the big bang. This is the back entrance. Normally I used the entrance from the library. We had better proceed with great caution if we don't want a nasty surprise. I quite outdid myself with this security system. Silly really, and quite unnecessary. Just an old man's game, for there are no real secrets amongst the Atema and the local natives were too terrified to come any where near here. I would have been most upset if anyone had been hurt. Follow me, and put your feet exactly in my footsteps."

"What's happening," called Garlita from the entrance between the rocks.

"Be patient, my dear," replied Rahitan. "We are entering a tunnel which I booby trapped before the big bang, and it will take all my courage and cunning to deactivate them. It is a secret entrance that leads to the scroll room. I used to enter this way when I wished to be alone with the scrolls. We'll soon find them." Turning to his companions he said, "Activate your extra sensory powers and tell me if you feel anything out of the ordinary. Now tread carefully."

Rahitan picked up a stone and threw it into the tunnel entrance. Immediately, sparks of blue light hissed and crackled across the opening.

"Device number one," chuckled the High Priest. "I'll deactivate it with my mind."

The electrical activity soon stopped and Rahitan cautiously entered the downward sloping tunnel, counting his steps. At the count of twenty he stopped. "Next one, chaps. Watch." He extended his staff forwards and a high-pitched noise echoed along the tunnel causing them to cover their ears and collapse with the vibration. After it ceased, Rahitan chuckled. "I thought one that was particularly effective. For an intruder, that noise would have made him permanently deaf and a total nervous wreck."

Twenty-five steps later they came to a heavy stone door. At its centre, a large engraved symbol of a serpent, similar to the tattoo on Rahitan's arms, sprang into life with it's golden eyes blazing. Overcoming any fear, their logical minds told them they were perfectly safe in the presence of their High Priest, the others looked more closely at the writhing serpent.

"It is a trick of illusion, made by the flickering lights," laughed Kaitewha in relief. "That could scare the wits out of an uninitiated intruder if he ever got this far."

Rahitan reached out to the serpent and pressed the two golden eyes in its head. Immediately the stone door swung open revealing a large, stone lined room. "Delighted it still works. I thought the big bang could have annihilated everything. Perhaps this room also went into another vibration, to return at this time for us to rediscover our lost wisdom. That is the way of the unknown. I still have so much to learn."

He stood aside and beckoned Thieron to enter. When the young scribe hesitated, Rahitan roared with laughter. "What, don't you trust me? Do you think a bucket of water will fall on your head?"

Sheepishly, Thieron grinned and walked into the room and held up his lantern. Initially golden colour shot around the room and then merged into one light to enable them to see. The others followed hot on his heels. A musty smell of kauri gum wafted through the dry still air.

"Good," said Rahitan. "The preservative still works. The gum of the giant kauri tree has kept everything from decaying, even here deep underground. We filled boxes with it help preserve our precious library. Now, let's see if the other lights still work."

The High Priest pressed a knob embedded in a niche, and uttered three words in the ancient language that only the highest initiates were taught, and light flooded the scroll room. "I'm amazed it still works. These three words of power never cease to impress me, even though I have used them for centuries. Thieron, see if you can find the scroll you were examining just before our last spectacular demise. It was the one with the rainbow light rods. Do you remember how to open the time proof case?"

Thieron moved to a shelf on which rested twelve large and twelve smaller cylinders, each with a different variety of gemstone embedded into the lid. He gently picked up a shining tube with a small circle of brightly coloured semi-precious stones. He was just about to open it when he said, "Master, I am afraid. I do remember that when the rainbow lights began to play around the room, they suddenly dimmed and you became very upset. What if that happens and we are about to be annihilated again."

"We are about to be blasted asunder again, my boy," said Rahitan, "but this one won't be quite so devastating. Tane has told me the great forces that control our earth mother can be held in check for perhaps another twenty years. That gives us a much longer time to prepare, and after that explosion it will only take us not quite two thousand years to regroup. By that time, the population growth and technology overuse on earth will be out of control and another form of cleansing may be needed. However, I do not foresee the rebuilding of our village and temple complex, for the way people will live in the future and their level of consciousness will not necessitate maintaining the old ways of living. There will also be political issues involving the ownership of this land by peoples who have not yet arrived on these shores. They will claim that they are the original inhabitants. It is not a time I relish returning to, but destiny is destiny."

Thieron pulled another cylinder from the shelf and pulled out a scroll with rods of greenstone, denoting its age and origin.

Handing it to Rahitan he asked, "Can you read this one instead, Master?"

Rahitan tenderly stroked the shining cylinder, walked to a stone table and removed the outer protective covering to reveal a roll of smoothly beaten gold covered with lexicography. Sliding one of the greenstone rods into a slot to hold it firm, he carefully unrolled the golden metal to reveal its contents. Morpheus and Kaitewha exhaled and Thieron gasped in awe at the beauty of the symbols etched in neat vertical rows along the entire length of the metre-long scroll measuring. From pocket in his robe, Rahitan took a pair of ground glass spectacles and put them on. He held a ball of light over the inscriptions, took a deep breath and began to read.

"This scroll tells of the creation and the interference by master geneticists of the human form on planet Earth. Life here has been periodically evolving for some three thousand million years. Beginning with a primordial mixture of chemical soup seeded with the potential for life by the creator gods, which slowly developed into aquatic cold and warm-blooded creatures, they eventually inhabited dry land. Some four million years ago, primates began to gather to live in tribes for protection and procreation. They walked on four legs and lived mostly in the great forests and jungles that covered the continents. These continents were in different positions around the earth than now. During the aeons, continental drift, impact by large meteors, and occasional polar shifts have drastically altered the shape of the world as mapped by the first extra-terrestrial visitors to this small planet. Around two and a half million years ago, primates began to walk upright and use stone tools. Around five hundred thousand years ago, certain primitive humanoids began to behave in a manner that interested the creator gods who monitored Earth. The manufacture and use of useful tools and of fire signalled that this species was evolving. Around three hundred and fifty thousand years ago, when the creator gods arrived on Earth they needed slaves to mine precious minerals, especially gold, found abundantly on certain continents, especially in the land now known as Africa, they genetically engineered a species of humanoid with special qualities and the strength to labour long hours. They did this by mixing the eggs of the primitives with the sperm of their own males which they inserted into birth mothers. A degree of intelligence was inserted into their brains to enable them to follow instructions. Mining was torturous work in which the other world visitors had no wish to undertake. So successful was the mutation that these sub-humans began to think for themselves, although at that time they could not procreate their species. Then a decision was made by the galactic federation that controlled this section of the universe, to abandon all activities on Earth and allow the creatures to develop at their own pace, and to see what would happen. The master geneticists were furious at this interference in their experiments.

Before they left, a series of mutations were seeded to enable the humans to increase their numbers, for without constant replacement they would soon become extinct. Until that time the women of the creator gods had acted as surrogate mothers. Two spiralling strands of the blueprint of life were inserted into certain individuals, one designed for the procreation of life and the other contained the necessary knowledge for survival in a hostile world. These humans had the ability to reproduce themselves and consequently. multiplied. Occasionally the creator beings returned to Earth to monitor their experiment. However, the pace of biological evolution was exceedingly slow, so around three hundred thousand years ago, teams of genetic scientists secretly landed in several areas on Earth and began to insert extra filaments into the blueprint of earth creatures, which forced their development at a vastly accelerated rate. Knowledge was inserted into ten extra strands of helix, enabling humanity to become exceedingly creative in every way. Connection with the Absolute creator of all things was inserted and the aspect of a human soul came into being. Art and science, architecture and stone masonry, music and drama, spinning and weaving and a higher mind capable of solving complex mathematical problems were inserted into the consciousness of humans. This was a profound change, as up until that time, they had lived in caves and hunted large animals with clubs.

Down through the ages, gods of myth and legend were given the credit for gifting humankind with these evolutionary tools. These twelve helixes plugged into twelve vibrating vortices of energy, seven that kept the body healthy and strong and five linked to the higher gates of consciousness.

Great civilisations rose and fell, for the male of the species was encoded with warlike tendencies, forever battling with his neighbour. The female of the species was designed to bear children and was worshipped at times, but denigrated at others. Occasionally, men became dominant over women, and in turn women began to have the upper hand, using beauty and inner power as unassailable weapons over men. It became a huge game, this battle of the sexes. It still continues in many tribes throughout the lands. Occasionally the earth mother convulsed and rolled over, changing her position in the daily revolution of her path around the sun. When this happened most of the humans on her skin perished along with their civilisations dotted around her body. Seas rose to become dry land and cities sank beneath the rising seas to be cleansed."

Rahitan paused, looking up at his companions who were now seated on a stone bench beside the script table. "Are you beginning to remember our mysterious history? Once upon a time each one of you knew how to read these scrolls. Who would like to continue the dialogue?"

Morpheus jumped to his feet. "I will. I have dreamed of this moment for lifetimes. Now the ancient information is available once again, we can instruct all our companions in its grand story."

Assuming a pose that made them all laugh, Morpheus bent over the golden scroll and began to speak, slowly at first because of the unfamiliarity of the script, but quickly gained increasing confidence.

"Some fifty thousand years before our present time, the creator geneticists once again visited this jewel of a planet to check on their progenies. The visitors were pleased that the humans they had so arrogantly interfered but also horrified with the great state of civilization and conscious advancement. Soon, it was feared, these humans would think themselves capable of becoming creator gods, with the ability to procreate life genetically and scientifically.

In certain groups of humans, millions of light encoded filaments were purposely rearranged in the helix structure of the body when the creator gods removed five of the double helixes, leaving the original two strands to enable humankind to be controlled by frequency modulation. Soul access remained intact as by then the karmic pattern of the Law of Cause and Effect was well under way, but emotions were curtailed. Emotions assist the physical body to excrete chemical reactions, hormones and enzymes that have a catalytic effect upon one another. Emotions are very necessary for human existence. When the light encoded filaments begin to line up with proper emotions, a being can move through its memories into other realities. Feelings connect the multi dimensional self to the Absolute creator. This discovery was not in the long term plans of the creators of humans as it would lead to an understanding of what had happened to their races.

A tremendous catastrophe for humankind was initiated by the creator gods before returning to their home planet. The earth reversed her magnetic polarity, the poles changed position and most of the untampered humans and their magnificent cities were deluged, leaving the lesser mutations to resurrect some semblance of civilization. Life returned to a very basic level of existence. Although most of the higher intelligence was removed, occasionally a genetic throwback surfaced who explored the higher mind, searching for the mysteries of the universe, and the meaning of all life. This being became famous for his or her wisdom, and revered as a great sage.

Small groups of highly intelligent people survived the cataclysms. In secret isolated valleys hidden from the creator gods they set up mystery schools, where the ancient wisdom was taught to each succeeding generation. The Atema are spiritually descended from these ancient survivors. Many thousands of years later, because of genetic abnormalities that developed as a result of a limited gene pool, they decided to incarnate within developing tribes to ensure stronger bodies. Later they devised a way of calling their own to gather at appointed times and places. This practice is still operating to this day and will continue until there are enough people on the planet to provide enough genetic availability for the vast majority of the human population to become enlightened. Then a different method of keeping alive the knowledge of our galactic inheritance will develop, for at the end of the next Piscean age, humankind will be ready to evolve into a higher dimension. This may be caused by the Earth once again convulsing to cleanse herself, of what may well be a very polluted and damaged body. All will be in order.

Historically our planet has been controlled by a group that has limited humanity and as a consequence has created chaos and fear, war and famine, and pitted man against man. This fear created emotions so charged with negative energy it emitted enough force for the creator gods to use for their sustenance. It was common knowledge that at times, they fed off our negativity. That is why they don't want anything to change. The role of the Atema, and other groups like us, is to change the imposed systems by raising the vibration of those on Earth, which is done by holding a certain amount of electromagnetic energy to assist in increasing the frequency in humans. We are the Keepers of Frequency. Whenever an age changes or a great conflagration is about to occur we incarnate to live and teach by example, to hold the focus of the Divine Absolute Creator on Earth. It is the mighty work for which we volunteered eons ago. To carry light is an awesome task. In future times, the true purpose of Earth's destiny will once again be revealed."

Morpheus straightened, stretched and smiled at his companions. "That is as far as this scroll takes us. I wish to know more about the frequency of Light. What colour are the rods of the next one, Rahitan?"

"I think that is enough for one day," replied the High Priest. "We must not be overly inquisitive and read them all at once. They are to be savoured, revered and understood on many levels. The one with the Rose Quartz rods we will take to share with the Atema. We will read a little each day and discuss the information. We have plenty of time now that Tane has promised to delay the destructive forces."

"Yes," added Kaitewha, "And every moment I spend away from my Princess is a moment wasted. I am so glad that it didn't take five days to find the scroll room. Are we ready to return to the others, Rahitan?"

The old High Priest laughed. "Ah, young love. Perhaps in a life far into the future I will be able to love a woman as much as you do. Garlita and I may just take an incarnation off and try it," he added with a rare show of intimacy, for he never revealed to anyone how deeply alone his inner essence felt at times. Rolling up the golden scroll he reverently replaced it into the shiny cylinder and headed for the door. When the others had passed through, he pressed the knob to extinguish the light and then touched the two golden eyes in the serpent on the door and stood back to watch the great stone door swing silently and smoothly into its original place, well camouflaged in the wall.

"Follow me," he boomed as his voice echoed along the passageway to reach the people anxiously awaiting at the entrance. A small platform had been lowered into the hole. Rahitan stood on it, and yelled "Haul me up," and disappeared up into the natural light of day. The others followed, and soon they were answering the excited questions of their people.

"One at a time," roared Rahitan. He loved to hear his own voice lifted above its normal pitch. "We have found the scroll room, and following the sunset meditation, we will all gather in the great temple where part of this ancient scroll will be read. Each evening we will read and discuss its contents until we have exhausted all possible misunderstandings. Then we will continue to interpret the eleven other large and twelve small scrolls still secreted in their nest. One large and one small for each month should suffice. Until evening, my friends." He motioned Garlita to accompany him to his special office inside the temple. At the propylaeum he paused. "This is a very special day, my dear. We will create an annual ceremonial occasion to celebrate the returning of our Princess and her consort, and the rediscovery of the scroll room.

Nothing like this has happened to us for centuries. Even I am excited."

"The next full moon would be propitious. Several of the major planets will be in alignment and the ancients tell me that a bright comet is due to pass through our southern skies at that time. This gives us a time to prepare. How thrilling it is to be able to create a new ceremony. Perhaps I'll even compose a new piece to play on the crystal bowl. That should raise the vibrations for miles around," replied Garlita, as she entered the small office. She sat on a large padded cushion covered with fine needlework depicting a colourful sunset, a gift from one of the many talented women who lived in the complex.

Rahitan clapped his hands and a man appeared with two tall glasses of golden liquid. Handing one to Garlita and raising the other he said, "To the future and the past" and drank deeply of the refreshing juice. "Now, how shall we begin the ceremony of the triumphant return? With so much else happening, the tapping into the secrets of the greenstone statue of the Princess will have to wait, although there is vitally important information contained within that could help us right now."

"Why not reconstruct Aloma's arrival, then Kaitewha's sudden appearance at our gates, and how he found out how to deactivate the blue protective beams with his courage. Then just as we have done during the past two days, we could replay the scenes depicted in the golden ball on the side of the temple, dance around the greenstone statue of the Princess, before rushing pell mell to the rock guardians behind the library. Even Morpheus's trick of moving stones and earth could be used to teach new arrivals how to maximise that aspect of the power of their minds. All we have to follow the actual events. They are amazing enough without inventing any new ideas." Garlita became quite animated, causing the golden flecks in her dark grey eyes to flash and power flow through her tall, lithe body.

Rahitan took her hand and looked into her magnificent eyes, saying, "How beautiful you are when in your power. Earlier I confessed to our young friends that I really looked forward to an ordinary life with you at the beginning of our next life. Now that I know that our demise is immanent, I feel less like the Priest I have always been and more like a man. We'd better be careful, my dear, or our vows will be broken, and we both know what the consequences of that are, though I wonder if it really matters any longer with the end of this epoch so near. Still we had better wait for a while longer to see which way the consciousness of the world is moving. Tomorrow I will open the canister with the rainbow rods to see how the light moves. I trust it will not confirm my suspicions."

"My dear friend and colleague, please don't stray from your self imposed path just yet. We still have a great deal to achieve in this lifetime, and can not risk our powers waning because of a moments temptation. That is for others, the intimate entwining of bodies in passion. Perhaps we can merge our souls in a cosmic embrace as that does not transgress our vows of celibacy. However, that must wait. The return of Aloma and Kaitewha seems to have unhinged you a little, but you'll get over it, my dear. Come now, we have work to do."

Rahitan smiled. "You are right as always. It has come to me that a group of the Atema must undertake a sacred journey to share the knowledge of the scrolls with other Enlightened Ones throughout this land of the great fish. As you know there are six other villages similar to ours, hidden in remote forests, all keeping intact the grid that promotes harmony and balance in the land. I once heard from Albinon, the High Priest of the village two weeks walk north from here, that there are also two such villages in the large canoe-shaped island to the south, in the area where our sacred green stone is mined.

We will prepare to leave at the time of the next full moon after the Ceremony of the Triumphant Return. Even though Aloma and Kaitewha wish to spend time in the Temple of Sacred Love, they also need to learn how to be sustained by light which, as you know, will take twenty-one days. After that I would like them to accompany us, along with Thieron, Morpheus and Zenita, your acolyte with the remarkable healing powers. She may be needed and I know Morpheus covertly watches her. Perhaps we can make a match there, as we cannot come together ourselves."

"What about Thieron," laughed Garlita. "He will be the odd one out if you keep up this matchmaking."

"Scribes don't need partners," snapped Rahitan. "They are far too busy. Besides I need him and we all know he is in love with Aloma and will never partner another."

"Selfish old humbug," shot back Garlita as she glided from the room.

Once left alone, Rahitan pulled the lid from the scroll canister, and gently placed the golden scroll on his large wooden desk, which was so ancient and extremely heavy piece of furniture that had been cut from one large slab of kauri set on two ornately carved uprights that could be detached. Well balanced and highly polished, it was the High Priests only personal possession. Several decades ago, when he had been called to rejoin his real family of Light deep in the forest, he had it carried by his birth tribe to the edge of the forbidden territory and subsequently arranged for several strong Atema to covey it the rest of the distance. At that time his use of mind control to convey weightlessness on heavy objects was not yet fully developed. Very few of the people brought personal possessions from outside, their needs being adequately catered for, but Rahitan felt his desk would be exceedingly useful in his roll of High Priest. And he had been correct. Now he pulled up a chair made of similar wood, arranged the light ball to hover directly above the scroll with the rose quartz rods, and lovingly unrolled it. Symbols leapt from the smoothly rolled gold, probing the recesses of his mind, awakening long forgotten knowledge and revealing themselves once again to the mind of a mystic and scholar. Charges of love swept into his heart and tears fell unchecked onto the scroll as he remembered his great and powerful love for the Creator of all worlds. That was the secret to his longing for love that he had expressed to Garlita. His soul was sensing the reawakening to the immortal aspect of himself that had never been separated from its source of light and love. A blazing light shafted through the top of his head, down along the energy centres of his spine and out through his feet into the floor and back again. Each cell of his body felt super charged, spinning out of control, fused with energy and power. Bubbles of light seemed to course through each limb to meet with explosive force within his abdomen, before moving up to his head.

Jumping to his feet he cried, "Io, my creator and sustainer, your love has reawakened me. I thought you had abandoned me. I tried so hard to keep the faith through distant memory of the sustenance. We have all been living on diluted sustenance thinking it was real. I thought I had power and knowledge. Now I know it to be nothing without love." He sank onto the deep pile rug on the floor and cried tears of awakening and cleansing from the depth of his being.

Dawn was probing her silver fingers across the land when he awoke for he had fallen into a deep sleep full of vivid dreams. He stood and stretched. *Today will be a new beginning. I must discuss my dreams with Morpheus, my desire for love with Garlita and thank our Princess most profoundly for her gift of love to help me awaken. How far from the path I strayed, thinking I had knowledge and power without the real experience of true love. This priestly illusion that celibacy increases power will be the first to fall. Ah, Garlita is awake; I hear the crystal bowl resonating.*

Hurriedly straightening his crumpled robe and running his fingers through his tousled long white hair, Rahitan hurried to find Garlita. He hardly noticed the flickering light casting flower shaped patterns on the shining floor. Usually he stopped to admire their lively dance. Sensing Garlita's presence he stopped and saw her for the very first time through the eyes of a lover. Walking softly towards her, he stopped just in front and took her long slender hand in his old brown gnarled one, looking deeply into her lustrous gold flecked eyes.

"Pleasant awakenings, my dear. Such a night I have just passed you wouldn't believe it. Somehow the energy from the scroll we found, combined with the return of Aloma has awakened me to my senses. What a game I have been playing. Last night I discovered that the one true path to the love of the Creator is through the love of another human to manifestly increase that power of love. The power of sexuality in its most ideal form can convey more fully what spiritual bliss, oneness and timelessness are, more than any other human experience. Will you practice these sensual delights with me, my Love? The rose rods scroll talks deeply of this aspect of humanness."

Garlita swiftly withdrew her hand from the intimate caress and stepped back. Gazing intently into Rahitan's beaming face she exclaimed, "Whatever has gotten into you, old man. I am dedicated to the temple, now and forever more. I cannot forsake my vows just because you have had an experience that tells you connubial love is a more superior way to the heart of the Creator than direct connection. If the situation was different you would be my first love, but when I was welcomed once again into the very heart of Io, I totally merged with that sublime consciousness. We are one and I would never betray that co-joining, even for you, my dearest."

"Come with me," laughed Rahitan, gleefully pulling the resisting Garlita along the corridor towards his office. Once inside, he sat her down on the desk chair and asked her to read the symbols. Slowly at first, but with increasing confidence and joy, Garlita absorbed their message from ages past. Finally, she stood up and immediately sank to the soft floor with a blissful look lighting her face, such was the vibration of love imbued into that scroll.

Gently, Rahitan pulled her to her feet and tenderly embraced the shaken Priestess. "You too have felt the power of the force of love contained within the symbols. Remember how we used to be together thousands of years ago, before the big bang? Remember how we loved each other, even though we were also then High Priest and Priestess? We chose a different route this epoch, but now that my memory of our deep and committed love has reawakened, I have no wish to continue with the distant formality of the game we have both played for the past four thousand years. Celibacy is not nearly so life enhancing as mutual desire, which is energised by the involuntary life force that creates an electrifyingly blissful feeling and longing. This longing for connection never ceases in the human soul. We have tried the celibate experiment and found it less than perfect. Come, my long lost love, share your god connected soul with mine and your purified body with mine, so our hearts may once again merge in bliss. I know Io has sent the Princess and Kaitewha back to us on the same days as we rediscovered the statue and the scrolls for a divine purpose. And this is part of it."

Giggling like a teenage girl, the stately form of the High Priestess softened to reveal a voluptuous woman in the prime of her life, awakening to the power of love.

Pulling him down onto the soft rug she murmured, "Come, Rahitan, show me what you say we have been missing this epoch. Or perhaps as we are both so inexperienced in this field, as much as I don't like to ask for instruction, we should take counsel with the teachers in the Temple of Sacred Love before consummating our union."

Rahitan's breath came in short panting gasps, "That would ravage the last shreds of my pride. As so many other understandings have returned, let us hope that of making love will follow. Later we can take instruction if we need to. It is though a switch has been pressed on and I can no longer hold my desire in check. Oh, Garlita, how beautiful and sensuous you are. Love me. Please."

In answer Garlita arched her back, pressing her body along the length of his and touched her lips to the bearded mouth. Giggling, she said, "You are a hairy old goat. How did this happen to us. It would seem most undignified if someone were to walk into your office."

Immediately Rahitan activated an energy field to prevent intrusion and turned again to Garlita. "We will have no interruptions," he mumbled.

SEVEN

Instruction

With only a short time to prepare for the inaugural Ceremony of the Triumphant Return, the Atema worked tirelessly. The entire Temple was cleaned inside and out, flowers and shrubs in planter urns arranged around the central courtyard, the statue of the Princess with the golden ball restored into her hand, polished until it gleamed. New gowns and robes were sewn, and ceremonial litters were built for the Princess and Kaitewha to carry them around the village in a triumphal procession. The moon waxed steadily and the first faint sightings of the approaching comet were reported. Finally all was ready, and the day dawned fine and clear.

As dawn rode in on silver wings lighting up the sky, Garlita rose and dressed carefully in her new turquoise gown with silver beads sewn in swirling patterns down the left side and sleeve. It contoured to her lithe, though no longer young body, falling to just above her ankles.

Looking at her reflection in the still pool beside her sleeping room, she murmured to herself. *My body feels different since Rahitan and I became lovers. Much more vibrant and supple. It feels as though I have been rejuvenated without the usual remedies I take periodically at the Temple of Rejuvenation. This must be what being in love does to one.* Smiling at her secret thoughts, she called to Aloma who was being dressed in the next room.

"Princess, how is your dressing going? You must be ready soon as we must greet the rising sun at the top of the platform in the Temple courtyard. You will need to be ready soon."

"I am nearly gowned," answered Aloma. "The women are having a wonderful time braiding my hair and applying colour to my face. I look completely different. No one will recognise me."

Garlita entered the room and gasped in surprise. Instead of the fresh, faced innocent looking young woman who had arrived only a couple of weeks ago, there stood a glorious example of a glamorous and perfected woman. *Love has also transformed her,* thought the High Priestess. Aloma's long apricot coloured gown was adorned with hundreds of small pearls gathered from the southern coasts, traded for the many wares that only the skills of the Atema could produce. These included herbal potions to heal sick bodies and minds, soft leather garments made with the hides of small animals, or pictures made from preparing flax leaves into smoothe parchment, and drawing on them with charcoal sticks and even soft coloured stones. Their knowledge of writing they kept to themselves, for it gave them a certain power over less educated tribes. Aloma's long blonde hair was coiled in plaits around the top of her head, interwoven with a long string of pearls. One large teardrop pearl hung suspended on her forehead between her brows. Delicate dyed leather slippers encased her feet. Dark charcoal mixed with fat enhanced the size of her eyes. Red berry juice stained her perfect lips and soft pink powdered chalk was rubbed into her cheeks, making them glow.

"Garlita," gasped Aloma. "What has happened to you? You look radiant. Your gown is a dream. Are you also in love? Now, don't try to deny it. Have you and Rahitan succumbed to the power of love?

It couldn't be anyone else. Oh, Garlita, I am so happy today, I think I will burst."

Much to her amazement and embarrassment, the High Priestess found herself blushing furiously under the scrutiny of Aloma and the women attending her. *What do I say,* she thought. *I am not ready for the whole village to know. Am I so transparent? I have tried so hard to shield myself from anyone knowing my secret. Do the people need to be aware of the change in the relationship between Rahitan and myself. We have always been so priggishly proper whilst encouraging every one else to find their true partner in love.* She needn't have worried, for the answer came as the four woman in the room laughed.

"So you and Rahitan have finally come to your senses," said Angelica. "What a relief to us all that the veils have been lifted. We knew something had changed between you two. Congratulations, my High Priestess, welcome to the human race, even though we are the enlightened aspect of it."

Zenita took Garlita's hands and danced in circles, compelling her Priestess to relax saying. "I cannot begin to tell you how happy I am," Garlita smiling in return. "A little bird has told me that you and Morpheus may soon come together in love. Is that so?"

"Oh, I hope so, Garlita. Morpheus is so bound up in his dreams and other world communications he scarcely knows I exist. My heart yearns to merge with his. Perhaps you can put a love charm into his drink?" asked Zenita.

"I'll ask Rahitan to let him read the golden scroll with the rose quartz rods. That is what awoke us. It's vibration is so high, I defy anyone reading it to remain immune to the awesome power of love," answered Garlita. "He can read it after today's ceremonies, before we venture on a journey to other parts of this land, after the next full moon. You and Morpheus will accompany us, along with Aloma, Kaitewha and Thieron. That should give you both sufficient time together to merge you energies.Then we will let nature do the rest."

"We are going on a journey?" asked Aloma. "I never want to go anywhere again now that I have rejoined my real family and my lover. Where are we going?"

"No more questions just now, my Princess. We have more important issues today. How beautiful you look. Every man in the village is already a little in love with you. And heaven knows how Thieron will react." Garlita mused. "Poor Thieron, I must find someone to ease the pain of his unrequited love for you, but there are so few young women here. Most of our women are past child-bearing age, but I will look out for a suitable girl to accompany him on our journey. Come, my friends, let us face the day."

Waiting outside Aloma's room were four attendants standing at attention. They were the litter bearers. A quickly stifled gasp of appreciation was uttered from each mouth as their Princess gracefully sat on the decorated seat, while their eyes shone with their love. Garlita mounted her litter to a similar reaction. It m*ust have been something they drank,* thought some of the bearers. *They are both women in love,* thought those who recognised the symptoms. Angelica, Zenita and Erana followed the litters on foot to the central courtyard, where a handsomely dressed Rahitan, his long white beard freshly washed and trimmed, awaited them. Graciously, trying not to give away his deep feelings of love, he took Garlita's hand and assisted her from the litter. Together they mounted the three steps to the platform on which stood the green stone statue of the Princess.

"How dignified you look, my love," Garlita whispered. "That sky blue robe makes your eyes look like shining sapphires. You look like a young man, and behave like one."

Kaitewha assisted Aloma from her litter, without taking his eyes from her face. He beamed such an aura of love and happiness that she couldn't resist kissing him lightly on the lips. The people gathered in the courtyard cheered, as Rahitan held up his arms, revealing the writhing serpent tattoos and aligned the two golden eyes with the suns rays. Very soon, light shone from his clear blue eyes, across the watching Atema.

"My friends" he boomed. 'Today, as you all know, is the inaugural Ceremony of the Triumphant Return. Annually will we will gather until the next demise of our village in some twenty years time, to celebrate the homecoming of Aloma and Kaitewha, the discovery of the green stone statue and golden ball, and the rediscovery of the scroll room. Never before in our history has such a momentous occasion been given to us by the gods who created us. There is great meaning attached to this time. Even though we will be destroyed once again, there is a purpose to all actions. There is a time, a season for every thing under the design of our creator. As we begin to read the golden scrolls, we will be able to ascertain if, or how far from the true path we have strayed, and if we have sufficient time to right any misconceptions before we, once again, face a long sleep. Already I have personally experienced a shattering revelation." A delighted titter could be heard, for within such a melded group there were no secrets.

Trying to maintain his dignity, Rahitan continued. "Most of the other tribes of enlightened beings who inhabit this fair land will also face a long sleep, for we are once again progressing too far ahead of the native population. For just under two thousand years this time we will be suspended as Atema, although we may incarnate in ordinary lives. We will come together at the end of the twentieth century when once again, great comets will pass close to Earth, and significant planetary alignments will occur. Millions of the earth's inhabitants, and there will be many, many millions scattered all over the body of our mother earth by then, will have awakened to the truth of the grand game and enough will be ready to rise to a higher dimension of reality. When all of those who wish to be incarnated for the final days of the grand saga of this epoch, only have to hold this desire when we next feel the breath of the totally destructive force that will cover our land. As you know, any who wish to leave our village may do so at any time, until we have the next Ceremony of Ascension."

Turning to Garlita and taking her hand, he continued. "But enough of the future. Let us celebrate the present. I have an announcement to make. Your High Priestess Garlita and I have been smitten by a force which emanated from one of the golden scrolls we rediscovered last week. A veil of ignorance was removed as I read the symbols late one night, whilst alone in my room. The following day Garlita was also exposed to the symbols and similarly affected. We have become lovers, something we both thought impossible in our sacred roles as dutiful interpreters and intermediaries between Io, Tane and the people. Now we know we were mistaken, and that through the power of love, each person can reach an enlightened state. Another experiment has been completed, but not one that we would choose to follow again. I do not wish to detract from the purpose of today's celebrations, but we had to reveal our true feelings to you all before we burst with happiness and shine all over the place."

With one voice the crowd roared their approval, some making ribald comments, some crying, others whistling, but most just yelling, "Hurrah."

Smiling broadly, Rahitan held up his hands for silence. "Following the next full moon, several of us will be undertaking a long journey around the land to check on various places and people. Even though we monitor every change from within our temple confines, there is a need to visit and exchange energy fields with other tribes similar to ours. I would like several volunteers to come forward after today's ceremonies have been completed. From these we can select a balanced group representing our special skills to teach those we encounter of the lesser tribes who may wish to learn."

The High Priest paused, and looked lovingly at the upturned faces below. "My dear companions, on the journey of life gathering experiences for our Creator, let the Ceremony of the Triumphant Return begin."

The spine tingling sound of conches rose from the ramparts, while actors and jugglers rushed into the courtyard to strut their talents, and large jugs of a mood enhancer, specially brewed by Pausanin the chief alchemist of the temple, were passed around the crowd. Within a short time everyone was singing and laughing, all imagined cares forgotten.

Morpheus mounted the dais and shouted above the clamour. "My friends, this is the day our Princess is returning to us. She nears the ridge above the village, so let us go to meet her. Grandmother Kelama, where are you? You must lead the procession."

Panting from her efforts, Kelama pushed her way to the gates of the village. "I am ready," she called. A choir formed to sings songs of praise to Aloma and Kaitewha while they all hurried up the hill.

During the beginning of the ceremony, Aloma and Kaitewha had silently slipped out of the village to take their allotted places. Aloma stood on the ridge, while Kaitewha hid himself until the others arrived, and then Aloma was settled on the litter and proceeded down the hill. With the events still fresh in the minds of the Atema, the re- enactment followed the original event without a fault.

Kaitewha smiled to himself. *I wonder if our memory of our arrival will remain true or become slightly obscured over the years. Ceremonies sometimes have a habit of evolving to suit the day, with the original true meaning forgotten.*

Suddenly he stood alone, wrapped in his long cloak. *Something has already changed as my cloak was not decorated with green blackbird feathers when I arrived. The craftswomen have given me a great gift.* Slowly he followed the cheering people to the gates and sat on one of the egg shaped stones.

The celebrations lasted far into the night, culminating with a colourful display of fireworks. The knowledge of the manufacture of fireworks was obtained by Pausanin many years earlier on a pilgrimage he and Rahitan made over the seas. They had travelled to a great northern land inhabited by people with yellow skins and slanted eyes, who called themselves Manchurians. These people had long been experts in the art of gunpowder production, and Pausanin had persuaded their chief alchemist to share this secret in return for his knowledge of rock levitation. Between them, the old Manchurian alchemist, Rahitan, Pausanin and two assistants had begun to build a great wall across that land. On their return home, the two men delighted in using gunpowder to terrify some of the native population with loud noises and dazzling lights. This had the additional effect of consolidating their fear of entering the forest surrounding the village.

Aloma and Kaitewha reclined close together before a small table in a sunlit room decorated with friezes of dancing animals and birds. Gauzy curtains moved lazily on the breath of a gentle breeze, and just outside water splashed down a series of cascades. On the table, a woven basket piled high with fruits of the forest added a depth of colour to the room. The lovers ate hungrily for this was to be their last real meal for a while. That evening they would be separated for twenty-one days while each learned how to be sustained by light and the forces of universal energy. Each person who had been called home to the village of the Atema underwent such a metamorphosis to raise their vibrational level to enable them to merge more fully with the spiritual forces that guided them.

"What a home coming we have experienced, my love," said Kaitewha. "How dull my life in the village of my birth now seems. My former tribespeople lacked of joy of spiritual ritual in their lives, they showed no interest in the natural world, and focussed only on surviving. It all seems so primitive compared to life with the Atema. Thank heavens the call came to me and not to Rongonui."

"Yes," replied Aloma, "I have no wish to return to the likes of Teringa and the jealous women of my birth village. I am also glad to be reunited with my beloved grandmother."

"Now that I have found you again my wife, I do not wish to be parted from you for one moment," sighed Kaitewha. "I want to sing you a song that has been occupuing my mind all day." He reached for the five string lyre that stood propped against the divan, cleared his throat and sang.

> I've climbed the high mountains, walked along valleys,
> swum over deep rivers, been down to the sea,
> Though my wanderings led me, through forests and
> grasslands,
> Nowhere did I find, some one who loved me.
> Now here with our people, I have found my true lover,
> You are my shining one, my eternity,
> And I know that I love you, my Princess, my own one,
> I can't live without you, here beside me.
> When we are betrothed, we'll merge in our oneness,
> To never be parted, by Io or Tane.

Delightedly Aloma hugged him. "Not bad for the songmaster's first effort. The tune is familiar."

"No wonder it sounds familiar, for a long time ago you used to sing it using different, more esoteric words." Kaitewha strummed the lyre. "Now your turn to sing, my little songbird."

Rich, clear notes rang from the little cabin in the centre of the circular garden, as Aloma regained her long unused voice and sang to the seductive music of the lyre. People stopped their work and listened with joy in their hearts, to the sweetness of the music and song, murmuring to each other, "Now we will have some real singing again."

Following the sunset meditation, Garlita appeared at the door of the cabin allotted to those who were preparing for initiation into the Temple of Love and asked "Aloma, Kaitewha, can I enter?"

Hurriedly they dressed, laughing at their efforts to appear unflustered, and replied, "Come in Garlita. How swiftly the day has passed. We have worked out how to manoeuvre the spinning bed and the other devices in the cabin."

"This is the first time I have ever entered this room," replied Garlita. "Soon I hope to spend time here with Rahitan when our official duties permit. Come, it is time for you to be apart for three weeks whilst you undertake the process of how to live on light. It takes discipline and courage but I assure you both, no one has ever died. You will be given much assistance from the higher forces who oversee this process, and the galactic surgeons who perform the operations."

"Operations, what operations." Aloma was somewhat apprehensive.

"I will explain. Please sit down, both of you." Garlita drew up three stools. "This process involves the abstinance of all liquid and food for seven days, and of all food for an additional fourteen days. After that you will not feel like eating again, but may if you so wish. Not one of the Atema who has been through this process feels the need for food, but most of us drink pure water, and occasionally, as you experienced during the celebration, herbal brews that fill us with ecstasy. There are those like Pausanin who are pure breatharians, who take no liquid. His brews are renowned yet he does not even taste them to test for potency and consistency. Others have that privilege. They are called Tasters of the Sacred Brew. Rahitan only drinks during special ceremonies to enhance his perception." She smiled to herself, remembering the golden liquid that had warmed their bodies on the night of their reawakening.

"The process begins at midnight. Soon I will escort Aloma, and Rahitan will come for you Kaitewha You will be taken to the Place of the Process, where you will be warm and comfortable for the next three weeks, isolated from communicating with any one but Rahitan and myself. Most importantly, no sexual contact is allowed during this time, which is a time of deep inner awakening. A time to cleanse body, mind and spirit; a time to release any old thought patterns that may restrict the spiritual connection with your higher selves. However, I know you two will sail through the process for you have so little to surrender, being young and healthy and pure of heart. Now, farewell each other. Wonderful. Come Aloma, follow me."

She led the young woman along a freshly cleared track to a small cabin built of wood from the tree ferns that grew abundantly in the forest. The floor coverings consisted of long fern fronds and the roof was well sealed with many layers of ferns and grass, making it waterproof. On a raised platform, springy ferns and grasses formed a bed covered with soft sheets made from woven flax and furs to keep in the warmth. A ball of light was suspended from the ceiling. Garlita explained.

"You have only to touch it gently to switch on the light and again to extinguish it. You can wash in the stream outside and sit in the sun in the glade behind the cabin. There is a rustic chair. You can do whatever you wish, except drink."

Aloma stared at her. "I was told by my step-mother that if I did not eat or drink I would soon die. Perhaps that was her fear, for she was an obese woman. I would not eat the food she cooked but, before she left, I enjoyed my grandmother's delicacies."

"That is one of the most entrenched beliefs in the world," replied Garlita. "That we would soon die without liquid or food. When our body is restructured to allow sustenance to be gathered from light, the energy of the sun and air, breath and spiritual connection, we can easily exist without food. In fact you will feel so much more energetic, for most of our energy is used up in digesting food. Do any of us in the village look as though we are starving? It is not lack of food that kills people, but the fear of starvation."

"No. I have never seen healthier looking people, nor such shining eyes and hair. No one carries excess weight. Such beauty as is within the Atema does not exist in the outside world, at least not to my limited knowledge. Many of the people in my birth village left their bodies before they reached fifty years, worn out by trying to survive the harsh reality of finding enough food and shelter to sustain them. Here everyone must be well over fifty, and some even look more ancient, but all are still strong and healthy."

Garlita laughed. "How old would you estimate Rahitan to be? Fifty, one hundred? He is one hundred and fifty years old and I am one hundred and twenty. Some of us have reached three hundred, before voluntarily leaving our bodies for a rest in the heart of the creator."

"I know you wouldn't lie to me, but still I find that hard to believe, and that at your age, you and Rahitan have just become lovers. Most old people relegate that part of themselves to pleasant memories. I will never reach that age as we only have about twenty more years here before the next big bang." Aloma bowed her head, ignoring the large tears sliding down her cheeks.

Gently Garlita wiped away the tears and said, "My dearest child, age brings wisdom to some and not to others. You are already wise beyond your years. Following the next eruption we will all have a long, well deserved rest in the heart of the creator, with perhaps a life or two in between just to hold our focus. Now I will leave you and only visit each morning and evening after the meditation time to the sun. Remember, you may rinse your mouth with cold water but make sure you don't swallow any of it or you will have to start again from day one. Goodnight."

Aloma lay down on the soft bed and closed her eyes. She awoke to Garlita's voice calling her. "I must have been exhausted," she exclaimed jumping to her feet. "Those days in the cabin in the garden near the Temple of Love were energetic. Good morning, my Priestess. I will go to the stream to wash my face with cold water and soon be fully awake."

Garlita smiled inwardly, rejoicing in her own recent memory of love making. When Aloma returned, wiping her face with a soft cloth, she said, "Since yesterday you look twenty years younger, you look radiant. Have you taken regeneration?"

"No, Princess, I know it to be the result of juices released within my body during the love making I experienced with Rahitan last night. The art of love not only refreshes the soul, but nourishes the body, making it more vibrant. I think it is the best youthing process I have ever tried." Garlita paused, then added, "And to think I decided to forego that pleasure for the past epoch. So many paths, but one destination. Now to the focus of today."

She began to instruct Aloma in the procedure to be followed for the next twenty-one days. "For the first three days, you will just rest and prepare for the following four days. On the third night your soul will depart your body, but not go too far away, keeping watch over the operations that will occur three times daily, with a two hour rest period between each session. Four of the top surgeons in the galaxy have volunteered to preform the intricate surgery. Three come from the Matariki, and the chief surgeon from a place so far away we don't even know its name. As your soul will be able to communicate with him, perhaps he will tell you if you ask. You will be amazed at what happens to your body. I will leave you now, for this is a time of stillness and inner contemplation, not chatter. Until this evening."

Left alone Aloma wondered how she would pass the day. She had never experienced a whole day, let alone twenty-one days with nothing at all to do. *How does a doer become a be-er. How can I slow everything down to the pace of a snail. Will I die of boredom or heartache for Kaitewha? No I won't. I lived without him until recently, and now I will not become dependent on him for my happiness. Perhaps I can contact him telepathically. No. This is his time to undergo a great change, as it is mine also. Kaitewha I love you.*

Aloma spent the day exploring the area around the cabin, making sure she did not go in the direction of the village, or Kaitewha's lodging. It passed quicker than she imagined possible. That evening she asked Garlita, "How will I know when to prepare for the operations and know when they are over?"

"You will have an inner sensing when the surgeons are ready to begin and again when they have completed each part of the reconstruction of your body. When it is over you may like to share your experience with me. I was never so fascinated in my life, when watching their expert hands wield unfamiliar devices whilst working on my own body. That happened well over one hundred years ago, but still I remember as if it was yesterday. Goodnight, my dear." Garlita kissed the young woman on the cheek before disappearing along the quickly darkening path, towards the glow of the village. Left alone Aloma slept, dreaming of making love to Kaitewha.

During the third night, she dreamed that her soul left to go on a long journey towards a brightly lit city floating in the sky. The inhabitants, some wearing long coloured cloaks, and floating in bodies of light, welcomed her as one of them, and told her the story of their eternal existence. She knew she was part of their family.

One glowing being came towards her, gesturing that she should follow along a corridor lit with shining globes. Before two large ornate doors, it paused, emanated a beam of light and silently, the doors slid open revealing an enormous domed room filled with light beings in a tightly packed circle. Their arms were extended towards a brilliant pulsing light at the top of the dome, and they were softly chanting. Rays of light poured down from the pulsating light into the open arms and heart centres of each being, as the chanting increased in vibration. Aloma's escort led her towards the circle which parted to allow her to join in. Raising her arms, she felt the impact of energy coursing through her own light body, filling her with a sensation of love and serenity. Surrendering to the bliss, she became part of the chanting group. When finally the outpouring of energy diminished, individual shapes emerged from the tightly united circle, and several greeted her. Hearing her name called, she turned to see a tall woman wearing a shimmering golden cape addressing her.

"Aloma, welcome. I am called Auralia. I am the commander of this crystal galactic city, and this is Jondra, my command captain. As the history making events of the last two centuries have been so important in the evolution of Earth's development, we have been orbiting your small planet to assist in a great transition. As you may have heard from the telepathic communications between priests like Rahitan and Garlita and those of far away lands, a very special event took place in a small country far, far to the north-west of your island. I will show you where."

Auralia led Aloma to a large glowing globe in the centre of a dais at the far end of the room, and spun it slowly. When it stopped she pointed to a place on the shore of a long sea that lay above a large continent and said, "This area is called the Holy Land or Palestine. by some. Nearly two hundred of your earth years ago, a son was born to a specially chosen young woman. This boy grew up to become a great teacher of righteousness. He was of a tribe called the Essenes who taught that love and peace were far better than hatred and war. Unfortunately, his teachings upset the powerful priests of different religions, who conspired with the foreign governor of that land to have the teacher crucified. At that time, that area of the world was occupied by a conquering army from a land far to the west, who used crucifixion as a common form of capital punishment in those barbaric days."

Aloma interrupted. "What is a crucifixion? I have not heard of such a death."

"Perhaps it is not for your ears, but I will tell you. Two large pieces of wood are connected to form an unequal cross that is buried upright in the ground. A man is either nailed or tied to it and left until he dies of pain, or is given poison by his relatives. Sometimes the procedure is reversed and the man is hung upside down, causing him to die of suffocation in his own blood. I am sorry to have to tell you of these barbaric practices, my dear, for we are the most loving and peaceful of beings. It sickens us to see what atrocities have been perpetrated on this planet. It was never part of the divine plan, that humans should suffer so much. I am sorry to say that it is the male of the species that is responsible for most of these acts of violence. During the next zodiacal epoch many wars will be fought on this planet in the name of our adored Creator. Many religions will claim Her to be a man who supports only their way of thinking which will lead to the true teachings of the righteous one being grossly distorted. However, during the following age, that of Aquarius beginning in just over two thousand years, humankind will become far more enlightened. Many on the planet will be so tired of conflict and war that a great shift towards a more peaceful way of living will occur. That is the divine plan, but if it does not happen, either a deadly plague will overwhelm the inhabitants or the earth will shift considerably, and the vast majority of her children will perish. This has occurred several times in ages past.

A vibration went out from the heart of the absolute creator that led us to this remote area of your galaxy, and drew us into its orbit. We will remain here for a little longer before returning to our home. We will return at the end of the time known as the twentieth century on Earth, two thousand years following a momentous occasion; the birth of the Christed teacher who is destined to live in the hearts of many people for a long, long time. Before we depart, we have a mission. Even though we are not allowed to interfere, for the vibration we bring to this planet is one of pure love and the ability to live on the sustenance emanating from the Creator, we are able to hurry the evolution of consciousness along a bit. You witnessed and partook of that sustenance just now. The process you are undergoing will allow you to live in that vibration. Being operated on, and reprogrammed from a totally human body into one able to be sustained by light is overseen by our best surgeons, who do this type of work all over the universe. They have been very busy during our time here. When an individual is ready a call goes out and a team of surgeons can immediately appear anywhere. Those humans who have undergone the transformative process whilst we in the Crystal City have been orbiting around Earth, have enjoyed the extra privilege of visiting us. They are all part of our soul family who volunteered for one epoch or many, to assist in the great experiment being conducted on Earth. You are also our Princess, and you have chosen quite a journey. We honour each and every one of our soul family who has contributed, for without your assistance the human race would still be living in caves, and wearing animal skins. As you would be aware, nothing happens anywhere in the universe without the knowledge of the Creator. Come, my dear, let me show you our city."

Auralia led the astounded young woman from the great room, along corridors, and up shafts of energy, finally arriving at a small room overlooking several towers that soared above the surrounding buildings. They walked through doors that opened at their approach and closed behind them. Light beings they passed smiled and greeted her by name.

"Have I been here before?" asked Aloma. "Everyone seems to know me."

"I will have to insert a memory chip into you. Of course they know you. You visit often in your sleep state. You are one of us, Princess. Here we are. Stand beside me, next to this column of light." said Auralia. "Jondra, activate the energy field."

The column burst into life, and became a vibrating, shimmering energy.

"Come, join me in ecstasy," Auralia whispered, urging Aloma into the centre.

Immediately the two light bodies shot upwards. Aloma felt herself disintegrating while Auralia's outline stayed firm. They were sucked into a tunnel that took them at an incredible speed towards a brilliant light. They soon stopped and were surrounded by a bubble of energy.

"Welcome back into the heart of the Creator, you who parted from me so long ago," Aloma heard the vibration of the words without sound. Joy flooded her senses as she merged completely into ecstasy, until she knew she and the force were of one essence. "We will merge for a brief moment in time so that you may be sustained until you join me once again, for ever. In subsequent lives you have chosen a long and difficult road to travel, but know that I love you, and am always within you. You will never be alone." Aloma completely surrendered and lost all sense of everything, until she felt a gentle tug on her consciousness. "Now it is time to return."

The next instant she was back in the cabin, in the village of the Atema. For hours she lay under the soft warm covers, crying warm tears of both joy and sadness. *I thought making love to Kaitewha was the greatest height I could attain in ecstasy. Now that I have touched the heart of my Creator, how will I ever again be content with physical merging?* A paroxysm of weeping overcame her and she yielded to its torment. Some time later she dried her eyes and thought to herself, *I was called home for a purpose. Was it to understand that there are many levels to this journey, many dimensions to traverse, and many ways to love? Why did I ever choose to leave such an embrace. I feel so lonely without it.* She thought of Kaitewha, and focussed her mind to his. *Can you know what has happened to me. Perhaps you have also experienced this bliss state. I will never be the same again, but now I love you even more than I thought possible. Through you I may be able to enter into the state of bliss once again. I really hope so.*

A picture of Auralia formed in her mind. *Thank you my Queen, for showing me what I had forgotten. How could I ever forget such merging? Surely I did not volunteer to forget.*

Auralia's mind answered. "If those of our family who volunteered to participate in the great experiment remembered their origins, how could they exist on earth, or indeed any of the thousands of other planets where similar experiments are happening. Divine amnesia is a blessing, not a curse; please believe me. When the consciousness of a developing human, which is actually one of us having a human experience to assist in the raising of all consciousness, reaches a certain level, they are shown their true origins. When they have enough strength to bear the pain of separation without being overcome with longing to return, and understand it is for the development of the experiment, they are given an experience such as you have just had. Never forget who you really are, Princess. We love you."

Unable to cry any more tears, Aloma fell into a deep, dreamless sleep. She was woken by the vibration of the crystal bell played by Garlita's mind, and the sun's rays streaming into the room.

Aloma rose, and walked slowly to the stream to wash her face. She was feeling weak and light headed. Her vision remained imprinted in her mind, and she knew it would remain there for the rest of this life, and hopefully into all subsequent ones. *How unfair if it doesn't. Why would any of us volunteer to be separated from such love. I know we did it for the Creator's evolution and therefore our own, but what a sacrifice. Even I who have the best life possible at this time on earth feel devastated after the revelation I have just seen. Don't be silly!* Aloma soundly berated herself. *I have made a choice and I will complete my mission.*

Back in the cabin, Garlita was waiting. "What has happened to you? You look radiant and distressed at the same time. Ah! I know. You have been on the most sacred journey any of us, on or off earth can be given. You have touched Io."

Aloma eyes began to water. "Oh, Garlita, how could any of us have left, let alone forgotten our divine truth. The love of Io is something I will always yearn for, even though I have the most wonderful of lovers here on earth."

"That, my dear," replied the High Priestess, "is a supreme secret Rahitan and I have only just rediscovered, as we thought we had evolved beyond the need for human love. Humans have a distant memory of the ecstatic embrace of the creator and try to rediscover it in the arms of a lover. Whilst we are in a human form, that is indeed the closest most of us will get. Two hearts and minds merged in love and harmony are better that one alone, trying to open the doors. Very, very few experience complete merging with the heart of the creator whilst still in human form. If that is what I think just happened to you, you are extremely blessed. During meditation or in the presence of a being who is of a higher vibration, a merging can happen spontaneously to awaken an unaware soul to its earthly role when it becomes too trapped. But I don't think that remains constant, nor do I imagine does the lover's role. However, I will deal with that if and when the force of that ecstatic experience begins to wane. How are you feeling otherwise?"

"I have a slight headache and am beginning to get very thirsty," replied Aloma. "I suppose it is the toxins being eliminated from my body as cleansing takes place. Angelica mentioned that might happen."

"An etheric drip has been inserted into your kidneys to prevent dehydration and damage. You will pass urine normally until you can drink again. Your first operation is due to begin soon, so I will leave now and return this evening." Garlita rose and left the cabin.

Aloma lay down on the bed and closed her eyes. Four light beings appeared, and gently lifted her onto an etheric operating table to began their intricate work. She was vaguely aware of her body on the table, but much more focussed in her mind as her soul aspect watched the procedure. Firstly a tube was inserted into her heart and all her blood drained into a bowl. This was taken away by a helper. To replace the old blood, new blood, filled with light filaments was infused until her inner body sparkled with light. This procedure took the entire allotted time, and afterwards she went outside to rinse out her mouth. After she had rested, .the next session began Even without having access to time she knew when to begin. During the second session a rod onto which all nerve endings were attached, was carefully withdrawn from her spine. During this proceedure, each nerve was cut. The old rod was very discoloured and dull. A new one was inserted and all the nerves connected and realigned. A dark gunky communicator crystal lodged in her medulla was removed, the area cleansed and a bright new crystal inserted. Her mind received a message. *This will allow your nervous system to accommodate a much higher level of vibration, allowing you to live on light and affect those around you.* The observer part of Aloma then watched in fascination during the following sessions, as her double helix blueprint was straightened, and rewound in the opposite direction. This was to speed the evolutionary process to allow the reconnection of the five double helixes that in order to manipulate humanity, had been removed by certain creator gods many millennia ago. Her brain was reprogrammed to enable far more information to be accessed from the guides of humanity, so she could teach others of the wisdom of the ancients. Her skin was flayed, dipped in a silver light solution and reattached, each nerve ending, pore, hair follicle and layer working perfectly, to allow light to be absorbed in greater quantities into the body as life giving energy and sustenance. Her eyes were also changed to utilize light better, and send it through her nervous system. In fact, not one part of her original body remained unchanged. Even her fingerprints were re-whorled. During the final session, her blood was changed again, this time with blood of a higher frequency, to carry light around her body.

At dusk on the seventh day Garlita arrived with a glass of pale liquid.

"Congratulations my dear. Now you can drink some diluted juice."

Shakily, Aloma stood and slowly walked from the cabin. Arcing across the sky was a brilliant rainbow celebrating a recent rain shower and confirming to Aloma that she had passed the initiation. A large eagle circled lazily overhead, screeching shrilly. Tears welled in the young woman's eyes and slid down her cheeks. Laughing, she said," I still have enough water in my body for tears. Now I will drink."

"Take it slowly," said the High Priestess. "Just a little now and more later. Tomorrow and for the remainder of your time here you will have to drink two jugs full daily. That will flush out any toxins and replenish your kidneys. You look a bit gaunt, but will soon round up again. Now rest and we will talk another day of your experience." Over her shoulder she added, "Oh! by the way. Kaitewha has also successfully completed his first seven days. I know you will have a lot to share when you come together again, but perhaps he does not need to know every detail. Best to keep some mystery."

"Good night, Garlita. Thank you for taking such good care of me. If you can, give my love to Kaitewha," called Aloma.

Lying in her comfortable bed she mused. *Mystery. My story. Yes. How could I possibly find adequate words to describe my merging with the heart of Io. Or about the etheric operations. If Kaitewha has also experienced such a mystery then we will not need to talk of it.*

During the second week Aloma's body healed and strengthened and she spent much of each day meditating and delving deeply into her mind and body to resolve and eliminate any old hurts, emotional pain and past regrets. *I forgive you Teringa, you tried your limited best. I forgive you father for dying when I was so young, and grandmother Kelama for leaving me when I was just a little girl. I forgive my mother for dying when I entered this world. Thankyou for bearing me, mother, wherever you are. I forgive the stupidity and jealousies of the local girls and the weakness of the boys who thought themselves great warriors. Now I understand why they behaved so. I am at peace.*

By the end of week three Aloma's soul prepared to re-enter her reprogrammed body as she completed the process. Daily new insights flooded her expanded mind and she began to communicate directly with angelic presences, high masters, other incarnated enlightened beings in other areas of the planet and for her, most exciting of all, with Kaitewha. Early in the morning of the twenty-first day a shaft of energy entered through the top of her head and flowed down through her energy centres along her spine to anchor in the second one, called the seat of the soul. *I am complete. My soul has returned. It is done.* Then a second wave of energy poured through her body and a third until she felt full of love. She began to laugh, a wild free laugh. The sound rippled through the forest and birds came to her door.

Soon Garlita appeared, saying, "Good Morning. How radiant you look. So full of light, I am almost blinded." Playfully, she put her hands over her eyes. "You must remain here until midnight to complete the process fully. Then if you wish, you can return to your room in the village or remain here until morning. You will be shown a couple of exercises to perform daily. One is how to receive light each morning at sunrise, standing in a column of light and absorbing it into every molecule of your body. Now, what do you wish to do tonight?"

"I will stay here," replied Aloma. "I feel a bit vulnerable about facing all the people. Can I stay here for a few days longer? Can Kaitewha join me so we can become reacquainted and share our secrets? Please, Garlita?"

"Why not," answered the High Priestess, bending down to give Aloma a peck on her cheek. "But don't over exert yourself. Soon we have a long and perhaps arduous journey to make around the land. I'll see you tomorrow and bring Kaitewha, that is, if he wants to come."

Expertly she caught the pillow that Aloma threw at her. "Get out of here you wicked woman," laughed the Princess.

Very early the following morning, before the blush of dawn caressed the clouds, there was a gentle knock on her door. "Are you awake, my love?" called a soft voice.

Aloma jumped out of bed and flung open the door. "Kaitewha, let me look at you. How gaunt you look." She activated a ball of light and inspected him more closely. Indeed he was thinner but his eyes shone, not only with love for his beloved but with an otherworldly quality that she sensed also emanated from her own eyes. "Hold me," she whispered.

EIGHT

The Journey

Two days later, Aloma and Kaitewha tried to slip unnoticed into the temple to find Garlita, only to find her waiting at the propylaeum with Rahitan and several of the temple acolytes. "Welcome and congratulations. You have easily passed the initiation, compared to some."

"Come with me," said Rahitan, indicating to Aloma and Kaitewha to follow. "You too, my dear," he added, looking at Garlita with deep love pouring through his intense blue eyes. His appearance had changed, and he looked more youthful and supple.

Aloma whispered in Kaitewha's ear, "Did you know he is one hundred and fifty years old and Garlita is one hundred and twenty? They look no more than fifty. Pity we will never reach that age."

Rahitan led them to his rooms and rang a small silver bell. Thieron dashed in, stopping just in front of Aloma. "My Princess," he exclaimed, "how beautiful and shining you look. And you too Kaitewha," he added reluctantly. "Living on light has its rewards. We don't have to waste time cultivating, hunting, or preparing food., and it makes journeying far easier." Turning to Rahitan he asked, "You rang, Master?"

"Yes, Thieron," replied Rahitan, "go and find Morpheus and Zenita. Erana also, for her skills as a herbalist and body worker will be useful in our travels. We will discuss preliminary plans for our journey which will begin the day after the full moon. It waxes quickly and we must prepare our itinerary, although already I have a good idea of our route."

After Thieron had left the room the High Priest continued, "I have been in telepathic communication with Albinon, High Priest of the village of the Matarau some distance to the north-west, and Carilan of the village of the Akariri even further north, along the western shore of the tail of the giant stingray. As you will discover, all our temples are constructed on an ancient grid pattern that criss crosses this land, and indeed the whole world. We are all connected by lines of energy that enable our thoughts to travel easily. They are expecting our arrival. Following our travels, all of the leaders from the six villages on the north island will gather together in our village, as it is the most central, and they are aware that we may not be around for much longer. They have invited any of us who wish, to join their village before our next annihilation. I will put that option to our people so each can decide."

A knock at the door announced the arrival of Morpheus, the dream master, and Zenita, master healer and maker of fine herbal remedies, followed shortly by Erana, whose capable hands soothed knots from tired bodies.

Rahitan requested they all be seated. "Greetings, my friends. Morpheus, you and Zenita know of our proposed journey, However, Erana does not." Looking directly at her, he continued, "I wish you to accompany those in this room on a journey to other parts of our land. We will leave at the full moon. Please arrange to be absent for one whole moon cycle."

Erana shot a covert look at Thieron, who blushed, as everyone noticed and laughed. "What ho, my boy," Rahitan looked amused.

"Found a replacement in your heart for the Princess already? Oh! I am sorry, I don't mean to tease you. We have other issues to discuss. It is a long and tiresome journey on foot and unfortunately the flying machines mentioned in the scrolls no longer exist. As the land is mostly at peace, attack is not a problem What we are confronted with is the density of the forest, the lack of roads and tracks and places to spend the night in comfort." He looked towards Garlita. "Please enlighten them, my dear."

Garlita stood up. "For some decades now, Rahitan and I have been perfecting the art of bi-location, the ability to travel in an instant to anywhere on the planet We have instructed Morpheus and Zenita. Indeed as you have witnessed, Morpheus has taken the art even further by learning how to move heavy solid objects, without effort. To catch up, the rest of you will undertake an accelerated course in transporting your body to another part of the country. Further insight has been revealed in one of the golden scrolls, which makes it easier for us to teach others. We will begin at once. Come with me."

The group leapt to their feet and followed the Priestess along the light-splashed corridor to the main temple room, housing the crystal bell and sacred objects of power.

"Stand in a circle around the bell and close your eyes. You also Morpheus, and Zenita. Rahitan will stand on the opposite side of the bell to me. We will imagine the plinth in the centre of the courtyard on which the statue of the Princess stands. Now concentrate."

A faint hum emanated from the great bell which was fashioned from a single piece of clear crystal. Soon their forms began to fade. "Hold the focus," was the last thing they heard before they found themselves outside, arranged around the green stone statue.

"How did that happen?" gasped Kaitewha. "I felt a tingle run through my body and then, here I am outside. Wow."

"You had a little assistance from us just to demonstrate how it feels," answered Rahitan. "Now we will return to the great bell to begin your instruction. Concentrate on the bell."

"It is necessary for you to learn this art," said Garlita once they were again standing around the crystal bell. "We could transport you on the journey, but that would take too much energy. Besides, you never know when you want to go off somewhere on your own."

She walked towards Aloma and stood in front of her, Rahitan did the same to Kaitewha, Morpheus, Thieron, Zenita and Erana. "Now close your eyes and think of the plinth in the courtyard. Good, now imagine you body standing in a column of light, and being filled with light. Now our two young friends have undertaken the Process of Living on Light, they should find this easy. Allow light to pour into every atom of your body and feel it becoming finer and lighter. Think of the body as an extension of your mind and move both to the plinth. Slowly Kaitewha, what's the rush. Concentrate on standing around the statue. Now move."

Seven shapes began to reform around the statue, but where was Thieron? They heard a scream full of terror. "Help. Help. I'm stuck in the wall."

"That often happens to beginners," laughed Rahitan.

"It really appears to be no laughing matter," countered Kaitewha.

"Easily remedied," said Garlita, moving towards the wall.

Sticking out of the wall they could clearly see Thieron's head and arms waving frantically. "What are you laughing at. I'm stuck in here forever. It's not funny."

"Hold still," commanded Garlita. "Now take three deep breaths to calm yourself. Good. Stay perfectly still. I don't want to leave your toes behind. Thieron, concentrate on dissolving your body into light particles. Don't argue. Of course you can. Relax."

Thieron began to struggle even harder. "I'll have to spend the rest of my life as a wall," he wailed. "Get me out of here. I'm finding it hard to breathe."

Rahitan said loudly and with great authority, "Thieron, look into my eyes."

The young scribe stopped struggling and did as he was told He relaxed and began to disappear. Soon he was outside the temple wall with the others who hugged him.

"Poor Thieron," laughed the Princess. "What a jester you are. I do love you."

"Enough levity. This is serious business. We do not want to attract too much attention, although only a few of our people have perfected the art of bi-location. Actually, some of them have also been stuck in the temple wall, Thieron, so don't feel too badly," said Garlita kindly."Now we will return to the bell. Ready. Concentrate, imagine the column of light, think of the bell and dissolve your body. Now."

Soon they all reappeared inside the temple, with Thieron visibly relieved.

"My courage nearly failed me, but that was much easier," he gasped.

"This time we will go a little further afield," said Garlita. "Visualise the vast lake south of us. There is a small island, just offshore at the end nearest to our village. Visualise it and imagine the column of light, merge your body with it and dissolve, all the time focussing on our destination. Let us go."

The eight forms slowly faded from sight, there was a momentary sensation of air moving past them, and they reappeared in a circle on the island.

Thieron let out a whoop of joy. "I did it. I did it. Amazing."

"Well done, all of you. Now, each pick up a small pebble, and then let us return to the bell," announced Rahitan, bending to select a round piece of grey pumice. "This will smooth my gnarled feet," he added.

They each picked a piece of pumice stone and standing tall, invoked their body to return to the temple. Soon their forms reappeared, tingling slightly but perfectly assembled.

"Huh, nothing to it," bragged Thieron. "I could travel to the other side of the world."

"Don't you dare try this without us. You might end up being mistaken for an alien in some superstitious land," advised Rahitan. "You are still very much a novice, and even though we helped you considerably each time, you are not ready to go bi-locating on you own. Nor are you, Aloma or Kaitewha and especially you Erana. Do you all understand?"

Each morning and evening following the sun meditation, the group of eight practised bi-locating, visiting a different place each day. As Rahitan forewarned, considerable practice was needed before this could be done individually. The hardest part was to travel to a place they did not know, having no visual image to lock on to and guide them. One tool they used was the vibration of a place name, or connecting with the mind of a person living there, but the novices knew little about these methods. That would only come when they were deemed proficient enough to be trusted to use the knowledge solely for the highest good of all concerned, and never for personal gain. Each evening Garlita and Rahitan prepared the way, mind merging with their counterparts in different areas, opening the doors of perception to enable safe travel through areas where darkness stalked the land, for not all beings worked for the realms of light. In spite of elaborate defence mechanisms and thought forms surrounding the coastline, a number of destructive people had found their way across the vast ocean to the land of peace, lying at the end of the long white cloud. They practised the black arts. Those dark rituals that brought enslavement not freedom to their followers, and those they conquered. The indigenous peoples had no words for war or weapon, nor any knowledge of warfare or how to fight with weapons. The power of love usually could not stand undefeated in front of a screaming, weapon wielding warrior intent on slaughter.

One evening before they were due to depart Thieron asked, "Master, there are many here who wish to start the reading of the golden scrolls. They claim you promised one a month would be revealed, and they are impatient to start. What should I say?"

"Tell them it will commence on our return," replied the High Priest, "I have other issues on my mind just now. Tell them I am very sorry, but we have to give the scrolls their due respect, and cannot rush the treasures about to be discovered. I need time to be able to focus on the interpretation and inspiration needed to fully understand what we are discovering. Now leave me, I have work to do."

"Is there anything I can do to help, Master?" asked the young scribe. "You look worried."

"No thankyou, this I must deal with myself. Good night," Rahitan said dismissively.

Indeed he was worried. Vibrations of distress had been received from the High Priest, Carilan, whose village lay in the far north, on the tail of the stingray. A visionary message showing tattooed, warlike people arriving in large canoes, intent on carrying off the young women was flashed to Rahitan's mind. He watched the inner screen in his forehead roll with scenes of rape and plunder, with several men killed trying to defend their women, and a look of destruction and desolation over the area. Even though he sent messages of encouragement and support, he knew that they we of little use against such invaders. He felt impotent to assist as he knew that the canoes were on their way south towards Albinon's village.

It was imperative that the group left the very next morning hoping to arrive before the marauders. Perhaps the village could be evacuated in time. He blessed the foresight of his ancestors in building his village in the centre of the island, and in the centre of an impenetrable forest that was only accessible to the invited. He reflected that to build shining white temples by the sea was foolish, as ignorant savages were no respectors of advanced architecture or wisdom and truth. Only war and power over others filled their twisted minds.

He focussed his mind to call Garlita to his side. When she arrived several minutes later, he said, "My love, I am disturbed. Vision messages are coming from Carilan showing that his village has been ransacked by wild men from across the seas, uncouth barbarians who have no understanding of how our gentle land functions. They do not have peace in their hearts, and are now on their way south towards Albinon's village. I think we should advance our day of departure and go tomorrow. What do you say?"

Gently Garlita took him in her arms and stroked his long white hair. "Dearest, I am ready to go wherever you say. But I have no wish to inflict even a hint of danger onto our young people. Perhaps they should stay behind."

"I can't see them wanting to do that, but if I order them to stay they will have no choice. No, I suggest they come, for they have to learn how to deal with all situations, not just the easy, loving ones. In the future all experiences will be valuable. I will call them," said Rahitan.

The other six in the travelling party soon, light heartedly, crowded into Rahitan's rooms, unaware of the serious situation confronting them. "Thank you for coming so promptly. I have some grave news," he said and proceeded to tell them of his vision message. As he had predicted, not one of them was willing to stay behind. Even Thieron who did not consider himself to have a brave heart wanted to go.

"We have packed our travelling clothes and are ready to leave whenever you say," said Kaitewha. "It makes a great difference to tour burden, not having to carry food."

Rahitan addressed the small group. "My friends, I trust you all to give your utmost on this most important journey. It will be different from that first proposed, for the forces of darkness will not welcome our presence. However, I have always said that light is more powerful than dark, so now we can put it to the test. We will all have an early night and be ready to travel at first light. I think the people have something prepared for us, so let us adjourn to the courtyard."

A great cheer echoed around the courtyard as the group of eight appeared at the propylaeum. The temple choir sang the song of protection and safe return for the departing travellers, the actors group did a comedy piece about travellers lost in a thick forest, and the weavers presented eight warmly woven, brightly coloured patterned cloaks. One of the lesser priests intoned a sermon about wanderers keeping to the straight and narrow path, although the assembled crowd wondered why on earth he would give a panegyric to his High Priest. He, soon had them laughing heartily as the sermon turned into a parody of Rahitan's favourite speech. Even Rahitan could not keep from smiling. He was a changed man since his awakening to the power of sexual love; he had become far more gentle and forgiving.

So much for an early night, as the Atema caroused far into the night. Pausanin produced an aromatic brew, made from herbs and berries that grew in the forest and precious spices traded with travellers from islands far to the north-east. This affected the usually sober people in a variety of ways. Once they accepted that only a score of years remained in this existence, they decided to enjoy life to the fullest, and that meant imbibing mind altering beverages. Garlita stood on the plinth beside the greenstone statue of the Princess and raised her voice.

"Listen to me, my friends." As the assembly quietened, she continued. "As you are aware, tomorrow at first light, eight of us are to embark on a sacred and potentially dangerous journey to the far reaches of this fair, green land. For at least a thousand years peace has laid its soft protective cloak over us all, but now the barriers have been breached, and warlike savages invade our shores. I wish you to meditate for our protection each morning and evening, visualising us a safe passage until our return. When that will be I do not know, but if we are not back safely enfolded within the arms of the Atema in one moon cycle, please send a party to find us. Many of you are very well trained in such missions, and have the mind power to know where we are at each moment. You will receive distress calls from us if anything goes wrong. We need to be prepared for unforeseen events."

A voice from the crowd called, "Who will be our leaders whilst you are gone?"

"You will all be responsible for yourselves," answered Garlita. "Now, make four circles around the plinth, and follow my instructions as you focus your minds on the statue beside me. It is time to see what she has to reveal." Turning to the musicians she added, "Get ready to play."

Quickly the slightly inebriated crowd did her bidding, with a little pushing and shoving to be in the front circle. Finally they quietened, lifting expectant faces.

"First we will dance the Dance of Divine Remembrance, which you all know," said Garlita, and nodded towards the musicians who lifted their wind and string instruments to play the haunting music that brought tears to the eyes and movement to the feet. Everyone joined hands and the first and third circles lifted their arms over the second and fourth ones, making two large interlocking circles that ebbed and flowed with the music. With eyes closed and hearts opened, the people swayed and merged, until they were in an altered state of consciousness. They continued swaying with hands joined after the music ceased.

"Focus your minds on retrieving the information from the greenstone statue," commanded Garlita. "I am not sure how this will be given to us, but trust the process."

Within seconds the statue began to vibrate, then emanate a soft green glow. Images whirled around it, forming and disappearing until they finally came into focus. Holographic visions danced around the statue and the watchers saw scenes from their former lifetime. Individuals began to exclaim when a memory was revealed in their minds, and received back the gifts that they had placed in the statue aeons ago, just before the big bang, and were able to compare them with their present day knowledge and creativity. Ecstasy reigned.

Rahitan gestured to the other seven travellers. "Let's slip away and leave them to it. They will be here all night, and we have to get some sleep. That was a brilliant idea Garlita. That will keep them amused for weeks. But I hope that they won't forget to send protection to us."

"Our people are far too responsible to allow us to walk into danger," replied Garlita.

As dawn rode her silver chariot across the lightening sky, the small party gathered around the crystal bell. Garlita played the morning wake up call with her mind, and then said, "Prepare to bi-locate. Rahitan, project a vision of our destination into the minds of each of us. Let's move."

Rahitan's image was the central pole in the courtyard of Albinon's village of the Matarau people. Soon the eight appeared in the midst of the morning sun meditators. Discipline was strong, and only a few of the younger ones looked curiously at the strangers. When Albinon finished intoning the prayers, he along with the rest of his tribe, opened their eyes. Gasps of amazement greeted the visitors. Many people jumped up and ran from the area, frightened and screaming of sorcery.

Albinon strode towards Rahitan, "Greetings, High Priest of the Atema. You and your escort are welcome and very needed. I received your message about the marauding savages heading towards our village and we have made what preparation we could, but unfortunately, we know nothing of defending our lives nor our temple. Most of us have never heard of one human killing another for any reason, let alone in cold blood. Carilan's messages have ceased and I fear the worst. It seems that many of the Akariri men have been slaughtered and their women taken captive. How can one group of humans treat another with such lack of courtesy and honour? It is evil."

Rahitan clasped the wrist of the other man and slid up the sleeve of his blue/green linen tunic, thinking, *What a splendid colour, I must ask him how material of such a colour is prepared.*

"Greetings Albinon, my friend. I see you have had your sacred tattoos reworked. They do look fine. Mine are fading. Remember when we underwent the trial to receive them. I'll never forget the pain, but that is something buried deep inside, and like many other things never to be spoken of again. Now to business. I was perturbed to notice that many of the Matarau fled at the sight of us. A fearful tribe cannot withstand the attack of a band of savages. Why are you are so filled with fear. How did this happen? You were once renowned for your spiritual courage."

"Ah, Rahitan, my friend, how good it is to see you. Thankyou for answering my call," replied Albinon. Turning to those of his people who had not fled he announced, "My people, do you remember the High Priest of the Atema, the Master Rahitan. He has come to help us, accompanied by some of his assistants. Please introduce them to us, Master Rahitan."

Rahitan gestured for Garlita to stand beside him, before saying, "People of the Matarau, greetings. This is Garlita, the High Priestess of the Atema and my consort. Many of you have known her for a long time, but not in her new role as my partner. I am very proud to say that we are united on all levels of our beingness. Our Princess, Aloma, has only recently joined us in this life with her partner, Kaitewha the songmaster. You all know Morpheus; he is the Master of Dreams and the contemporary of your own Dream Master, Menanata. Beside him stands Zenita our Master Healer. I thought it advisable to bring her along and I was right, as many of you do need emotional healing, for fear has entered your hearts. Thieron here is my scribe and invaluable assistant and Erana, is also a healer and clever masseuse. Her hands can magically dissolve knots and pains in the body. We are on a journey of discovery around the island, which was planned before the savages invaded the Akariri. It is probable that they have attacked other villages which are not inhabited by enlightened ones, who could not send out a distress call on the thought wave grid."

Those of the Matarau who had run away, began to filter back into the courtyard, ashamed at their cowardly behaviour. Indeed, fear was infecting their minds.

Rahitan addressed them directly. "In the state of fear you cannot live in freedom. Freedom has no limitations and therefore cannot conceive the state of fear. Fear is one of the oldest companions we walk with on this planet and imposes boundaries. In its positive form it signals danger, and for most people it lets them know when life is under threat. But as enlightened ones, as people who have supposedly risen to the frequency beyond fear, it is sad to see the low vibration of fear capturing you again. That emotion is generally felt by those still living the mundane life in villages. What has happened to bring you to this state?"

Albinon replied, "Three days ago, at sunrise as we gathered around the central pole to greet the sun, a form manifested in front of us. Its great loathsome smoky shape writhed and its red eyes shot daggers of energy impregnated with fear into our hearts. Darkness blotted out the sun, the skies darkened. We fled in panic, as we were totally unprepared for such an invasion of our psyches, being in a state of openness during meditation to the sun, the symbol of our creator. For the last three days we have been in turmoil, living in fear, unable to sustain the protective shield around our village. How it initially breached the shield we do not know, for nothing of a low vibration should be able to penetrate it, so you can appreciate that, when you appeared in our midst, it was too much for some of our people. Most of our young ones have not been infected. It was the older, more vulnerable men and women who succumbed. We do not know where this evil form came from or what to do about it."

Garlita put her hand on Albinon's arm and started stroking the writhing serpent tattoo with its glowing red eyes embedded into the back of his hand, and asked. "Do you know where your copies of our ancient set of golden scrolls are hidden Albinon?"

"Yes," he replied. "They are secreted in a stone room deep within our library. No one is allowed to read them any more, not even me, though I forget the reason. Why do you ask?"

"They hold the secret to this mystery, for all has been foretold. With your permission, Morpheus will induce an hypnotic state to fall over you. In this state you may remember why studying the scrolls is forbidden, or what information they contain that could be relevant now. We could give you the answer, as they are identical to our scrolls, that we have only just rediscovered. But it is your responsibility to work out the solution to this predicament yourselves, and we as have not read all the scrolls, we are unsure of the procedure you should follow to erase the fear overwhelming you all. In any case, we must work quickly for we do not have much time to reactivate the protective electro-magnetic force field surrounding your village. We will stay and assist you in any way we can."

Morpheus took Albinon aside and quietly said, "Master Albinon, do you wish me to work with all your people simultaneously or just you first?"

"Work on me, Morpheus. I was the one reckless who dabbled in things outside of our laws and I fear I may have attracted the evil serpent into our midst," replied Albinon gravely.

"How so?" askd Morpheus sternly.

Quivering slightly, Albinon confessed. "During the time of the last full moon, Carilan of the Akariri and I decided to form an alliance to develop our powers of manifestation. We met secretly in a secluded cabin situated between our two villages. Also with us was Lonikai, the High Priest of the Arariki, and Honehe of the Gadumi. We needed the power of six to successfully complete our experiment. At the last minute Rakaheke of the Waitaha, those people with reddish hair and fair skins, and Ioannes of the very ancient tribe of the Levanti, those with white skins, dark beards and blue eyes, decided not to join us. In our vanity and ignorance we proceeded with only four. Not that I am condemning Rakaheke and Ioannes for our failure. They showed far more wisdom than we did and tried to stop our foolishness. The blame lies solely with we four."

"What did you hope to achieve?" questioned Morpheus. "I think Rahitan should also hear this confession."

"Please don't involve him just yet. I am so ashamed of my actions that I could not bear the humiliation when he looked into me with his penetrating blue eyes. He would make me feel like a naughty boy instead of a great priest," pleaded Albinon.

"You may no longer be a great priest," replied Morpheus. "Or a living one if we cannot reverse whatever you released. I suppose the other villages are also in mortal danger, now that this demon has been unleashed. I sincerely hope it is not the same taniwha that was entombed under our great lake aeons ago, following the great explosion. Something is stirring under the lake, threatening once again, to blow us to smithereens. Tane has agreed to hold it in check for another twenty years, but if you have meddled in its imprisonment mechanism it may have escaped prematurely. Now it is weak, but as you know it feeds on fear, and will grow daily more powerful and vengeful. In its present fearful state your village is a great source of sustenance for it, as is Carlian's and probably the other two. I am going to call Rahitan. This is far too serious to keep from him."

"Yes, you are right," admitted Albinon. "My pride and ego became overly inflated. That a group of puffed up priests should inflict such terror and destruction on this land of peace and harmony is unforgivable. There will be a terrible price to pay if this monster is not subdued."

"These savages marauding along our coastline may have been called by the taniwha," said Morpheus angrily. "Such primitive life-forms are designed to create fear for their sustenance. What a fool you have been. What were you playing at?"

"We were attempting to manifest the expansion of the boundaries of our minds to enable us to bring in higher powers to try to control the elements. We were aware that Nature is a jealous god and does not reveal her secrets lightly. That is why we met in such a secluded forested area. We wished to exert control over the seasons, extending the warmer months and decreasing the colder ones, or even eliminating them, to stop the suffering that cold brings to the people of the land. As enlightened ones, many of us know how to prevent coldness seeping into our bones. We were not doing this for ourselves, but for the more primitive tribal peoples," said Albinon.

"Nonsense," snorted Morpheus. "Don't forget, I can see into your mind. You were doing it to exert power over the primitives, so they would worship you as gods. First, let us talk to Rahitan, and then go to your scroll room to see if we can find the answer."

"No one is permitted to enter the scroll room," whimpered Albinon. "The punishment is death."

"I had no idea you had become so superstitious. I think you have been tampered with," Morpheus responded.

Rahitan's stern voice made the other Priest start. "What on Earth is going on here?"

Albinon prostrated himself before Rahitan. "Forgive me, I have transgressed the law and released chaos over the land. Now none of us knows how to bind the monster."

"What are you talking about, my good chap?" a puzzled Rahitan asked. "Morpheus, what is this all about?"

"Well, Master Priest," replied Morpheus, "it seems that a little coven of renegade priests has opened the restraining door on our not so friendly taniwha, imprisoned beneath Lake Taupo. As you well know, twelve of these hideous creatures that feed on fear emanating from humankind, were transported to earth from a galaxy that wanted to be rid of them. They sent them to this small out of the way planet thinking that would be the end of their problem, and that the small population here would not be harmed. They were seeded aeons ago from a parallel universe that pushed them though the time tunnels into our sector. Each creature found a deep lake or sea in which to make its home. Our particular nasty one lay dormant until the century before we began to rebuild our temple, some four thousand years ago. Through mischief and ignorance, it was awakened and rose to the surface of the lake. Those who glimpsed it were terrified, and many legends were created. Its name is Narcobath, the sleeper of the deep."

"Don't tell me these fools have summonsed him from his sleep? How could I forget the incredible danger that stalked our land when he last awoke. It took the combined powers of all the High Priests to contain him. As well you remember, Albinon. Who played this foolhardy game with you? Lonikai, Carilan and Honehe I'll bet. I have a good mind to return home, and leave you to your fate, but I cannot turn my back on all those who are innocent. You were warned that if ever any of you meddled again you would be severely punished." Rahitan was so furious that his beard emitted sparks of electricity, and his usually sparkling blue eyes turned very dark.

"What can I say?" Albinon wheedled pathetically. "It is done and now we don't know how to contain this creature. The first thing it did when the gates opened was call its mate. She responded and right now is heading south from Lake Bratan under the shadow of the mighty volcano Argung Agung, which stands in the string of islands that lie like a garland far to the north west. If they mate and spawn, there will be little monsters looking for a home in every lake in the world. What have we done?" Albinon sobbed like an hysterical child. "We did not intend to release it, only tease it into telling us how to manipulate nature. It knows how to survive in all weathers, both on sea and land, and the legends state that wherever it goes the weather patterns change and it becomes warmer."

"Fools," snapped Rahitan. "Stop drivelling man, there is work to do. It is probable that Necrobath's mate, whom I seem to remember is called Gameling, is driving before her groups of fiends who emanate enough fear to sustain her on the journey. She travels at a great rate and may be here in only a few days. The fiends invade peaceful villages causing panic and terror, which fear provides a banquet for their monsters. Only Io knows what will happen when the two monsters meet. Perhaps an earthquake will rock the land as they thrash in passionate embrace. If they meet at sea, a great tidal wave could inundate us all. They have been separated for thousands of years. Now, concentrate. We must summons Honehe and Lonikai and also Carilan if he still lives. Perhaps the two who had the wisdom to resist your foolish scheme will be of some assistance. We will call on Rakaheke and Ioannes to attend this conclave. It has been a very long time since such disaster stalked the land and we will need to delve deeply into the recesses of our minds and study the ancient scrolls. Where is your scroll room?"

Albinon blanched. "If you enter you will die. The guardian spirit will not tolerate your intrusion."

Morpheus said contemptuously, "That is only an illusion created to keep out the uninitiated. It seems you have been tricked by your own game."

Rahitan added, "These dire warnings were put in place aeons ago by the ancient Priests to protect the precious knowledge. The Atema are guardians of the only set of golden scrolls in this land. Other sets are safely hidden in various parts of the world, under the protection of learned men and women. Your scrolls are parchment copies of the originals. Have you not seen them? In the event of a global catastrophe at least some of them would survive, along with those who can read them."

By this time Albinon was thoroughly demoralised. "Not in this lifetime, although I do have a vague memory of previous times when the scrolls were freely read by scribes and scholars. The existing tapu was in place when I became High Priest of the Matarau and I never questioned it."

Rahitan turned to Morpheus. "We left this journey too late. It should have been undertaken years ago, but we were awaiting the arrival of our Princess before proceeding." To Albinon he added, "When this catastrophe has passed we will make an annual pilgrimage around the island to ensure all is in order."

"That is fine with me," said Albinon, "but I am not sure that all of the other leaders would agree that you should become the Chief of Chiefs. They might feel you have overstepped your position."

Rahitan looked deeply into the other's eyes. "I did not let loose the taniwha. Now will you take me to the scroll room or do I have to find it myself?"

"No, I will show you the entrance door. Come with me. My High Priestess Marita has the key." Albinon walked towards his temple complex, followed by the Atema who had all gathered at Rahitan's mind call.

"What is going on?" asked Kaitewha. "We have been talking to some of the Matarau and they seem terrified."

"As well they might be," replied Morpheus seriously. "This twit of a High Priest, along with a few others have loosed the monster that has slept for aeons under our great lake. We were not aware of it until just now. It is called Necrobath and he has summoned his mate living in a lake on an island far to the north west. She is now on her way here, causing destruction and havoc wherever she passes. Preceding her are hundreds of warrior savages who are just now to landing on our shores to create enough chaos and fear to feed the monsters. We have to prevent these two taniwha from meeting and mating."

Rahitan added, "The only way any of the taniwha can be released is by human intervention. Thus was the law set down for our protection. It is part of the great game plan the creator gods invoked aeons ago. If we in human form evolved to such a high mental degree that we could challenge the gods, great destruction would befall us. A group of four black priests have so challenged and now we are all in grave danger, unless the light can prevail."

"How could they have been so misguided?" asked Aloma.

"I suspect they have had an implant inserted into their bodies," replied Garlita. "I noticed a small dark chip behind Albinon's left ear. Perhaps some of the creator gods thought we were developing too slowly for their liking, or becoming boringly light, so they interfered once again. And he is lying about the scroll room. Is that not so, Albinon?"

"You are right," replied the stricken man. "I can hide nothing from you. We were aware, as I am sure you are Rahitan, that there is a greater plan for this planet, a plan which was to design a new world where there would be extensive exchanges of information. The great mind of the Creator functions as a network of information that connects these worlds on many levels. Earth's place in the new world was designed to be extremely beautiful, rather like a living library. Information was to be held in the cells of each and every creature and molecule of consciousness designed to exist here. Consciousness was to be inserted into all living beings and also into the mineral world, as in this vast realm of creation, myriad forms exist. They are all playing the greatest mind game imaginable. The system of worlds has become continuously self-evolving, so much so that even the creator constantly surprises itself with the new rules and possibilities of this substance that has been endowed with consciousness."

"That is written of in the scrolls," growled Rahitan. "You told me that it was forbidden for anyoe to read the scrolls. How could you have such knowledge without access to the scrolls?"

"I created the tapu to keep anyone else from entering the hidden room," sobbed Albinon. "I wanted to be the most powerful priest in the land, even more so than you, Rahitan. Now I see how vain and foolish I have been. I used the other priests, stroking their egos by promising them great powers if they assisted me. They have much knowledge but little wisdom. I beg for your help in reversing our folly."

"Folly, you call what you have let loose folly. I call it the ultimate disaster," fumed Rahitan. "Now, for the last time, where is the scroll room?"

Reluctantly, knowing he was outwitted, Albinon let the Atema to a small door at the far end of the temple, and bent low to swivel a knob and stood back. The door swung open revealing a corridor lit with light balls, leading slightly downwards. "Follow me," he said.

Soon they all crowded into a small, musty room lined with shelves containing dozens of papyrus scrolls with various coloured rods protruding for identification, clay tablets covered with symbolic writing and wooden boards depicting scenes of ancient times. One shelf was covered with rocks made of clay covered with pictograms of animals, maps and scenes of the solar system. After pulling a scroll with dark wooden rods from the top shelf Albinon said, "This is the scroll that we used containing the information on how to set loose the taniwha. Unfortunately, I have not been able to find its companion telling how to restrain it again. I didn't think that we would need to know."

Rahitan turned to Thieron. "My boy, to save time and frustration, I ask you to return to our village and bring back the relevant scroll from our archives. Everything here is such a mess, it would take too long to locate it. You know how to enter our scroll room. Look for a large scroll with garnet rods. Now be as quick as you can, for I feel we are running out of time."

As Thieron slowly disappeared from sight. Albinon pleaded, "I know you have the knowledge of bi-locating. I have been working on that for years. Please show me how it is done."

"Not on your life," snapped Rahitan. "You are in enough trouble already. Now let us see where you went wrong and what we are going to do about it. When Thieron returns with the original scroll we will be able to fill in the missing pieces."

They all bent over the brittle papyrus scroll which seemed so crude compared to the golden masterpieces they had previously seen. Rahitan exclaimed, "Aha, this is a clue. Listen. 'Humankind has often been influenced by a few individuals designing its mass experience. When this is being done, certain rebellious people believe they can be liberated through their own thinking and perceptive abilities. They are further encouraged into doing this so that they can truly realise what their boundaries are, and that every action is part of the game. Sometimes those entrapped in the game forget that it is a game, and take themselves and it too far by interfering in circumstances beyond their control. Control forms the boundaries of safe behaviour. When they are about to change the equilibrium on earth, certain re-evaluation must be allowed to establish what are considered safe avenues to pursue. To become impatient leads to being ignorant of why it takes so long to move from one state to another. It is quite simple. Humans are not making the decisions. They may think they have clarity of mind but in reality are ultimately controlled by the creator gods.'"

Turning to Garlita he said, "My dear, you mentioned you could see an implant in Albinon's head. Any idea what it is?"

"Let me look more closely," she said. After a while she continued, "Albinon, was there a time when you were unconscious for a short period?"

"Yes, it was strange,' he replied. "About two years ago I suddenly fell into a coma for three days. Everyone thought I was dying, and when I awoke I felt different. Since that day I have been plagued with headaches and nosebleeds. It was soon after that I began to dabble in mind power and plot with the others to control the power of nature. Funnily enough, Lonikai, Honehe and Carilan all slipped into a coma around the same time. They also experience similar symptoms to mine We had to be very careful when sending our regular communication messages to you that we let nothing slip."

"Then you have indeed all been tampered with," said Rahitan. "I wonder for why. What is the reason for releasing the taniwha? Did the creator gods wish for a little excitement in this land of peace and harmony? We have worked so long to reach this point, why do they wish to ruin it all? Perhaps the scrolls will tell us." He continued to read for a while and then straightened and looked at his companions and said sadly. "I suspected as much, listen."

'When humankind slips into boredom, certain entities come to earth to join the game, and push things along a little. Sometimes they come from realms of the highest connection of spirituality. They keep humankind tethered to great beings of light who communicate through making a connection. When a spiritual entity chooses to become entrapped in human form, it often forgets what is ultimately possible, and so it is easily manipulated by those who control the game called Life on Earth. At the beginning of each zodiacal era certain evolved beings incarnate on Earth to act as catalysts for change. Sometimes the resulting change may not appear positive to those who are negatively impacted by it. At times the darkness of unconsciousness increases to affect cultures and planets and the coming era is one such time. Dark ages alternate with more enlightened times. The world is currently entering into a very dark epoch. In two thousand years, the following zodiacal era, the next Aquarian Age, is scheduled to be one of much greater compassion, enlightenment and awareness, coupled with immense technological inventions. Most of the creators of change will be incarnate at that time."

Rahitan looked up from the scroll. "My friends, I fear we are soon to enter another Dark Age. For the Atema it will certainly happen when Lake Taupo blows up once again. For the rest of the country it will happen when an invasion of great canoes arrives from the eastern seas. In other parts of the world it has already begun. In Europa the powerful Roman empire is in its demise, the far northern lights of Hyperborea become dimmed, and in the large continent far to our north west, great hordes of conquering hairy barbarians ride into innocent villages, pillaging and plundering at random. Their leader is so misguided that he thinks that the only humans who have any value are those who create beautiful works of art or can fight and kill. He has built a great column from the skulls of his victims. Now here we face the monsters of the deep unless we can find the secret to stop their rampage. When it was released last time we were able to contain it, but, Albinon, that was before you and the others were tampered with. I grow so weary of this eternal game of the alternating dance of light and dark."

Suddenly, a glowing shape manifested in the room. Thieron let out a shout of joy. "I did it. I did it all by myself. Here is the scroll you asked for. I even managed to dematerialise it for the journey." He handed the carefully wrapped object to Rahitan.

Lovingly Rahitan unwrapped the scroll and laid it on a bench. Its rods of garnet glowed dully. Unrolling it, the High Priest silently read its contents. The others were beginning to get restless when he finally looked up.

"It will not be easy to contain the chaos, but it can be done. Let us mind merge and summon the others involved in this foolish deed. They must be made aware of my displeasure and the seriousness of their actions."

Leaving the scroll room, the party returned to the temple and sat in a circle around a great stone statue of a woman dressed in a long feathery cloak.

"She is Ohinetaha, our legendary navigator, the one who led us to these shores many generations past. Her presence, when invoked., still overshadows the statue. Perhaps she will be of assistance," said Albinon, feeling more confident now that he felt he was on familiar territory.

Sitting cross-legged on cushions arranged in a circle they closed their eyes and following Rahitan's instructions, prepared to mind merge. "Firstly we must create a dome of protection over this temple to prevent the creator gods from finding out what we intend to do. No doubt they are aware that something is happening, for it was they who instigated this fiasco."

Angrily, Garlita interrupted. "Rahitan, before we begin it is imperative that the implants are removed. Albinon, I must first remove yours. Where can we go?"

Visibly Albinon cowered before the wrath of the High Priestess and meekly replied, "We can use the small room at the back of the temple. There is an altar there used for healing rituals that I can lie on. It will not be easy for the implant is well attached. I might die in the process."

"Tough," replied Garlita, pulling him to his feet and marching him to the room. "This should not take too long. Zenita, please attend me. You others, create a circle of protection around me."

The healer leapt to her feet and ran to keep up with the disappearing Garlita.

When Albinon lay down on the altar, Garlita raised her arms causing the tatooed entwined serpents to writhe, and their jewelled eyes to glow. "Great Spirit of Healing, overlight and work through me. Use my body as a pure channel of the healing force. Keep us all safe from harm during this operation to remove the implant from this man," she invoked.

For a long time Garlita strove to remove the implant, being careful in the process not to leave any small pieces behind that had the ability to regrow. For ttotal success she needed Albinon's assistance to release the psychic attachment to power and glory, while Zenita's strength of mind and powerful healing energy held a dome of invisibility over their actions until finally, every piece was successfully removed and disposed of.

"It is done," said Garlita, relaxing her tense body. During the operation, charges of power had rippled through her continuously and she felt now exhilarated. "How do you feel, Albinon?"

The Hight Priest of the Matarau threw himself at her feet. "Oh, Priestess Garlita, such a load has been lifted from my shoulders. My head no longer aches and the pressure behind my nose has gone. Thank you, and also you Zenita. I feel like I have been reborn."

"Get up you silly man," snapped Garlita. "Understand that you will have to regain my respect before I will treat you as a High Priest again. Now, let us join the others."

Seeing the trio emerge from the room, Rahitan rose to his feet. "I see you have succeeded, as the man looks completely different. Now let us continue the work."

"Just a moment, my dear. I think we need something to drink first." Turning to Albinon, Garlita said, "Call one of your people to bring us some nectar."

Refreshed, the circle of ten including Marita, the Matarau priestess, reformed around the ornately carved greenstone statue of Ohinetaha, the navigator ancestor. Rahitan invoked Tane, the great guardian force of the land, who responded with a deep rumble of thunder and a flash of lightning. The High Priest then communicated with the protective force. "Oh Great Tane, keeper of the land, protector of our villages, it has come to our knowledge that great destruction is about to overwhelm parts of this country, unleashed by the unfortunate curiosity and foolishness of a few. Seemingly natural disasters are often triggered by the unthinking actions of humankind. Can you bring to my vision the condition of the grid system suspended over our land?"

Rahitan remained motionless for several minutes before opening his eyes. "My friends," he said solemnly. "Tane cannot directly assist us in our dilemma but will do so indirectly. Because of the Law of non-interference, it seems that the grid system is damaged along the line of passage created by Gameling, in the area over Australis, the large continent to our west. I have been in contact with some of the clever men of that great barren land. They are aware of the danger and will assist us. Their powers are great and they should be able to seriously weaken the charge of the monster as she makes her way by sea down their eastern coast towards us."

Hearing a disturbance outside the temple, the group turned to see the three renegade priests enter, loudly demanding that everyone kneel before them.

"Good, you have arrived," said Rahitan, ignoring their request. "We kneel to no one. The messenger was swift. Now sit down amongst us, for we have serious business to discuss. Carilan, what news of your village?"

The High Priest of the Akariri was furious. "You were told to kneel before us. We have been elevated above all others, even you Rahitan."

Glaring at Carilan.the High Priest of the Atema stood his ground, "Rubbish," he snorted, "you have been interfered with by the creator gods who wished to have a bit of sport with you. Poor deluded fools, you have been implanted with a chip meant to control you even more than usual. Now Garlita and Zenita need to remove them. You first Lonikai. I wish to question Carilan about the condition of his village and the whereabouts of the fiends. He called us for help."

"I will not," shouted Lonikai. "There is absolutely nothing wrong with me." He moved swiftly to strike Rahitan but Kaitewha, rising swiftly to his feet,.blocked his path.

"You'll have to get past me first," the young man said "I will let no one strike my Master, especially one such as you."

"Young upstart," snarled Lonikai. "Young impudent whelp. Stand aside or I will put a curse on you." Lonikai was an enormous man of large girth, thighs and buttocks that were tattooed with spiral markings. His black eyes glittered with an unnatural light, and saliva dribbled from the corners of his mouth as he turned on Kaitewha. A second later his great bulk was sprawled on the floor. Kaitewha laughed. "Thank you, Morpheus. Levitation also works on humans I see." Staring into the eyes of Honehe he added, "Care to join him? Have you anything to add, Carilan?" Both men, equally large, stopped their posturing and sat on the floor. "Ha, the bully coward syndrome is alive and well in some priests of this land," Garlita laughed. "Morpheus, flatten them for good measure."

"I won't waste my energy on them just now, but if they don't cooperate you may need my assistance to restrain them whilst you remove the implants," answered the Dream Master.

The great bulky body of Lonikai began to float towards the healing room. He yelled, "Put me down. How dare you lay hands on me"

"Look, no hands," laughed Morpheus.

Lonikai was unceremoniously dumped on the altar and although he tried to struggle, he couldn't move. "Release me, I command you. I will have you boiled in oil and fed to the sharks. Do you hear me?"

"Idle threats cause no harm. Now be quiet while Garlita removes your implant. Don't you see what is happening, you great oaf? It is possible that the creator gods have twigged and are trying to prevent their puppet from being deactivated," growled Morpheus through his teeth.

The implant was soon removed, for Garlita and Zenita had found the patterning. Light poured through them as they worked, assisted by the overlighting presence of Tane.

"Your turn now," said Rahitan to Honehe. Although the big man struggled furiously, he was no match against the combined mind powers of Morpheus, Rahitan and Garlita.

"Thought you had it all worked out didn't you," said Garlita as Honehe lay meekly on the altar table. "It will take a great deal of co-operation to put the monster to sleep again. You do not treat Nature with disrespect and then expect her to teach you. Now close your eyes."

A short time later Honehe was released from the restraining forces and stood up. "The side of my head feels awfully sore around," he moaned. "What have you done?"

"Stop whinging and thank us," said Zenita. "We have not only saved your life, but possibly the lives of countless thousands. Do you feel any different?"

"Yes, I feel like I did a couple of years ago, before I fell into a coma. The clarity of vision and thought is getting clearer by the minute, but I have a feeling something awful is about to occur," the bewildered man replied. "What has happened?"

"Rahitan will tell you all about it whilst we work on Carilan. Please ask him to come," said Garlita. "Zenita, my dear, can you summon Erana? She can assist me on this one. She also needs to know how to do this work, for I fear we will meet others similarly affected."

Within a short time, Carilan emerged from the healing room saying, "I am amazed that my trusty guardian spirits allowed such a thing to happen. I suspect they were no match for the creator gods. It seems we need greater protection, Rahitan. What do you suggest?"

Rahitan stroked his fine silver beard and looked intently at the four wayward priests.

"I have summonsed Rakaheke and Ioannes to join us. They will be with us shortly, for they have the secret of bi-location."

As he spoke, two shadowy shapes slowly took form in the temple.

"You called us and we are here," said a tall thin man with a very black curly beard, dark bushy eyebrows and a hooked nose. He wore a long woven robe of natural flaxen material with a loose plaited belt tied around his middle, and shoes that turned up at the toes. Facing the fascinated group standing around Rahitan he said, "I am Ioannes of the Levanti. My tribe lives at the tip of the western fin of the great fish, under the benevolence of the volcano Taranaki. This is my colleague Rakaheke the Hight Priest of the Waitaha, who live in the far north along the tail of the great fish. We declined to join in the foolish prank concocted by Carilan and Albinon and thought that would be the end of it. I am sorry we did not take them more seriously."

Rakaheke bowed to Rahitan and Garlita. "Greetings, my old friends. I am delighted to be in your presence again. I have heard of your awakening to the power of love, and congratulate you. How can we help you, Rahitan, my esteemed friend?" Rakaheke was a giant of a man, with flaming red hair the colour of lava pouring from a volcano, and eyes the colour of the deep green sea. His fair skin was freckled from the kiss of the sun and he exuded an aura of power.

"Greetings to you, Ioannes, Rakaheke. Let me introduce you to my fellow Atema. You know the High Priestess, Garlita. She has consented to become my partner in life. Together we have rediscovered an ancient and powerful secret. Next is Morpheus the Dream Master, and this is our Princess Aloma, hiding behind her partner Kaitewha, our Song Master. Don't be frightened, my dear, they won't bite," laughed Rahitan.

"How do you do," whispered Aloma. Never before had she seen such fearsome, spiritually powerful men. She was used to Rahitan and saw that he wasn't as awesome as the others.

Rahitan continued, "This is our greatest healer, Zenita and her assistant Erana, and last but by no means least, my faithful scribe Thieron. He has recently rediscovered an ancient golden scroll that has led us all to a new level of existence. I believe there are parchment copies in other areas, Now, we have work to do."

The enlarged group sat on the floor in a circle around the statue of the navigator and closed their eyes. Rahitan began to chant in the ancient language and was joined by Rakaheke and Ioannes. Several of the other men took up the refrain, toning in deep masculine voices their reverence of Io. The women joined in, adding their harmonious voices to the hymn. Ripples of energy started moving through the air, expanding in ever increasing circles around the village of the Matarau, moving out over the land to create a dome of protection over each village lying in the path of the approaching destructive forces. The object was to make them invisible to the taniwha. Once that was done, the ripples of force continued to expand until they created an enormous force field strong enough to stop Gameling and her fiends.in their tracks and envelop them. The ripples kept expanding until they pushed her back home under Lake Bratan.

Howling indignantly, she was thrust deep under the lake waters and bound with such force that she could not be released, even if, in the future, the creator gods tampered with human destiny. Although she could still emanate thought forms to create fear in the land to sustain her energetically, she could not move from the lake. Rahitan knew that at the beginning of the next age she, and most of her family would be released from the Earth, after each being divided into four separate portions and sent to an uninhabited, primal place in the universe where they could live in freedom. That dangerous work would be done by Ratihan, Garlita and Aloma in different bodies more suited to the times. By then humankind would be in plague proportions on the planet, and the emanation of fear caused by wars, intolerance and hatred rampant, would provide enormous amounts of food for the taniwha. They would become bloated, greedy and slothful on such a daily banquet of psychic pollution.

Next their attention turned to restraining Necrobath. He was furious that his beloved had been bound before they could mate, and sent waves of viscous hate across the land. He began thrashing his enormous tail, felling forests with each swish and his fiery breath set fire to the resulting devastation. People ran screaming from his foul emanation, and finding nowhere to hide, perished. With the element of surprise gone and Necrobath's mind closed by wrath and fury, it was nearly impossible to approach him.

145

Rahitan called for a stronger effort. "Concentrate. Focus as you have never done before. Give this your all, or we may not survive. Necrobath, hear me," he shouted. "You will be restrained. No longer are you allowed to destroy our land, lay waste to our forests and kill our people. Tane will help us, assisted by Io, for your wrath cannot continue. Hear me, Necrobath. Return to Lake Taupo and live peacefully under its waters. Soon the Atema will all be destroyed again when the waters of that great lake are turned to steam. We will help you to find another home before then, so you will not be annihilated. There is another lake to the north east in which you can make your home. This is your choice, Necrobath."

Long into the night the merged minds of the fifteen people in the temple of the Matarau fought to contain Necrobath, and force him to return to his home under the lake. Exhausted and overcome by the battle of will Marita, Carilan and Albinon gave their lives in sacrifice. By the time the fiery red fingers of dawn spread over the land, .the battle had been won and Necrobath imprisoned.

For two days the remaining twelve rested, cared for by the grateful Matarau and homeless others who found their way through the forest. A new High Priest and Priestess were chosen to care for the spiritual life of the Matarau. The Atema did not have enough energy left to bi-locate home. Finally on the evening of the second day Rahitan called them together. "It is time to return to our village. I had planned to visit other parts of the country first but we must gather our strength. Being in our own environment will hasten the healing. Then I have a surprise for you all."

Turning to the gathered Matarau he added, "Thank you for your hospitality. We will return in two moons with some of the golden scrolls. We intend to share their knowledge with you and any from other villages.who would like to join us here. At present we have barely enough strength to return home."

Joining hands and forming a circle the group slowly disappeared before the amazed onlookers and were soon in their home temple, surrounded by those who loved and strengthened them. A few days later, Rahitan called the eight together. "I said I had a surprise. Are you all well rested? As you know, I had intended to travel much further afield than Matarau and now that we have recovered, we will make a quick trip around the great stingray to visit several of our kindred villages. After that how would you like to travel far over the great Pacific Ocean to the lands of our ancestors? To begin with I thought we'd travel through Hawaiiki, Rapanui and Hawaiikinui. If that is successful, we will spend time with our Rishi counterparts in India, and then move on to the lands where Asia and Europa meet. After that, our Druid friends in the small islands directly north of Europa, on the opposite side of the world will welcome us. In far future times many settlers from those Islands will find their way to our land to settle and prosper. Many will intermarry with those originally inhabiting these shores. The people presently residing here came from diverse lands but have common ancestors. The ancestors of those like Aloma and myself, who have fair hair and blue eyes, came from across the great eastern ocean. The forebears of Garlita, those with olive skins and straight black hair and green eyes, originated far to the north west and found their way to these shores a long time ago. Those like Kaitewha, with black curly hair, flat noses, deep brown eyes and dark brown skins, arrived from the islands to the north, the islands of the people with beautiful smiles and a love of fun, dance and song. Totally without prejudice we interbred and merged our qualities and colours and became the integrated and healthy people of today. In the far future other changes will occur."

The others reacted with pleasure as Rahitan told them of his plans. "We will be ready to travel around this land at the darkest time of the moon. That gives us just over a week to prepare. There is a lot to learn before we venture from these shores. We will use the golden scroll with the coral rods to open your minds. When the next two full moons have passed we will travel over the seas to connect with High Priests and great magicians in many lands. Now leave me, I wish to be alone with Garlita."

NINE

Wisdom of the Scrolls

Following the morning salute to the sun, the High Priest of the Atema summoned his scribe Thieron and asked him to call the others. The previous evening, after dismissing his companions he and Garlita went to the scroll room to collect two scrolls, one with the coral rods and the other of with rods of turquoise. Throughout the night, by the light of a luminescent ball, they read their contents. It was a rather tired and grumpy Rahitan who greeted them, while Garlita had managed to get a few hours sleep and arrived looking fresh and ready for action.

"Good morning, Master Rahitan," chorused Aloma and Kaitewha, who arrived with a large cup of nectar for the older man. "Have you some exciting news?"

As the others crowded into the small office, Rahitan cleared his throat and commented. "How fresh and rested you all look. I must be getting old. It seems, I can't work through the night without getting tired."

"You, old? Never, my dearest," soothed Garlita, laying her hand on his arm and stroking the serpent tattoos. When the golden eyes began to glow, she stopped, as energy flowed through her into Rahitan refreshing his body. He straightened and smiled in satisfaction.

"This scroll," said Rahitan, holding it up for them all to see, "has rods of coral. This particular red coral is exceedingly rare and is found high in the mountains of Tibet along with the turquoise which forms the rods for a companion scroll. That land was once deep under the sea and is being slowly pushed up to create the Himalayan mountains to the north of India where some of the greatest sages in the world have their abodes in remote caves. That gives us a clue as to the origin of this scroll. I frequently communicate with several of the Rishis, as these sages are called. Many of them hold the knowledge of the ancients that is contained in the scrolls."

Morpheus arrived, his streaked red and orange beard in disarray, his eyes rheumy. "Sorry I am late. I have been in meditation all night, communicating with the Lord Ashteroth of the Sirian Federation who has a great interest in our welfare. He has given me some very interesting insights into why our land is going through such turmoil."

Rahitan sighed. "Morpheus, you know what I think about your communication with space beings.There is only one God, who is Io. He is responsible for our wellbeing, and expects our help to interpret His wishes. These space beings only confuse our role on this planet."

"You are wrong, Rahitan," answered Morpheus. "Io needs beings on each inhabited planet to assist in the great work. You acknowledge the guides of humanity on Earth, why not those on other planets. We all work for the great Father and Mother of the creation of all things. We are like a great community in this galaxy who need to support each other in the great cosmic battle between light and darkness that Io has instigated for he understands the duality of all things. Together, we are all in this cosmic game, and cannot deny that others are also involved. Some of these civilisations on other planets are far more advanced in the rules of the game than we on Earth, and wish to prevent us from making some of the more potentially catastrophic mistakes, some of a magnitude that we cannot even imagine. He has shown me visions of a dreadful holocaust called nuclear war."

Rahitan replied sceptically, "Yes, that possibility is mentioned in one of the scrolls. But, as you may remember, the devastating effect of the cataclysmic natural explosion that wrecked our village and annihilated the land many thousands of years ago was far more destructive, and affected the whole world. It took thousands of years to recover from that event. Tane and the Earth Mother can be extraordinarily destructive when necessary."

"Master Rahitan, I get your point, but there is a vast difference between a natural disaster and a man made one. A natural one comes unannounced taking the people by surprise. Not the Atema or other enlightened ones who are in touch with the forces of the Mother and can transcend, but this kind of great destruction usually negatively affects those who have lost their connection to nature. A man made disaster is premeditated by perpetrators and involves the taking of one human life by another, either through hand to hand battle or on a larger scale, the use of weapons of mass destruction."

The High Priest sighed. "I am not in the mood for a philosophical discussion just now. I would rather read the scrolls to you and reveal the wisdom of the ancients who wrote them. They knew all things. You and I, although we know far more than most on this planet, are only guessing. I promised the Atema that we would read the scrolls to them when we returned from our journey. I will begin this morning. Garlita, please use the crystal bell to call the people to assemble in the temple courtyard."

Soon everyone stopped whatever they were doing, and gathered in response to the call of the crystal bell. No one ignored its summons without a good reason. Early on they were taught the bell's every nuance, ranging from a gentle to an urgent summons. Now it emanated a gentle call, meaning everyone was to gather for an important announcement.

Zenita did a quick healing and balancing on Rahitan, combed his hair and beard and brought him a fresh robe. Revitalised, it was the old familiar, controlled High Priest who mounted the central platform to stand beside the green stone statue of the Princess.

"My friends," his voice carried with authoritative power across the packed courtyard. Three hundred pairs of eyes focussed on the tall man standing with his arms outstretched towards the sun, activating the tattooed serpents on his arms. Power flowed through his deep blue eyes into every attentive pair. "When we rediscovered the golden scrolls, I promised that I would share their wisdom with you. Today I will begin, and each day following the sunrise meditation will devote time to their interpretation. If you wish to form small study groups to further discuss the wisdom of the scrolls whilst I am travelling again, I will assist in choosing discussion leaders." Rahitan held out his right hand and Thieron handed him the rolled scroll with the coral rods. Forever the showman, the High Priest of the Atema paused, scanned the crowd with sparkling eyes and slowly removed the attaching clips. Handing one coral shaft to Thieron to hold, he began to unroll the thinly beaten gold. It reflected the dazzling rays of the sun, now nearly overhead, making many of those nearest to squint. An aura of awe settled over those gathered and they became very quiet.

"This scroll, and indeed all of the others, has not been exposed to sunlight for many thousands of years. Each is mounted to a different coloured rod so as to be organised and recognisable when stored. Though this one with coral rods is not the first, for they are in a sequential order, it is one I thought you might first like to hear. The first scroll has rose quartz rods and reveals the love of the Creator for all creatures. It is the one that affected Garlita and myself so deeply. The second has rods fashioned from a rainbow coloured meteorite and is the one that depicts the rising or falling of consciousness on our planet and the evolution of our species. This coral for the scroll I am about to read from, comes from high in the Himalayan mountains to the north of India, where some of you visit to communicate with the holy men there after you learn the secrets of bi-locating. It is easier to visit that land than most others, as their level of the understanding of spiritual law is stronger. They have a focus for interdimensional travellers to lock on to for directional guidance. This scroll was written by the creator gods who, in very ancient times, travelled from their home on faraway Matariki by a means now lost to us, to assist in an earthly experiment. They were not the creator gods who genetically engineered the primitive human to be a slave to mine minerals, but their geneticists did adapt certain primates to evolve a higher intelligence. Relatives of these ancient primates still roam the jungles of many lands, but they never reached our isolated shores. Nor did they reach the great barren land to our west. That land has been continuously inhabited by a more developed version of the primitive, black men and women who reached those shores by flimsy raft and have lived there for longer than any other modern humans have inhabited their lands. Their ways are very different from ours. They build no earthly temples or villages but their knowledge of nature and art is quite advanced."

Rahitan paused and looked at his people. Their eyes were wide open with interest, and silence reigned. *Good, I've got their attention. I won't give them too much to ponder on today, but they can understand what I am saying. I can see by the yellow light of intelligence around each body.* He continued reading.

"When the creator gods who were connected with the divine experiment first came to Earth, they brought with them many gifts to assist in the development of humankind. One of these was law and order, and a system of justice, for the primitive humans behaved no better than some animals. Compassion and altruism did not exist in their minds, and nor did assisting any to whom they were not directly related. Theirs was a system of survival of the fittest, who bred and passed their stronger genes on to the next generation. The creator gods realised the desperate need for an organised and orderly society and achieved this by using the concept of kingship, and a system of justice. The one appointed the ultimate leader or king was required to be righteous and to proclaim and uphold the laws of the land, provided by the gods to wise men and women who advised the ruler. The laws were upheld by a judicial administration. These laws applied to every aspect of society, from rights of widows and orphans, marriage contracts, rules of succession, all the way through to commercial transactions and foreign trade."

Rahitan paused and looked at the crowd. "Many of the things mentioned in these scrolls as yet, have little relevance to this land. In many countries far to the north, in Asia and Europa, commerce and trade, the buying and selling of goods, animals, land and people, is commonplace but has not yet reached these remote shores. This will not happen for well over seventeen hundred years, when settlers from the land of the Druids come to live here, bringing with them many new ways. The indigenous inhabitants of this land are today still very primitive and live by tribal lore as most of you well know, having grown up in that way. Since coming here to live as an Atema, in a very short time, you have all had to undergo dramatic changes in the way you live and think. This tribal way of life can never lead to industrial development or great architectural wonders as it is self-defeating and in some ways does not encourage incentive. Also a change of consciousness happens very slowly with them. Some of their spiritual leaders have a degree of knowledge of the stars by which they navigated to this land, but keep such mystery to themselves. Others know herbal lore and the art of healing. Still others till the land and fish the seas but that is basic compared to how some citizens of far away lands live their lives. They do not know of writing or mathematics. In some other lands the inhabitants are similar to our tribal people but do not have such as The Atema to protect the land. Here we have no savage beasts or serpents that can inflict fatal injury on the unwary, nor droughts and floods to ruin the crops. Centuries before superior technology is brought to this land, we will be long gone, as will most of our companion villages, for the dark ages once again will overwhelm the land."

In silence Rahitan read for a short while and then looked at his people and said, "Wisdom handed down by the early gods contained knowledge of science and art, writing, music, metalworking, medical treatments, astronomy, mathematics and much other knowledge as yet unknown to us. Today, hardly any of that wisdom is known in this land. For instance even few of the Atema are versed in the science of mathematics. It is an ancient unspoken language of dimension and numbers." He paused and looked around. "I think that it enough for today. Most of you have never heard of medical treatments where the body is cut open and the diseased part removed, before being sewn up. Nor do we practice sacred geometry or metalworking, although I have some small understanding of these things from my contact with learned men in other lands. The Levanti brought the craft of smelting metals to this land but hold its secrets close to them."

He gestured to Thieron to roll up the scroll and secure the pins. "You may all return to you tasks but feel free to discuss anything I have told you. Tomorrow we will have another gathering at the same time."

Rahitan turned and walked briskly to his quarters, followed by Thieron and Garlita.

"That will exercise their intelligent minds," he chuckled.

The following morning, the entire village of some three hundred and fifty Atema gathered in the temple courtyard for the sunrise meditation, and to hear Rahitan read from another scroll. The sun rose a fiery orange, tingeing the few clouds with brilliant colour, which turned to red before fading to a soft pink. Rahitan mused. *It will rain before evening. Better make sure all the cloth laid out to dry in the sun is taken inside. Now that some of the women have perfected that splendid blue/green shade, I wouldn't like the results ruined.*

The High Priest of the Atema mounted the dais on which the greenstone statue of the Princess glowed with fiery light, and raised his arms. Soon the two golden eyes of his tattooed snakes began to glow, and the ceremony for the greeting of the sun began. When the great orange orb regained its normal daily colour, Rahitan motioned to Thieron to hand him the scroll which he carried. Thieron removed the outer casing and handed the golden roll to his master.

Rahitan said, "Thank you, Thieron my boy." Then turning to the crowd he held it aloft. "Today I was going to read the scroll with the turquoise rods, but late last night, as I perused some of them, I came across this one with amber rods that contains some remarkable information, which I would like to share with you. Not that the others are less informative, but this one I know will fascinate you all."

Motioning to Thieron to assist, they unrolled the scroll and held it aloft. Those closest could see that, instead of tightly written symbols, much of this scroll was covered with drawings. Some were maps of unknown continents, others of large animals and people, and still others seemed to indicate some sort of ritual.

"I spent most of last night attempting to decipher these drawings, and then realised that one of the smaller scrolls might contain the key to this knowledge. I was right, thank Io. This is what they say." Rahitan paused to create a greater impact on his onlookers.

Garlita thought, *How handsome and impressive he looks, but he doesn't really need to posture like that. He is always the showman shaman.* She flinched as Rahitan looked directly at her. *He can read my mind. For the time being I had better veil some of my deeper thoughts*

The High Priest became excited as he continued. "We can take from these scrolls only that which is in our limited range of understanding. The information that we can understand can be put to good use. We know our rebuilt temple complex is far inferior, in every aspect, to the previous one which now probably lies deep beneath us. The fact that we discovered the statue of the Princess is a miracle, thanks to young Thieron here. Occasionally a piece of marble is unearthed, and if we were to excavate below our village no doubt the whole complex would be revealed. But as we only have another twenty years before this village is annihilated, there is no point. We have a great deal of other work to do before we are blown sky high. We must interpret these scrolls and put into action anything that can be of assistance to this land, before they have to be hidden again. Now, let me begin before I interrupt myself again."

To catch a glimpse of the scroll, the crowd moved closer to the plinth, threatening to overwhelm the High Priest.

"Move back, and sit down please," he implored. "Afterwards you can all file past and take a look and while I am away from the village, you may study the scrolls as often as you wish."

Raising the scroll again, he continued. "Do you see these shapes at the beginning? They depict the known continents of Earth. There used to be seven as shown on this scroll, but now only five remain as the result of cataclysmic turmoil experienced by the earth mother, Papatuanuku. I myself have visited most of the five remaining continents in my light body, but now a few of us prepare for a group journey."

Pointing to the diagrams on the scroll, he began. "This is the hot land of Africa, said to be where humans first developed, aided by the creator beings. The people of that land have blue-black skins. To the north, the much colder Europa where those with white skins live. Over here is Asia, the land of those with yellow skin, whose slanted eyes protect them from the glare of the sun. These people have quite a high degree of civilisation. This is India where the holy Rishis reside and to the west is Sumeria, thought by some to be the cradle of the civilised world. Far to the north east of our small islands was a vast land called Mu, the Mother land. It sank beneath the ocean without trace around the time when our previous village was annihilated. We were part of that great land which at the time had advanced technology and an enlightened lifestyle. Today, all that is left are our two small islands, with the anchor stone island way to the south. In fact, even though we may seem enlightened compared with our tribal cousins, we are in fact but a shadow of our former glory."

Rahitan paused and looked at his people. They represented quite a mixture of skin and hair colour, and eyes of blue, brown, green and black, but no one had eyes like Garlita's magnificent gold flecked orbs. *Concentrate, old man. Don't lose yourself in the eyes of a woman.* Even though their stature ranged from short and squat to tall and lithe, they all had one thing in common, the light of intelligence showed in their faces. Not the flat, dull look of the primitive. This same light that had caused many of them a lot of trouble in the tribal situation before being called to join The Atema, especially those born of lower class mothers, for the hierarchical system was present and powerful.

"Over to the east of Mu, stands the north and south Americas, inhabited by brave and noble red skinned men and women. In the future they will be discovered by white skinned explorers from the west who will wreak havoc on the tribes. In the centre and south Americas, invaders from Europa seeking gold, decimated great civilisations, using superior weaponry and introduced diseases to which the native peoples had no immunity.

Further east was Atlantis, a great continent that no longer exists, for it met its demise during the great cataclysms and resulting flood that covered the earth some ten thousand years ago. Many of her inhabitants were our ancestors who, being pre-warned, fled before the break-up of their continent, taking with them many of their precious treasures, including copies of these scrolls. Far to the south lies a great cold land which consists of two large islands totally covered with ice and snow. Ancient maps show that this was not always so, for before the earth shifted on her axis, tropical vegetation once grew in abundance. This polar shift happens periodically, but the next one is not due for another couple of thousand years, possibly soon after we reassemble, after the next bang at the beginning of the twentieth-first century. Our earth is a living, breathing being, forever growing and changing. Every now and then she heats up. Look, that is shown in the next series of drawings. There is a diagram of how the planet can regress to a crisis situation because of atmospheric contamination. The abandonment of traditional and cosmic knowledge to embrace egotistic ideals that lead to the misuse of natural resources and contamination of the atmosphere happened in the remote past, and will happen again in the future. But to avoid, the plan is that humanity will be aware enough to take preventative measures before another great catastrophe envelops the earth. Let us hope that is the case. But is not only contamination by humans that causes the climate to change. We know that our earth orbits the mighty sun and imagine it does so in an circular orbit. However, great sages have discerned that earth is actually on an elipitcal orbit taking one hundred thousand years. The orbit becomes either more round or more elliptical at these intervals. A related aspect is a forty-one thousand year cycle in the tilt of the Earth's axis. This can also cause periodic changes to the climate. Occasionally ice covers the Earch causing temperatures to plunge and humans to adapt to freezing conditions.

But when the planet is highly polluted, a condition almost impossible for us to imagine, she overheats and immense blocks of ice break away from the polar regions and melt. Such immense quantities of cold water cause changes to the climate in the areas they affect." He paused before asking, "Will the surface of the earth experience another global flood, such as the one mentioned in our ancient texts? That, my friends, will be up to us as future incarnations of ourselves.

Never forget who you really are; for you are children of Io inhabiting human bodies for a short span of time. Now, that is enough to think about today. Tomorrow we will see other drawings showing great monstrous reptiles walking with humans; animals from distant lands we have not yet encountered; and yet others showing detailed medical operations. We have plenty of time to uncover the mysteries of the scrolls. Until then."

Rahitan motioned to Thieron the roll up the scroll and follow him.

Later that night, when the moon was sliding along its silvery trail down towards the horizon, and before the sun god began his fiery gallop across the vast blue sky, Aloma and Kaitewha were fast asleep, entwined in each others' arms. Suddenly they were awoken by a strong jolt, as the ground swayed violently beneath their hut. They leapt out of bed and ran towards the temple courtyard, meeting many of their people all rushing in the same direction. Then the crystal bell began to hum loudly. The ground stopped shaking, the panic subsided, and an eerie silence filled the village. A silence so loud there was no room for sound. A few minutes later everyone began to talk at once, until Rahitan appeared in the propylaeum, his arms upraised calling for quiet.

"My friends," he boomed, "there is no need for panic. We have just received a small warning from Tane not to forget our fate. Also, during the night he moved Necrobath to a new home. The monster was a little reluctant to leave his familiar place under Lake Taupo and to travel to the safety of Lake Rotorua. Necrobath's destiny is not to be blown to pieces when the next volcanic eruption occurs beneath Lake Toupo's great waters. The transfer happened under the cover of darkness, so the villagers whose dwellings he passed would not flee in terror or lose their wits. You know how superstitious some of them are. Tane still assures me that we yet have twenty years before the small bang occurs, but that is nothing in the lifespan of Necrobath and his kind who unfortunately live for aeons." Lowering his arms, he continued, "Now, please return to your beds until the morning sunrise ceremony. Sleep in peace."

But no sleep came to the young lovers as they lay awake talking.

"I have no wish to be blown asunder again, my beloved," whispered Aloma. "That earthquake opened a memory bank deep within my mind, and I saw our previous village, one far more splendid than this one, being covered with deep layers of ash and lava last time. I am afraid, Kaitewha."

Kaitewha held her close and kissed her. "I will ask Rahitan if memories of ancient events affect us in subsequent lives. For now, let us focus on the fact that in three days our betrothal day dawns. It is fun being betrothed in each lifetime. I cannot imagine spending even a small part of any life in the arms of another woman. Get some sleep, my Princess, for there is much to do tomorrow. There is nothing to worry about. We can always leave for another village when the time comes."

Aloma sat up, astonished by his suggestion. "You know we cannot leave our people to face the conflagration without us. That would change the course of destiny for us all. How can you even suggest such a thing? I thought you were worthy of my love."

The intense young man moved to put his arms around her. "The thought is not in my heart but in my head. I love you so much, the thought of being separated from you again in this lifetime is unbearable. Am I being selfish is wanting our love to last for a whole lifetime, and not have it extinguished once again? I know our intervening lives have been long and fulfilled, but each time we inhabit a mortal body, mine aches with desire for yours." He smiled deep into her eyes.

Aloma snuggled down beside him and asked, "Do you remember if we have ever shared the joy of conceiving a child together?

My memory is not yet fully restored. I know it is against temple regulations, but a deep urge is rising within me to fuse my seed with yours to produce a perfect child. I will ask Garlita for her opinion, and after we are betrothed, perhaps we can prepare in the Temple of Love to call a soul to us who wishes to incarnate through our combined love vibration."

"Many lifetimes ago, my love, we bore a child. At first the elders were furious, as tradition states that the Atema are born within the tribes, and only called when they are ready, which is usually in middle age. As you know, if the women who are called still bleed each month, they are given poroporo tea to prevent conception until the moon flow ceases. We were the exception. This happened several incarnations ago, and our girl child whom we called Manicarita, meaning the jewel of the temple, brought much joy and happiness to everyone in the village. While it is sad that the laughter of children does not fill our homes, it is also true that they are a great distraction to the important spiritual work being carried out here. Many of our friends miss the company of their grand-children and the opportunity to impart their wisdom, but if the child is a true Atema, it already has much knowledge."

"As a precaution, since we have become lovers, Angelica has been insisting I drink an infusion of poroporo tea each day, so I will not conceive. We are so much younger than most of the Atema, so conception is possible."

She put her arms around Kaitewha's neck and kissed him on the mouth. "What a pity we must sleep apart for the next two nights, until we are betrothed. Erana says it is to make us so mad with desire that we will spend the whole of our betrothal night making love. While Garlita assures me there is a deeper reason, she would not reveal it." She kissed his lips again before continuing with a sigh, "All the same, I can dream. I wonder if our child had blue or black eyes. Perhaps they were brown. Do you remember what she looked like, my love. She must have been beautiful. No one has mentioned her to me."

Kaitewha breathed deeply. "When I was taken to the great library where the soul records are stored, I saw in my life scroll another child destined to us. A girl born and grown to a young woman before the second bang of annihilation. This I can share with you, Aloma, to let you know that we shall have a child within the next full circuit of the sun."

"Oh! How wonderful," she laughed. "Do you think anyone else suspects?"

"They probably all know. There are no secrets here once memory is fully restored. Past, present and future are all fully open to exploration. While she may be lonely as a child, with no other children to play with, she is no ordinary soul and will delight in serving the temple. Garlita will instruct her in the wisdom of the Divine Feminine essence and you, as her mother, will just teach her by example, for you are the most feminine woman I have ever encountered."

Kaitewha's voice became thick with desire as he began to explore Aloma's body with his lips.

She giggled. "What do you mean, the most feminine?"

"You have all the qualities of a goddess. Beauty, laughter, intelligence, inner strength, compassion, a joyful and loving heart, and best of all, you love me. Now stop talking my adorable one, and let us get on with some serious loving. Remember that soon after our betrothal, we resume our journey around the land, and probably won't have many opportunities to enjoy unreserved love making."

"As soon as we return from the journey I intend to stop drinking the poroporo infusion. My love, I think I will burst with happiness," sighed the young Princess.

Only moments later, or so it seemed to the lovers, the clear vibration of the crystal bell danced through the village, carrying the early morning wake up call for the greeting of the rising sun.

Following the sunrise greeting, Rahitan called them to his room.

Before he could speak, Kaitwha askd his question. "Master Rahitan, following the earthquake, Aloma had a very disturbing memory of the destruction of our previous village on this spot. It caused her great distress as visions flashed before her eyes. Do you think we carry past trauma deep within our memories?"

"Most certainly, Kaitweha. It is written in the garnet scroll that there were two possible causes for humankind's original trauma. The human race has experienced some huge catastrophies during its development on Earth, both self-inflicted and caused by natural events beyond its control. Self-inflicted causes are wars, overpopulation leading to starvation, abuse as children, or a sense of abandonment. A much more likely contributing factor is the fear and trauma caused by natural disasters, both originating on the Earth, like earthquakes, floods, fires, volcanoes, and the changing climate, and from comets, and meteors colliding with the Earth, causing great conflagration, or fluctuations in the energy from the sun,. The scroll informs us that the Earth's climate is constantly changing, for it has experienced long ice ages, and in between, some periods of drought and heat, causing crop failure and starvation. There have been several ice ages and a few pole reversals since the time humans were created on Earth by the creator beings, so our memory covers many thousands of millenia. Then there is the memory of the destruction of Lemuria and Atlantis and other great civilisations. Around ten thousand years ago, it is recorded that a large comet hit the Earth in the area to be known as North America, causing the covering of thick ice to melt suddenly, leading to a great flood that affected every part of the Earth. Many of the myths and legends of earlier peoples and even present day tribes, tell of such a calamity that everything changed rapidly, with sea levels rising and whole villages being inundated, with their populations destroyed. However, it is written that there have been many catastrophes contributing to the surfacing of unresolved traumatic memories during subsequent disasters, leading to fear, and superstition. Indeed, many cultures view comets and unusual celestial events with extraordinary dread. Many myths also blame humans for bringing misforturne on themselves, or believing it is the wrath of the gods who are displeased with them. On our return, I will read the rest of the scrolls to everyone, so we can all have a better understanding of history. Now, on to a more pleasant subject."

Beaming widly, the High Priest of the Atema continued.

"Children, two days after your betrothal ceremony we resume our journey around the land of the giant fish. I have a delicate matter to discuss with you." He cleared his throat and slowly paced the sparsely furnished room. "This mission we are about to embark on is a most diplomatically important one, for great damage has been done in the land by the renegade actions of the four wayward priests who unleashed Necrobath's mate, Gameling. Albinon and Corilan paid for their folly with their lives. New spiritual leaders have been chosen in the villages of Matarau and Akiriri and we must make their acquaintance, as well as smoothing over any difficulties they may have in adjusting to their new roles. We must determine if they are suitable candidates to learn the art of bi-locating, and, if they do not yet have that knowledge, teach it to them"

He stopped pacing and looked directly into the eyes of the two. "Now to a, er....., delicate matter. This task would be so much easier had I not read the Rose quartz scroll that had such a magical effect on me. We will be visiting in the official capacity of the Atema, and as such must conduct ourselves accordingly. What I am trying to say is that you will be sleeping in separate rooms on the journey. We will be guests wherever we travel, and as is customary, men sleep in one room and women in another. Betrothed couples are no exception. No doubt Garlita and I will also find this a burden, but our years of training will make it easier. Occasionally you may find the opportunity to come together, but we need to keep our senses about us at all times and so need no distractions. There is no guarantee that we will always be safe on this journey, but our powers of protection are strong, and I have no fear for our safety. However, it pays to be cautious. There, I've said it. I must be getting weak in the head to baulk at such a task. Now leave me, I have much to prepare, and so have you."

The betrothal day of Aloma and Kaitewha dawned clear and bright. Following the sunrise meditation, many helpers swept the pathways clean and sprinkled scented water to settle the dust. Garlands of flowers bedecked the village, and sweet perfume scented the morning air. The ceremony was to culminate at noon in the temple courtyard around the statue of the Princess standing proudly on her granite plinth, her lapis eyes sparkling in the sun. Thieron lovingly placed a necklace of highly perfumed white flowers around the statue's neck and then kissed its feet. *My Princess, whom I have loved since the beginning of time, how I wish you were being betrothed to me. Will we ever spend a lifetime together in love and intimacy? My heart aches with my love for you, but you have only eyes for Kaitewha. How I envy him. Were he not around, would you instead look lovingly into my eyes? I cannot harm him, for to do so would hurt you deeply. I love you too much to cause you the pain and suffering which you would feel if he were to die. I will partner with Erana and dull my longing for you, my dearest love, but I will always love only you.*

Two large tears slid slowly down his tortured face, and dropped unchecked on the statue's toes. Thieron rose and walked slowly across the courtyard towards the temple where sounds of music began to waft on the air. *Today I will wear my heart on my sleeve, tomorrow I will bury my grief and talk to Rahitan about betrothal to Erana. Life must continue.*

The entire population of the Atema gathered to greet and bless the young lovers, as they sat on decorated litters, carried around the village by strong men. A betrothal celebration rarely occurred in their village as most were older and wiser when they arrived, having completed the child bearing years in their birth village, although later they were encouraged to find a lover. Today was an exception. Laughter and song followed Aloma and Kaitewha, carried on separate litters until they were escorted back to the temple to prepare for the ceremony.

"Angelica, I had no idea I could be so happy," sighed Aloma as she lay in the Temple of Rejuvenation, on a long table covered with soft towels Under the expert hands of Angelica, the Princess's perfect body was oiled and massaged until she felt soothed and relaxed.

"Now, my Princess, your bath awaits," said Erana, offering her a soft warm towel. "Follow me."

Aloma settled into the scented water, let out a long, contented sigh and totally relaxed. She felt the surface of the bath move and opened her eyes to find Erana placing handfuls of brightly coloured petals around her. Laughing, she arranged them in a pattern on her breasts, stomach and face. "Would these do for a betrothal gown?" she asked.

Excitement mounted towards noon when Rahitan and Garlita mounted the central dais, and called all to gather around.

"I see you have prevailed upon one of the craftswomen to make the turquoise cloth into a most attractive ornamental robe," said Garlita. "That dark swirling pattern sewn down the side is a nice touch. How distinguished you look, my dear."

"Thankyou Garlita," replied Rahitan. "I must say you look pretty fetching yourself. What colour do you call that? I'd guess light yellow, but you know I am not too knowledgeable in such mysteries," replied Rahitan. Then, raising his voice he boomed, "Atema, please leave a path on each side for Aloma and Kaitewha to join us."

A murmur increased to a loud cheer as Kaitewha walked down the temple steps between the parted onlookers, towards the central plinth. He wore a simple white leather tunic that hung to his knees, and belted with a chain of copper rings. Red highlights touched by the sun glowed in his long curly black hair and his dark eyes danced with joy. Rahitan embraced him and said, "Stand beside me until Aloma joins you then turn to face me. I will conduct the ceremony in full view of all our people."

Alerted by a group gasp, the young man turned to see his adored soulmate walking, with great dignity, slowly towards him, followed by Zenita and Erana. They all looked resplendent. He tried to move to assist her up the stairs but could not. He was overjoyed as he watched every lithe movement of her precious body glide towards him. Her long golden hair was piled high on her head and secured by ornately wrought golden pins. A string of pearls was entwined within its curls, one perfect tear shaped pearl hanging between her brows. Her shining blue eyes, enhanced by ash mixed with a little vegetable oil on her long lashes, looked enormous as they smiled at the crowd of happy people. A long, soft white gown hugged her figure and swayed around her ankles. Long sleeves covered her arms, hiding the scabs of the newly formed tattoos encircling her forearms. She could feel the material caressing the serpents as she walked. *When we return from the journey I will have the jewels implanted into their eyes to enhance my vision. My jewels are to be pearls gathered from the far northern coast of the great brown land to our western shore. I know Rahitan had to pay a great price for them. How they must really love me. What have I done to deserve so much happiness. Ah, there is my beloved standing beside Rahitan. How handsome he looks. I am growing weak at the knees. I hope I can conduct myself with dignity until this ceremony is over. Of course I can.*

Aloma mounted the dais to stand beside Kaitewha and looked deeply into his eyes. She glimpsed an image of herself. *Yes, we are one, for he is also in my eyes.*

Rahitan took their hands in his and faced the crowd. "Today I have the great honour of formally joining our Princess with her beloved, Kaitewha. They assure me they have found each other acceptable on all levels of being. They are twin souls having left the Heart of the Creator in unison, and always finding each other at each incarnation. Not all incarnations have been as Atema, nor as happy as this one, but they have always incarnated within the same land at about the same time. Only twice did they mistime. The first time was three hundred years after the big bang. Kaitewha was a village chief and well advanced in years when Aloma was born into a neighbouring tribe. When he first saw her in her mother's arms, he knew instantly who she was, but had to constrain his impatience until she was of age. His constant visits to a family of the neighbouring tribe had everyone wondering what he had in mind until he asked to take her as his wife. By then, as was the custom, he had many wives and children who, being jealous, did not relish the thought of Aloma coming to live with them. Even under the threat of dire punishment from the chief, whenever she visited with her father, they taunted her, threw stones and generally made her life unbearable. Kaitewha knew that she would not be safe in his village, so forsaking his position, his family and everything he owned, he convinced Aloma to live with him in isolation, by the shores of the great central lake. The area of the original temple was totally buried, and the entire area was still mostly uninhabitable and therefore, greatly feared and avoided by the tribes of the land, so they were left to live in peace. They lived in great harmony and love until he died at an advanced age. Aloma built a pyre for his body, and in her grief, threw herself into the flames.

The second mistiming was a reverse of the first, with Aloma being a great deal older than Kaitewha. This caused even more consternation amongst their respective unenlightened families, so that again they lived separately from the tribe, in the aura of great love and contentment that only twin flames can know. This time it was Kaitewha's turn to immolate himself on her pyre and join her on the other side of life. However, enough reminising. Let us commence the betrothal ceremony."

Two musicians, each standing on the rear steps of the dais raised a conch shell to their lips, took a deep breath and blew. Resonant notes filled the air, leading everyone to become silent, and look towards the dais. They were soon joined by two more musicians who played reed pipes that made a haunting, strangely familiar sound like the wind playing in the reeds by the lake. Two more joined in, playing hollow gourds with finger holes arranged along the top.

Garlita whispered to Rahitan. "Kaitewha spent days composing that music during the twenty-one day process in anticipation of this ceremony. He has done, well for it is melodic to the ear. How romantic."

"My dear friends," Rahitan said, projecting his voice so that all could clearly hear. "We are gathered together on this auspicious day to join our Princess Aloma and her consort Kaitewha, in union with each other and the Atema. As many faceted Rainbow beings we are composed of all the rays of light and knowing. This enables us to blend energy across the entire spectrum of expression, bringing forth the presence of the One God, Io. We are responsible for our self-creations, and have the ability to remain totally in the radiance of Io's presence at all times, whether in safety or danger. We have surrendered the veil between our outer and inner self unto the empowered fulfilment of the universal will through our unique expression of our Rainbow being, and know that we live within the body of our Earth Mother who bore us. Our father and mother creator join with us in welcoming our beloved Aloma and Kaitewha, as fully integrated members of the Atema and the greater Rainbow tribe."

Looking up he shielded his eyes from directly gazing into the sun, saying, "See, Uenuku has blessed this day with his rainbow presence. This is indeed a great omen. He bowed deeply and chanted in his deep resonant voice, a long greeting to Uenuku, the rainbow god.

All the people shielded the direct glare of the sun, and looked into the heart of its encircling rainbow. The cosmic rays of energy flowing through the circle increased the heat and penetrating capacity of the sun. It was an awesome moment.

Then Rahitan took the couple's left hands and placed one on top of the other. Thieron handed him a plaited, rainbow coloured length of fibres which he placed over their wrists, and tied with a bow. Overhead a great golden eagle spiralled on a thermal of warm air, and the brilliant rainbow grew in intensity as it encircled the sun. In the surrounding trees small birds sang their hearts open with joy. Butterflies danced around the lovers' heads, and even the flowers seemed to glow more billiantly. Strong perfume wafted on the air.

"You have my blessing and that of all the people on your union. More importantly Uenuku has honoured you with his presence. You are now truly betrothed. Live in peace and harmony and do not feel beholden to remain with the Atema when the end time again assails us. You will soon bear a daughter, to be called Maricarita, as was your last child. Take her to the village of the Waitaha occasionally so the people will know her and allow her to live amongst them, after the next demise of our present village. It is not her destiny to ascend with us, for she carries within her the seeds of our ancient line and our future. The purity of her blood line must be continued for hundreds of generations, until we are ready to incarnate as a group once again. The son of Thieron and Erana, to be named Haeata, 'a beam of light,' will be her partner and that line will run true until the time when nobility of spirit will be more important than nobility of blood."

Several people pointed to the sky and this caused everyone to look up. Encircling the first rainbow was another, showing a reflection of Uenuku, and around that, a third. That display caused most of the people to fall to their knees, raise their hands in supplication, and begin to chant. They were totally overcome, for the third rainbow was pure white.

Rahitan responded. "Oh, mother rainbow, we are greatly honoured that you should bless us with your esteemed presence. Only once before in my long life have I seen your beauty shine translucently on our village and that was when the previous incarnations of Aloma and Kaitewha were betrothed. Also, during that life they were blessed to bear the soul of Manicarita, who became a very special child."

Garlita in a trance like state, raised her arms causing the two serpents eyes to glow with life, and their bodies appear to writhe along her forearms. "I am Aniwaniwa, the goddess of the white rainbow, and the consort of Uenuku. I greet you, people of the Atema. You are especially favoured by me. The child Manicarita is an earthly incarnation of my self, chosen to continue the true blood line until the time when nobility of spirit is so strong in most of human kind that no longer will pure blood be required to preserve my very essence on earth. That day is far into the future, for it will take one whole cycle of the zodiac to pass before the consciousness of this land rises to a high enough vibration to allow this to happen. She and Haeata, the earthly incarnation of Uenuku, will bear several children to be placed amongst the tribes whose seed has grown weak and needs to be replenished. As most of you will leave your earthly bodies within twenty years, these children must be grown and betrothed before that unavoidable catastrophe. They have much to learn from you, but they also have much to teach you during your final few years, about how to more successfully survive the transition. Last time it took you over twenty thousand years to regroup. This time it will be less than two thousand. We will overlight these aspects of ourselves every step of the way. The parents we have chosen to bear them are totally suitable. We have waited a long time for this moment, and now we thank you for the privilege of appearing before you. Farewell."

Garlita opened her eyes and stared at Aloma and Kaitewha who stood hugging each other.

"Look," cried someone in the crowd, pointing up. "A white eagle has joined the golden one and they are dancing the sacred spiral between the rainbows. What does that mean?"

"It means", continued Garlita, "that the destined children of our young lovers will also have the protection of the great eagle spirit. Unfortunately, through ignorance, that great bird will become physically extinct in this land, but its spirit will live on forever. But we are witnessing an even greater omen, for very rarely are the two seen flying together. Usually the white female is hidden deep in a cave, where many aeons ago, she was imprisoned by an evil sorcerer from an unenlightened tribe to the south of our forest. Fortunately, his power is insufficient to contain her when a special occasion such as this arises. For a short time she manages to free herself and fly with her mate, who tries to restrain her from returning to the cave, but his strength is not sufficient, so she stays hidden awaiting the next time. One day, in the future when the Atema find each other again, someone will come to this land from over the sea, who can break the spell, and free the white eagle forever. That one will be an incarnation of the sorcerer who imprisoned the bird. She will be in a woman's body and understand that for this land to fulfil its destiny, the white eagle must be released to fly free. The woman will meet the living incarnation of her mate in a brown body, an incarnation of the golden eagle, and when their auras fuse the spell will be broken. Once they're together, they will have much spiritual work to do to restore this land ravaged by fighting between tribes and with those from distant lands who will come to settle amongst its green hills. Until that day the white eagle must remain a prisoner of the sorcerer. Such is the game of life in this dimension."

Garlita moved closer to Rahitan and whispered, "Why don't you perform another ceremony now? That of joining Thieron and Erana in sacred union. I am sure the people will approve, and Aloma and Kaitewha will not feel it an intrusion into their day."

Rahitan responded with surprise. "Is it not perhaps a little premature? Does Erana know of Thieron's intentions?" Quickly he glanced at the two who were standing close together, holding hands. "I thought his heart would be broken today, seeing his adored Princess betrothed."

"Young men are very resilient," replied the High Priestess. "But I will ask them."

She walked over to the couple and smiled. "Rahitan suggests that you also seal your love in betrothal this very day. Do you agree to this?"

Thieron blushed furiously, making his red hair seem pale in comparison. "Are we so obvious? I thought not to spoil this day for Aloma and Kaitewha."

Garlita laughed. "Nothing could spoil their happiness, and you will only add to it if you agree."

Erana hugged the High Priestess, causing her some concern that the delicate tracery on her gown might be spoiled, but Garlita said nothing.

"We agree. I would have liked a special gown, but I know that is not possible. Yes, Thieron, let's do it." Erana laughed and looked lovingly at him.

"Why not," replied the young scribe. "You look beautiful in that crimson gown. My broken heart will mend as our love grows, especially when the destined son is born."

Quickly Garlita returned to the dais and nodded to Rahitan. "They have agreed."

Rahitan called for quiet and summoned the shy couple to him. "My young scribe, Thieron, and our excellent healer, Erana, have been blessed by the prophesy of the white rainbow. We have suggested they become betrothed on this day so that their son and his future partner may be conceived on the same night. They have consented. Please be silent while I recite the blessing." He repeated the words he had previously spoken for Aloma and Kaitewha and thereby, sealed the union.

A loud cheer rang out from the crowd, for Thieron and Erana were also particular favourites of the Atema.

Morpheus, who had been in the background for longer than he could stand, came forward and whispered to Rahitan. "Can I add something?"

"Of course, old friend, the stage is yours."

Morpheus smoothed his ginger beard with his gnarled hand and said in a loud voice. "With your permission, I would like to make this a triple betrothal, for the master healer Zenita has consented to become my partner. Just why she would choose to commit such a foolish act is not for mere mortals to understand. Rahitan, would you also seal our betrothal?"

"Delighted," smiled he High Priest, while copying Morpheus' hand on beard stroking. "Zenita, my dear, are you sure. I always took you to be a wise woman."

Zenita mounted the dais and stood in front of Rahitan and Garlita. "Do not mock me, Rahitan. I know Morpheus is not much to look at on the outside, but within beats a heart of gold, and he is a kind and gentle friend."

"I apologise," replied Rahitan. "I meant it only in jest. I see you are serious and will gladly conduct the ceremony." Turning to the onlookers he enquired, "What say you. Should these two be betrothed?"

With one voice they shouted, "Yes". Someone in the crowd added, "While we are at it, what about you and the High Priestess?"

Rahitan glared for an instant and then laughed. "No my friends, that is not to be in this lifetime. We are still controlled by the vows we made. Before I read the Rose Quartz scroll I would have had whoever said that, severely punished. I must be getting soft. Now Morpheus, Zenita, stand before me and hold out your left hands."

So the ceremony was repeated for a third time, but without the overlighting presence of Uenuku and Aniwaniwa's rainbow, or the golden and white eagles.

"By the signs, it looks as though we are not to bear a child, my dear," whispered Morpheus. "What a relief." After giving Zenita an enormous bear hug, he yelled, "Pausanin, master brewer of potent herbal brews, set up your jugs. We have some celebrating to do."

Zenita shrugged. "Morpheus, I will not try to change your ways, as I have more sense than that. However, as we are yet to become lovers, I would ask you to be gentle, for I have yet to know a man intimately, and I do not wish my first time to be with a man in his cups."

Totally surprised, Morpheus stared at his new wife. "What, am I betrothed to a virgin? How extraordinary. I had no idea. I assumed you were experienced in the ways of men." He picked her up and whirled her around in his arms. "I have an idea. How about we get that over with right now, and then I can enjoy our party? Come with me, my love."

Grabbing her hand, they rushed through the crowd to his hut, where he pulled aside the entrance curtain, picked Zenita up in his arms and deposited her on his unmade bed. She wrinkled her nose at the unwashed smell that pervaded the bedding. She was given no time to say anything before Morpheus was peeling off his clothes. "Now it's your turn," he panted, tugging at the ribbons that held her gown together. "It's been so long since I made love to a woman, as my interests have been elsewhere. That changed when we truly saw each other for the first time in the village of the Akariri. I then realised what a magnificent woman you are and wanted you more than anything I have ever wanted in my life. I have thought of nothing else but this moment."

Morpheus roughly pulled her gown apart to reveal an ample but firm figure, which he fell on, his breath coming in short gasps "I am a little unpractised, my dear. Can you help me."

Zenita whispered like a young inexperienced woman. "I don't know what to do. Would you believe I have instructed initiates in the Temple of Love without ever having experienced intercourse myself."

Morpheus barely heard her, as his lust took over. "Zenita you magnificent specimen of womanhood. Open your legs and heart to me and I will show you what you have missed out on all these years." With that he thrust himself deeply into her trembling body, and groaned as a stream of blood and semen flowed onto the bed. The startled woman gave a stifled scream as Morpheus withdrew his rapidly shrivelling penis and wiped it on his shirt.

"Thanks, love," he rasped. "We are going to have a wonderful sex life, but now get up and clean yourself, before we return to the party. Tonight I intend to have a skin-full. I rarely drink the potent brew, but tonight is an exception as it is party time."

Zenita remained on the bed, mortified, tears rolling like fat raindrops down her cheeks. "That's it? It's over. Just like that. What a foolish woman I have been, saving myself, believing in some romantic notion that my first time would make the stars spin. Morpheus, that was the greatest anticlimax of my entire life. Not a performance I ever want to repeat. Unless you can do better than that, you will never penetrate my intimate space again. Do I make myself clear?"

Morpheus looked crestfallen. "What are you talking about? That's what it is and I thoroughly enjoyed it. It is always a quick thrust, ejaculate, deflate and out. You'll get used to it. Come on, let's join the others." He pulled her from the bed and thrust her clothes into her arms. "Get dressed. I'll see you in the courtyard." He had been dressing whilst talking and took his leave.

Zenita, shocked and deflated, was slow to get up. *I do not believe that is all there is. Why do Aloma and some of the other women look so radiant after being with their lovers. They talk of foreplay and long sessions of kissing, stroking, gazing into each others' eyes. What about the ancient teachings about the fusion of masculine and feminine energy that joins initiates in a greater understanding of the creative ecstatic unity of bliss and love. The body is vitalised, the mind becomes freer, deep insights are discovered and a deeper blending of two souls in true love occurs. Are the teachings wrong, or is Morpheus totally ignorant of them. His recent effort showed no appreciation of love over lust.*

She struggled into her gown, making sure no blood stained its cream coloured folds.

Does he not know how to hold his semen and focus his energy and thoughts, or how to transfer the stimulating delight and increased energy to the more limitless ecstatic capacity of the higher centres. Is he not aware that the balance obtained by such actions supporting a more loving, fulfilling and expanded awareness which leads to the merging of sexuality with the spiritual path? What have I done? The join with Morpheus.was such a spur of the moment decision, otherwise I would have talked to Garlita about her experience with Rahitan,. What was it that influenced the old High Priest to change so radically? Of course. reading the Rose Quartz scroll. I must arrange for Morpheus to read it at the first opportunity, and if he refuses, this will be the shortest betrothal in history. Angrily she marched from the hut towards her healing temple, feeling pain between her legs. *I must anoint my damaged loins with a soothing balm. This is not right, and I am not some silly girl to be trifled with by an inexperienced and selfish lover. I am a woman who deserves much more. No wonder I kept my virginity for so long. It was not worth losing.*

In the courtyard, the influence of Pausanin's potent brew was already having an effect, as it made people happy, funny and playful. Lines of dancers formed around the young betrothed couples. At first, Zenita's presence was not missed until Morpheus returned alone.

Rahitan clapped him on the shoulder. "What ho! master of dreams? Why the long face. Surely this is the happiest day of your life,?"

Morpheus grunted "I wish to partake of a mug of ale and then I will tell you my problem, Rahitan my old friend." He filled a large mug to the brim with foaming brew, and drained it in one swallow. "Rahitan, I think I have done a terrible thing. I only just discovered that Zenita was a virgin, so I rushed her to my hut to deflower her before I got drunk. The mating didn't take long. She seemed very angry when I left. She said something about 'if I couldn't do better than that, I would never again penetrate her intimate space. What do you think she meant, my old friend?"

Rahitan removed his arm from his friend's shoulder, and looked him squarely in the face

"What exactly did you do." he enquired.

"I followed the traditions of my former tribe and did what every red blooded man is supposed to do following his betrothal. I ripped off her gown, threw her on the bed, penetrated her quickly bursting her maidenhead, shot my load and withdrew," Morpheus answered defensively.

"What, no kissing, no stroking, no telling her you love her, no foreplay?" said Rahitan. "No wonder she is a bit miffed. Have you ever sampled the delights of a woman before?"

"Not for a very long time, in fact not since I was a youth, when as a lad of fifteen I first experienced lust. Couldn't call it love. Since then I have known few women. You know I have not desired a partner until I met Zenita." Morpheus hung his head.

Rahitan groaned. "Poor Zenita. She instructs acolytes in the Temple of Love in the art of connubial love, and this happens to her. She must be dreadfully disappointed. Where is she now?

"I really don't know. I told her to join me here when she was dressed," Morpheus replied. Then naively, he asked, "Have I done something wrong?"

"I am sure you can rectify the matter. But first, have you never had instruction in how to please a woman? Remember, it is part of the Atema training when we are called to the village."

"Because I never thought I would become betrothed, I bluffed my way out of it by saying that I was very experienced in the art of love I thought I'd be safe from those problems," he moaned. "I am very fond of Zenita and her massage blisses me out of this world."

"I suggest you read the scroll with the Rose Quarts rods. It talks about every aspect of love and the art of lovemaking. I think you will be pleasantly surprised by what you learn. In fact, you may never be the same again. It certainly has had a profound effect on Garlita and I. We have become accomplished lovers since reading that exquisite text on love." beamed Rahitan.

"I have heard the rumour about you two," replied Morpheus. "Isn't it forbidden for the temple priest and priestess to copulate, because it supposedly reduces the effectiveness of your powers?"

"Yes, we did think that, but since reading that scroll, we now know that celibacy is but a path we chose, a different direction to walk along. Now we realise the folly of that choice, and instead, enjoy the bliss and fulfilment that leads to transcendent experiences of making love with the one partner your body and soul loves deeply and truly. However, we waste time standing here talking about such matters, when they are best experienced first hand. When we return from our impending journey, you are to read the scroll and experience its transformative qualities. I guarantee that Zenita will have nothing to complain about after that. But that joy will have to wait, as you will not be able to sleep together during our trip, and have other things to take care of. Best to be patient until you have enough time to concentrate on putting what you discover into practice. Understand that it is no loss of face to be a bad lover. What is inexcusable however, is to do nothing to improve your performance once you realise this. I am sure Zenita could assist you if you but ask her. Now, have another drink and lose yourself for a while." Rahitan turned abruptly on his heel and strode away.

Morpheus filled his mug and joined in the frenzy of the party. He forgot Zenita, his sacred role, and his inadequate performance in the depths of the mug and caroused long into the night. When Tira Whetū, the long river of milk that flowed across the black night sky began to fade, and Te Taki o Autahi, the cross of light, had slipped below the horizon, he crept to his hut to sleep. It wasn't long until the vibrant sound of the crystal bell penetrated his brain, causing him to groan, roll over and try to sit. To his amazement he found he was clear headed and alert. *Pausanin said something about a hangover cure he added to the last vat. It has certainly worked. I must congratulate him. I wonder what is in it. Perhaps he can exchange its secret with other master herbalists on our journey and get some of their recipes. I feel wonderful.* He leapt to his feet and quickly crumpled in a heap on the floor. *Whoops, It appears that I am not immortal after all. I realise that I am lying on the floor, my head is clear but my body will not work. Come on body, you can do it. First one foot and now the other. That's it. Stand up and walk slowly to the wash trough. What happened yesterday. I think I experienced something very special; not a supernatural experience but a very natural one. Zenita. Oh! Io, Zenita is my wife. I must find her. I've missed the sunrise meditation. I never do that.*

Morpheus stumbled from his hut to wash, and then made his way to the healing temple. Rather shyly he knocked at the entrance to Zenita's room. She gave him a frosty reception.

"Zenita, I am truly sorry. In my ignorance as a lover I treated you badly. Though not a justification, I only did what I had seen the people of my old village do. My elders said the act was only for procreation of the tribe and not to be enjoyed. I had no idea there was a whole spiritual side to copulation. As I have never been interested in procreating the tribe, I spent my time learning more useful pursuits. Now Rahitan tells me what a fool I have been. Will you forgive me, my love?" he asked.

Zenita stood her ground. "What did Rahitan tell you?"

"He told me about a Rose Quartz scroll and also that you instruct couples in the art of connubial love. He suggested I read the scroll as soon as we return from our journey. Perhaps during our travels you could enlighten me on exactly what it is you teach couples. Right now, I feel like such a fool. Morpheus, interpreter of Dreams, Morpheus of the massive ego, Morpheus who communicates with the great spirits of the land, is in your eyes, a failure as a man. Please do not tell anyone, Zenita," he pleaded.

"Humility becomes you, my husband. Relationships have a way of showing us exactly what we need to learn. They are more challenging when one has an inflated opinion of oneself." She paused and walked towards him. "However, if you are truly repentant and willing to learn, then I forgive your ignorance in this matter. A successful partnership takes courage, honesty and co-operation, as well as compromise. Our courtship was practically non-existent. We have not shared our secrets and dreams or talked about the more intimate side of life. But that will have to wait. Come, Garlita wishes to see us."

They walked arm in arm towards the temple.

Following their betrothal Thieron and Erana slipped away from the party walking along the path leading to the stream that supplied water to the village. This well worn pathway led past the reservoir dammed to create a permanent source of water. It continued up a gentle slope towards a massive tree, known by the Atema as the grandfather of the forest. Traditionally it was an area where lovers came to whisper their secrets. Many new arrivals in the village, although past their prime years, still found passion beating in their heart and bodies. Thieron led Erana to the huge moss covered rock, carved into the likeness of a man. It was reputed to be extremely ancient. It was discovered deep in the forest by Morpheus several incarnations ago and levitated to this spot near their sacred tree.

Thieron held Erana's hand and gazed deeply into her eyes. "I will need some time for our betrothal to sink in, Erana. Before our union, I had planned on allowing myself time to heal the wound of seeing Aloma betrothed to Kaitewha. You know that I have always loved her. But miraculously, today a great healing has occurred. Perhaps the scars will heal very quickly now you are with me. Garlita is a clever woman. No wonder she is the High Priestess."

Erana smiled. "Thieron, my husband, I am s skilled herbalist. I will give you an infusion to make you forget Aloma completely, and have eyes for no other woman but me. Come with me, I have something to show you."

She led him a short way along another path, until they were in front of a small hut.

"This is the place where the twenty-one day process is undertaken. It is also has other uses Lovers are encouraged to spend quiet time here away from curious eyes. I think we will find it in good order." She gently opened the heavy curtains and peered in. "Yes, it smells sweet, and the bedding is fresh. Enter, my husband."

Cautiously Thieron looked around before entering the hut. "What if somebody sees us."

Erana laughed. "I hope they do. We are betrothed, and it is expected that we spend our first night here. Aloma and Kaitewha will be in the Temple of Love, while here we will create our own temple. I will not try to verbally teach you anything for the present. Experience is worth many words"

"I have never known a woman in this life, Erana," confessed Thieron. "I have no experience in the art of loving. I managed to avoid the teachings given by Zenita and yourself and Rahitan never encouraged me. I think he selfishly wanted me to be always at his beck and call. And I thought that if I couldn't have Aloma then I would never partner anyone. Now I regret that I have no experience."

"I am told you are a fast learner, and I know that I am a good teacher. Trust me, my soon-to-be lover, relax and enjoy the love that will last at least until we are again blasted to pieces, and very possibly beyond the physical."

She guided Thieron towards the bed and began to remove his clothes, one piece at a time. Firstly she removed his footwear and placed them by the door. She then untied the cord around his waist which held up his rust coloured tunic. Next came his woven trousers, dyed blue black with the pulped bark of the hange hange shrub. Unable to look at Erana, Thieron tried to conceal his rapidly rising manhood behind both his hands.

She laughed. "Ho, now I know you are a virgin. How unusual in a man past puberty. I am going to have fun with you." With a lithe shrug, her long crimson gown slid to the floor, revealing her naked body. He let out a small gasp as he stood transfixed by the sight of her small breasts, crowned with dark erect nipples. Slowly he reached out to touch her. Erana remained quite still while Thieron, with shaking hands, explored her breasts.

"I have never seen anything so beautiful," he signed. "What do I do now?"

"Follow your instincts, and let nature be your guide," she replied. "If you become careless, I will guide you." Erana moved in very close to her man and tenderly kissed his lips, exploring his firmly shut mouth. "Open your mouth a little," she whispered.

Thieron's breathing quickened as he responded to her caress, while a flame of energy shot up and down his body. He felt blood surge towards his genitals and engorge them more and more until he felt he would explode. All the while, Erana caressed him with her mouth, her fingers and her long shining brown hair. Her dark brown eyes burned into his, looking deep into his soul, telling him she loved him, and wanting him to return her love. His knees grew weak and finally, he toppled with Erana onto the bed.

Erana pulled him towards her and stroked that part of him that would soon enter into her divine temple. His excitement was rising as he asked, "Erana, what are you doing? It feels wonderful."

She then guided his hand to the wet space between her legs and whispered, "Explore me with your middle finger. It will excite me."

Clumsily he thrust the finger deep inside. "Gently, slowly, caress me. Do you feel that hard area towards the front. That is the place that sends a woman wild with passion. Tease me, my love, while I do the same to you."

Thieron set to work and soon Erana was writhing and groaning. "Oh, you are a fast learner. That is perfect. How do you feel?"

"I feel as if I am about to explode through the end of my penis," he panted. "Please, let me enter you. I don't think I can wait any longer."

"Yes, you can. That is the greatest secret to successful lovemaking. Man is like the sparks that combine to make a fire. Woman is the space in which it all exists. Draw deep within you the sparks that are about to light that fire. Draw that energy back along your penis, up through your body's energy centres to the area between your eyes and hold it there. Good. How does that feel?" she whispered.

"Now I feel as if my head will explode," he answered. "A bright light has come on deep in my head and my body is tingling all over."

"Just relax into the sensation and follow the light," Erana instructed.

"The light is taking me back to my penis, where the energy started," he moaned.

"Splendid. Now let's stop talking and merge our essence. I invite you deep into my sacred temple, my husband." She pulled Thieron on top of her, parted her legs and guided him towards her waiting, sacred place, using her hand to guide his penis into her. She stroked her lubricated lips with its tip, arousing them to fever pitch, so that Thieron lost control and thrust deeply into her temple, and kept thrusting until with a loud groan, he climaxed with such intensity that he nearly passed out.

"I think I have died and gone to heaven," he whispered.

Gently Erana rolled him aside and snuggled her head on his shoulder. "Now let us sleep for a while in the bliss and afterglow of our union. Then you may like to continue."

"I have left my body and gone to a higher realm," he said. "Nothing will ever be the same again. It is no wonder that since he read the scroll of love, old Rahitan has been walking around with a great grin on his face. I must read it soon and find out what wonders it can reveal to me."

With that he began to breathe slowly and deeply, and fell asleep. Erana looked lovingly at his curly red hair and boyish face, and noticed for the first time, pale freckles across his small nose. *How cute he is, and how malleable. Thank you Garlita. You have done well in selecting him. Soon I must begin preparing our bodies to receive our sacred child.* Soon she slipped into a deep, contented asleep. Their union had been mutually successful.

TEN

Travelling

Two days later all was in readiness for their journey to travel to several other villages. They were the Matarau to the west, the Arataki to the south, the Akariri to the east and a large Gadumi temple to the north, with four others in between. For several days, telepathic communication between the High Priests were sent and received. The eight travellers arranged themselves around the crystal bell in the main temple and activated the bi-location technique, as instructed by Rahitan.

"Now, remember our destination is the carved pole in the courtyard of the Matarau, so focus on that. A great cone shaped mountain dominates the whole area so use it as a guide. There are legends of large ancient reptilian creatures that once inhabited the area and that still live in another dimension beside the mountain's protective aura. ...... Close your eyes and imagine your body becoming particles of light able to move through solid walls, across space and reassemble around the pole. All is in readiness for our arrival. This time they will not be taken by surprise and run away in fear. Ready?"

The eight human forms slowly disappeared, slid through the molecules of air and slowly reappeared to each other and the awaiting Matarau, who were gathered expectantly in their temple courtyard.

"Bi-locating gets easier and more fun each time," said Thieron.

Rahitan looked intensly at him and thought. *"Mmm, he is no longer my faithful scribe, though he will still continue to produce excellent work for me. Surprisingly, he seems to have forgotten his undying and eternal love for Aloma and is already merged with Erana. She must have given him some sacred herbs for binding the heart of one's beloved, which seems to have made him much more mature. Splendid."* Aloud he said, "Well done, Thieron. Soon you will be ready to roam the world."

He turned to see a tall, slightly stooped man with very white hair walking slowly towards him, using a carved stick for support.

"Welcome to the village of the Matarau, Atema. I am Mohiotanga, the newly appointed High Priest of the temple."

Rahitan was the first to fully appear and speak.

"Greetings, my friends. I hope this will be a much more auspicious meeting. Since we last met, the taniwha are again restrained until the end of time as we know it, and those who released them have been punished. As you may be aware, our village has but twenty years to exist. We have come to discuss our united futures and share our knowledge of the scrolls with you all."

Mohiotanga put out his hands to receive the scroll offered by Rahitan. "This scroll is a work of art of great antiquity," Rahitan whispered, "a gift from the gods to be revered by humankind. Io must think it is time for us to read it again."

Holding the scroll aloft for all to see, Mohiotanga said, "Behold, the scroll of the rainbow rods my friends. While once we knew its contents by heart, now we have all but forgotten its message. For years have I sought to obtain such a specimen with perfect rods. Our poor paper and wood copies are in tatters and barely legible. How many did you say there are in your library?"

"We have recently rediscovered twelve large and twelve small scrolls," Rahitan replied. "I have not had time to peruse them all for since we found them and the greenstone statue of our Princess Aloma, our life has been exceedingly full. With your permission Mohiotanga, together this evening we will read the scroll with rainbow meteorite rods. It tells of the creation of our planet and solar system."

The visiting group relaxed among the Matarau, who had prepared a welcoming feast. The host village still enjoyed eating food while many knew that the Atema lived on light and cosmic energy and were eager to learn the secret of being sustained by manna from heaven.

Following the meal, the villagers and guests feeling relaxed and contented, sat on wooden seats around a large fire in the courtyard.

One old woman stood up and spoke. "Atema, tell me of your village and how you spend the time saved without the need to prepare food. It takes a great part of our day gathering the roots and berries needed to sustain our needs."

Garlita sat up straight, pulling her feathery cloak around her body, before responding. "It means that have more time for artistic pursuits such as music and singing. Kaitewha here is our songmaster. Perhaps he can be persuaded to sing for us later. We weave fine cloth from the flax plant that grows in abundance along the great lake and make vivid dyes from herbs, leaves and mosses, to colour our world. We also share our dreams with Morpheus here, our Dream master. Aloma, our Princess, spends much of her time laughing and story telling, while lifting our spirits and loving us unconditionally. Zenita is a master healer using universal energy to compliment her skills, and also takes groups of acolytes into the forest to learn the mysteries of herbal lore. She is more than happy to exchange herbal recipes with your healers. Our chief Alchemist Pausanin, who unfortunately is not with us, has offered to share a few of his more famous secrets. He makes wondrous concoctions and mind enhancing brews from the plants and berries collected by the women. Thieron here is our scribe who is kept busy by Rahitan, taking notes, keeping the scrolls updated, and generally being indispensable. Next to him is his partner Erana, a gifted masseuse and healer. She has offered to smooth away knots and stiffness from aching bodies. If you have soreness, talk to her tomorrow about a time to enjoy her skills. I am sure a hut can be set aside for her use. Thieron will organise her appointments. She will teach her art to any one interested. All of us spend a great deal of time meditating, and are in touch with many beings on other realms of reality who guide our progress. If not for their guidance we would be as primitive as the majority of the tribal people of this land." She paused and looking around asked, "Would anyone else like to speak?"

A tall and proud young woman stood to speak. "Greetings Atema, I am Astarte, youngest daughter of Mohiotanga. Many times, unsuccessfully, I have I asked him to allow me to learn the art of healing. Now I ask in front of our people and the Atema. Father, will you allow me to learn the ways of the healer? I wish to travel to the village of the Atema to learn from Zenita." Her challenge rang loud and clear.

Old Mohiotanga, slowly and painfully rose to his feet, his strong carved stick grasped firmly in his gnarled left hand, and for several minutes he silently surveyed the onlookers, before turning to Astarte with a furious glint in his eyes.

"My daughter, how dare you make such a request in front of our guests. You put them in an awkward position of not being able to refuse. I forbid you do this study."

Zenita responded swiftly. "Oh Priest of the Matarau. I would be delighted to take Astarte with me to teach her the healing arts. I can see from her colours that she has the gift. Why do you object to such a noble wish?"

"Do not interfere, Zenita of the Atema," the old man hissed. "You do not know the full story, or the reason for my reluctance to allow my dearest and youngest daughter to become a healer."

Rahitan, while outwardly calm was inwardly seething that the old man should speak like that to Zenita, "Perhaps yould would you care to enlighten us, Mohiotanga, or do you wish me to give my version of the truth? Remember, I know what happened and I also knew her mother, who was a great healer."

"We are already playing games, my old adversary. When her mother sought help from your people whilst carrying Astarte in her womb, I knew the day would come when I would have to reveal the real reason to my people if ever I was made High Priest, for such a role carries with it, great humility and openness." He paused to look at each member of the Atema and continued, falteringly at first, but then with more confidence.

"Astarte is twenty summers in age. At the time of her conception I was fifty-six summers and her mother, Tawhita, was only thirty. Tawhita had an older sister called Amarita, who was considered the most beautiful and desirable woman in our village, and many of the men wished her for their wife. As you know, Rahitan, our village is not totally comprised of Enlightened beings, but those from many levels of consciousness. Amarita, was as evil as she was beautiful, but kept her true nature well hidden. As a small child she tore the wings off butterflies and laughed at their pitiful attempts to fly. As a young woman she led suitors on a merry chase, only to mock them when they pleaded for mercy. Her sexuality drove men wild. I was in love with her myself, even though I knew her cruel ways. I could not help myself. It was as if she had some sort of hold over men, both young and old."

He turned to Astarte and continued, "My dear, I know you have never been told the true story and now it is time the younger members of the tribe were told the truth."

A groan was heard from several of the older Matarau. "Some things are best left unspoken, Mohiotanga," said one old woman.

"No, I am compelled to talk of this matter," he responded. "It is a black cloud that hangs over us all, and perhaps the Atema can help us lift it."

The old priest, taking his time, looked at his daughter. "Astarte, you deserve to know my reason for refusing your request. Tawhita, your mother, was very beautiful and a gifted healer, the opposite in her purity and light from her dark, older sister. Amarita became very jealous when the son of our late Head priest Albinon wished to partner with Tawhita. However, Amarita saw it as her role to eventually become high priestess of the village, and to achieve this, she needed to become the wife of the High Priest. Secretly Amarita put a curse on the young man and poisoned his drink, causing him to stiffen with paralysis and die, for she was determined that if she could not have him, then her sister certainly would not. Albinon was distraught at the death of his son and mourned deeply. I think that was when he decided to learn something of the black arts in order to deal with them, so contacted Carilan. How Amarita learned the black arts no one knew, for such despicable ways were not practised by the Matarau, but explained why no one recognised what was happening to Albinon's son. It was thought he had eaten a poisoned plant by mistake. Tawhita was so distressed by his death that she stopped eating and talking, she just sat and stared into space.

This caused Amarita much unhappiness, as even though she had a black heart, she still felt some love for her sister Tawhita. So she prepared potions for her younger sister, in the hope of restoring her to normality. She had learnt her craft well, although none ever claimed they taught her, and soon Tawhita was restored to physical health, but not to sanity. Part of her soul never returned and she wandered our village in a trance-like state. I suspect Amarita didn't want her dead but definitely didn't want her available to suitors. Then Albinon's wife died suddenly and Amarita was blamed. Incensed by her callous indifference to his grieving heart, when she thrust herself upon him, and demanded he make her his new wife, something snapped deep inside Albinon. I will never forget the look on his face when Amarita boasted that she had killed his son. He grabbed her by the hair, pulled her along the ground into an abandoned and desecrated forest altar and with a sharp blade, cut her female organs from her belly. First her womb and then her egg pouches and the connecting tubes. She took a long time to die, all the time cursing and screaming that he would be overtaken by the dark forces under her bidding, and that they would use him cruelly. Her womanly parts, he buried beside the altar while shouting that she did not deserve to be called a woman, but a thing of no consequence. He was quite mad according to someone who watched the dark actions from a hiding place. Later that evening he staggered into the courtyard, covered in blood and gibbering that he had saved the village from her evil. We washed him, gave him nourishing food and put him to bed. It took a whole moon cycle for him to return to some sense of normality, although in a reduced capacity. He was my teacher then, training me for the priesthood and I loved him dearly."

Mohiotanga wiped tears from his eyes before continuing. "Following Amarita's death, her body was cut into many parts and buried across the river on barren land in the hope that she could never reincarnate. Tawhita's mental health improved from that day, and I fell in love with her. We became betrothed and conceived several children. Astarte is our last child. Around four months into her pregnancy, Tawhita had a dream that frightened her badly. She dreamed that Amarita's soul had entered her to merge with the body of her unborn child. Next morning she took strong herbs to try to abort the baby, but no matter what she did, it remained firmly implanted in her womb. In great distress, she told me of her dream and we decided to consult Albinon, who said he couldn't help and suggested we visit the village of the Atema. He contacted you Rahitan and you came here instead of allowing us to go to your village. You said that nothing of such a low vibration was permitted through the protective barriers surrounding the forest and we would not be able to enter. A small hut was made available some distance from our village where we spent several days wrestling with the black magician who controlled Amarita's soul in Tawhita's womb. He was determined another female would physically carry on from Amarita, and who better to bear her than her sister, Tawhita. It took all our strength and knowledge to defeat the demon but eventually Rahitan, in a moment of pure inspiration following a dreadful night, stood and bared his arms to the rising sun streaming through the door onto poor Tawhita, who lay as dead, and hardly breathing. The serpents tattooed along his arms began to writhe and four golden eyes came alive at the touch of the sun. Through the serpents' eyes, Rahitan directed the rays of Ra to shine onto Tawhita's swollen belly, and shouted an invocation. Immediately, taken by surprise, a black cloud hissed from between her legs and hovered in the centre of the hut. A dreadful smell of sulphur filled the air and we shivered, not with fear but with relief that the evil thing had left its victim. Then a beam of light shot out from the heart of Ra right into the black cloud and shattered it. Just like that, it was gone No residue or stench, no more dread dreams. Just perfect peace. Tawhita cried healing tears for many days, but eventually got over her fear and became her cheerful self again. The rest of the pregnancy went well and just before the birth, she felt a strong light enter her womb and envelop Astarte so she knew her daughter would be safe from evil. Unfortunately, still weakened, Tawhita died during the birth. I brought Astarte up on my own for I had no wish for another to partner. She is dearer than life itself to me and I refuse to allow her out of my sight. Learning to become a healer would mean she would have to travel to a place of teaching, such as your village. Understand that I am not prepared to release her, even for a short time."

Turning to look at his daughter her continued, "I am sorry for my possessive ways. Perhaps you wonder why no suitor has claimed you? There have been several, but I discouraged all of them. I cannot let you go."

Astarte put her arms around her sobbing father and whispered, "Father, you have to, for I am a grown woman and feel an urge deep inside me to learn the healing crafts and bear a child of my own. For that I will need a partner. Please. It is time to release me."

"No, I cannot. My heart will wither and die. Rahitan, can you help me," he pleaded.

Rahitan was unimpressed "Pull yourself together, man, no one dies of loneliness when his daughter weds. I will have Zenita make a potion to calm and strengthen you. As High Priest of the Matarau, you have obligations to the whole tribe, and must rise above personal attachment. Now, you choose; is there a suitable young man who is brave enough to claim her, or does she come with us to learn the healing arts?" Turning to the young woman he assumed his most kindly expression, not easy for a man of his mien. "What is your heart's desire, Astarte?"

"To learn of healing, please Master Priest," stuttered Astarte, a little in awe from the recent revelations. "Yes, I can always find a partner later, but now I wish to learn something useful. My father kept me ignorant of many things. I have a lot to learn."

A sceptical Garlita, who had been silent until then, asked, "How do we get her back to the Atema temple? She cannot bi-locate, and it will take weeks to go overland."

"That is easily solved," replied Rahitan. "It will take us at least another month to visit the remaining villages. If she sets off now with an escort, they should arrive about the same time as we do. It was easy to teach Thieron and Erana to bilocate. They are Atema and live on light. But for someone like Ashtarte who still eats flesh food, it is impossible. I will give directions to the escort, and communicate with some from our village to meet her at the edge of the forest. She has not been called in the usual way, so cannot follow the song line. Do you agree with this arrangement, Mohiotanga? Good. It is the best for everyone, old chap. I'll talk more of this in the morning."

Astarte was beside herself with joy, but also a little concerned. "I will be sorry to leave you, father," she said. "But when my training is over, I will return to our village to teach and heal our people. It is what I must do."

"I know, my daughter," replied old Mohiotanga. "I know. Now let us ask the songmaster to entertain us, and to lift our hearts."

Kaitewha rose to the occasion and sang several of his own compositions, accompanying himself on a small stringed instrument he had fashioned from the wood of a rata tree and the dried intestines of a kore rat. It looked crude but played harmoniously when plucked by his experienced fingers.

When the applause died down, Rahitan stood and said, "My friends, tonight your High Priest has shared with us something deep from within his being and I honour his courage. It seems a huge healing has taken place as the whole village is of a lighter vibration now. In return I will read some of the Rainbow scroll to you."

The Matarau busied themselves stoking up the fire, setting out comfortable benches and mats, and filling mugs of herbal brew before settling down to listen to and absorb the wisdom of the scroll.

Rahitan cleared his throat and began. "This is the scroll about the creation of our species. I will read until the sun is about to set, for at that time we conduct our ceremony to the setting of the sun. Some of you may care to join us. Now, let's begin."

He turned to Thieron and said, "I need your help to hold the scroll."

Thieron jumped up, took the scroll and carefully removed the securing pins, so as not to damage the fairly fragile rainbow coloured meteorite rods that flashed luminous colour. Slowly he unrolled the thinly beaten gold and held it in front of Rahitan.

The High Priest's voice assumed the rich timbre he used for important occasions. "From afar we greet you, who read these scrolls. Your planet which we call Eridu, meaning home in the faraway, is not our true home. We of the Nefilim who arrived here to settle for a time, came from Nibiru, a large planet with a vast elliptical orbit that infrequently visits this area of the galaxy. Its arrival causes great chaos amongst your solar system, and great upheaval to your home, that you now call Earth. Originally we inhabited this planet looking for gold, a precious and rare metal on our home planet, but very useful for our purposes. Our slaves mined this solid light in great quantities from rich sources in the hot land far to the south of our original settlement on the shores of Persian Gulf. When a rebellion broke out amongst our slaves who refused to continue with such menial and exhausting manual labour, our master geneticists created a primitive worker from the seeds of our men and the eggs of the indigenous, primitive female creatures. This took time to perfect, With some failures, until eventually, our efforts succeeded using blood and fused seeds and eggs implanted in breeding women brought from our planet for that purpose. Some time later they also rebelled at being constantly pregnant to produce workers, and upset at the unlovable sterile creatures they were birthing. In our special place called the House where the Breath of Life is born, further experimentation on these offspring allowed them to breed amongst themselves. With the partial intelligence of our race but the body of a more primitive creature, they successfully reproduced and migrated around the planet.

To make them more in our image, variations were introduced, creating higher types of wiser males and females with different coloured skin, hair and eyes to enable them to adapt to the changing climatic conditions. We taught them to become skilled miners and makers of tools necessary for their primitive needs. One gift we did not confer was that of the extended life span that we enjoy. To achieve this, we ingest a white powder made from the gold they mine. They could partake of the Tree of Wisdom but not the Tree of Life. Nature took over, and the evolution of the species forged ahead after we abandoned Eridu. Each reading of this scroll means the evolutionary tree has progressed, as each reader must be an intelligent human after our own image.The way of evolution is extremely slow and tedious, but occasionall the process is speeded up by the assistance given by more highly evolved species. The meaning of the symbol drawn along the edge of this scroll, showing entwined serpents is the emblem of Enki, one of the master creators of your race. His role will be re-discovered by scientists far in the future of this planet. We tell you now, it shows the structure of the genetic code, the secret knowledge that enabled Enki to create the early humans, and later gave them the ability to procreate. It is also a symbol of healing that can be utilised by those who have that ability."

Rahitan paused and looked toward the rapidly descending sun creating splashes of brilliant pink and orange colours on the clouds over the western sea. During his reading he had become increasingly uneasy, as the previously brilliant rainbow colours flashing along the rods dulled and became lifeless. He looked at his captive audience, sitting in stunned silence, and decided to stop reading. *No use going beyond their ability to comprehend. I am not one to cast pearls before swine. Perhaps the Rose Quartz scroll would be more appropriate for the Matarau. If they wish more information I will read that one. It works through the energy of love instead of intelligent understanding.*

The dulling of the rainbow colours demonstrates their low level of consciousness. Aloud he said, "That is enough for now. We must prepare for the sunset ceremony. You are all welcome to participate."

Later that evening, Rahitan summoned Mohiotanga. "Let us walk a little by the seashore. I have not done so for a long time. It will refresh my heart."

Together, the two old High Priests left the village. Garlita saw them go and noted with pleasure the strong, vital stride of her lover compared with the slow, tired steps of his companion.

Rahitan pulled off his shoes and sighed with pleasure as his tender feet felt the cool, soft black sand that was rapidly releasing its stored heat back into the atmosphere.

"There is something you didn't tell your people, you old rogue," he said.

Mohiotanga looked startled. "What do you mean?"

"I mean that for the last ten years or more you have used Astarte's body for your own pleasure. You must realise that nothing escapes me. No wonder you do not wish to let her leave you."

"So what," sneered Mohiotanga. "It is common practice for a father to lie with his daughters. It gives them experience and an understanding of their future role when they get a husband."

Rahitan replied. "Not in our village. We arrive as adults and try to find our soul mate as soon as possible. As a result, there are very few young women living there. This has allowed us to rise above that despicable practice which betrays the sacred trust of fatherhood. That trust is meant to protect young girls, not harm and mutilate them. If that is your attitude, no wonder the rainbow rods have faded."

"But surely in the village where you grew up, such practices were accepted?" said Mohiotanga.

"No, fathers held their daughters close to their hearts, not to their genitals," answered Rahitan, feeling the distinctly uncomfortable sensation of judgement creeping on him.

"What is so wrong about this practice? It stops unwelcome seeds entering our daughters until they are betrothed. If accidently they become pregnant by their father, herbal brews are given to cause abortion. You are a strange one, High Priest of the Atema," replied Mohiotanga.

Rahitan could no longer hold his temper. "What is wrong with incest?" he yelled. "I'll tell you what is wrong. Firstly it does irreparable harm to a young girl whose access area is undeveloped, and not ready to be penetrated by an aroused man. Her sensitive areas can be torn and desensitised, and when she is betrothed, sexual pleasure may not come to her. Secondly, she has learned to love and trust that her father will not hurt her. When he betrays that trust perhaps she will never trust another man again. How do you think that could affect her betrothed? Thirdly, often the father puts terrible fear into her mind by threatening to kill or harm her if she tells anyone. She has to keep this dark secret, even from her mother. That denies her the intimacy of deep friendship and open sharing with others. Often the pain and betrayal are too much for her to cope with, and sometimes she leaves her body during the outrage. When she returns, something is lost, and it can have an effect on her mind. Furthermore, if she becomes pregnant, she has to go through the trauma of aborting the baby, an act that can further harm her body and soul. If she carries the child to term, it can be deformed by the closeness of the genes." Rahitan was so incensed he could barely contain himself.

"You foolish man," he shouted. "You have the gall to ask me what is wrong with incest. We will leave your village early in the morning.

You are obviously not ready for our gifts and teaching. It's no wonder Albinon went astray." He turned and strode back along the beach leaving old Mohiotanga wondering what had happened.

The pale light of dawn tinged pale pink on the snow cap high on the great cone shaped mountain dominating the area. Soon after the sunrise meditation, the eight Atema gathered around the central column of the navigator in the courtyard of the Matarau village and prepared to depart. Earlier, Rahitan had selected eight strong young men to escort Astarte to the Atema village, and given them specific directions, he took the precaution of putting the fear of the taniwha into them, and threatening that if any of them so much as thought about violating her body or emotions, he would know, and immediately that one would become impotent. It was a drastic and powerful way to ensure obedience.

Most of the Matarau were quite bewildered by the turn of events. They had hoped their guests would remain for several days but Rahitan was adamant. The Atema were leaving. During the night he had contacted Ioannes of the Levanti to the south west, and announced his intention to bring forward their arrival date.

Rahitan called for silence and explained. "People of the Matarau. Last evening I discovered a shameful custom that is followed in your village. It appears that Mohiotanga is one of its worst offenders, as he knowingly and callously is committing incest with Astarte, his youngest daughter, and I have no doubt his older daughters suffered the same fate. He told me it was common practice in this village. A people who inflict such suffering on to their daughters do not deserve the teachings of the higher realms. I am not saying everyone is guilty of the act, but anyone who knows and does not speak out is just as wrong. An enlightened people do not harm their children in any way. They are your future. How you treat them is passed down to their children and beyond through the generations. Abused children become abusers themselves, and do not know peace in their hearts.

So we are leaving. When this immoral practice has been totally eradicated, if you wish, you can contact me and we may visit you again. But right now, I will not waste my time on such barbarians."

Taking his place in the circle of Atema he said, "Ready to bilocate. Visualise the great river that flows past the village of Levanti. We will focus on the central courtyard, where there is a large rock carved into the shape of a head. Now, together."

A rush of wind was all the watching Matarau felt as their guests disappeared.

The bi-location to the Levanti was successful, and soon Ioannes was greeting the group.

"Welcome, Welcome to the village of the Levanti," he beamed. "What a pleasant surprise that you have arrived earlier than expected. The Matarau must have given you a hard time, old chap."

"Greetings, Ioannes. Let me introduce you to my companions. We will talk of other issues later," replied Rahitan, and introduced everyone to the Levanti.

Later when they were comfortably lodged in a long house made of plaited fibre, with a strong waterproof roof of woven reeds, Kaitewha asked, "Why are they called the Levanti. It is a name like no other tribe I have ever heard of?"

"I will let Ioannes tell that story, as it is his to recount. Ah, here he comes," Rahitan said.

"Let Ioannes tell what, my friend?" said the Priest.

"Kaitewha was wondering why your tribe is called the Levanti. He noticed that it is different from most others in form and sound," answered Rahitan.

"Very observant, young songmaster," said Ioannes. "Yes, we have a long genealogy that dates far back in time, long before that of any other tribe on this large island home of ours. We belong to one of the so-called twelve lost tribes who were dispersed several hundred years ago, from a very holy land, a dry and arid place that lies at the end of a wine dark sea, called the Mediterranean, For aeons we had lived in peace and harmony until we were made prisoners of the mighty empire of Khem, situated to our south. They wanted slaves to build great monuments to their gods and chose us. Also for them it was an unfortunate choice as we were not good slave material, being too fierce and independent. Most of our people belonged to twelve different tribes descended from twelve brothers. Once captured all were forced to work together, something that led to great tension and rivalry.

For several generations they toiled until a great breakout occurred, led by a natural leader called Moses. Ironically, he was educated by the rulers of that land, the Pharaohs. Many people followed him across deserts and seas back to their homeland, but those of our tribe, of the Levanti, preferred to choose our own escape route.

Under the leadership of my ancestor, the High Priest Abram, allegiances that had been developed during the time of enslavement were honoured, and four long ships were provided to transport us to a far away land, one that very few had heard of, let alone visited. Legends referred to it as the Footstool of the Gods, or the birthplace of the Gods, and it was thought to be the furthest place from Khem that could be inhabited. Ancient mariners circumnavigating this watery planet discovered it by chance, when mercilessly driven far off course by a terrifying storm that dumped them dazed and battered on this strange shore. These sailors were clever map makers and managed to chart the location of the land that was to be their home for the next twenty years. Finally they were able to rebuild their damaged ships and sail north to the Celebes Islands, where they encountered a crew of Phoenicians, also very far from home. As these sailors regularly traded in that area they knew the route back to our homeland.

By the end of the following year, most of the shipwrecked had sailors returned to their homeland, telling strange tales of a land populated by giant birds that couldn't fly but ran along the ground at great speed, and large eagles whose wingspan covered fifty feet. They had encountered very few people for the natives kept their distance, although occasionally, they glimpsed, flitting through the trees, tall light beings of whom they were so terrified that they did not investigate further, and stayed close to the shore where they landed. That story of a strange land was told by my ancestors, around campfires in Khem, the alien land of their capture. So a decision was made to find this lost world, the Footstool of the Gods and live in peace far from the known world. As we were a tribe of priests and scholars, not of slaves and merchantmen, the journey took a very long time. Unfortunately, one of the ships foundered during a storm near the high cliffs of an immense, inhospitable southern continent. The ship's crews were terrified during the entire journey and, at every chance, threatened to turn back. Great whales nearly collided with the ships, unfriendly natives often chased those who tried to land on their shores hoping to replenish food and water, and storms constantly battered the small ships. Because of the expert navigation of the captain of the lead ship, my people managed to land safely on these shores some twenty generations ago now. Of the three ships that survived, the crew of one ship chose to remain here, rather than face the return voyage, while the other two sailed north to catch the favourable winds that blow around the equator.

We still speak our ancient language Aramaic, and conduct many ceremonies in the old ways, but since arriving we have had to develop new customs, especially with regard to the path of the sun. As you know, here it passes to the north of us and not to the south or nearly overhead as of old. Here the climate is much colder and wetter but more fertile and green. We have adapted well and increased the size of our tribe by selectively interbreeding with native women. While they are often of great beauty but lacked the knowledge of the ways of civilised people. With patient instruction, they soon learn and are found to be highly intelligent in many ways. They make good mothers, and are free with their sexual favours, far different from our women because of the strict upbringing they received as girls." He paused to look at his listeners.

Even Rahitan listened intently. "I had not heard your history, Ioannes. Thank you for sharing it. No wonder you didn't support the mad Albinon and Lonikai in their quest to rule the world. I think there is much we can learn from you about the ways of the ancient world."

"Whatever we have is yours, my friends, but in return we wish to know the secret of bi-location. It would be interesting to visit our ancient homeland, and return with a few comforts available from merchants who traverse the long Silk Road, and trade in merchandise from the land of the Manchu. There they make excellent material for garments and our old sacred robes are just about worn out. Even though we are accustomed to the everyday rough clothing, silks and fine damask make better garments for sacred service. Come with me. I will show you what I mean," said Ioannes.

From their long hut, he led them to the shining white temple that stood at the far end of the courtyard. "I believe this is of a similar design to your temple, Rahitan. One day, so the story goes, as we were struggling to adapt to a new way of life in this unfamiliar land, a magician appeared in our village. His name was Wanenga and he brought with him a parchment on which was drawn the design for the temple in the star shape of two interlocking triangles, one of blue and one of white. We were astounded as this design was an ancient symbol for our people. He convinced our elders to allow him to erect the structure with the assistance of our people. Raw materials appeared overnight, and our people who had learned from their exile in Khem, to be expert builders of stone and shapers of marble went to work. When the temple was completed, Wanenga disappeared, never to be seen again. Since that day we have kept the construction secrets alive and as you can see, we have built some fine structures similar to those we left behind in our land of exile. Some said Wanenga was an architect of the Pharaoh, sent to make amends for the shameful treatment we suffered at their hands. Others said he was one of our people, come through the air from our homeland to assist us to settle in this land. I do not know, but whoever Wanenga was, he left us a great legacy. Do you know where the plans for your temple came from?"

Rahitan thought before answering. "Our temple is built over the site of a previous one that was destroyed when our great lake was created by the convulsions of the earth mother, Papatuanuku, some twenty-four thousand years ago. Silence descended onto the land after we were all annihilated. Then some two thousand years ago, with the assistance of our creator gods, remnants of the Atema began gathering in the area, drawn by the vibrational resonance of the great crystal bowl now situated deep underground.

When I arrived I remembered the details of our star shaped temple, formed by two great interlocking triangles. It took a long time to rebuild the complex, but we were successful, although on a much smaller scale. The sacred crystal bowl reappeared in the holy room on the day it was completed, which also happened to be the day before Garlita joined us. Between us we tried to resurrect the old ways, but evolutionary changes decreed that we also needed to adapt. Without the recently rediscovered golden scrolls, we have lived from memory of those distant times. As part of the experiment, we formulated new teachings, new customs, and new laws. I was told by my divine master who overlights me, that Garlita remembered how to play the crystal bell so she was able to call many others to rejoin us. Mostly those who answered were incarnate in tribal villages, but did not really fit in to that primitive way of life." He became quiet for a time before saying, "And now, my friend, the Lord Tane tells me that in twenty years we will once again be blown asunder when the great lake explodes. Hence, this journey around the giant stingray to communicate with as many High Priests and their people as we can. Then our plan is to travel along the lines of bilocation to other lands, to learn new ways and record them on a scroll."

"You mentioned golden scrolls. We do not have a set of gold but only of papyrus that are rather tattered. Is it possible for me told see some of them?" said an excited Ioannes.

"I have not yet read all the scrolls we recently found hidden deep inside the hillside behind our temple, nor the one I dictated to Thieron just before we were blown up. But the ones I have seen reveal a great story of our creation on this planet by creator gods, experimenting with early hominoids. The finest scroll we have read so far tells of love. Reading it had a profound effect on Garlita and myself causing us to reconsider many of our beliefs. I carry with me one with Turquoise rods and another with Coral. If you wish Thieron can return to our temple to collect another. Perhaps every High Priest in the land should experience the vibration of the Rose Quartz scroll," offered Rahitan. "Then we will surely experience peace and harmony throughout the entire domain of the giant stingray."

"I will announce to my people that tonight will be a time of feasting and song. Then starting tomorrow we will devote ourselves to more serious matters, such as sharing our wisdom and the reading of the scrolls. Your visit is a good omen, my friend, for at this particular time we begin to enter our most holy days of the year, the time when we remember our exodus from slavery under the rule of the Pharaohs of Khem, and of finding our new home here in this green land. We would be honoured if you would stay and celebrate with us."

"We would be honoured," replied Rahitan. "I am sure I speak for us all, for this is a journey of discovery as well as one of teaching.

Please let your women know that we do not eat food so they will not have to prepare any for us. I look forward with delight to exploring your stories. How came you by your name? It is strange to me."

"Ioannes is a very ancient name handed down from father to son right back to the first of my ancestors who bore that name when they first landed on earth. The founder of our line was a commander of the Nefilim from Nibaru, a large planet with a vast elliptical orbit, that only visits this galaxy every three thousand six hundred years, bringing chaos and destruction to this world. A number of Nefilim settled on Earth to mine its gold, and in due course rebelled at the backbreaking physical labour involved, so their geneticists created primitive workers to do the heavy manual work for them. These workers bred and evolved into the people living as the tribes of this land and many others. Those such as the Levanti and your Atema are star seeded, not earth seeded and therefore, have greater intelligence to understand the wonders of the universe. I suspect that is what your golden scrolls reveal."

Rahitan managed to look suitably impressed at this revelation, although he had heard it several times before. "You are saying that this knowledge was brought with you from your holy land and that you have known this since you arrived on these shores nearly five hundred years ago? Why did you not share it with me, or others?" he added.

"What purpose to cast pearls before swine, Rahitan?" replied Ioannes."The ancient writing of Sumeria, the area where the first Nefilim inhabited Earth, describes Ioannes as half man, half fish, holding a communicating device in his right hand, while around his wrist he wears a device for marking time. Unfortunately, we have lost that knowledge and have become very primitive compared to our exalted forebears. Sometimes, when we relate the tales of the ancient ones, we feel very isolated from the civilised world in this faraway land. Now, after five centuries, even we would be like aliens if we could return, for we have lost the way. Perhaps using your knowledge of bi-location, some of us could visit there and gain new insights into the ways of the old world our ancestors left behind. I am sure it is far more populated and advanced than this land that we now call home."

"When we return from this sojourn, Ioannes. we are planning an extended journey to visit several holy places and temples around the world. If you learn quickly, I can see no reason why you and your High Priestess, Seraleah, along with another couple, should not accompany us. That would increase our group to twelve. I'd prefer a woman who sings divinely and a man who knows the art of illusion, for I have a feeling his skill may save our lives on more than one occasion. The dwellers of some lands are very suspicious of strangers who exhibit exceptional talents, but an illusionist is always accepted. I mentioned earlier that we of the Atema do not eat food but occasionally drink clear water, nectar and herbal brews. Do any of your people live only on the life force in the air?" asked Rahitan."

"How so, Rahitan?" said Ioannes. "It is my belief that if one does not eat or drink, the body dies of starvation."

"People die of fear, not starvation. Fear of lack, fear of death, fear of everything. When you trust the love in your heart and drink the vibration of the morning dew, when you inhale light through the skin and the eyes, when you progress beyond the need to be sustained by food, then you can bi-locate. Until such time, your body is too dense to be able to move through the molecules of air to reach another location. What do you say? Are you willing to try living on light? It takes twenty-one days for the process to change your physical body from being sustained by food or water, to using light as a sustenance."

"I am willing to undergo this conversion, and I am certain Seraleah will agree. For the other couple, I have two candidates in mind. If they are successful in eliminating the need for food, I am certain they can also learn to bi-locate. When can I have the first lesson, Rahitan?" asked Ioannes.

"We will begin one week after you have realigned your body to receive sustenance from light. Who else do you have in mind to join you and Seraleah?" asked Rahitan.

"Let me ask the two I have in mind, Where will we undertake the twenty-one day process?" said Ioannes.

"I suggest you travel to our village. We have specially prepared huts for the fasting, and our crystal bell speeds up the ability to bi-locate. Can your people do without you for some time? Do you have a priest who can fill your shoes whilst you are away? The entire process, including the bi-location training and subsequent travelling could take some months, perhaps even a year."

"Yes, to take my place, there is one whom I trust with my life. He is my son, Jondra, whom I am training to be my successor. It is time he was given some responsibility. During your visit I will encourage him to act in my place and watch him carefully. His wife is becoming a gifted healer. You know, our forebears who inhabited our homeland, were very patriarchal. Women were never allowed to walk beside men, to learn sacred scripture or to become priestesses. Several generations passed before those ancient restrictions were lifted. With equality, women blossomed and the harmony in our village increased. We realised that a tribe or religion can never prosper when one half of its people are considered inferior by the other. We discovered that the male was domineering because he was afraid of the power of women. When that power is given expression, then the whole tribe prospers. Now, when can we begin the process?" asked Ioannes.

"Firstly, we have several more villages to visit," replied Rahitan. "I would suggest that when we depart, you, Seraleah, and the chosen couple, along with several strong escorts, set out at once for the Atema village. Walking, tt will take you at least four weeks. I will give you the directions later. I must first contact our people to have them meet you at the edge of the Kaimanawa forest, for it is impenetrable and dangerous to outsiders who have not been specifically called. When the four of you have been conducted to our village your escort will return here. Hopefully, nothing will prevent us from returning in time to greet you. Right now, I see the sun is about to set so we must farewell its magnificence. Without his beneficial rays we could not exist on this planet."

Rahitan rose and called his Atema to accompany him to the courtyard near the large head of a man. "We salute you Ra, our exalted sun," he intoned, thus beginning the melodious prayer chanted at this ceremony.

Five days later, the Atema prepared to leave. Their destination was Arataki to the south east. This was the village of Lonikai, the High Priest from whom Garlita had earlier removed an implant that had caused him to act with arrogance and pride. Rahitan was anxious to know if he was still clear of influence from renegade aliens, who delighted in interfering with and causing suffering to the lives of humans. The eight Atema gathered around the carved head in the courtyard of the Levanti and disappeared.

On arrival they were pleased to find Lonikai was awaiting them in front of an ornately carved pole in the centre of the temple courtyard of the Arataki. The visitors were pleased to note he no longer huffed and puffed with the illusion of his own importance, but instead humbly bowed. Even his voice was softer, yet seemed more authoritative. "Welcome, my friends. I am honoured by your visit. Perhaps one day you will teach me how to just arrive in a place without the need of travelling over land, through the dangers of the forest and deep swift flowing rivers."

Rahitan turned towards him and they embraced. "Many ask and few succeed, Lonikai. However, I will consider it if you are completely free of any remnants of the implant Garlita removed. Now, let me introduce your people to mine."

Although the few days went without a hitch, at the time of departure Rahitan made the decision not to teach Lonikai to bi-locate. Something deep inside told him not to trust the man, and he always took note of this inner voice for it served him truly.

Lonikai was extremely disappointed by Rahitan's decision and became abusive. "Why," he yelled, "have you shown Ioannes and not me? Do you think that because I was once weak I will reveal its secrets? I have changed. I no longer care to amass wealth and power. I care for the children and the aged, the dying and the sick. I would treasure the secret, and never reveal it."

"I am sorry Lonikai," said Rahitan. "I see something deep inside you that makes me uncomfortable. There also remains a spark of arrogance. While I am certain the whole implant influence was removed, there is still something that is not entirely of the light. Perhaps a shadow. On my next annual visit, I will reassess the situation. I feel sure you will be completely clear by then. But you will need to purify your heart, overcome pride and ego and the wish to dominate others, as you just tried to do to me. When light emanates from your heart and eyes and healing flows through your hands, then I will reconsider. When you overcome the need of food for sustenance, and can live on the vibration of the universe then you may be ready. But until then it is not possible for you to bi-locate. It is a vibrational ability, nothing more or less. I am not excluding you, only protecting you from the disappointment of failure. It will give you a goal to attain and a desire to rise above the mundane aspects of life. As spiritual leader of the Arataki, you are responsible for their well-being. Please continue to practice the methods of healing and meditation we have taught you. Do you have any questions?"

"No," murmured Lokikai. "Deep down I know you are right. I have much to learn before receiving the gift of bi-location. I will encourage my people to do as you have taught. You have certainly impressed our Chief and his wife.They are good leaders and deserve the respect and honour of their High Priest. We have prepared a ceremony to farewell you." Raising his voice he sent a shrill call across the village, and soon the Arataki gathered in the courtyard to sing songs of farewell to the Atema who stood around the central pole and prepared to leave.

"This time next year we will visit you again to check on your progress," announced Rahitan. "You have learned well, and I ask you to keep practicing the ways we taught you. I will keep in telepathic communication with Lokikai, so if there are any concerns, please tell him and I will do my best to answer. If something very serious occurs, perhaps you will need to visit me and personally. Now farewell."

He faced his companions, said, "Prepare to bi-locate, we next head to the central pole in the courtyard of the Akariri, located on the eastern fin of the giant stingray."

The eight disappeared to the astonishment of the Arataki.

The remainder of the hikoi wairua - spiritual journey - went well. The Akariri Chief had replaced Carilan, who had died recapturing the taniwha, with his eldest son, Tohera, a clever and able young man. Several couples in other villages were selected to join the special training with the Levanti and given instruction on how to find the Atema village.

Before returning home the Atema made a discovery that would dramatically change their lives. Ronaki, the High Priest of the Gadumi tribe living to the north east of the great lake, where the Atema made their home, let slip one day that he and his people regularly bathed in a sacred spring that bubbled warm, soft water from deep under the ground. They had made a stone walled bath in which to sit and enjoy the benefits that the water blessed upon them. Kaitewha remarked that it was amazing how youthful all the Gadumi looked, even those he knew to be of advanced years.

Ronaki agreed to share the secret of the waiora a te tane te - fountain of youth - with his guests in return for all the gifts they had already bestowed on his tribe. As the party walked towards a lion shaped hill, Ronaki told them the legends associated with the area.

"In ancient times," he said, "when the land was still forming, this hill was part of a much larger land known as the Motherland. It was always revered as a holy place and acted as a vortex of power and energy to enable beings from other dimensions to enter through the inter-dimensional based portal built there. The portal no longer operates, or if it does, we do not know how to activate it. When a great portion of the continent sank in a cataclysmic movement, this hill called Te Aroha, the hill of love, remained as a beacon over the land and the hot soda spring gushed up from its base. Our people revere the springs for their youth-giving waters. We drink it, bathe in it and use it for healing. To fully receive it's gift you must remove all your garments and wallow in the pool. If you are prudish we have separate areas for men and women."

"I will consult my companions," replied Rahitan.

The others jumped at the opportunity to indulge their bodies in the healing fountain of youth, with no thought of embarrassment.

Kaitewha said, "Why should we be ashamed of our body. It is a thing of beauty created by the gods who designed us. Surely they chose the most beautiful form imaginable. When I look on my beloved, I see perfection."

Morpheus was the only one to exhibit shyness in revealing his body and chose to enter a small private area. But he soon joined the others when he heard his friends' laughter.

"I can't bear to miss out on your fun and enjoyment," he said. "I am so pink that I look like one of those delicious sea creatures with the hard shell, that the Levanti cooked for us."

Garlita sighed as she lowered her body into the pool, "Ahh! This is one of the most wonderful things I have ever experienced. Even better than our sophisticated bath houses. I am so weary from our travels, but I feel younger already."

Ronaki joined them. "Do not stay too long in the hot waters or they will have the disturbingly opposite effect of prematurely aging the body. We have worked out that the ideal time to remain is until we feel a little light headed. Then we jump into the cold stream just over there to refresh us. You can then re-enter the hot healing waters again for a short time, before a final cold dip. Come, that is long enough in the hot water. Follow me." He leapt from the bath and rushed to the stream, jumped in and yelled with pure pleasure. The others followed him and soon were also screaming, but more from shock as the cold water awakened their senses.

"Ronaki, you old trickster," gasped Garlita. "This creek is freezing."

"We stay in for but a moment. Don't you feel your body coming alive and tingling with health. Is it not pleasurable?" he asked.

"I have to agree. It is," Garlita sputtered, after she had immersed her whole body and head under the clear running water and then climbed out. "Where does this stream come from?"

"It is birthed deep within Te Aroha. Strangely, one stream of water emerges hot and the other cold. While we do not understand the reason for that, we are eternally grateful for the gift."

"Truly a gift from the gods," agreed Rahitan, running his fingers through his wet beard.

"This is an enchanting land. Full of beauty and power, life and destruction, tranquillity and turmoil in its thermal areas. I have enjoyed our visit with you, Ronaki. With your permission, we would like to return on a regular basis to wallow in Te Aroha. And we will bring our own towels, for ours come from the land of Khem where cotton grows. These primitive flax things you use are too rough on the skin. I suppose on fine days, you let your body dry naturally in the sunlight."

"I was admiring your towels," said Ronaki.

"Then I will present mine to you. I can always nip over to Khem and get some more," responded Rahitan. "The weavers there eagerly trade them for pounamu, the green stone from the south land of the great whale. Now we must prepare to continue our journey."

Returning to the Gadumi village refreshed and ready for the next leg of their journey, the Atema gathered around the central dais and bilocated home.

They returned home to find the invited visitors had all arrived safely. Within a month each had successfully transitioned to living on prana, and glowed with health and beauty. Lessons in the art of bi-location took another month, after which Rahitan felt they were all ready to go on longer journeys to foreign lands. Before their departure, each had surprised their own village with a quick visit and left before anyone made a fuss of them or asked how they managed to live on light and fly through the air like a bird.

During that time, Morpheus read the Rose Quartz scrolls and was so overwhelmed that he cried for days, much to Zenita's concern. However, the healing crisis soon passed and he revelled in the loving relationship with his betrothed. No one could remember ever seeing him so happy and gave him quite a ribbing, which he good naturedly accepted. The villagers spent much of their spare time gazing at the greenstone statue of the Princess, delving into the secrets they had once energetically placed within her, and retrieving aspects of their former selves.

ELEVEN

The Small Bang

Rahitan read and explained the rest of the scrolls to the Atema, and daily their wisdom grew. Three months later, as the date of departure for the chosen twelve couples to journey around the world approached, the excitement mounted. Teams of people were recruited to perform continuous meditation designed to keep the travellers safe. Rahitan estimated the group would be gone for around three months. He chose a route that would ensure favourable weather and a warm climate at each destination, for they could take only the minimum of extra clothing. Each tucked a quantity of gold, the universal form of exchange, in a pouch tied around their waist. One gift the Levanti had given to all the receptive tribes, was the knowledge of how to extract gold from the abundant local rock, especially in the southern island of the great whale. Their ancestors had brought this craft with them from their homeland, where it was already an ancient art.

Rahitan told them, "Far in the future of this land, thousands of tons of gold will be wrenched from the belly of the great whale by men from many lands who will be affected by a disease of the mind, known as gold fever. They will have scant regard for the local people or the land, and will leave much of it desecrated. However, over time it will recover as will the miners, once the fever has passed. I have seen it in my scrying of the future."

Someone asked, "What else do you see about the spiritual destiny of this land, Rahitan? What will happen following the next bang?"

"I will speak of that on our return, but for now you have enough to think about," was his reply. "How are the preparations for our farewell celebrations coming along, Thieron?"

"Pausanin has been busy for weeks brewing special concoctions for our journey to keep us well and different brews for us to enjoy tonight," replied Thieron. "He also made a pile of fireworks to light up the night sky. The party will start after the sunset meditation, and hopefully be over before the moon rises as I for one wish to have a good night's sleep."

"Splendid, my boy," the High Priest said.

I wonder if he will ever stop calling me 'my boy'? mused the scribe.

In spite of Thieron's wishes, the Atema caroused far into the night and it was a groggy group that gathered at sunrise the next morning. Rahitan and Garlita were their usual sober and efficient selves, as were Thieron and Erana, but the others had overindulged, not being used to Pausanin's potent brews. Morpheus, who should have known better was in the worst shape of all.

"Oh, my aching head. Why didn't you give me the antidote, you old rascal?" he said to Pausanin. "Last time it worked like a charm. I thought I could get away with getting sloshed again. To feel like this today of all days. My vibration is probably so low that I won't be able to bi-locate and come with you, Rahitan."

Pausanin came to the rescue, giving him a long green drink made from kawakawa and minguningi leaves infused in hot water. "Here you old soak, drink this. It will clear the alcohol from your liver and stop your head from aching. You should soon be good as new," said the master alchemist. "What did you think of my firework display last night?"

"Amazing. In fact, even better when seen from the altered state your brews induce. You learned that art well on you travels to the land of the Manchu," replied Morpheus.

"I am instructing two of our guests, one from the Matarau and one Levanti. They will be able to surprise their people on their return. They'll probably be full of other surprises after being with the Atema for the next three months. They are all to remain here until your group returns, so they can take back any news of world events," said Pausanin.

Rahitan joined and greeted them, "Good morning, my friends, and to you Morpheus, O interpreter of dreams, a word of warning. As we travel to many lands, you will no doubt encounter some fearsome brews, for most people have discovered a way of dulling their senses and their minds with alcohol or drugs. I wish you to promise me one thing. That you will not indulge in any mind altering substances until we return. What you do here is your business, what you do elsewhere, as a representative of the Atema, may endanger us. Do I make myself clear? If you can not make that promise we will have to leave you behind."

Before he could answer, Morpheus turned pale, excused himself and rushed to the side of his house where he threw up the contents of his stomach. Pausanin's herbs had worked well, and soon he felt much clearer.

Returning to Rahitan he said, "I promise. Without old Pausanin's magic fixit brew I might just die in some foreign land."

The shimmering rays of the rising sun began to warm the cobble stones and the group of twelve who stood around the base of a golden pyramid, recently excavated from underneath the ground. This device, they were to discover, held a great power. Earlier Rahitan had found detailed descriptions and instructions in one of the golden scrolls. Used properly, its energy field gave one with the knowledge, to construct a triangle of light through which to travel interdimensionally. Various triangles were connected by a thin cord of golden light, rather like a necklace. On arrival at the destination the triangles of light faded until invoked again. The scrolls had revealed to Rahitan, who taught the others, a safe and effective way to travel over long distances without the need for personal exertion. The twelve couples practised controlling the triangles many times before feeling fully confident. Each couple stood in the column of light that overlighted the pyramid, invoked the triangles and were enveloped, linked and projected to a predetermined destination. Rahitan had re-discovered a very ancient system for global travel that seemed to have been forgotten around at the time of the great flood, some ten thousand years earlier. He hoped other such pyramids still existed along the route as boosters, but wasn't prepared to depend on that method of travel alone.

The entire village turned out to farewell them, some looking rather the worse for wear.

"We wish you good speed. Travel safely and well," they chorused

Rahitan instructed his group. "Ready to bi-locate. Our destination is the great red rock in the centre of the vast land to our west. Remain conscious of my presence at all times and stay close. There we are to meet with a group of Aboriginal clever men who await our arrival. In all future travels we have to be aware of time differences. On our arrival we will find that area still in darkness, but the sun will soon rise and cover the great rock with its warm rays, making it glow red. It is a sight you will enjoy my friends. We will watch the sun rise for a second time today. Now, all together, let's go."

At the base of the great red monolith, several black men adorned with white symbols covering their bodies sat around a small campfire beside a waterhole. They were waiting in absolute silence for something to happen. Finally, dawn rode in on silvery fingers interspersed with shafts of deep pink, lighting up the sky. The wind died down, suddenly tired from its ceaseless game of chasing spinifex balls across the desolate land. No birds sang, and no frogs croaked. The usual dawn chorus slept late that day. Suddenly, with a loud, startled shout, one of the men leapt to his feet, grabbed his spear and ran away. The others stood their ground, seeing not only their fellows, but five times that number standing around the fire. One man wearing a tall headdress of black and white feathers and covered in symbols painted on his naked body, stepped toward Rahitan, and smiled.

"Greetings, my old and esteemed friend from the land at the end of the long white cloud. We have spent the night in meditation awaiting your safe arrival. We are honoured by your presence but a little surprised at the number in your party. I notice that half of them are women."

"Greetings to you, Warrumbidgi, my old friend. You see correctly. In our tribe men and women are considered equal in all things. Without them we would not exist. They are our sacred half," responded Rahitan.

"Unfortunately, this is a place forbidden to women. Our society treats them differently. We will have to leave this place and go somewhere allowed by our customs," said their leader and spokesman.

"Then we are not off to an auspicious start," said Rahitan. "When we last met, our whole assembly was male, so the question of male and female equality never arose. However, if the women are not included in the talks and ceremonies, then we will not stay. Can we not reach a compromise?"

"Our women always perform their own ceremonies to which men are not welcome. Our ways and needs are different. We do not have room in our minds to include women in our sacred mens world. Your women will have to accompany our women and perform their own rituals," said Warrumbidgi, trying to stay calm, but feeling dreadful anger rising from deep within his belly.

"Then we will continue our journey westwards," responded Rahitan. "Pity, on our last meeting I took you to be a much more enlightened man. We would have loved to wander around your land and circumambulate the rock. I am trying not to be intolerant. We are not on this journey to change the ways of others, for if everyone on this planet was the same, what a boring place it would be. Rather, we are here to teach by example and if we cannot do that, then this is no place for us and we need to move on," responded Rahitan.

Garlita stepped in front of Warrumbidgi and challenged him. "Greetings, Warrumbidgi. I see from your field of colours that you are a highly evolved man, and a star seeded being. Usually such souls rise above the tribal customs and limitations imposed on them. While I do not wish to insult you or interfere in any way with your belief system, I do ask that you consider talking with all of us to our mutual benefit. I see that your companions are also high beings, and ask that you suspend the imposed customs for just one day?"

"I will talk with the others," the man replied. "Wait here."

Six of the men walked several paces from the Atema and began to discuss the situation, quietly at first, but it soon led to raised voices and gesturing spears. The Atema stood silently around the dying fire, engrossed in their own thoughts. When the discussion rose to a fever pitch, Rahitan said softly, "Mind merge. Though I have no wish to interfere in their customs, we must send them harmonious thoughts."

Twenty-four powerful minds sent love and light to the arguing men. Their bickering suddenly stopped, and as one, they turned and walked back to the fire.

"We have reached an agreement," informed Warrumbidgi. "We will elevate your women to honorary men. As they are not of our tribe, our laws and customs do not apply to them."

Just as he finished speaking, dozens of black men, shouting and waving sticks and spears. advanced menacingly towards the newcomers. The man who had initially fled at their appearance had returned to the tribe jabbering about people from outer space invading their territory. He was the only one of the original group who had not been informed of their method of arrival.

Warrumbidgi strode forward to confront them, held up his spear and yelled, "Stop. They are our friends. They are holy men and women from across the sea, far to the east of our rock. They will not harm you. They have only come to exchange wisdom. There is nothing to be afraid of. Stop I say. Stop."

Rahitan quickly made up his mind. "I do not like the look of their energy fields. We need to immediately dissolve our bodies into light and reassemble on the other side of this rock. Together. Now."

In the growing light the advancing warriors stopped, and stared in amazement as the strangers disappeared before their eyes. Frantically, they searched behind rocks, inside small caves at the base of the rock, and even behind the stunted trees growing about the waterhole. "Too much magic" they muttered. "Warrumbidgi, you told us to expect strangers, but you didn't tell us they would come from the air. We need to understand this, old man. What kind of sorcery is this?"

"It is not sorcery," replied Warrumbidgi, thoroughly shaken by the reaction of his people. "In this world there are many things we do not know. Our legends tell us of the journey our ancestors made from the stars, how they created all things; the mountains, the rivers, the animals and the people. We should not be so overcome by superstition and ignorance that we are afraid of the unknown. Just because you do not believe in something, does not mean that it cannot be so. Now control yourselves, and prepare to receive our guests with dignity. Remember that we are not savages who kill what we don't understand, but are noble men and women. Behave so, or we will miss this exceptional opportunity to learn something new. I regularly communicate with their High Priest, Rahitan, and I also can disappear and relocate to another place. Up to now that has been solely my secret, handed down through a long line of my clever ancestors. Please, my people, do not disappoint me with your actions," he pleaded.

One of the six who first encountered the Atema, joined Warrumbidgi, and said, "They have no weapons so cannot harm us. There is an equal number of men and women. As women are forbidden to enter this area, we have made their women honorary men. Otherwise they threaten to leave without talking to us."

Not all were convinced and several of the weapon waving men grumbled, "How much more do we have to hear?"

"If you promise not to harm our guests I will call them back, for I know where they have gone," said Warrumbidgi.

He put his fingers to his forehead, closed his eyes and concentrated. To the amazement of the tribesmen, several men appeared around the campfire. Men of different skin and hair colour, dressed in unfamiliar robes but with no fear on their faces. Rahitan stepped forward holding his hands out in front of him.

"My name if Rahitan, High Priest of the Atema, a tribe living in a large forest in the centre of the great stingray shaped island far to the east of your land. We travelled here through the air, an arbility we learnt from our ancient ones. We come in peace. I have the gift of many tongues and learned to speak your language from Warrumbidgi several decades ago when we first made contact." He paused to allow his words to sink in, then continued. "It is better that our women stay with some of our men on the other side of the rock, until this misunderstanding is sorted out."

One old man stepped forward. "Rahitan of the Atema. You are welcome to our land. It was wrong of Warrumbidgi not to prepare us for your arrival. I am Gullanjingi, the head man of the Mantatjula people. Please, summon the rest of your group."

Rahitan put his hand to his brow, and concentrated. Soon vague shapes began to appear around him, and materialised a short time later.

"We have resolved the problem," he informed them. "This is Gullanjingi, head man of the Mantatjula tribe who live in this area. It seems Warrumbidgi neglected to inform them of our method of travel and sudden arrival. The six who greeted us were also ill prepared, judging from our welcome. In future, I must remember to get my contacts in each land to inform their people of our arrival and have them prepare a proper welcoming committee. It's not that they could harm us, but because of their ignorance, we gave them a nasty fright."

Gullanjingi turned and summoned several young men. "Go and kill a great red kangaroo for a feast. It should be ready by sundown, and it is one way we can make amends to our visitors."

As the men dashed off, Rahitan addressed the chief. "I have another surprise for you. None of my people eat food, especially the flesh of animals. We live on light, and there is more than enough light and energy here to sustain us during our time here. You see all those dancing silvery particles in the air, that is what sustains us, combined with the spiritual food from our creator, Io."

A collective groan of disbelief came from the black men. 'Not eat food. Impossible. If you do not eat you will die. That is the law.'

"No," answered Rahitan. "That may be your law, but it is not ours. I am telling you this because I do not want your women to be upset when we do not eat the food they prepare for the feast. We do not mind watching you eating your kill. We look forward to dancing and singing your songs and hearing your stories. But we will not share your food."

"I think you have a great story to share with us, Rahitan of the Atema. We will sit in the shade of the great rock and listen. Then later we will tell you our story. This promises to be a day of great learning, one we will speak of for many years. Perhaps we may even make up a dance to convey the meaning, but we will have to omit the part where you just appear from the air. We can't emulate that. But if Warrumbidgi has the knowledge of moving through the air, perhaps in the future, he can teach some of us."

By the time Rahitan, with the assistance of each of his group had finished talking. the sun had ridden high across the sky, shrinking shadows, causing heat to shimmer across the desert, and the listeners to become drowsy. Rahitan had insisted calling the tribal women to listen. A place had to be found where men and women could sit together. Millions of little black flies drank from glistening sweat, swarmed into eyes and noses seeking moisture. Hands constantly slapped and swatted the irritation, until Rahitan called a halt to the story telling.

"You have listened well. This evening, after the sun has set and the sky has darkened, we have another surprise for you. One I trust you can cope with, now that you know our story. We will rest for a while in the shade of the rock while you prepare your feast, and decorate your bodies for the corroboree Gullanjingi promised us. We will see you following our sunset meditation, for we always greet the rising and farewell the setting sun," he said.

A large fire blazed in the centre of the aboriginal camp, creating dancing shadows, and strange movements when reflected onto decorated bodies. The eerie night noises, amplified by the intense silence of the land, echoed like forlorn ghosts around the outer perimeter of the light from the fire. None of the Atema were afraid, but all the same, they stayed close together. The singed red kangaroo was greedily pulled from the fire and people tore off chunks to satisfy their hunger. All the while, the Atema watched impassively. Appetites satiated, the women began a slow, shuffling dance around the camp fire, moving their hands, while singing an ancient song that told of the Dreamtime, that ever changing timetable of events that forged this great land. When the women finished, the energy changed and decorated, plumed men jumped to their feet, gesticulating wildly, running, crouching, sliding and feigning a hunt. Their movements told the story of the hunt for the great kangaroo they had recently slaughtered. When they reached the kill scene, most of the Atema women hid their eyes. The actions were too lifelike for them to watch.

For what seemed like hours the men danced, swayed, sang and generally enjoyed themselves. Countless stars appeared in the squid black sky and The Atema realised that in the dryness of the desert, far more stars were visible than through the moisture laden air of their homeland. Familiar constellations followed each other across the sky. Orion chased the Seven Sisters, those they called Matariki, through the river of milk that ran thick and full across the clear night sky. No moon rose until the dancing finished.

Rahitan whispered to Gullanjingi that their surprise could keep until the following night, for what they had just witnessed had brought the natural world to life and now they needed to sleep. Wrapped in their warm cloaks, the Atema lay in a circle on the ground, with feet pointing towards the now cindering fire, and slept soundly as the zodiacal signs rose and fell towards the dark, vast horizon. No one noticed or heard the scorpions scuttling around looking for food nor the dingoes howling in the distance.

As the eagles soared on the morning thermals created by the warming of the sun's rays, Aloma slowly awoke, yawned, stretched, and sat up.

"I feel so dusty," said Aloma. "I wonder where they wash."

"I don't think they wash in water, but use sand," said Zenita. "I overheard two women talking about it last night. Water is precious here and they never pollute their drinking water by washing or swimming in it. We can always bi-locate home to the hot pools if we feel too unclean."

"Rahitan said there was to be no backtracking on this journey," replied Aloma. "Perhaps there is a river or hot springs around here somewhere. I'll ask Kaitewha to scout around."

"I think he has gone with Rahitan and several of the others to greet the sun," said Zenita. "They were whispering about not waking us. There they are. Perhaps we should join them. I don't like to miss the sunrise ceremony; it makes my whole day go better." She dashed off, leaving Aloma alone by the cold, dead fire. She looked over to the camp and saw several women carrying long stout sticks, walking towards a distant clump of trees in the distance. *I wonder where they are going. Perhaps they will show me how they find food and I can discover if they use any herbal medicine. Zenita would be interested in that.*

Aloma put on her shoes and dashed after the women. She was a little breathless when she finally caught up and they laughed, pointing at her shoes. Their feet had never seen shoes and were hard and callused, like the rough skin of sharks. *The women would not believe me if I told them about the actual size of the ocean and the large creatures that live in it. I didn't believe it myself until I visited the Akariri, who live by the great Ocean. Until then I thought our lake was the largest body of water in the world.*

Though the conversation was stilted, action speaks many words and soon Aloma, armed with her own digging stick, was fossicking for witchetty grubs and tubers. While she declined to eat a fresh grub, she didn't mind touching them. Soon the dilly bags were full and the women returned with Aloma to the camp. Curly-haired children danced around her, touching her face and hair and pointing at her eyes. Never before had they seen blue eyes and felt sorry that she could not see properly. Perhaps she was like the old men with opaque eyes who could no longer see.

"No," she assured them, "I can see as well as you. In my land and in other countries, many people have blue or green eyes and fair or red hair."

The women pondered on what she meant by other countries. Surely they were the only people and this the only world. They could accept her and her friends because they could see them, but to imagine unseen people in an unseen country was beyond their understanding.

The day passed with fun and laughter, interspersed with discipline for the children and the usual arguments amongst the women over petty things Following the sunset meditation, as the night advanced rapidly, Morpheus called everyone together.

"After you have finished eating, my friends, we will present our surprise."

Rahitan translated as the language still tied Morpheus's tongue around his teeth. Along with Kaitewha and Ioannes, he had spent some time preparing a fireworks display with the materials given to him by Pausanin. Ten large and ten small rockets, wheels and bangers were hidden in the sand and on nearby stumps. The children sat wide eyed with excitement and the adults looked apprehensive as he lit a fire-stick and walked a little way across the sand, where he put the fire-stick to the ground and jumped back. A loud whirring noise scared the people, but they relaxed when an explosion of coloured light high above them brought forth ooh aahs. However, several people ran from the camp screaming that the debil debils were aloft. Rahitan's mind sought them, overcame their fear, and gently pulled them back to the camp. Morpheus lit one after another until the sky blazed with sparkling coloured light, then he quickly set off a spinning wheel that shot sparks across the ground. Their initial fear turned into delight as the people became entranced by the display. They wanted more and were disappointed when Morpheus set off the last one. It was a long time before anyone in the camp slept that night, as such wonders there were to be retold over and over. Meanwhile the Atema lay in a circle around a fire some distance from the noisy camp and slept soundly.

The third day passed quickly with both peoples sharing secrets. Zenita taught several of the women how to pass healing energy through their hands, and in return they showed her their ways of treating wounds, bites and fevers. She recognised none of the plants, but saw the results were effective. In this harsh land, one either survived or died quickly and was buried with much ceremony.

Following their third sunset meditation, Gullanjingi called Rahitan over and announced, "Now I have a surprise for you. Please be seated."

Into the arena strode an apparition with a white painted face and body markings, stilts attached to his feet and tied to his legs, making him look much taller. A dingo skin was slung over his right shoulder, and his long matted hair hung to his waist, and was covered in twigs, feathers and mud. The people cringed. They had heard descriptions of the Kadaitcha spirit-being but very few had actually seen him. The being strutted around the circle looking at the Atema with dark deep unseeing eyes. They sat very still. Suddenly he let out a fearsome shriek, and rushed to the centre of the circle, where he stopped, silently lifting and lowering his arms like a bird in flight. Then he began to spin, faster and faster until he became a blur of white and black. Above him appeared a large blue light that descended to hover just above his head. He played with the light, throwing and catching it, spinning and bouncing it, until it doubled, and then tripled in size, expanding to fill the arena, and still it grew. People moved back as it touched them.

Rahitan whispered to the Atema. "Prepare to disappear. I have heard that this trick sometimes has an unhappy ending. Gather in the cave on the other side of the rock. Now."

The Atema disappeared just as the blue light expanded to envelope them. Finding them gone, it let out an angry hiss. The kadaitcha man emitted a piercing scream, and ran toward the place that until a second ago had held the Atema. *I tricked that old fool Gullanjingi into letting me perform tonight but not for the reason he thought. I want the secret of bi-location from the Atema and I also want one of their women, the one with hair the colour of the full moon and eyes like the blue sky in summer. She is a woman of great beauty, not like a woman at all but more like an angel. Her man doesn't look like he can satisfy her. What she needs is a real man of the earth, not some star seed. Now they have tricked me. The old priest must have had prior knowledge and warned them of my intentions. I won't stop trying to get the angel. After I saw her alone with our women today I decided that she will not leave with the others. She will be mine. HaaaHaaaa.*

Laughing hideously, he gathered the blue light into a small ball and threw it high in the air. It returned to earth like a flash of lightning, struck the ground with a crack and disappeared. In a rage he ran from the arena screaming that the Atema had tricked him and that he would extract a dreadful revenge. That night the Atema did not sleep in a circle around the fire, but in a monastery set high on a clifftop in the mountains of India. Rahitan guessed the kadaicha man's evil intent and thought it discreet to leave. If necessary, he would deal with him later.

Following their time in India where they spent several fruitful days with holy men and women who lived in monastries among the misty mourntains to the north of that ancient land, the travellers went to Aftica to visit Kirinyaga, the Home of the Gods; a high mountain standing above the green plains of Kenya, to be welcomed by a man as old as any on the planet. He called himself Swahalal, the witch doctor, a dispenser of good and evil, one who knows how the world plays its eternal games, who told them,

"On top of this mountain your soul group anchored their energy to the earth to enable them to remain here. It was extremely difficult for souls to incarnate because of the heaviness of Earth's atmosphere back then. One day, Aloma, one of your future incarnations will climb this mountain to release the hold and free them from the eternal cycle of birth and death on this planet, but that time is far into the future."

Two days later the group travelled further north and found themselves standing at the base of a gigantic pyramid, gazing in awe at a head of a man wearing a Pharaoh's headdress on a lion's body, partially covered with sand.

"Behold, the Pyramids and Sphinx of Giza. Ah, there to greet us is Ptolomy, a High Priest of this land. We should not have to make a hasty getaway from here, but be alert just the same.

"Greetings, Rahitan of the Atema. It is a pleasure to meet you again. It is unusual for you have come with an escort, as normally you travel alone. Follow me please." Ptolomy turned and headed towards a large stone structure beside the largest pyramid that had several rows of stone missing from its top.

"You also speak his language, Rahitan," commented Garlita. "Oh, to have a large brain like yours."

"My brain, as you put it, is no larger than any one else's. It is what I do with it that makes the difference," replied Rahitan. "Note that the capstone is missing from the great pyramid. There is much speculation as to its material of construction and its purpose. Some say it was made of gold, others of copper and yet others are sure it was crystal, and that it was removed when darkness invaded the land of Khem. I think the priests of the Brotherhood here know the secret. Perhaps one of you can discover the answer."

The Atema entered a cool, high-domed stone building to find several richly dressed men waiting. One with a long black curly beard, black eyebrows joined in the middle, and a large straight nose advanced towards Rahitan. "Welcome Rahitan, member of our Brotherhood, and welcome to your entourage." Turning to them he said, "I am Horemheb, High Priest of this temple of Isis, our divine Mother, whom we worship above all others. No doubt you have heard of the tribulation in Palestine to the north of Khem. One who was hailed as a Messiah, or Anointed One was crucified by the Roman governor, which caused no end of unrest. Much of what is written in their Holy Books about his virgin mother also relates to our revered goddess, Isis. But I am remiss. We will talk of this later, but fow now we have prepared some refreshments. Please quench your thirst and satisfy your hunger."

Several women, dressed in long close fitting gowns, glided amongst the visitors offering, delicacies such as smoked eel and cooked lotus seeds.

"Thankyou," said Garlita. "While we do not need food for sustenance we will gladly drink that delicious looking nectar. Tell me, what fruit is it?"

"You do not eat?" remarked Horemheb. "How do you sustain yourselves?"

"On light, the prana in the air. It is abundant in our land and in places away from large settlements. However, we do drink nectar and pure water occasionally."

A tall, graceful woman came forward to explain. "This drink is a mixture of pomegranate and apricot. The pomegranate is deep red and the apricot orange, the mixing of which makes a delightful colour. Please take one." She offered a highly polished tray of beaten bronze on which stood several fine goblets. Garlita took one and sipped it.

"Astonishing," she said, and took another sip. "All our fruits are sour, while this is wonderfully sweet."

Handmaidens offered the rest of the party a drink and they all raised their goblets, before sending a prayer to Io for safe arrival, and drank.

"I would like to know the secret of living on light," said Horemheb. "I have heard there are hermits living in caves high in the Himalayas who take no food but, apart from them, had no idea others lived so."

"The process of transition takes twenty-one days," replied Rahitan. "You would need to travel to our land to receive the teachings, but that you cannot do unless you travel through the air as we do, for we do not think it is possible to bi-locate whilst one still eats food, especially animal flesh."

He gestured to Ioannes to step forward. "Ioannes here is of the Levanti tribe who originated in the land of the Hebrews, but were taken as slaves by your people many long years ago. When the Hebrews returned to their homeland, some of the Levanti wanted their freedom, so sailed to our island on the other side of the known world, guided by maps made by shipwrecked sailors who had found their way home. The Levanti have lived now on the giant stingray shaped island for twenty generations, but still keep their ancient language and teachings. Ioannes has recently undergone the process to be able to live on light. Perhaps he will show you a map of the route to our land, but only if you are truly prepared to undergo the perils of the voyage. We will talk more on this later, but now, if it is permissible, I would like to see your complex, the pyramids and the hall of records under the Sphinx."

"Of course. We have saddled a team of camels in anticipation of your wish. Marmouk," he called, "please escort our visitors to the stables."

At the sight of the huge, snarling beasts most of the Atema recoiled in horror.

"What are we supposed to do with these," whispered Aloma to Kaitewha. "They smell awful and do not look very friendly."

"I think we are supposed to sit on that contraption tied to their humps," he replied. "Look, that man is getting his camel to kneel, and asking us to mount."

"I am not getting on that without you," she said. "Can't we ride together?"

"Rahitan, Aloma and I wish to share one beast. She is not too keen to ride alone. Will you tell the driver?" he asked.

"Kaitewha, Aloma, they are camels, the ships of the desert, for without them, this land would be much poorer. We cannot offend our hosts or show ignorance of these beasts. However, I will ask," said Rahitan.

Soon everyone was mounted and the beasts got their feet, encouraged by shouting and prodding from their keepers. Aloma and Kaitewha shared one camel as did Thieron and Erana, while the others all chose to ride alone. Before long, as the fear of falling off diminished, they began to relax and look around as they rode across the sand towards the smallest pyramid. The camels trod daintily over sand, littered with fossil shells and sea creatures.

"It seems as if this area was once under the ocean," said Morpheus to Zenita. "Just look at all those tiny shells. I wonder if that was before or after the pyramids were built, for Ptolomy said they are much older that their history suggests. He said that the Pharaoh Khephren merely restored the greatest pyramid for his tomb, but did not build it. It is not known how, why and when they were built."

"I think the ancestors who built our first temple complex before it was covered in volcanic debris knew of these. Remember the engravings on the old stone in the forest shaped like a pyramid without its cap?" replied Zenita. "Anyway, thank heavens they didn't bring any camels with them to our land when they arrived. If we'd had them we may not have learned to bi-locate. Beasts of burden are handy things."

"They could never live in our green and fertile land," Morpheus replied. "A blessing really, for I too prefer life without these noisy, smelly beasts."

They became silent and concentrated on keeping up with the others, while listening to the constant flow of information pouring from Ptolemy's lips.

When the sun could no longer see the shadows it loved to cast, along the ground, the party dismounted in front of the Sphinx. Ptolemy led them to a heavy door between its paws and signalled the to guard to open it. Resistant at first, the door swung smoothly on its hinges to reveal a dark opening. Ptolemy disappeared inside, and descended a long flight of steps lit by flaring pitch torches that send a cloud of smoke along the passage. The Atema covered their noses to prevent breathing the stale air and followed Ptolemy down into a cavernous room deep under the belly of the enigmatic sphinx. Awaiting their arrival was an old bent man, his grey beard nearly touching his waist, his clothes dark with soot and age. His smile revealed holes where there once were teeth, but his eyes were alive and piercing.

"Welcome, Rahitan of the Atema." Turning to the others he said, "I am al-Zaoud, keeper of the Hall of Records. I will guide you to the secret place where our most sacred records are kept. As you know, few get to see them, but your people are of an exceptionally high vibration, I am assured by those who can see their colours. And I have known Rahitan for a very long time and trust that you will not reveal the knowledge you are about to receive to those who would use it unwisely. Please, follow me carefully for there are a couple of booby traps along the way, designed to prevent uninvited intruders"

"Now I know where Rahitan used to disappear to during his long absences from our village," remarked Morpheus to Zenita. "He was so secretive, we never knew about his international life."

"Halt," commanded al-Zaoud. Stopping in front of a heavy wooden door decorated with great metal studs and bands, he inserted a large key into a hole and turned it. A loud clicking sounded and he swung the door easily on its hinges.

"I have never seen a key before," whispered Aloma. "We have no need to lock secrets away. We just place them in a higher dimension where those of low vibration cannot access."

"There are many wonders so hidden here also," replied al-Zaoud, whose hearing was extremely acute. "But some of the larger items take too much effort to hide, so we lock them away and guard them from robbers. If a thief or uninvited man tried to pass through this door, a large metal lever would swing from this recess and break his back. An even nastier surprise awaits along the passage."

"Rahitan used booby traps to protect the golden scrolls in our last temple library, before the big bang," said Kaitewha to Aloma. "I saw them on the day we discovered the scrolls and we found Aloma's statue. He is full of secrets, our High Priest."

"Yes," said al-Zaoud, "I showed him a few tricks."

"But they were placed there over twenty thousand years ago," gasped Aloma.

"Yes, I am very old, my dear," smiled the toothless old man.

No one said a word, and kept close together as they proceeded along the smoky passage. Soon al-Zaoud stopped in front of a solid wall covered with symbols and pressed the pupil in a drawing of an eye. A large part of the stone wall in front of them swung aside to reveal a room full of golden objects, stacks of papyrus and golden scrolls, furniture inlaid with precious stones and metals, an enormous sarcophagus covered with thinly beaten gold, statues of long dead Pharoahs, and countless other unfamiliar objects made of a shiny grey metal.

"Welcome to the Hall of Records," said al-Zaoud. "It is a sight very few get to see. We decided to invite you all out of respect and trust for your High Priest. He wouldn't bring with him any who would use this information to harm others. For the moment, it is safe from unenlightened eyes and minds and will only be brought out into the open light of day and common knowledge when the consciousness of the planet has risen high enough to understand what is contained here. A fanatical mind will only wish to destroy or own such treasures, not to learn from them. Let me show you around."

"You mentioned another booby trap," ventured Ioannes. "Where is it?"

"Oh that. If I had pressed any of the other symbol written on the lintel or the wall but the pupil of the eye, the ceiling would have collapsed showering us with tons of rubble, killing us instantly. There is one more trap, a psychic one that if wrongly penetrated sends a man mad with fear. He sees horrifying monsters pursuing him and feels them tearing at his flesh. He doesn't live long. I will not show you the room that trap protects, for it is our Holy of Holies containing our most sacred relics. Even I have only been inside twice in my long life," said al-Zaoud. "Now, listen and I will explain what is kept here."

Time stood still as the wonders of the universe were paraded before the eyes of the Atema. They had always thought themselves rather knowledgeable compared to the tribes of their land, but now felt like small children in a hive full of honey as the old scholar opened their minds to far greater knowledge. Even the golden scrolls did not reveal such information, and they certainly possessed no objects or instruments like those revealed here. Only Rahitan understood what they saw that day.

"What are these large disc shaped objects with holes along the sides?" asked Kaitewha.

"They once flew through the air, transporting people from one land to another. Unfortunately, we have forgotten how to replenish their power source. I suspect it came from the capstone of the great pyramid, but that was removed when the creator gods who populated our land, departed. They obviously thought we were not ready for this knowledge and so now the objects lie here, hidden until a power source is found once again. Over here are delicate medical instruments for operating on a diseased person. One scroll shows how surgeons performed life saving operations on hearts and other body organs. As we have also lost that knowledge it is better these instruments are also hidden. These long hollow tubes with an ornate head, are dreadful weapons of destruction, depicted in the scrolls as firing death at the enemy. I am glad we no longer have that knowledge, and hope it will never resurrect in the minds of men. While our creator gods knew far more than we will ever know, they did give us the gifts of agriculture, art and music, and to my mind, the most important gifts of mathematics, writing and language. These enable us to build fine temples, calculate the movement of the stars across the heavens, and to communicate with each other. Having this knowledge, the gods sped up our evolution by over a million years. We have much to be grateful for, even though they originally bred us to be slaves to mine gold."

"That is exactly what our golden scrolls say," said Rahitan. "We rediscovered our set only recently and have been astounded by their contents. Once you showed me your set of scrolls but I did not get to read them. Now we have found the set hidden in our land, I will not have to travel so far to learn."

"Please continue your visits, Master of the Atema," replied al-Zaoud. "I always enjoy your company, for you are not puffed up by ego like some other scholars I have met. Now any more questions?"

The Atema continued to ply him with questions until he called a halt, declaring that they had other wonders to see before leaving his land. He guided his visitors from the bowels of the earth back into the surface, carefully resetting the booby traps.

The following evening the Atema were invited to a special ceremony in the subterranean rooms beneath the step pyramid of Zoser, some two hours camel ride to the south of Giza. Horemheb told them he had received a special dispensation from the Brotherhood, allowing them to attend. Just after sunset a party of nearly fifty priests, priestesses and attendants set off along the wide road. The string of camels protested as only a camel can at having to work at night, but the skilful drivers soon had them under control. Though bruised and battered around their thighs from the unaccustomed hardness of the saddles, the Atema successfully alighted in front of a small doorway in the side of the step pyramid. *I wonder why the skins of those little white goats are not used to make the saddles softer, thought Aloma. If I have to ride another beast I will insist on a goatskin seat cover.* Horemheb escorted Rahitan towards a small door and ushered him inside. Each visitor was paired with a priest or priestess and taken down a long flight of more than one hundred steps, to a large room, lit by smoking torches.

"Why don't they know about our balls of light that illuminate the night?" whispered Thieron to Erana. "I must mention it to Ptolomy. He seems the most approachable."

Aloma stared at the night-blue ceiling, adorned with luminous stars depicting the night sky; Orion, Matariki, the Great Bear and other familiar constellations illumnated by torches.

A thrill shot down her spine as her thoughts were interrupted by two jackals bounding into the room from a small alcove. In the gloom they looked real, but on closer inspection she saw thay they were two men wearing wooden jackal masks and pelts, cavorting around the priests. Soon they were joined by a man wearing a hawk's head, and a woman with a golden disc suspended between long golden horns on her head. She was joined by a woman with a lion's head and a man wearing the head of an ibis, the sacred bird of Khem.

Horemheb chanted in a deep rich voice, intoning the story of their gods, of the creation of their land and of their cosmology. Other actors entered the room, wearing different masks depicting ancient gods and goddesses, until at the stroke of a loud gong that slightly deafened everyone, they rushed out, the torches were extinguished and the stuffy room was plunged into a darkness so black that the end of the world seemed near. Not a breath or a whisper passed unheard. Just when Aloma thought she would pass out from lack of air, a faint breeze wafted through the room, followed by the barest glimmer of light. The light increased as Horemheb intoned, "Once our land was ruled by capricious gods and goddesses, whose wishes were interpreted by corrupt priests. Darkness ruled until a great Pharaoh came to sweep away the old gods with a new form of worship.

His name was Ankhenaten, who lived in the late eighteenth dynasty, and with his wife Neferititi taught that there was only One True Being that overlighted this world, and all others were his subordinates. They caused the old priests to be replaced with true believers in the One and built a new city called Amarna. Their reign was short lived when the priests of the old religion successfully rebelled and destroyed his temples. Ankhenaten's name was expunged from all historical records, and the old gods reinstated. Nearly everyone returned to the old ways, except those of our priestly line who knew the truth of his teachings and vowed to secretly keep the One True God always upper most in our hearts and worship. The White Brotherhood, which has always included women, who are after all, the embodiment of Isis, our Queen of Heaven, was born and has remained strong to this day and will do so until the end of time on earth as we presently know it."

"Most of the priests of the old religion sold their souls to Set, the martial, dark brother of Osiris, who still demanded sacrifice. It was a dark and evil time for our country, but we held a glimmer of light in our hearts, hence the symbolic dousing of the lights and the new glimmer you have just witnessed. As you can see, that faint light grows stronger and will continue to do so throughout our land; sometimes weakening, but it will always remain alight, until one day, far into the future the light of the Law of One will spread across the whole earth. It will dispel ignorance and darkness, and dissolve false religions such as the one that will overwhelm our land during the next century, and grow to become a fanatical force, until Isis calls a halt to the oppression and control of all women who were forced to cover their faces and bodies from the sight of bigoted and lecherous men. Her image will appear in the sky above Giza, astounding her citizens. Then teeming millions struggling for survival in a great city, will fall to their knees and realise the folly of the belief system imposed upon them by misguided mullahs." He paused and took a deep breath of the foetid air.

"Isis will not be mocked. She is the creator and nurturer of Life, and the sustainer of our souls. Without her sustenance, men cannot survive for very long. That is why she has been resurrected in the image of the mother of the Great Teacher of the new Christian religion spreading in the lands to the north of us. That religion will cover the earth, vying with those already established and others yet to come. Although they are all based on the Law of One, they will often disagree between themselves, sometimes with devastating consequences." Raising his voice he called, "Isis, Queen of Heaven, appear before us, we beseech you."

The room fell quiet as a bright blue light shone from the alcove, before a heavy damask curtain parted to reveal a living incarnation of Isis. As one, the tall, stern priests dropped to their knees and the priestesses curtsied low. The Atema stood immobile, staring at the apparition of beauty glowing before them. She seemed opaque yet of flesh and blood, ethereal yet alive, young yet as old as time. Isis was real and still lived. Her long, straight black hair, braided with precious jewels, shone in the glowing light, and her kohl enhanced eyes penetrated all who were brave enough to meet them. Contact brought a strong thrill of recognition through those touched by her eyes. Slowly the form glided around the room until she stood directly before Aloma. She took her hands and gazed deeply into the clear blue eyes of the young Princess of the Atema.

"I have known you from the beginning of time, Princess of Heaven, my daughter. Every one knows I conceived my son, Horus, after many travails, but the birth of my daughter is a great secret. You are my daughter, now and forever more. Embrace me."

Aloma opened her arms and her heart, and Isis embraced her. Aloma was surprised to find her soft and warm instead of cold and distant. Tears rolled from her watery eyes to splash unchecked on pale shoulders as waves of love radiated between the reunited mother and daughter. Soon everyone in the room felt tears well and slide down their cheeks, not tears of sadness but of joy. Gnarled old priests cried beside fresh young acolytes, the actors removed their false masks and cried, the Atema wept openly. At last Isis released Aloma and stood back to look at her again.

"I have searched heaven and earth for you. Where have you been, my daughter?" she asked, drying her tears on a wisp of silk pulled from her long sleeve.

"Am I truly your daughter? My home is on a small island shaped like a giant stingray, far to the south-east of here. In my memory it has been my home since I came to this planet thousands of years ago. I remember falling in a ball of light from a great height and landed unhurt in a forest glade, not far from a gleaming white and blue star shaped temple. That evening a woman found me, crying that her prayers had been answered. She became my mother, and took me to live in her village hidden deep within that forest. She told me that my birth mother had died when I was born. I returned there for several long lifetimes and was loved as their Princess. Then a great explosion blasted that whole area into oblivion, and we all wandered in a void for a very long time until about four thousand years ago, when a vibration passed through my soul and I was pulled back to the forest. I have been called back there ever since, incarnating into several different bodies. Soon that place will be blown asunder again and we will need to leave before that happens. Why do I have no memory of you, Queen of Heaven?"

"My darling one. When you were born, your wicked uncle, Set, called the God of Chaos, was so jealous of his brother, Osiris, my husband, that he stole you from my arms and took you where I could not follow. He wanted me for his wife and lover and to bear his children, and could not look on you as you were a constant reminder of his unrequited love. So he kidnapped you, but all the time I knew you were not dead. Eventually he slew Osiris, dismembered him, and distributed his body across the land. With great determination, I found and gathered together fourteen parts and reassembled them. One part was missing however, but with the aid of a little magic I managed to conceive Horus, my only son. But that is enough talk for now. I have found you and will never let you go again."

Aloma looked aghast. "Isis," she said. "This is such a shock. I can't go with you. I have a partner, my twin soul, Kaitewha. We have only recently rediscovered each other and I love him more than life itself. Within the year we are to bear a child who has an important destiny to follow."

"I am sorry," replied Isis. "In my joy at finding you, I have forgotten everything else. So I am to be a grandmother? I am sure that, once this has sunk in we can come to some satisfactory arrangement. I am so very happy, my true daughter." Turning to Horemheb still on his knees, she added, "Rise O Horemheb, you will be well rewarded for you devotion. Rise all of you and be happy with me. This is the best day of my long and tortured life. You dried up old priests couldn't possibly know the joy of a mother's heart at finding a long lost child. I have something to live for at last. And she is so beautiful."

Horemheb got stiffly to his feet, trying to maintain his stern mien. The tall headdress balanced on his head tilted forward obscuring his vision, and as his hand rose to straighten it, he dropped his long carved staff. It clattered on the floor, causing Isis to laugh. Soon the whole room was laughing, not exactly at Horemheb, which was just as well, for he was a proud man, but with the contagious joy emanating from Isis and Aloma. The traditional ceremony became a shambles as everyone broke with protocol and hugged each other. Loosely fitting tall headdresses became skew-whiff, stern faces softened, and veneers crumbled as the Divine Feminine Principle worked her magic on men and women alike. Amid the revelry a lone voice wailed, but no one noticed al-Zaoud crouched in a corner.

"My work is over. Now I can leave this ancient, worn out body. Thankyou, Aloma,"

Nor did anyone notice a bright light leaving his body to ascend through the ceiling.

True to her fervent wish, Aloma, along with the rest of her people, bi-located back to their comfortable accommodation near the pyramids of Giza, as the idea of riding camels again did not appeal to them.

Two days later, a convoy of wagons pulled by sturdy horses left the Giza temple and headed south for Karnak and the temples of Luxor. Horses were another strange sight to the Atema, for no large animals lived in their land. No one, Horemheb said, could visit his land without gazing upon the great and mysterious temples of Karnak and the Temple of Man in Luxor, where an avenue of rams guarded the entrance flanked by enormous statues of the Pharaoh Ramses III, who built it to honour the Theban triad of Amun, Mut, and Khonsu. The Atema told Horemheb they preferred to bi-locate rather than spend a week rumbling over rough dusty roads, and sleeping under the wagons. However, Horemheb planned on using this opportunity to check on various temples and sanctuaries under his control. They would not have to sleep rough. Comfortable accommodation would be provided along the route. The uneventful journey gave the Atema a chance to see first hand a completely different culture, and witnessing farming and other implements far more advanced than those used by the tribes people of their land, and often by themselves for that matter.

Finally, dusty and a little bedraggled, they arrived in Luxor and were taken to a comfortable villa, bathed in warm perfumed water and given new cotton clothes, far more suitable for the hot climate than the crudely woven garments they wore. Erana massaged Aloma's tired body, and she sighed, remembering Angelica ministrations back home. Kaitewha whistled in appreciation when she met him in the garden.

"Wow, my Princess, what a vision of loveliness. My body is responding as my eyes feast on your body. It remembers and aches with longing to join with yours. Can we find a quiet place for a few hours to make love. I am a desperate man, my beloved," he groaned.

"Kaitewha, you know the rules. But I must admit, there is something in the air here that kindles the fire of passion. Perhaps it is the sun's warmth, or the heady perfume of the bright flowers growing in this garden. I wonder if they would grow at home?" she replied.

"Aloma, please, stop it. Ease my need. I am about to burst with desire," Kaitewha huskily whispered. "Come with me. There is a grotto by the pond, over behind those trees. Take my hand and come with me. Pleeeease."

"Yes, my love, I will come. There is nothing wrong with two lovers spending private time together. I do not care if we are seen. We are betrothed. I have not seen Isis here. I wonder if she will join us." Aloma took her lover's hand and together they strolled through the perfumed garden towards the small cave with water flowing over its crest, fed by a series of buckets pulling water from the Nile that glided sluggishly past the edge of the villa's garden.

As soon as they were out of sight, Kaitewha pulled Aloma to him and kissed her passionately. She responded, and soon they were entwined on a rug that Kaitewha had laid on the soft sand, with their senses open only to each other. Some time later Aloma stirred, opened her eyes and looked straight into the dark eyes of Isis, who stood watching them.

"Isis," she gasped. "Mother, what are you doing here?"

"You have just conceived your daughter. It is fitting that her seed should be sown in my land. I have been on a long journey to beyond the beyond, to claim her soul. This will be her first incarnation on earth. She was very nearly lost to us and about to incarnate on another planet, one far more advanced than this. I had a lot of persuading to do to convince her she was not making a retrograde step in entering your womb. That is why you have not seen me these past days," said Isis. "She is to be called Annaraleah, she of the sacred heaven come to earth,"

"I thought she was to be called Manicarita, who has birthed through me once before."

"No, that soul will now go to Jondra, the son of Ioannes and his wife. And now a high soul must be found to be Annaraleah's earthly partner, to incarnate through Thieron and Erana. It is one of the many things I am working on," said Isis.

"I don't know whether to be pleased or angry," said Aloma. "I not used to having anyone interfere in my life. I have to decide how to deal with this. Can we talk?"

"I'll go and have another bath," said Kaitewha and quickly walked away, leaving them alone.

"My daughter," began Isis, "for aeons I have searched for a small child with round cheeks and long dark hair. I never expected to find my daughter fully grown, betrothed and with pale hair and eyes. I looked in all the wrong places, my judgement overcome by grief. Set hid you well. It will take some time for me to get used to your physical presence. No matter. I want to be with you anywhere on the planet."

"Isis, mother," said Aloma, "You will also take some getting used to. In this incarnation my birth mother died when I was born and I grew up in a primitive tribe, before being called to the Atema. By your standards that is also a primitive village. Are you sure you can cope without servants and priests to worship you. We have great equality amongst the Atema. Following our pilgrimage, I mean to return with my people to the island at the end of the long white cloud."

"All I can do is try," replied Isis, giving Aloma a great hug. "But I know, in my happiness I can do anything. But I will not remain with you all the time, for I have heavenly duties to uphold."

"Tell me of the daughter who I am to give birth to," said Aloma.

"Annaraleah is of the ancient line of Nefilim, who first seeded this planet with intelligent humans. They used the seeds and blood of their males fused with the eggs of a primitive earth dwelling creature and implanted them in the womb of one of their birth goddesses. I see from your eyes that you know this story. Your daughter will be of the pure race. Her role on earth is to bring civilisation, art, music, and writing to your area of the planet. She is to be brought up as an ordinary child, if that is possible amongst a group of older people, but she will have the son of Thieron and Erana as her playmate and eventual partner. You will need to teach her very little, for she comes with the wisdom of the ages in her soul. She needs love and understanding and perhaps a little discipline and education into the ways of your tribe. And of course, a doting grandmother to take her on the occasional intergalactic journey." Isis laughed. "Don't look so shocked, it will be fun."

"I hear Garlita's call to assemble the Atema, mother Isis," said Aloma. "I must leave you for a while. I'm pregnant? I thought something special happened during our lovemaking."

"I will overlight you always, now that I have found you I won't lose you again," said Isis. "If ever you need me, just imagine my image. Farewell for now, my beautiful daughter."

When Aloma joined the Atema, they were excitedly preparing to go on a day trip to Abydos, the fabled ruined palace dedicated to Osiris, built by the long dead Pharaoh Seti I, who was a great innovator and builder. He was the son of Ramses I and father to the great Pharaoh Ramses II. Garlita looked at Aloma and asked, "What is the matter, my dear? You look different and very happy. Even more light than usual shines from your eyes. Is it anything to do with Isis?"

"I'll tell you later," replied Aloma. "First I must find Kaitewha."

Two days later, the Atema stood among the great carved columns of Karnak, in awe at their size and permanence. Built by Ramses III and reputed to be the largest religious building ever erected, it was dedicated to Amun-ra, the greatest Egyptian deity. The sightless eyes of long dead Pharaohs looked down from their lofty statues. An old priestess guided the Atema women to a small temple standing some distance from the main temple. After fumbling with a stiff lock, she opened a small wooden door to reveal a gloomy entrance room, which she led them through towards an opening filtering pale light. The twelve women crowded into a small room lit by a hole in the roof, and stared silently at the apparition standing in the centre. They saw a black stone statue with the head of a lion and the body of a woman staring knowingly back at them.

The old priestess walked to the statue, placed her hands on its knees and said, "Behold, the goddess Sekhmet, the protector of women and children and their secret desires. She is of the old religion.

Many of our older priestesses still worship her, for she understands the ways of the female and is much more accessible than Isis. Often Sekhmet grants our wishes, so we keep making offerings to her statue. She greets you, women from the faraway land and asks if you wish to ask anything of her."

The twelve Atema woman formed a circle around Sekhmet's statue and held hands, silently tuning in to her vibration. Several moments passed in utter stillness and it seemed the statue breathed in their essence. Suddenly Garlita from broke the circle and rushed from the room crying, "This is not of the light. We must leave at once," and ran outside.

The other women quickly followed their High Priestess outside into the warm sunlight and back to their men.

Rahitan opened his arms as Garlita rushed towards his safe embrace. "What is the matter, my dear?" he asked.

"I have just seen something I do not wish to talk about just yet. Please hold me for a little," gasped Garlita.

"We have been talking," said Rahitan. "I think it is time we moved to our next destination and the others agree. We could leave from this great temple, as it stores enough magnetic force required to assist our bi-location. That would save us the tedious trip back to Giza. We will leave as soon as we have had a look around this great temple and after I inform Horemheb that it is time for us to continue our journey. We cannot just disappear without saying goodbye."

TWELVE

The Journey Continues

That evening the Atema slept in a hut beside the great stone walls of Ggantija, on the Island of Gwadex in the great inland sea, created when the Pillars of Hercules parted to allow the Atlantic Ocean to flood the land. Ggantija temple, shaped like two giant flowers was dedicated to Calypso, the ancient goddess of the sea. They remained there for several days, exchanging wisdom and laughter with the keepers of the temple, who entertained them royally. This temple, reputed to have been built by a Giantess many millenia ago, was designed by the ancient ones as a transmitter/receiver, and still operated to communicate with the heavenly home of its builders. The following morning, Gilju, the High Priestess of Ggantija, explained that several star gates still operated in secret locations on the planet, one of which was this temple complex, but they were gradually being shut down until human consciousness, once again evolved to a level of operational physical safety. However, some could still be accessed through a higher dimension, but only used by those with the knowledge to operate them.

Rahitan asked, "Do you know the location of Nibaru, your home planet? Could we go on a galactic journey through this temple?"

Gilju answered, "Nibaru? Yes, that is my spiritual home. I return often. We can travel this evening as the moon is in her dark phase, the easiest time to travel through the windows of space. I think you will be surprised at what you will see."

The Atema hugged themselves in anticipation, as the Priestess continued, "First there is a little preparation to undergo. I see from your energy fields that you are very light beings, and as you refused refreshment, can live on light, but you must be shown the correct procedure. As you already have the ability to bi-locate we can speed up the preparation time to just one afternoon. Now I will leave you. My maidens will show you around and answer any questions you may have."

As the crescent moon rose above the eastern hills, the Atema were escorted along the flower strewn path leading to the great stone flower-shaped temple, built before the arrival of the present population on the island. Kaitewha noticed several large egg shaped rocks similar to the one he had sat on outside the gates to his village, when he had been transported to the akashic library. All the while, an air of familiarity embraced him. Each of the group stopped at the stone doorway, focussed on the destination, walked to the first left hand petal, and spun quickly several times before moving to the first right hand petal, then the second left and right before spinning very fast on the large flat altar stone in the head petal. As their consciousness left to go on the journey, their vacated bodies were gently caught by waiting assistants and carried to a chamber lined with sleeping mats, where it was laid to rest until the journey was over.

Rahitan with the High Priestess Gilju went first to open the way, followed by Garlita, Morpheus and Zenita and finally the rest. Within seconds it seemed, as balls of light, they were 'home' being greeted by familiar faces. One tall woman stepped forward to greet them.

"Welcome by brothers and sisters, from Earth. This is the first time so many of you, who long ago, volunteered for duty to assist the evolutionary process of that jewel of a planet called Earth, have returned as one group. You are only granted a short time with us, for sometimes memories of home can make the sojourn to faraway places harder to cope with. Occasionally it is necessary to update your memories and keep you vibrationally connected. As you are aware, for many of you, your present incarnations will soon be over, when your village is destroyed. It is all part of our plan. This is a trial run to make sure you are able to beam home just before the explosion."

Rahitan said, "Greetings, Ninti. It is a pleasure to meet you again. Many of us are so very soul tired and wish for a long rest in the bosom of our creator. Though we communicate at a distance through my mind, a long earthly time has passed since we last saw each other.As you know, Nibaru is not the home planet of us all as some have come from the Pleiades. But I am certain we are all welcome here."

Turning to his group he introduced them all, feeling as though he was doing something irrelevant, as Ninti and her companions already knew them better than they knew themselves.

"You will each have a room prepared and awaiting your arrival when your village is destroyed. Many of your people may not make it through the portals and may remain stuck on earth, until released in the future by one who knows the way. I cannot guarantee your safe arrival here, but Rahitan, you may begin to prepare your people for their transition. Now it is time to return to your bodies, for to dally too long from your sleeping bodies can be harmful," said Ninti.

For the next few days they visited several other ancient temples on the main island of Malta, which they reached by boat, crossing the rough strait separating the two islands. Some sites were abandoned and a few were still inhabited by priests and priestesses. They entered each building along the central avenue of the façade, leading along a monumental passageway, into a paved court, uaually containing a stone altar. In the interior of the buildings, semi-circular apses, symmetrically arranged on either side of the main axis, graced the temple. Through holes in the ceiling, light filtered into the apses revealing brightly coloured frescoes depicting various flora and fauna. Astrologer priests used these holes to plot the journey of stars across the heavens. Following the tour of Malta the group returned to Ggantija. There they conversed with Dreaming Priestesses who could foresee the future, whilst lying asleep on stone benches deep within the temple complex. Rahitan returned from one conversation, deeply concerned for the future of the islands, but was told to remember that each place and person has a pre-determined destiny a fact of which he was well aware.

Leaving Ggantija on the island of Gwadex, the Atema continued their pilgrimage around the world. In the lands of the Celts they met at a giant stone henge with learned Druids, who taught them of the Celtic gods and goddesses who they worshipped. Usually their ceremonies were held in forest clearings and stone circles: goddesses like Aine - Goddess of love, summer, sovreignty; Arianrhod - Goddess of beauty, fertility, reincarnation, the sky, weaving, enchantment.; Blodeuwedd - Goddess of flowers, lunar mysteries, wisdom; and gods the Amaethon - God of agriculture, animal husbandry, and Arawn - God of the dead, hunting, revenge.

Like the Atema, the Druids fulfilled a wide variety of roles among their Celtic peoples - as philosophers, teachers, judges, the repository of communal wisdoms about the natural world and the traditions of the people, and as mediators between humans and the gods. With no written word, the Druids committed most of their knowledge and teachings to memory, and some said it took them twenty years of study to complete the teachings.

The Atema listened respectfully, but were unimpressed with the need for an individual god for so many different conditions, for they knew that Io was the Supreme One, who overlighted them all. Garlita and Aloma complimented several of the leaders for their variety of clothing, for the Druids wore white robes in ceremony, grey bull hides in battle and many speckled robes on state occasions, such as banquets and court appearances. The kings usually wore robes of crimson or red, while the foster sons of kings wore cloaks of scarlett, purple or blue.

One point of interest to Rahitan, that much-travelled priest, was the story of the Greek, Partholon, who reached Ireland after a big flood. It was said that he came from Macedonia or central Greece with his wife; his three sons, their wives and three Druids, Fios, Eólas, Fochmarc.The names of the three druids meant cognition, knowledge and inquiry. Myths such as this carried a core of truth. In this case the story could signify that knowledge was brought to Ireland by Greek settlers who brought with them wise men to spread knowledge and educate the locals, accompanied by their holy men and women – the Druids.

However, it seemed the reign of the Druids was coming to an end. Following the Roman invasion of Gaul, their religious orders were being suppressed by the Roman government under the 1st century CE emperors Tiberius and Claudius. Ratihan invited those who wished to flee their northern land to relocate to the land of their original people far from the influence of Roman conquest. Few chose to do so, for like the Atema, the Druids preferred to care for their people until it was no longer possible. With heavy hearts, the Atema left the sacred groves of the Druids with a feeling of dread, as they realised that they might never meet their new-found friends again.

From the land of the Druids, the Atema bi-located to meet with shamans dressed in seal skins, who lived in igloos made from blocks of ice, in the cold, desolate northern land of the midnight sun. Their next destination was the land inhabited red-skinned peoples whose Chiefs wore colourful eagle feather headdresses that fell to their feet and whose people wore buckskin clothes and lived in movable teepees. Theirs wise medicine-men and women were aware of their future demise at the hand of a white race that would inhabit their vast tracts of land and descimate their buffalo, but for now they lived in peace and harmony, with only the occasional skirmish with neighbouring tribes

Most of them knew Rahitan, and all were elevated and grateful for the contact with so many Atema.

Their last visit was with their legendary ancestors living in cities and villages made from great blocks of stone, situated high in the Andean mountains, and overlooking a vast jungle spread out below for as far as the eye could see. When the Atema materialised around a large stone placed on a circular plinth in a village high above a fast flowing river, the local inhabitants gave a loud shout of joy, for they had been well prepared for the arrival of visitors from across the wide ocean. The Chief, Haykuy, welcomed them with a song of praise as they stood surveying the colourful costumes worn by their hosts. Shy children peeped from behind their mother's voluminous skirts while sturdy boys chased each other around the crowd.

Striding out from the group, a large man dressed in a short belted robe, began to speak.

"Welcome to the misty mountains of the Chachapoyas, and our fortress village of Keulap. We are called the Cloud People, for our homeland is often hidden by clouds. I am Valqai, the High Priest of my people. We received your telepathic massage. I am happy to greet you, Master Rahitan of the Atema. I have heard of your great wisdom, even in such an isolated village as we inhabit. Our healers and story tellers often communicate with other tribes who are closer to the coast, and exchange stories with sailors who occasionally visit the ports to trade. When your request to visit was received by our Priestess, I prepared the way."

Rahitan smiled. "Greetings, Valqai. We never expected to find your secluded village, but somehow we were connected with a vibrational beam that drew us here. Perhaps you can tell me how this occurred? But before you do, let me introduce my companions."

Each of the twelve travellers was introduced and began to relax. Valqai led them to a large round stone house with a steep roof thatched with reeds and drew aside a colourful curtain, behind which several women and children were seated.

"This is my family," he informed them in a language they all understood. "They are in seclusion, for some families are hidden when strangers arrive. In the past, some savage warriors have invaded our village, so I always take precautions to protect our loved ones."

Speaking in the local Runa Shimi tongue, he gestured to the closest women to come forward, and they shyly complied. Three looms were arrayed along the wall, behind which sat women busily engaged in weaving fine looking cloth. Garlita was intrigued and moved closer to inspect the work.

"This weaving is as fine as any I have seen, except in the land of Khem," she marvelled. "Where and how did they learn to do such exquisite work, Valqai?"

"Ah, that is quite a story which I will relate to you all later this evening when we gather for our evening ritual of blessing Pachamama, our Earth Mother. Now, please accompany me on a walk around our village and meet some of our people. Many have never seen a person from another land, or of a different skin colour, especially that dark skin of your song master. They will ask many questions, and I will endeavour to translate."

The afternoon passed quickly, and towards evening fine misty clouds began to engulf the village, shrouding it in a cloak of invisibility.

The Atema were ushered into a large round hut, with soft, colourful blankets folded in a sleeping area. Several women bustled around bringing dishes of food they had prepared.

Rahitan looked embarrassed. "Oh dear. I forgot to mention to Valqai that we don't eat food. I must find him before it is served." He rushed outside and immediately became disorientated in the thick mist swirling around the hut. "Valqai," he shouted at the top of his voice, "Where are you? I need to tell you something important."

Valqai materialised beside him, a look of concern on his handsome face. "What is it, Rahitan? Is the food not to your liking?"

"I am so sorry, Valqai," replied Rahitan. "I omitted to mention that the Atema do not partake of solid food. We occasionally drink nectar and water, but have transcended the need to take sustenance in the form of food. Instead we receive it from the energy in the air and sunshine." Looking at the thickening mist he added, "But if we lived in such a climate, with so little sunlight, we could starve. Please tell your women we are sorry to have inconvenienced them."

"Ah, that means all the more for us. They will not understand but will believe anything you tell them, so ignorant are they of your existence. They already think you are Gods. This is something I also wish to understand, so I can share it with our people, as it is hard to find sufficient food during the cold months." Valqai turned and went into the hut to inform the women to take the food to the men's quarters.

A short time later, Valqai invited the group to accompany him to the Chief's hut, where several other men and women were seated on large cushions. Haykuy invited them to sit and opened the evening with a welcome and a local song. He then invited Kaitewha to contribute one of his songs. A smoky fire burned in the central grate, its smoke wending its way up to a hole in the roof and dispersing in the mist. In this air of friendship and openess, Haykuy began to talk.

"You wanted to know how our women discovered the art of fine weaving. They knew how to collect the wool from our wikuna animals and spin it by twisting it in their fingers, but this technique was rather crude. One day a woman appeared in our midst with an elegant spindle and a distaff to hold the unspun fibres. She taught a few of our women how to spin fine thread, then showed them how to construct a loom on which to weave the fine thread. Our cleverer women quickly learned how to spin both flax and wool, and create colourful dyes from local plants and rocks. When they were totally proficient, the stranger just disappeared. We never saw her again, but her legacy lives on in our beautiful fabrics and designs. We never found out anything about her.

Now, I wish to share some our creation stories with you, and to hear of yours. It is possible they came from the same ancient source. Indigenous peoples have been inhabiting the Amazon basin and these mountains for several thousand years, sustained by crops grown in the rich black soils maintained with fire and fertilizer. Those of us chosing to live amongst the clouds trade with the people of the lowland for food, exchanging our holy nectar which we call caapi. It is made from pounding the root of a vine into a paste and boiling it with another plant until it forms a dense liquid, which is then mixed with water before being drunk during our ceremonies. It has a bitter taste which takes some time to get used to. It has been known to our people for thousands of years and is used mostly as a medicine to prevent diseases. Caapi can cause bowels to become very active, and induces vomiting, but this leads to a healing effect, enabling the body to get rid of toxic substances. We know that the body needs regular cleansing to remain healthy. Caapi also affects the mind, causing visions, which can lead to a greater understanding of reality."

Morpheus could not longer contain his excitement. "We also have a wisdom drink. Our master brewer, Pausinin, has such a recipe although I suspect he uses different plants. It has the effect of opening the mind to the higher realms, while leaving the body unaffected, except for a certain weakness of the muscles. Can we do such a ceremony with you, Haykuy?"

"Certainly," replied Haykuy. "We can merge our higher minds, for as long as such rituals are practiced by learned men and women, we will continue to exist. We are able to share a link between our plane and higher planes of existence, linking to the spirit world in order to heal, contact deceased ancestors, influence the weather and uplift consciousness. This we will do in a ceremony tomorrow evening, as the drink takes a while to prepare and should be drunk fresh. You will have noticed that our skin is very white and many of us have fair hair, caused not from lack of sun at this altitude, but from our ancestors who came from across the sea, a long time ago. They left many sarcophagi as the final resting place of our wise men, a process we still practice and will show you tomorrow. The body is mummified before being placed in a wooden coffin, which is then plastered with clay, straw and gravel, before their likeness is formed on the front. We then stand them in a niche high up on a cliff so they can watch over and protect us against our enemies, and also provide a link between the living and the dead. Now Valqai will tell us one of our creation stories."

Valqai stood in silence for several minutes, as though summoning another level of himself, then began to speak in the voice he used for relating long stories. Finally, he opened his eyes and looked at the Atema seated around him.

"My friends from the land of the long white cloud, I am delighted to share our story. Then we look forward to hearing yours, although I suspect you are star-seeds." Valqai took a deep breath, and began....

"Once upon a time, a long, long time ago a woman named Yaye lived among us. She was the first woman of creation, who drowned men in visions. As a result, to our people intercourse is a visionary experience in which men are drowned in visions. Yaye became pregnant by the sun-god who had impregnated her through the eye, and their child was born in a flash of light. Yaye cut the umbilical cord and rubbed the child's body with magical herbs, thus shaping its body. The child, who lived to become an old man, became known as Caapi, after a narcotic plant. He jealously guarded his hallucinatory powers, his Caapi, which was the source from which our men received their fertile seed. The myth essentially tells the story of the alchemical marriage, in which woman seeks union with the god-source, the divine power of creation. As a result, the religious experience is also always a sexual one, as we seek to make it sublime, to pass from the erotic, the sensual, to a mystical union with the mythic era. This union is the ultimate goal, attained by a mere handful but coveted by all."

Zenita nudged Morpheus. "That is similar to what we teach in the Sanctuary of Love, a knowing that I hope you will learn when we return from this amazing journey. Listen well, my husband."

Valqai frowned at Zenita before continuing. "There is a slightly different version of this story told by some other local tribes who say that the first people came from the sky in a serpent canoe, and that Father Sun had promised them a magical drink that would connect them with the radiant powers of the heavens. While the men were in what was called the House of the Waters, attempting to make this promised drink, their first woman went into the forest to give birth. She came back with a boy radiating golden light, whose body she rubbed with leaves. This luminous boy-child was the vine, and each of the men cut off a piece of this living being that became his piece of the vine lineage. In another variation of this myth, the serpent canoe came from the Milky Way, bringing a man, a woman, and three plants for the people – cassava, coca and caapi. They also regarded them as gifts from the Sun, a kind of container for the yellow-gold light of the Sun, that provided the rules for the first people on how to live and speak. There are other versions of these stories, but they will have to wait until another time, as we retire early in our village. So I will bid you all good night."

Valqai turned and disappeared out the door to return to his own hut, as did the rest of the people in the mountaintop village.

Next morning, after a fitful sleep, the Atema rose to welcome the rising of the sun and give thanks to Io for their ongoing journey. During the night, Aloma experienced a powerful dream. All through the night she was charged with energy rushing though her body and tingling her nerves, until she felt she would burst. Constant communication with an intense Being of Light filled her mind with information. She saw herself in a verdant garden filled with large, colourful flowers, butterflies and singing birds. A stream along which small waterfalls cascaded gave the garden a sense of serenity.

On waking, she told Rahitan, of her dream who took her to meet the oldest man she had ever seen. He cracked a toothless smile and said in a voice hoarse with time, "Ah, my little one. You have been touched by our great Mother, who is our giver of life. Remember what she told you, for it will be one of your greatest gifts in this life and help you to teach the girl-child you are soon to bring into this world. Teach her well, for she is to be a great Princess."

Moving his head slightly the old man became silent and gazed at Aloma with rheumy eyes and after closing them, seemed to disappear into himself.

"We had better go." whispered Rahitan. "He spends long days out of his body travelling among the stars. His brothers never know if he will return so keep his body warm."

Kaitewha looked at Aloma. "What did he mean about the girl-child you will birth?" he inquired.

"I will tell you later tonight, my love. Now we don't have time, as Valqai is waiting for us," she responded.

Valqai greeted them at the altar stone.

"Greeting, my friends, I trust you spent a restful night. Today we will share some more wisdom and prepare for the ceremony of the caapi journey that will alter your perception of how you see your existence."

The day was spent harmoniously, sharing knowledge and practical ways to make life more comfortable, such as the making of a more refined pottery, weaving reed mats and constructing basic furniture, for the Chachapoyas had not known of these arts. They, in return, showed Morpheus how to prepare the concoction they would drink and explained its expected effects.

Valqai explained, "The earliest effects of the liquid tend to be a warming of the stomach, followed by a spreading feeling of physical relaxation and mental calm. While there is no loss of vigour or alertness, you may see visual images, along with more acute hearing and smelling sensations. Weaker doses of caapi produce a mild detachment from one's body and surroundings, which allows one to critically examine small details without identifying with feelings and thoughts. Stronger forms of the liquid create the visual apparitions of irregular shapes; recurring and colourful geometric patterns, distorted and fleeting images, and out-of-body experiences or dream-like visions filled with the familiar and the fanciful."

Turning to Rahitan he continued, "As your people do not partake of physical food, you do not need a strong brew, and will have no trouble with the negative side-effects experienced by some unprepared people. Those on the spiritual journey have at least modified their diet to lighten their body. We do not encourage the use of caapi by unenlightened ones."

Following the settng of the sun, and the evening meal of the villagers, Valqai called everyone to an open area containing stone seats surrounding a blazing fire. As they took their places, the ancient Priest, whom Aloma had met only that morning, shuffled into the centre of the circle and held up his arms, revealing tatoos of writhing serpents with eyes of gold, very similar to Rahitans. The Atema let out a collective gasp, realising there were still more mysteries to uncover. Slowly he lifted a jug of liquid and muttered an incantation into its contents, and with the assistance of a Priestess, filled a number of beakers with the muddy-looking brew. She then presented a beaker to each of the Atema and to several of the Chachapoyas, while the old Priest continued his prayers, occasional blowing into the jug. The Priestess explained that he was filling the caapi with the universal power and its protection to assist those taking the journey that the caapi would induce.

Aloma whispered to Garlita. "I would prefer not to drink this liquid, for I know I am to bear a daughter in several moon's time. It may do some damage and I am not prepared to risk it. Please say nothing to Kaitewha about the child, as I wish to surprise him at the right moment. Now is not the time."

"Oh, how wonderful news, my Princess. You are wise, for I believe this concoction causes vomiting and purging, not a good idea in early pregnancy. Why not pretend to drink it and then watch how it affects the rest of us, and copy us. I don't think they would like you to refuse their offer," Garlita replied. "The old man would understand, as he guessed you were pregnant, but how he knew is a mystery. I am not sure about Valqai, although he has a wife, I do not think she is involved in the ceremonies."

At the invitation of Valqai the group raised their beakers and drank the foul tasting liquid. Morpheus nearly spat his out. "Great Io, that is awful. I bet Pausanin could improve on the taste." Dutifully, he drank the rest of the contents, then sat in silence with the others before they all lay down to surrender to the effects of the caapi. Aloma managed to pour hers out into a small hole in the ground beside her stone seat. As the group relaxed, visions began to arise. They lay around the fire for some time, before staggering to their hut to sleep. Garlita later described her experience.

"I was immersed in a swirling light of many colours, intense and somehow familiar, which lifted me into a higher level of consciousness and filled me with such love that I could hardly breathe. It was even more intense than the love I feel for Rahitan. That feeling lasted for some time and then I seemed to enter into my body and explore its state of health. The only condition I found that needed healing was an imbalance in my right hip, which was causing me some pain. Now it is released and normal again. Finally I was lifted at great speed towards an intense electric-blue light which had a circular pattern decorating its edges. As I sped into this light, I exploded into millions of shards of light and just disappeared. There was no more I or even We. I merged with the body of Io and became a cell in its body, feeling so loved and blissful that I never wanted to return to my physical body, which I reluctantly managed to do. That is what we have to look forward to at the end of our long sojourn on Earth. That vision will sustain me for a very long time, until perhaps I forget it if I have to in the future, incarnate into an ordinary body, which I trust will be in one destined to become a member of The Atema."

"Yes," addd Kaitwha, "It is not unlike my journey. I was surrounded by the coloured lights but I didn't need the healing. Instead I was taken to a place where music is created and immersed into its mysterious allure. It is hard to believe that such a tiny amount of liquid can induce sensations so overwhelming and unlike anything I've ever felt. My heart rate increased and my body heat rose and fell. I was sweating one moment and shivering the next. My hands and feet tingled and I could feel the liquid circulating around my body. My stomach wanted to expel the stuff several times and felt like demons were having a battle in there, until I finally succumbed and released the lot, trying not to disturb you all. But I was aware of the same vomiting happening around me. I was entranced by a million stars in the sky and the smell of burning sacred herbs. At no time did I feel uncomfortable, except during the purge, and now I am just content to be blissed out for a while. How did you go, Morpheus?"

Morpheus growled and wiped his beard clean. "I felt pretty irritable for a time so shifted my focus back to the intention for taking this journey, as suggested by Valqai. My senses became very acute and I could feel each organ in my body groaning under the assault of this stuff, although I enjoyed the sensation of floating up into the light surrounding Io after I had chucked it up. When we get home I will work with Pausanin to improve the taste and purging effects but Valqai told us that it was to bring on cleansing of toxins from the body. However, as we do not partake of food and our land is fresh and clean, I do not see how we can have absorbed toxins into our body. I have no idea if a similar plant grows in our land, but we can take some back to compare and perhaps cultivate. Our master brewer does have knowledge of a similar recipe. A funny thing though; my body feels very weak and I have little control over it although my head is clear. Let me just lie here for a while."

Rahitan said he had been reluctant to drink the caapi for he did not want his ability to commune with Io diminished, which he thought might happen. But, as he surrendered to the experience, his visual and spiritual perceptions were considerably enhanced, and as his soul wandered around the universe filled with amazing colours, he became part of the universe. Great Beings welcomed him to their worlds and he experienced teachings far in advance of the ones he had learned during his long life. If this was a product of his own mind, then what was the greater mind which overlighted him. Perhaps this was where the information written on the golden scrolls originated.

But it was the journey Thieron took that really amazed his Atema family. He looked different.

"I came to the realization that I was inadequate and tried to deny the fact that I am a lost cause. However, it was just my ego defending itself, threatening to lead me into a deep, dark place, which I had to resist or I would have been lost. I accept my failings and this plant knows me better than I know myself, and that I am not in complete control of my actions and reactions, thoughts and feelings, but a projection of my soul which is connected to the universal mind. My ego was getting a bit inflated so I surrendered it as a step toward this long and difficult road we are on to bring me back into balance. I hope Erana loves the new me."

Eran embraced her husband and smiled. "After the trip I have just undertaken, I will love you for all eternity. I know you are my true soul mate, dear Thieron. I so look forward to the end of this journey so we can continue practicing our connubial bliss, and conceiving our son."

"What about you Aloma?" asked Kaitewha. "What did you experience?"

"I only pretended to drink the caapi because we have a baby to bring into the world. She was conceived in Luxor. Now it is time to go home, my love," Aloma said as she hugged him.

"Yaaaahoooo," yelled Kaitewha. The cry echoed around the encircling cliffs causing birds to startle. Great faces of the Apus imprinted in the surrounding mountains smiled benignly down from their perpetual homes. "I am going to be a father," whooped Kaitewha.

"Rahitan, take us home please," said Aloma.

"First, let us say farewell to our hosts and thank them for their hospitality. They have shown us more than we expected. Have you packed the items we collected during our great journey?"

The Atema gathered in a circle around the central stone revered by the Chachapoyas and bid their farewells, promising to return just before their next annihilation.

Addressing his people, Rahitan smiled. "We will take the fast route. Concentrate on our village centre. Now, bi-locate," he said.

Alerted by Rahitan's telepathic message, the Atema were waiting around the courtyard outside their home temple when the travellers materialised in a circle around the greenstone statue. The entire village turned out to welcome the travellers home. Murmurs of approval met the group when the clothes they wore were fondled and inspected. The delicate craftsmanship of gold jewellery caused the most admiration. Each had managed to transport a large bundle of gifts home. Angelica whisked them all away soon after they arrived for a cleansing bath, massage and a change of clothes and give them all a physical check-up to see that no parasites or fleas had stowed into their hair and Pausanin gave them a strong purgative although they protested that they were thoroughly purged by the caapi root. Within an hour they appeared refreshed and clean, dressed in new garments, on the dais in front of the greenstone statue. A great cheer erupted from the people, delighted to have them return safely. A riotous evening of celebration and story telling merged into the rising sun meditation. Pausanin had not been idle in their absence and great quantities of his herbal brew disappeared down the hatch that night.

Three months was the longest time anyone had been gone from the village, except when taken by death.

Life returned to normal until Aloma's daughter, surrounded by a protective ball of light, entered into the world. One month later, Erana gave birth to a son they called Haeata - a beam of light. The babies grew rapidly, blessed with loving and protective parents and an extended family of three hundred and fifty doting aunts and uncles. Haeata inherited the bright red curly hair of his father, Thieron, and strangely, Annaraleah's hair was also brilliant auburn, growing long and straight. They were nicknamed the Twin Flames, and showed a great ability to learn, absorbing the teachings of their elders. Shortly after their sixteenth birthdays, Rahitan decided it was time they were betrothed, for only three years remained until the predicted demise of the Atema and their village. Three weeks after the ceremony of binding together, Rahitan, Garlita, Kaitewha, Aloma, Thieron and Erana accompanied the young couple on another world tour, revisiting the places and people of power to introduce sights and ideas yet unknown to them. Isis, who became the perfect grandmother, always being there when she was needed, but not interfering when she wasn't, had insisted the Twin Flame's destiny was to remain in their bodies to carry the spark of the Atema, passing it down through the generations until the time came for its next reunion. She had also insisted they meet the important people of the world, those who kept the secret knowledge true. They could choose to live anywhere, within any tribe, or could roam around spending a short time in different countries. Their children would interbreed with tribes of different skin, globally seeding the Atema.

Finally, as Tane had predicted, the long anticipated time arrived. The greenstone statue of the Princess holding the large golden ball, recharged with love and blessings of all the people was removed to the etheric plane for safe keeping, along with the golden scrolls and other precious objects not destined to be destroyed, only hidden until the next epoch. In the full knowledge of impending events the people were given an opportunity to leave for a safer part of the country. No one thought to save their bodies at the expense of a glorious ascension of the group soul of the Atema, except for Annaraleah and Haeata and their small red haired daughter, Annibale. Isis came to escort them to stay for a while in her sanctuary high in the Himalayan mountains, until all danger had passed. As before, the Princess suggested a large party made merry with copious quantities of Pausanin's herbal brew liberally laced with caapi, to assist their passing into another dimension. The Atema sang and danced as the earth shook, the buildings collapsed and their world changed. This time the effect was different. As a caldera opened up under the great lake, its huge volume of water drained into the molten chasms below causing towering columns of sulphurous steam loaded with pumice pellets to shoot high into the sky, before reigning death and destruction across the land.

The Atema lifted their voices in one long praise of their creator, Io, and felt a column of light surround them, pulling most of them towards it the instant before the ground subsided and their spirits watched safely from above while their bodies dissolved into ash. A lesser number than previously didn't make it through the shock and sound barrier soaring around the area and were destined to wander as before, suspended in time and space until released by the future selves of those who were freed.

One evening Annaraleah called Haeata and their daughter, Annibale, to the balcony of their bungalow to see the sunset. They knew the volcanic cataclysm had occurred when the evening sky turned bright red. This spectacle lasted for weeks and nightly glowed red with reflected ash captured by solar winds encircling the earth. Although they mourned for the physical passing of their parents and extended family, they knew better than to grieve for their spiritual passing, for they never died. Their destiny lay in life everlasting, with their genes destined live on in the red haired people of the world.

Their spirit overlighted a noble soul wherever one awakened to the light.

Isis joined them to watch the sun set over the snow capped peaks. "The land of your birth," she told them, "has a great destiny to follow, and will begin to realise this at the end of the next millennium, in about nineteen hundred years. Those of us who are scheduled to be involved in this great time will reincarnate, either directly there or in another country and find our way to the land at the end of the Rainbow. The call will be very strong, unable to be denied."

She turned to the south-east, raised her arms high and called in her rich melodious voice. "Sleep long and rest well, noble Atema, until the time of awakening, for then you will be very busy and need all the strength and courage you can muster. My love and blessing on you all."

A voice came floating on the gentle wind, "Farewell, my daughter. Travel well, as will we. We will all be together again to help prepare for the time when the earth is due to enter the next Golden Age, when wars will cease, no people will go to bed hungry and prosperity will be available to everyone. Perhaps you can visit me in between some of the many incarnations you will have on earth before that glorious time. I will train your daughter to soul travel." Looking into the emerald eyes of her flame-haired grand-daughter Aloma sighed. "I love you, Annibale."

THIRTEEN

The Reawakening – Aotearoa – 1992

The sensation of being watched felt very strong as the people in the cavalcade of cars drove slowly along the narrow dirt road leading deep into the ancient growth Kaimanawa Forest. The road twisted past fallen trees and climbed up and down steep hills, while dappled sunlight played through the thick forest growth, plunging the cars into light and then shadow. Startled bird calls split the silent air and the sense of spirit became intense. When the group of around a dozen excited people gathered in the small car park just past their destination, called The Wall, they shared their feelings and insights of the twenty-five kilometre drive from the turnoff at the main road between Taupo and Napier. Their guide, Vernon from the Tauhara Centre in Taupo called for silence. "Welcome to The Wall. This is my third visit," he told them, "and each time I have brought a group here we have all experienced strong recollections. I suggest we walk in silence back to the Wall and approach with respect."

The chattering ceased as the group moved slowly in twos and threes to stand by the sentinel stone still guarding the wall of cyclopean blocks, some with bevelled upper surfaces, built by ancient craftsmen in some unknown time of the history of New Zealand. Four levels comprising over a score of perfectly aligned blocks of granite were all that remained. A tree covered tell hid secrets from prying eyes until the day archaeologists could excavate the ruins once all the controversy had died down, and the reality that a far more ancient people than the Maori once inhabited these shores. In awe they stopped before the altar shaped stone to make invocations and ask permission from the guardian spirits of the place to be allowed to enter this sacred area.

Judith separated from the group and made her way up a track through the native beech towards a circular group of trees. She had travelled from Australia to Aotearoa - New Zealand following an insistant inner call and to participate in the planetary event known as Time Shift. Now she felt a strong urge to follow the track she had found. *Seems to have been a few visitors here over the years for such an obvious track to be worn. I wonder where it leads.*

The track led right through the centre of a circle of native beech trees, and continued up the hill. Stopping before the largest tree in the circle of five she raised her hands in greeting. From the palm of her left hand streamed forth light showing a symbol in the shape of a large blue eye in the centre of an orange diamond, projecting upwards for some six meters. This showed an image of a universal symbol recognised by all sacred-site guardians, her spiritual passport, enabling her to show her credentials to the guardians of the area. From her right hand beamed her personal symbol; that of a shining gold and silver cadeus surrounded by rainbow colours flowing in an arc around coiled serpents. A few moments later came an acceptance in the form of a strong breeze. The keepers of the area knew her timeless symbol and opened the dimensional gateway. Judith's mind communicated.

Greetings, I come in peace and memory of ancient times in the hope of reconnecting with you.

In the centre of the circle of trees, a fine clump of moss sprouted tiny cream flowers nodding on invisible stems. Light appeared to emanate from the ground below it. *I'll stay here quietly and tune in. This is a place of ancient energy and perhaps those who live here in spirit body will communicate.* Judith sat on a tree root just outside the circle and closed her eyes. Almost immediately her inner vision opened and she saw the area in a very different perspective. With her fourth eye activated, she scanned the area for beings who can not be seen with ordinary sight as they inhabit a different dimensional frequency than the one with which most humans are familiar. A tall shimmering light blue haze appeared before Judith and she smiled as a form emerged in the shape of a woman clothed in a flowing feathery cloak that swept over her feet. Her eyes shone with an intense blue sparkle and her golden hair hung down in long gossamer strands over her shoulders. Around her head she wore a bright band woven from natural fibres, with a clear quartz crystal attached over her third eye area. Strongly resisting the temptation to open her eyes for the vision was so strong, Judith communicated with her mind.

"Greetings. I am Judith. My present homeland lies across the sea to the west, but I remember this land and love it well. Who are you?"

The tall feather cloaked woman responded. *"I am the memory of you from an ancient time. Soon your recall will be total. I am called Aloma of the Atema, the tribe who once lived in peace and harmony in this great forest. We were one of the tribes of Enlightened Ones who cared for this land shaped like a the great fish, floating in the Southern Ocean. Our world was annihilated nearly two thousand years ago when Lake Taupo blew its body of water all over the land, causing great death and destruction across the entire area. Twice we have been blown asunder. We have lived as the shadow of ourselves until now. Some five years ago we began calling to our long lost people to gather once again in this forest. But few have come. With magnetic shifts about to happen on Earth, we need to regroup the*

Atema, the Enlightened children of the Rainbow to assist in raising the consciousness of the land and her people."

Another blurry light appeared and formed into the figure of a tall man, also wearing a long cloak, but his shimmered with a green black haze. His eyes glowed darkly and long black hair hung down over his shoulders. He appeared to merge with Aloma then the two separate forms appeared again.

"I am Kaitewha, the songmaster of the Atema, our Princess Aloma's twin soul. I welcome you to the remnants of our village. Several years ago a vibration passed through this area activating this aspect of us from a long sleep, although our souls could fly free, and even incarnate in other bodies for an intermittent life. It seems like the time to regroup has come, but I think we will not rebuild the temple this time. What time frame are we in? We know nothing of the outside world as an electromagnetic barrier was placed around this area to prevent any from straying. It can be easily penetrated by insensitive humans. Others like you who are more aware can free us to move on. I see you also have a companion."

Judith opened her eyes and saw no one near so closed them again. Into her inner vision came her old friend Gudjewa, the light dreaming man from her home in Australia. He always appeared when clearing work of trapped spirit beings needed to be done. Gudjewa had been the Aboriginal guardian spirit of a area of sacred land in the western Blue Mountains, where Judith and her husband ran a spiritual retreat centre. During a transition time a few years earlier releasing many guardians from their ancient roll, Gudjewa had moved from his traditional Aboriginal form to enter again into the Universal light stream from whence all beings come, and to which they ultimately return after a sojourn on earth or wherever they choose to spend a series of incarnations. He had chosen to assist Judith in her planetary healing work. Judith smiled in welcome.

"Let me introduce Gudjewa, from Glastonbell in Australia. I think you were aware of such a land. It lies over the western sea and is a great continent now inhabited by people from every country on Earth. There are nearly two hundred separate nationalities who intermingle and share their seed to create a land of tolerance and compassion for refugees fleeing from war torn countries. It is similar in this land. As Gudjewa has appeared to us, it means there is clearing work to do. Are some of your people ready to ascend to the Lifestream?"

In answer, Aloma sent out a long, clear call. Soon several other beings appeared and telepathically communicated. One who wore the dark blue robes of the priestly caste came forward.

"Greetings, you who are one of us from the future. I knew the present aspect of you, who was once Aloma, would soon come. I see you have already made her acquaintance. My name is Rahitan, High Priest of the Atema. I look forward to meeting my future body. You will be bringing him here in four years. I wish it could be sooner, but he is not yet ready to receive this information. This is Garlita, our High Priestess. Our future lives now enjoy a normal married state, as we wished before we were suspended. This is my scribe, Thieron. He has faithfully kept records of all past events. Yes, there are many here who wish to ascend. I have been awaiting the energy pattern to release them through the sacred vortex. Many have reincarnated into the present time frame who will need to come to this place to integrate the remnant of themselves left here to become completely whole, although many are still unaware of this. I will call my people."

Rahitan put his fingers to his forehead and closed his eyes. Soon silvery-blue shapes began forming into recognisable beings, all very tall and wearing similar long feathery cloaks, who crowded around the circle of trees on the knoll above the wall. The people Judith arrived with were nowhere to be seen, although she could hear them talking. *Surely they must be able to see these beings. If not, I must have slipped through into another dimension.*

Telepathically Judith addressed Rahitan. *"How is it that you live here? I am aware that when a traumatic event occurs, it can be constantly replayed holographically, but you don't appear to be trapped in a hologram like those who die in battle and are forever fighting the final battle. What has happened here?"*

"It is a long story, one that I wish you to write. I know you can do it. When you leave here Aloma and Kaitewha will accompany you on your travels around the island of the great fish so they can become acquainted with civilisation in the late twentieth century, for I know that is the date prophesied in the golden scrolls. They tell of our reawakening and release from being trapped in this place. Now, what do you wish us to do to prepare those who are soon to depart?"

Judith stood still with her hands held in front of her chest, palms facing outwards. Gudjewa instructed those who wished to ascend to form two lines, one for men and one for women on either side of the vortex now appearing in front of Judith. Its shimmering coils merged together to create a solid looking funnel of light. Then he beckoned them to jump in. Because the vibrational rate of men and women is different even in spirit form, the vortex was slightly adjusted on each side to accommodate either men or women and children. Slowly at first, then with increasing confidence, nearly two hundred of the trapped souls entered the vortex to be transported to the realms of the Lifestream, so they could either reincarnate, merge fully with a present incarnation, or return to the heart of the creator. As the last being ascended in the vortex, it disappeared. Soon only about a dozen remained. Rahitan's mind reached out.

"There is still work for us to do on this plane. When the key figures are reunited, for you are all presently incarnate and living in or visiting New Zealand, we in this spirit form can be reabsorbed into you. I do not know if you are aware, but during every life you leave an impression of your presence wherever you have spent intense time. You Judith, have a lot of yourself to reabsorb here but the greatest part of you will be

discovered in Peru, at an abandoned city high in the Andes. You will visit this place soon. Some of us have travelled there in past eons to commune with the enlightened ones who guard that magical land. I am aware that you have been planning a visit for many years. Now it is timely."

That has to be Machu Picchu or Kuelap. I do long to visit those places, thought Judith. *I have already absorbed many aspects of myself during my previous travels to sacred sites.* Then focussing on Rahitan she asked, *"How is this communication talking place? I have communicated with light beings before but never understood the principle."*

"*Information from higher realms travels on thought beams and light beams. Thought and light are intertwined. Thought is the feeling level, and light more intellectual. We are all portions of glorious beings designed to express joy, who are striving to become greater. We have the ability to learn through thought, although we are connected to the multi-dimensional self through feelings. It is feelings that are the weak points in most humans, but are what make us so human. Of course, that is when we are not fragmented, as we are now. Those who have recently ascended can either find their multi-dimensional self and merge with it, whether or not it is incarnate anywhere on this or another planet, or rest in the heart of the Creator of all worlds. A number left permanently during the Small Bang, as we call the second erruption. Those of us who remain know that our soul has entered another body and we will soon be reunited. You and Aloma are ready to merge. Kaitewha is not an aspect of your present husband from whom you will soon separate. The one of whom Kaitewha is an aspect, will arrive on these shores soon and find you, for you are twin flames for once and future times. You will have a challenge to create balance in your life, but soon will undergo a rearrangement of your light encoded filaments that form the strands of each helix. These will be increased again, for once long ago, thousands of light encoded filaments were purposely rearranged in the helix structure of the human body, when certain creator geneticists*

*removed several of the helices to enable humankind to be controlled,
when they began to think for themselves. The time of control is very
nearly over. It is an awesome task to carry light, but many in human
form are now ready, as the Earth is due to move into her vibrational
shift. very shortly. That is why the call has gone out to bring a number
of you to our secret village and let you walk through the dimensions of
yourselves. To walk between the worlds. It may take many more years
to complete our mission, even into the next century, for enough souls to
awaken to their true destiny, but the event has been set in motion and
will move to its conclusion. We have no way of knowing when and Io
cannot tell us. It all depends on humanity awakening from the illusion
that it is not just a body but a soul.*

Judith sat with tears falling down her cheeks. Not tears of sadness,
but of love, for her memory of the time spent with the Atema was
returning, and the element of love was so strong. Into her mind came
the message,

*You are a light being of steadfastness, power and beauty expressing
those qualities wherever you travel. You have the ability to manipulate
form through thought. Travel well our companion, and return soon, for
there is much more to learn. When you depart, Aloma and Kaitewha
will leave with you. Teach them well.*

Judith opened her eyes as all the light beings dissolved and
disappeared from her vision. She heard her human friends calling
her name and watched their surprise when she reappeared, sitting
calmly on a fallen log above them.

"I'm sure you weren't there a minute ago," called Veronica, the
woman in whose car they had travelled. "What has happened. You
look as though you have seen a ghost."

"I have just met the guardian spirits of the area. They say they are
the Atema, the Enlightened Ones who used to live in a great temple

complex here before Lake Taupo blew up nearly two thousand years ago. They have been in a sort of energetic suspended animation ever since. They have finally been released by our visit. Two of them wish to leave with us and travel around the island with Philip and I on the pilgrimage we have planned, to prepare for Time Shift. in mid-July. They wish to catch up on human behaviour and development in the latter days of the twentieth century."

"Hmmmph," was all Veronica said, then added, "I suppose they will want to travel in my car? What do they want to learn? If they are so enlightened, what can we teach them? Humankind has reached such a low level of development I think we have gone backwards, not forwards."

"I think they can teach us more than we can teach them. They just need to be able to function in the new energies pouring down onto Earth at this present time. There has to be a reason for the increase in these energies and I think it has to do with the coming Time Shift ceremony to be held on your land," said Judith. "As we align ourselves to the light and the greatest fulfilment of our being, we must draw into ourselves all that we need. Time Shift is due to change the spiral of descent from clockwise, bringing spirit into matter, to anti-clockwise to become the spiral of ascent, taking spiritualised matter back to a higher dimension. That is the start of our journey home."

"Home? I trust you are right. Because of Time Shift I have invested a lot of time and money in my property to create a suitable home for the new energy pouring down into the Spinner wheel that you and Philip activated, and now overlights this Taupo region. Let's hope it gives me the ability to learn through thought, as I grow tired of the constant flow of chatter and information bombarding me," replied Veronica.

She was a sprightly white haired woman with roadmap lines covering her weather -beaten face; a fit woman in her early seventies who spent much of her life outdoors, working tirelessly to create a garden from animal ravaged land. She had very recently sold her comfortable home on the East Coast to buy land and build a Light centre across the road from the Tauhara Centre, a spiritual retreat overlooking Lake Taupo. To prepare the land to receive the incoming energies, Philip spent an hour each day as the sun rose, receiving and emanating light. At sunrise he stood in a column of light created above a large rocky outcrop, to absorb it into every molecule of his body and emanate it around and into the earth. This and many other secrets he had been taught by spiritual masters in Kashmir, who had contacted him during a visit to that mystical land some ten years earlier. He knew that the body is a magnificent transmitter of energy and any energy can be transmuted by aligning thoughts to clear blockages, so used this method to prepare the land to receive an influx of light by reciting a mantra.

"I am light, I am love, I draw light into my life and emanate it around to all beings and to the earth. I am a being of light and love."

He taught this mantra to any who joined him on the rocks for sunrise meditation.

Vernon called the group to reassemble in front of the wall and asked if any one had experienced an inter-dimensional communication. Judith kept quiet for she was not yet ready to tell others of her encounter or that Aloma and Kaitewha would be leaving with them. Veronica was about to say something when she quickly put her hand on her head. "Who pulled my hair?" she demanded to know. Everyone laughed for no one had touched her.

A short, plump blonde woman called Kerry spoke. "I have a feeling that a clearing has taken place here today. When we arrived the area felt very heavy and uncomfortable, full of sadness and fear. Now there seems to be a lot more light. I guess our presence here has helped clear the area."

Vernon smiled. "There are laws in the universe that make it possible for us to create exactly what we choose. These Laws cannot be violated, nor can they be ignored. We chose to have an effect on this place and it happened. After all, we call ourselves Lightworkers do we not. Now I suggest we leave before it gets dark."

They all trooped back to their cars. Judith cleared the back seat of Veronica's car so that Aloma and Kaitewha would be comfortable. They laughed.

We do not occupy the same space as you do. It doesn't matter if there are garments strewn over the seat. We will not be disturbed. What is this machine called?. We must have no fear about what will befall us. I never imagined humans would bi-locate within a moving vehicle. It is so much easier to travel around just with a thought. However we will sit quietly and join you in whatever you have in store for us.

Judith was uncertain about mentioning the extra passengers to Philip who occupied the front seat. Veronica drove her white BMW expertly along the dirt road, back towards Taupo. *At least they will be introduced to moving at speed by a good driver in a car worthy of them,* she thought. She was kept busy pointing out modern day wonders as they neared Taupo, a thriving modern city nestling along the northern shore of the great lake that now seemed so tranquil. Aloma and Kaitewha wondered at the paved street, neat rows of houses and gardens, street lights, shops and every thing else they saw. The culture shock appalled them.

"However are we going to adapt to this?" moaned Aloma.

"I will allow you to merge with me to see through my eyes and understand with my mind," said Judith. "I know of the art of merging. I suppose I take all this town development for granted."

"Pardon? Did you say something Judith?" asked Philip turning around.

"I imagine she is talking to our two invisible passengers," said Veronica. "How are they coping with civilisation?"

"It is a great shock for them to see the development around the lake. It should not take them too long to adapt though, for Aloma, that is the female, is an aspect of me and I have a pretty good handle on life in the present," replied Judith.

"What are you talking about?" said Philip, turning around to look at the back seat. "I can't see anyone. Don't tell me you are seeing fairies again, Judith."

"Not fairies," countered Judith. "The two beings in the back seat are Atema, enlightened ones who lived in a temple complex deep in the forest before Lake Taupo blew up nearly two thousand years ago and destroyed their world, leaving certain aspects of themselves in a state of suspended shock until recently. They wish to travel around the North Island with us on our pilgrimage."

"O.K." replied Philip. "I see no harm in that. They won't eat much or take up any room. Accommodation should be cheap."

"Don't discount them. I have never doubted your connection with that long dead Kashmiri saint whose influence changed the direction of your life," snapped Judith. "When we arrive at the Tauhara Centre, I will take them to the meditation cabin and introduce them to the Angel of Tauhara. She can fill them in on the missing two thousand years of development in this area. I'm sure she has been overlighting the area for centuries."

For the next three weeks, Philip and Judith travelled around the country giving talks on the importance of Time Shift, meeting people, wallowing in thermal pools, visiting sacred places dowsed by Richard, a colour healer, as resonant with the rose/peach vibration of the Matrix line that flowed around the circumference of the Earth, and anchoring transformational energies into the land. They returned to Taupo to imprint the sign of infinity around Lake Taupo and the Tongariro national park. This area of high electro-magnetic force had been activated as the water spinner or driver wheel of the great Matrix line through which vast amounts of cosmic information had poured since 1990. Kaitewha and Aloma survived and prospered on the journey, delighting in the freedom experienced by the people now living in the land at the end of the long white cloud. The travellers finally returned to Taupo just prior to the celebration of Time Shift on the 26th July, 1992, to find a large number of people gathered at the Tauhara Centre. They had all been inspired by the importance of the occasion and wished to add their beneficial energy to the ceremony.

Philip addressed the assembly when they gathered in a large room.

"Friends, welcome to Tauhara and Time Shift. Let me explain a little of what is happening for those of you who don't know. As you are aware, the Earth contains a complex of energy points and meridians upon which her health depends, similar to those which enhance our physical bodies. The dawn of each Astrological Age seems to be typified by a global spiritual centre. Persia was dominant during the Age of Aries, Jerusalem during Pisces and for the Aquarian Age, a north/south balance centred on the Avebury/Glastonbury area in England and the Taupo/Tongariro energy wheel in the centre of Te Ika a Maui - the fish of Maui- the North Island of New Zealand. Much of the earth's future depends on strong leadership coming from New Zealand. Foundations created over the past few years should endure for millennia. A special area of land overlooking Lake Taupo, lies across the road from here. Over the years, several people have etherically connected it to a series of sites resonant with the Southern

Hemisphere Spiritual Pole consecrated at Raurimu early last year, and a global network of Light and Earth keeper Crystals

During the years since Harmonic Convergence in August, 1987, unprecedented changes have occurred on this planet, and the light has penetrated many places once in darkness. Nature has assessed humankind, wrought changes and with the assistance of overlighting Beings, has sought to raise the consciousness of those who make the choice, albeit often unconsciously, to evolve with the new era. This change is often made easier by being in the presence of those who have made or are making the transition from personality centred materialism to Earth and Universal centred spirituality, called ascension by some, as a moving from third to fourth and fifth dimensionality. Many are already living between these two worlds, for who has not had an experience beyond the five senses which seems to transcend the mundane?"

Removing his glasses, Philip looked at those listening to him. "Why have you all come here at such short notice? What was the inner prompting?" No one spoke.

He paused for some time before continuing. "You are all assisting in fulfilling the destiny of this country, as she will be the first to make the transition. From high up in space astronauts have reported seeing a purple aura over New Zealand. Perhaps that is caused by the active Pinatubo volcano on the island of Luzon in the Phillipines that erupted last month. That is why several of us from Australia and other countries are now here We know that Australia cannot move forward until New Zealand has opened the doorway. This has been prophesied by, amongst other seers, a man from Findhorn, that celebrated new age community in Scotland. He said that New Zealand and Australia, esoterically speaking, are a single continent, that they are a linked country, though in some aspects they are very different and embody different qualities of energy. In Australia is the presence of an ancient force, a primal paradise. The contact point with it is through New Zealand, which is a land of vast natural power. Within Australia lies a focal point of an energy which helped create this earth, and whose attention is inward dwelling within the Earth. But in New Zealand there is a point of power, an alignment with a force that does not originate upon this earth. There is a line of energy passing from the more masculine energy of Australia into the feminine New Zealand and back again via Mt. Taranaki, and if you are to contact certain of the ancient forces, and draw them forward into integration with the forces of present and future, New Zealand will be the initial point of contact. That is why many of us working for world harmony in Australia regularly travel to touch the consciousness of this clean green land. I see Australia as passive fire, energy held within the land, and New Zealand as active fire, spurting it out through volcanoes and steam vents. Thank you all for responding to the inner call. As you know, the more who gather together to perform such rituals as we will be doing at sunrise tomorrow, the more powerful the effect."

Philip, a tall, thin man with a greying beard and penetrating clear blue eyes that looked deeply into one's soul, sat down. A man with presence, he had once been a school teacher and knew how to project his voice and talk clearly to groups. For twenty years, he had been taking groups to camp in the bush to reconnect with the earth, in an attempt to renew the Dreaming in Australia, knowing that the Dreaming was a continuing occurrence, not something that happened a long time ago, before white people arrived on that great continent. As the custodians of a large and spectacular property located high in the Blue Mountains west of Sydney, he and Judith were host to hundreds of visitors annually, who benefited from his wisdom on the ways of earth's development.

Watching him Judith thought, *I am surprised he is not a incarnation of Rahitan. He has similar penetrating blue eyes and the presence of an ancient priest. Pity we need to part. I wonder what my true soul mate will look like.*

Then Vernon announced it was time to dance.

Catherine, a small, round, cheerful woman from the cold northern part of the world, said in her lilting voice, "I will lead you through the dances. They are not difficult and set the scene for us to become more integrated."

Expertly, she instructed the large group in sacred dance and soon even the most bumble footed were lightly dancing in circles around Catherine. Several dances later, everyone began to flag and dropped laughing to the floor to relax before Judith began to lead a meditation connecting the group through their hearts to the land.

During most of the evening celebrations, Judith had remained in the background, preferring others to take the front line. Now she sat in a chair directly beneath a large portrait of the Angel of Tauhara, painted by a visionary artist a few years ago. In the mediation cabin the previous evening, after Judith had introduced Aloma and Kaitewha, she had been given a powerful meditation by the Angel of Tauhara, centred on the human heartbeat. The Angel had made her presence known to many who visited and stayed at the Tauhara Centre to spend time in the silence of the meditation cabin overlooking the lake.

To Judith she had explained, "The majority of humans are conditioned beings, not encouraged to live in unity with heaven and earth, nor open to the ever changing universal dynamic. Hence, there is the need for expansion of consciousness if effective Earth rebalancing work is to be done. Before this energy work can be undertaken, three stages of cleansing need to be accomplished."

In the darkness of the cabin, Judith could just see the shimmering form who communicated. She felt no fear, only a tingling sensation running through her body and a sense of being deeply loved. Her two Atema companions stood silently, adding their love.

Communicating to Judith's mind, the Angel continued, "The first stage is a time of cleansing and healing of both body and emotions. This is often experienced by an influx of energy or depression, chaotic or irrational behaviour as the personal and collective shadow is revealed. A deep desire to cleanse the physical body by fasting, liver cleanse, developing fitness and receiving bodywork such as massage and rebalancing out of alignment structures, often follows deep emotional release work.

The second stage is an emptying of all negative and irrelevant attachments in life. Relationships that are no longer beneficial or supportive, work that does not make one happy and fulfilled, dwelling places that are not beautiful and comfortable, all conspire to keep the illuminative stage from entering and need to be reassessed. This stage is typified by experiences of light in meditation or prayer, inner guidance comes and effective healing is channelled. Awareness of higher dimensional beings becomes common, enabling people like you to connect with Angels like me." The Angel began to shimmer more brightly until Judith could discern her form.

"You are not at all like Aloma and Kaitewha in your essence," commented Judith.

"No, as I am from the Angelic family I have never incarnated on Earth, although I have a deep knowing of its inhabitants' struggles towards enlightenment. Aloma and Kaitewha, and indeed yourself are star seeded members of the family of Light who incarnate regularly. You and Aloma are of the same soul and you and she are but different aspects of your Oversoul. She is you in a past life, enabled to appear now because of the traumatic events that held an aspect of her suspended. This will become clearer to you in due course."

The angel paused and looked deeply into Judith's blue eyes before continuing,

"Now, the third stage of the expansion of consciousness that humans need to undergo is the unitive one. At this stage, personal identity is not just body, mind and spirit but is centred in transcendental consciousness and united with the universal light dimensions, the fifth and beyond. Once the purgative process begins, there are usually glimpses of the illuminative and unitive consciousness, so one does not have to wait to be perfect to begin to work for Earth harmony. Most of the one hundred and forty-four people gathered here at present are well on the way to an uplifted consciousness. This time of being together will inspire and uplift their inner beings many fold. Nowhere else in the world could so many of such spiritual quality gather together at such short notice. It is an indication of the interconnectedness of those living in this land. Many have been called from other lands to relocate here to assist with the great changes being instigated. Likewise, untold numbers of beings of the fourth and fifth dimensions also inhabit this land, living parallel lives, assisting those humans who awaken to their higher mission."

By this time, Judith could clearly see the Angel of Tauhara. Her long gown shimmered with rainbow colours, her golden hair hung down over her luminous shoulders to which large, very elegant glowing wings were attached. In her hand she held a large wand with a shining jewel fixed to one end. The very tall figures of Aloma and Kaitewha were dwarfed by the Angel's presence and Judith felt like a midget.

"I have two gifts for you Judith," came the silvery voice of the Angel. "I know how long and tirelessly you have worked for the highest vision of humankind and the earth. You have endured much pain and suffering during your purgative stage of development and have shown tremendous mental and physical effort in order to attain the degree of luminosity you emanate. No longer are you concerned with the acceptance or approval of others, and are not satisfied with the mundane life. You have had enough of this world as it is at present. You are tired of the game of illusion played by so many others. You seek a newer world, one that is in alignment with your highest thoughts. However, further pain and suffering lie just ahead of you when you realise that the partnership you are presently in, no longer sustains you. On your return to your homeland, you and your husband will separate, for he does not cherish your being and still seeks approval from others to support his ego. Deep inside you know this is so. I am sorry, for I know you love him but you can no longer tolerate such emotionally abusive behaviour. Is that not so, my dear one?"

Tears flowed down Judith's cheeks. "Yes, you are right. Rahitan said the same. I have tried so hard to please him, but can no longer stand in his shadow. It is my nature to love unconditionally, but how long does one pour love into a bottomless pit. I am no longer interested in being someone I am not, just to please others. No longer do I care what others think of me. I must live in my own light and truth. I can't keep ignoring the problem, pretending it isn't there. How I wish an aspect of Kaitewha was incarnate in Philip and we could have such a loving relationship as twin souls. But if it not to be, then so be it. In future I will direct my energy wherever I am called."

The Angel gently touched Judith's forehead with the tip of her wand, and before her vision flashed scenes of her life. It had been an interesting and varied one, full of travel, fun, romance and adventure interspersed with times of deep suffering, which had honed the template of her soul, preparing her for a more spiritual role. She saw herself as a six year old girl running, deliriously happy, into her parents room after finding that the tooth fairy, whom she thought had forgotten her, had indeed left a threepence. She had utterly believed in fairies, making little clothes and beds for them, leaving food each night, to find that in the morning they often left a penny. *How did they ever carry such a large coin. I'll bet they were delighted when decimal currency was introduced.* In later life she'd wondered at her mother's love in playing the game. Her overworked mother of four, living in a remote farmhouse, still had time to indulge her eldest daughter's fantasies.

Next Judith saw herself at the age of thirteen in a hospital bed writhing in pain, with her anxious mother at her side. Rushed in with acute appendicitis, it had burst and the pain subsided. Following a bright light, she felt herself rise through the ceiling, and float gently towards a glowing being surrounded by a bright light, waiting for her. The Being communicated that it was not her time to leave her body and bade her return to it. Behind her she heard the frantic cries of her distraught mother, who had once been a nurse and was familiar with the symptoms leading to death, calling her back. Reluctantly, she returned to her body. It was difficult to remain in it whilst the offending appendix and its spattered contents were removed. *I only found out two years ago why I chose to go through that experience. I didn't want to grow up to become a woman. My unconscious memory of being a woman was strong. As women in this country are no longer considered inferior creatures I am safe; for I have a memory of wrongs done to me in past lives because I was outspoken and threatened the male power base. Now I would much rather be in a woman's body.*

A scene of her late teens flashed by. She saw herself with a number of other very nervous young women, all beautifully dressed, parading before a panel of leering judges. *The Miss Australia contest. How could I have been so silly as to enter that. Still it was a lot of fun at the time and I learned a great deal about people, poise, and raising money for charity. Glad I didn't win. That would have taken my life in another direction entirely. The winner's life has not been happy. But then neither has some of mine.*

Next she saw herself, at the age of nineteen, aboard a large ocean liner, with three girlfriends travelling to England, on a five week voyage through the Suez Canal, before docking in Southampton during one of the coldest winters on record. How they loathed

London besmirched by dirty snow, pea soup fogs and penetrating cold. The English pubs kept them amused, for men and women actually communicated with each other, something unheard of in Australia at that time, and they met some new friends. Deciding never to spend another winter in England, they travelled to Israel to join an archaeological dig at the ruins of Masada, deep in the Negev desert overlooking the Dead Sea. *That experience changed by life and awakened me to a whole new concept of reality.* Following her return to Australia she became an Air Hostess with Qantas for three years, until marrying a Cambridge graduate now working for a major oil company, whom she'd met whilst hitch hiking in Sweden four years earlier. They left Australia for England the day after the wedding. Fourteen years later, she returned to Melbourne with three small sons, the marriage over. A year later, her oldest girlfriend lay in the arms of her husband.

They said they were soul mates. Talk about the run over by a truck syndrome. I was hurt far more by the perceived betrayal of my girlfriend than by my husband's weakness. After all he was only guided by one thing, the need to be needed. He didn't think I needed him enough. I eventually forgave his weakness, as that was the catalyst for my spiritual growth. The agonising cry that there must be more to life than this unbearable emotional pain echoed in my heart. I soon found a spiritual teacher and a great group of women who were in a similar situation, searching for answers as to the meaning of life."

Intrigued, Aloma and Kaitewha also viewed the pictures Judith saw. *I had no idea that humans would still suffer so much. I remember how emotional the unenlightened used to be, but thought that the pain and suffering would have lifted by now. It seems to help people awaken to the understanding that there must be more to life than their painful situation and help them to search for methods to help them rise above it. Not that it should restict feelings, but also teaches them not to take on the pain of others.*

"Don't feel sorry for me, Aloma" flashed Judith. "There are many, many others on the earth who have had a far worse life than I ever experienced. I actually thanked the man for leaving me. It enabled me to search deep within my psyche and find that I did not need him to feel worthwhile. It taught me that there was a far greater source of love available to me. Because of his deep karmic love for me on the unconscious level, he freed me to explore my own journey. This benefited my sons greatly as well, although the eldest rebelled in his early teens. They are now all fine young men getting on with their own lives."

Next, scenes of fifteen proud recipients of diplomas flashed into Judith's mind. *Ah, yes. Graduation evening from the College of Natural Medicine. I became a Naturopath in my search for physical and mental answers. The Church of the Mystic Christ fulfilled my spiritual searching for a time, until I moved into my own knowing. Then a few years as a Lifeline counsellor followed, while I worked though much of my emotional pain. Then the second marriage, which you tell me will soon be over.* Judith looked at the Angel of Tauhara. *Does that really have to happen? Can't he be zapped with something to knock some sense into him?*

Sadly the Angel smiled. "No my dear, your time together has nearly run its course. Between you a great deal has been achieved. You have learned to deal with anger in males and together created the foundations for a light centre that will shine for many years to come. You have other work to do now, work that he would hinder, but you will be friends with this man for a long time to come. You have much travelling to do for the next few years, channelling light, moving energy around the planet, clearing trapped spirit beings and anchoring cosmic energy along the grids. The old grids are due to be replaced and you are one of the team incarnated to assist in this work."

Yes, thought Judith, *but I will always love the area of sacred land where we live in the Blue Mountains. Perhaps one day I will build a home of my own there, overlooking the valley.*

The Angel continued, "Far beyond time and space is the mystery that veils the source of all Creation. In the very centre of your being is the spark, which connects you to that ultimate mystery, the mystery which no one will ever unfold on the living side of the grave. All you can achieve in a lifetime is to embark on that journey to the centre, discover the indwelling Creator and fight to continue that journey no matter how many obstacles are thrust in your path. To serve the mysterious transcendent Force you must continually work to align yourself with the God within to become the person God created, not a poor image concocted by cosmic geneticists. Your task is to be whole, not fragmented, to be fully human, not a naked ape; to reach upwards towards the Light, not to dive headlong into the dark and to always remember that the Creator of all things is there in both its masculine and feminine aspect, calling you to integrate, self-regulate and move towards eternal life, by impressing images on your psyche to lure you towards Itself. You have had to struggle through the labyrinth of the unconscious mind on your inner journey, as have most of humankind, but the guiding light is always there ahead of you at the source of the stream of life and light within."

How amazingly she understands my inner journey, sighed Judith.

The images continued to roll, showing Judith her past and her future lives on Earth. One she particularly enjoyed reliving was the time of her intense spiritual awakening. She saw herself, sitting in a large room some ten years earlier, with many other people, listening to a large man with a greying beard and hair, talking to them with an American accent from the deep South. Suddenly she felt an intense jolt of light hit the top of her head and course down through her body to her toes. Stunned, she sat there unable to move as light filtered into every cell of her body, feeling like champagne bubbles tingling through her insides, coursing around her arteries and veins, making her body numb but alive at the same time. Her eyes took on a glazed appearance and she sat rigid in her chair. Several minutes later, when the spiritual teacher finished his talk, Judith's companion noticed her entranced state and called the teacher's assistant. The woman took Judith outside and suggested she hug a large rock to ground the energy. This helped a little but the experience stayed with her for weeks, even being repeated several times during deep meditation. Judith's life had changed dramatically from that day and her appearance also altered. Some commented she must be a Walk-in, but Judith had laughed and responded that no, it was because she had been so fast asleep and stubborn that she needed to be zapped by a bolt of spiritual lightning to awaken her from the pain that she was experiencing; that of separation from her husband, and to put her firmly on the path to her Higher self.

Judith recalled her first Earth walking journey the following year, with a group led by the spiritual teacher responsible for her instant awakening. He led them around Egypt, to ancient temples and tombs. Many had past life memories of their time when Egypt was in her greatest power, and they released emotions attached to those lives. One day when Judith had been walking near the second Pyramid, a man dressed in a djelaba approached her, saying "Come with me." Unable to resist, Judith allowed him to lead her to one of the three small Queens tomb pyramids beside the larger one. The man lit a candle, gave it to her and indicated that she should crawl along a small tunnel, into the centre of the tomb. With no thought or fear of spiders or scorpions, Judith did as he bid, and moved some five metres along the dark tunnel, where she sat, blew out the candle and began to meditate. Firstly, she heard a low mechanical noise deep underground, followed by a sweet high note, before being inwardly told her spiritual name, the one she was known by in the higher realms to which she belonged. She thought it important for Aloma to know of this event, for it had opened in her a whole new ability to contact the higher entities inhabiting the next dimensions of Earth, when she was given her note, her spiritual name and earth mission.

The Angel then communicated to Aloma. "These visions serve a twofold purpose. The first is to instruct you on this aspect of yourself at this time and to the range of feelings that Judith has already experienced; the second is to heal Judith from past trauma in her life by bringing up some of the major events, both happy and painful, to show the balance. Humans tend to remember the bad things that happen to them, for they make an impact deep within the cellular level of the body, but they tend to forget the happy times, which enhance their soul with joy and laughter. They are more able to access physical and emotional pain than soul joy, as it is held in very cell of the human body, not just the mind. It is a strange phenomenon. They judge themselves, often harshly, unable to access their soul's desire. All the soul wishes is to experience the highest form of love attainable when in a human body. It wishes feeling, not knowledge for it is already imbued with all the knowledge it can ever need, although many pursue academic knowledge for the sake of being educated above others. The soul wishes to experience a broad spectrum of feeling, so manifests many situations throughout its incarnation to do just that. The highest feeling a soul can reach when in a body is the experience of unity with the great Creator of all that is. It yearns to return to the essence and truth of itself, to experience perfect love. Love is not the absence of emotions, be they positive like joy and passion, or negative as with anger, jealousy, hared, lust or greed, but the combination of all feelings. So, for the soul to experience perfect love, it must experience every human feeling. Do you know that one purpose of the soul when in a physical body, is to experience all the broad spectrum of feelings, both joyful and painful, so that it can encompass all of them. It all comes down to a matter of choice and courage. This, in turn, is also felt by the Creator who wishes to experience every permutation of human existence, whether good or evil. It is part of the cosmic game. Humans are born with a clean slate, so to speak, determined to redress past wrongs, but soon unconscious memory of past lives can cause them to relive certain situations. Forgetfulness is also a blessing in many cases, as it would be distressing for a child to know of its difficult past lives until it is awake enough to release the emotion. Either they sink into forgetfulness and fall asleep, because very rarely do their unwakened parents encourage their true expression of feelings or past memory, or super natural talents like seeing auras, the ability to read minds, or, if they become a prodigal, encourage them unconditionally. Judith's sons were lucky that she encouraged them to remember that they were old souls with a journey to undertake on Earth. From the short time you have had to observe humanity of today, do you think they have progressed much since you were last incarnate?"

Aloma looked deeply into Judith's energy field. "People of this land today are certainly much more able to freely express themselves without fear of being punished by the Chiefs or elders of the tribe. They can choose where to live, what to think, what to wear and how to work and, perhaps the best of all, with whom to become partnered. But they are far less connected to the Earth and her needs. We have certainly witnessed some sad desecration on the journey we undertook around the great stingray, but we feel that people are beginning to awaken to the folly of abusing the Mother. The Atema were not restricted like the ancient tribal people and enjoyed a freedom like modern people. In some ways we were more advanced spiritually and we cared deeply for the Earth. I cannot comment on the present situaton in other countries on Earth."

She looked to Kaitewha for his comments and he responded.

"When we last travelled this land nearly two thousand years ago, we had no roads or vehicles. We were able to use the power of our minds to move our bodies wherever we focussed. We have been trying to teach Judith and Philip to bi-locate, but everything is much denser than in the past, and the air much thicker with pollution. Cars are very crude transporters. They use so much energy just to move around the land that is criss-crossed with long black ribbons scarring the mountains and valleys. We hear that other countries in the world are in far worse shape than this one. I am sorry Judith must travel across the sea."

"Don't worry about Judith, she is very good at travelling." The Angel smiled. "You can go with her if you wish."

Aloma shuddered. "No, I would rather remain here. We travelled the world a number of times in our past incarnations by bi-locating. If I need further experience in the world, surely I can access another aspect of myself in another body or country to feel what they are going through or bi-locate there. Now that we are released from our dormant state, we can be anywhere in the pulse of a thought, as can you, dear Angel. Why inhale the conditions of so many others by being crowded into one of the flying machines Judith has told us about after we saw such an object flying in the sky?"

Just then the door of the meditation cabin opened and Philip entered, after taking off his shoes.

"I thought I would find you here," he said. "You have been behaving strangely all day. Is anything the matter?"

"Oh, hello, Philip. The Angel of Tauhara has been communicating with me and also Aloma and Kaitewha." Judith was a little put out that he had interrupted before the Angel had imparted the second part of her gift. "She hasn't finished yet."

"You were missed. There are some who wish to talk to you about tomorrow's plans. More productive than talking to an Angel I can't see," Philip replied.

"Tell them I will be there in about fifteen minutes, please," said Judith.

Replacing his shoes, Philip left and the Angel spoke again. "The sparks of love do not charge between you. He is angry, not only with you but deep within himself. He is angry that he incarnated, and has not achieved his soul desire and he will not let you help him. Now for my second gift. Tomorrow evening you are to conduct a meditation to join the hearts and minds of all those gathered. There is one woman who has travelled here from your land who carries very destructive energy that does not wish this shifting of time to happen, because she is jealous of you. She has an inflated ego and will try to damage the vibrational fields that have been placed around this whole area to seal it from such as those who use her, which enables them to penetrate the hearts and minds of others. She will nearly succeed, but of course will not be allowed to destroy what so many have worked for so long to achieve. The reason she will nearly succeed is to show those here the energetic difference in a tangible way, between one who works for the dark and one who works for the light. Most only think they know. She will blame you and Philip for not allowing her to succeed and when she gets home, she will give you negative publicity. That is something you can cope with, for one who tries to damage the reputation of another is not a Lightworker."

Judith stood under the apex of the roof below a downward pointing filial that drew energy into the building. Outside, darkness had totally enveloped the sky, and covered the land with its night time cloak. From the filial, an electric blue line charged into the top of Judith's head, coursing through her body. She heard the voice of the Angel.

"Stand calm, my dear. Open your inner sight and receive what I am about to insert into your memory bank and your heart. This is for you to share with everyone you contact, if you feel it is appropriate. Tomorrow evening, following the time of near disaster, you will call everyone into the great meeting room and send this loving energy to them. I will be overlighting you to reach deeply into their hearts and minds. Now, Judith, receive."

The vision of a beating heart was strongly imprinted into Judith's mind and she felt the light coming through the top of her head connect her to a great source of golden light high above. She saw her heart fill with light, and with each beat, expand ripples of light, like rings made by a stone thrown into a still pond, and through her body until every part was filled with light. She felt healing energy also rippling with each heartbeat, caressing each cell and washing away the pain felt between her shoulder blades. Her whole body became one huge beating heart until it could no longer contain the light, which increased to spread around her in ripples until it filled the cabin, and continued to the Tauhara Centre, over the lake, all across the North Island. Light spread from that small cabin around the planet, increasing in vibration until the whole Earth became a pulsing heart, sending love out to infuse into everyone who was able to receive its essence. From high in space the Earth could be observed pulsing out her message, "I am ready to receive the change in the spiral of time. Let it shift."

For a long time, Judith sat on the floor under the filial, unable to move, still charged with light and love. She had no wish to join the others to talk about plans and worldly arrangements. Everything would be taken care of by the great beings overlighting them tomorrow. How could they think otherwise. *It should be an interesting day with the various egos competing for recognition. As long as the higher beings are overlighting us, their plans to compete will come to nothing.*

The following evening unfolded just as the Angel had predicted. Using Judith as her channel she entered the heart and mind of all present, and dispersed the negative energy built up by the one who was being used to sabotage the event. She had very nearly succeeded in luring most of the participants outside to sit under the stars, thereby dispersing the energy built up in the central hall, but Judith had alerted Philip to her plan which he twarted quite cleverly by arranging for Vernon to recall them inside. The planned events flowed smoothly after that, and the woman disappeared to her room, deflated and defeated. She emanated anger and dislike towards Judith, who absorbed it into her loving heart to neutralise the negativity.

FOURTEEN

Time Shift

At five o'clock the following morning, one hundred and forty-four people assembled in the pre-dawn light to walk from the Tauhara Centre, along the road, to the land called Zuvuyaland, lying in preparation for the anchoring of a major infusion of energy. Overnight, a bulldozer driver had carted great rocks from the road works above to create a spiral on the land. Crisp grass crunched underfoot as a single file of people wound its way down the steep slope, along hastily made tracks, to stand around a large white Earth keeper crystal planted on the site. Disaster struck for one woman who missed her footing in the dim light and fell heavily, breaking her leg in several places. Attended by a few helpers, she lay in pain until an ambulance came. The rest of the participants continued the ritual, unaware of the sacrifice made by one of their members. The ambulance men tried to contain their surprise at seeing such a large number of people braving the winter morning to watch the sun rise over Lake Taupo. No one attempted to explain what was actually happening.

Gathering in two large circles around the Earth keeper crystal, the group chanted during the rising of the sun, glowing orange and red, reflecting on the waters of the great lake below. One dark haired woman dressed in white called, "We are the Keepers of Frequency, come to change the illusions flooding the present world, by our example and dedication. We are the Keepers of the new time, the changing of the spiral to move anti-clockwise back towards our creator's heart. We are going home."

Slowly, and with great reverence, individuals placed the sacred objects they carried around the Earth keeper crystal. Pendants, crystals, stones, jewellery, flowers and many other items all lay on the cold grass, giving and receiving of their owner's energy frequency so that it would merge with the great crystal and be spread wherever they travelled in future. A sacred dance of divine remembrance completed the ceremony, before most rushed back to the warmth and comfort of a sustaining Tauhara breakfast. However, some remained, silently gathered around a large pointed anchor stone in the centre of the rock spiral, to connect more deeply with the essence of place and time and deeply integrate the momentous occasion of the last two days. They were the ones who put their spiritual needs before their physical ones, who had learned to transcend the distraction of matter over spirit, the core people focussing the energies of the group who had all contributed to the occasion.

Later in the evening when most of the participants had left to return home, Judith went alone to the meditation cabin, where she found the Angel waiting with Aloma and Kaitewha. The cabin was centrally heated during the winter to allow meditators to sit without freezing. Judith took off her shoes and entered, then sat on a cushion on the floor. The Angel glowed magnificently, her aura expanded to touch the main building. She communicated to Judith.

"Congratulations to you and Phillip and all the others involved during the past two days of ceremony here, and in the months of preparatory work. The spiritual energies have increased exponentially. New Zealand's future leadership role in the events unfolding before the end of this century and into the next one is assured. You may write or talk of this time, for Time Shift has duly been achieved, and the journey back to the heart of the Creator has begun. Soon you will return to the country of your birth, but this land is your spiritual home and your rainbow light is well known here. In due course you will be given the gift of a rainbow cloak by the spirit ancestors who live along a great river to the south. But first you have a lot of emotional clearing to do. Farewell my spiritual friend. Aloma and Kaitewha have decided to remain here for the time being. They wish you to write the story of the Atema when you are able. They will assist."

Judith watched her brilliant shapes fade and was soon sitting alone in the darkness of the cabin. Not wishing to break the flow of energy coursing through her body, she remained for many hours in meditation, before returning to her room for a short sleep before breakfast. Phillip wondered where she had been, but she just smiled. "I'll tell you later," she said.

Each year Judith returned to New Zealand for a few weeks to continue the connecting work between the two countries, until she was ready to spend several months living there, focussing on the work. Much of her time was spent anchoring the Auralia energy that had arrived on earth and merged with her, following a long inter dimensional journey to bring it down. Auralia embodied the highest aspect of the Divine Feminine, a quality sorely lacking in Australia, but in abundance in New Zealand. As predicted, she had separated from Philip soon after the Time Shift and moved to a log cabin in the Blue Mountains, although she was still participating in ceremonies held at Glastonbell. She also continued her job in a health resort in Katoomba, where she had worked for many years.

Four years later, destiny played its part in the unfolding story when Judith returned to New Zealand and encountered two people from Coromandel, whom she took to the Wall. From the car park the three walked barefoot for nearly one hundred metres along the gravel road to the guardian stone. At Arthur's suggestion three tightly curled fern fronds were laid on the stone in front of the wall and immediately he, Lynda and Judith jumped backwards in surprise as a dimensional shift opened like a garage roller door between them and the cyclopean blocks that made up the wall. Slowly, they climbed to the area where Judith had first met Aloma and Kaitewha and stood within the circle of gnarled native beech trees. Lynda placed her large crystal beside the mossy knoll in the centre of the trees and they opened their inner senses to the place. Aloma and Kaitewha appeared saying they had returned to the place where the Atema had once lived to instruct those who remained in the vagaries of late twentieth century living. They were all glad to remain hidden deep in the forest until they merged with those aspects of themselves who would free them from being stuck in time.

Lynda looked up and gasped. Standing half hidden behind a tree further up the slope she saw the vague outline of a woman with long black hair, dressed in a silvery blue flowing robe. As the woman moved towards them she was joined by a stern looking man wearing a long blue robe with a feathery cloak thrown over one shoulder, his long white beard and hair just discernible. Arm in arm they entered the small circle and addressed the astounded couple.

The man spoke to their minds. "Greetings again Judith and friends. Welcome to all that visibly remains of the once great temple complex of the Atema. You have met our Princess, Aloma and her consort, Kaitewha. Now let me introduce myself and this beautiful woman." He bowed deeply then stood and looked for some minutes directly into the eyes of Arthur, Lynda and Judith until they were infused with light and a tingling sensation.

"I am Rahitan, High Priest of the Atema, and you are the ones we have awaited for so long. When Judith first made contact with Aloma we knew she was once one of us. Others have visited the wall and made contact with aspects of themselves, but you Arthur, are my incarnation in present time, and you Lynda are Garlita.

Let me introduce you. Garlita is the High Priestess of the Atema. Long ago we promised each other that, in a future incarnation, we would meet to become husband and wife. Welcome. We could not come to you even though we knew where you were, for we are bound here until released by the modern aspect of ourselves, so sent telepathic messages to guide you to Judith, who knew where to find us. Those who left through the vortex activated by Judith and her Light Dreaming friend when she first found her way here, were not at present incarnate but many soon will be now they are released from suspension in time, for they are preparing to merge with the body of a baby to experience first hand the new energies pouring into this area. They are the future hope of this land. Now I have a favour to ask you and a gift for you."

Lynda and Arthur exchanged glances. Who was this woman Judith they had just met, who had brought them deep into a thick native forest, taken then to this old pile of stones that looked like a ruined wall, and now drawn them into a circle of trees with these tall light beings? Telepathically they communicated. *"We have a choice here. We have the free will to accept or refuse whatever Rahitan and Garlita ask of us. We will support each other in whatever decision each makes."*

"O.K." said Arthur, "Ask away." He was a well built man of medium stature, sporting a slightly greying, short black beard. His wife Lynda, looked deeply into Garlita's eyes and saw herself reflected in the gold-flecked greyness that gazed intently back. Lynda was of medium build, with short brown slightly wavy hair. She did not possess Garlita's imposing prsence.

"We wish to merge with you to enable us to move from this place and experience the present aspect of ourselves," said Rahitan. "Since the small bang, as we call the last annihilation, we have not been able to resurrect our power of bi-location or much else for that matter, but have been in a sort of suspended animation until the electro-magnetic energy field that surrounded this area keeping it invisible to most visitors, was deactivated a few years ago. Since then we have been calling to you. Aloma now wishes to merge with Judith. That didn't happen last time they were in contact as Judith still had a lot of emotional trauma to resolve and Aloma considered it was not her lesson, even though she felt great empathy for her present self. But the contact enabled her to leave here. She remained with Kaitewha and the Angel of Tauhara until she learned sufficient knowledge to adapt to this prsent life and they returned to us last year." Turning to Judith he added, "We still wish you to write our story. One day soon, you will find a place where you can write undisturbed. Will you consent to Aloma merging with you?"

The three in human bodies exchanged glances, and agreed. Arthur knew they had been receiving messages for some time but from whom he didn't know. He also knew that they needed this infusion of energy to move forward in the important work they were starting to do all over the North Island. That of anchoring and connecting energy, clearing entities trapped in the spirit worlds, and much of the type of work Judith had been doing for the last fifteen years since being zapped with light and woken up to her true path.

"We are ready," he said.

"Just a minute," Kaitewha interrupted. "If you all merge with your present soul aspects what will happen to me? My body has not yet arrived in this land. Your ex- husband is not a reincarnation of me. I don't wish to stay here without you, Aloma."

"You can come with me, er us, until your human aspect arrives," Judith answered, "but not interfere or show jealousy or any other all too human emotion. Then we will have to convince him to accept you, if he is not already aware of his role. During his world travels, he has almost certainly absorbed past aspects of himself, both from male and female bodies, as have I. Let us hope he is not too far away."

"Now," said Rahitan, "are you all ready. Stand in a triangle, close your eyes, open your senses and chakras and permit us each to enter."

For several minutes the three felt nothing, and then a strong tingling sensation ran down their spine and a sense of becoming much taller. Their minds expanded to receive far more knowledge. Each felt a symbol in the shape of a silver-crafted young fern leaf placed along the chakras at the front of their body and a smaller one implanted into the right shoulder. Judith was told to take her larger leaf to a special site on the South Island, a place once called The Home of the Gods, now called Kura Tawhiti, and throw it from a high cliff to the wind to the Atema related family in spirit living there.

Rahitan's voice spoke from Arthur's mouth and he said, "The leaf is revered as the symbol of life force. Life force is energy and in the human energy field it takes several forms. It is used in the production of body heat, for movement, the function of organs, to keep the heart beating, to move body fluids, and for feelings, thought and will. Ordinary humans are not able to adapt their organism to use energy that does not come from food. This is true of both solar and cosmic energy, with cosmic being the more powerful. The leaf can signify human life or a given form of energy with which the leaf is associated The symbol of the curled fern leaf that has been placed along your chakras will enable you to utilize both solar and cosmic energy much more fully. You Judith, are already able to do this, for I sense from your auric field that you have undergone the process of learning to live on solar and cosmic energy. And very recently it seems. You know what I am saying is true."

When it was over they opened their eyes.

"You don't look any different," laughed Lynda looking at Arthur. "I was sure Rahitan's eyes were a bright blue, but yours are still dark brown. Do I have any gold flecks in mine. Garlita's looked so unusual."

"This will take a while to get used to," said Judith. "But we have not finished our work for today. I have a feeling we need to visit Mt. Pihanga, a small mountain at the southern end of Lake Taupo. She is the pivot for the great water spinner wheel covering this whole area of Taupo/Tongariro. Do you feel I am right?"

"Yes," answered the other two, or were they now four. "It is only mid afternoon. Let's go. Ready Kaitewha? How do we look to you?"

"I feel very left out of this whole adventure. I know I can accompany you but will miss the human sensations. You all look wonderfully at home with each other," he answered.

Half way along the gravel road leading back to the highway, Judith yelled, "Stop the car." She grabbed her camera, opened the door, got out and pointed to the sky. "Look, how exquisite. A rainbow around the sun. That is a good omen. And over there, two hawks circling. Whenever I see a rainbow around the sun and hawks I know something very special has happened. Not that I doubt what we just experienced, but confirmation is always nice."

Arthur smiled. He had spent most of his life farming and knew weather patterns. "It is just the sun reflecting on crystals of ice. Not so unusual at this time of year."

"But why do we see one now, and why do I always see one or a great rainbow cloud in confirmation that something special has happened?" asked Judith.

"Blowed if I know," replied Arthur, getting back into the car. "But if it makes you happy Judith, enjoy it."

Ah, Rahitan would be proud if he had said that, thought the Garlita aspect of Lynda.

During the drive, Lynda turned to Judith in the back seat and said, "What did Rahitan mean by saying you had already undergone a process and knew how to be sustained by light?"

"A couple of months ago, last August actually, I spent three weeks in a tent in a paddock in southern Queensland going through an astounding process, so that I no longer need to eat food for sustenance. I have a choice. I was etherically operated on for four days by four galactic surgeons who totally restructured my body to enable me to be sustained by light, or solar and cosmic energy as Rahitan put it."

"I wondered what was different about you, a certain glow," said Arthur. "But you don't look as though you are fading away. I'd have thought someone who didn't eat for so long would be skin and bones by now. Come to think of it, I haven't seen you eat anything since we met. You drink fluids though."

"One of the most fundamental beliefs on this planet is that we have to eat and drink to survive. I know that is not true. It is fear and the belief that if we don't eat we will die that kills us, not lack of food. And being in a certain state of consciousness, one beyond basic survival level" answered Judith.

"Well, I'm not ready to give up food yet," said Lynda and Arthur in unison. "Although," continued Lynda, "with the influence of Garlita now within me, who knows what will happen?"

"I am certain Aloma influenced me to follow this course," replied Judith. "I first met her four years ago. About a year later I began to seriously follow a detoxification programme and had several colonic irrigations. By the end of the following year, I had lost weight and was feeling so full of energy and healthy that I looked years younger. Two years later when I heard about the Twenty-one day process I knew I had to do it, so the following week I was in a tent in a paddock, being supervised by a medical doctor I might add, who had eaten nothing for six months and looked wonderful. But it is not something one should undertake unless there is a deep feeling that the time is right. It is also essential to have someone who has done the process to look after you during the three weeks. The whole time is a deep commitment to one's spiritual growth and has nothing to do with any outer teaching. If you ever want to do it, I will undertake to caretake you both."

"We'll let you know," replied Arthur. "In the mean time I know a great little cafe in Taupo overlooking the Lake that serves enormous afternoon teas." He mentally ignored the nudge from Rahitan regarding this statement.

Lynda looked at Judith. "Recently I heard the old Maori legend of a great battle by the fiery mountains in the centre of the North Island, probably a distant memory of violent volcanic eruptions. Have you heard the story?"

"No, I once saw some dramatic illustrations on a postcard, but do not know the legend," replied Judith

"In the ancient past, many magnificent mountain gods lived in the centre of the North Island Te Ika a Maui – the fish of Maui. The male mountains called Tongariro, Ngauruhoe, Ruapehu, Taranaki and Tauhara stood proudly on the Central Plateau, alongside a graceful, lone female mountain called Pihanga, which was robed in native bush, and still stands between the other mountains and Lake Taupo. All the mountains wanted to win the heart of pretty Pihanga, but none more so than Taranaki and Tongariro. The two fought so fiercely that the earth shook, lightening crashed, and lava flowed down the warring mountains. In the fighting Tongariro lost his head – some say he broke it off to throw at Taranaki, others that Taranaki sliced it off with a powerful blow. Either way, the top of Tongariro fell into Lake Taupo, where it formed Moututaiko Island.

Tongariro emerged victorious, and a defeated Taranaki was banished westwards, led to the coast by Toka a Rahotu, a small guide stone with great mana (importance). As he travelled, Taranaki carved out the Whanganui River, before he settled beside the beautiful mountain range Pouakai. Mt. Taranaki last erupted in 1755, although it's hard to imagine that the peaceful looking mountain hides such a dramatic past. There is a saying in New Plymouth; that if you cannot see the mountain it's raining, and if you can see it rain is coming. The area of Taranaki is very green and fertile."

"What a great story, Lynda," responded Judith. "There is usually an historical truth behind most legends. They are not only just folk tales."

Two hours later Arthur parked the car a the bottom of the track leading towards Mt. Pihanga. They had stopped at the cafe in Taupo for afternoon tea, a ritual thoroughly enjoyed by Rahitan and Garlita.

Judith said, "We have to walk half way up the hill to a clearing. Are you aware of anyone around us?"

Arthur bent down to pick up an imaginary object. Lynda said, "There are hundreds of Maori spirit beings welcoming us. They have thrown down a God-stick which they call Whaka-pakoko rakau and Arthur has just picked up. We are very welcome. They know who we are and have gathered here to greet us. Can you also see them, Judith? Some over there are preparing a feast for when we come back down the track."

"We are each being given a feather cloak to wear and a Chief is uttering long words of welcome," answered Judith. "Now they are leading us along the path up the hill. How wonderful. I suppose they have been caring for the great spindle, cog and pearl that was planted here by myself and two other women during the Time Shift, well over three years ago. It was put here to turn the spinner Taupo wheel. Look at all those adorable children."

The procession wended its way up the mountain until it reached the end of the road and stopped at a large cleared circular area. Lake Rotoiti glistened in the late afternoon sun and an eerie stillness enveloped the area. Suddenly a great wind tore into the clearing, shattering the air and disturbing the trees and the three people.

"Looks like we have visitors," remarked Arthur. "Stand quietly and let them introduce themselves."

Into the circle stepped several large Maori spirit warriors, gesturing wildly. Wind swirled around the small group as they stood their ground. The impulse to run was strong but the desire to remain was stronger. One particularly large spirit man stepped in front of Arthur.

"Who are you and what are you doing here?" he demanded. Looking at the assembled spirits he yelled, "And why are you all gathered here? We have not been told of a gathering. What is going on?" He began to gesture threateningly and do a haka with his companions.

The Rahitan aspect of Arthur grew to his full height, bristling. "Savages, killers of the gentle people who once inhabited this land, how dare you threaten us. You are not the true guardians of this area, only usurpers. Now stop that silly display of intimidation and let us get on with our ceremony."

The chief of the group nearly burst with rage, his energy field spreading to engulf the group, but Rahitan was ready and with a gesture of his hand, rays of light shot out towards the still posturing men, causing them to diminish in size and strength.

"No one," he said almost mildly, "interferes with the Atema."

"You are the High Priest of the Atema?" stuttered the chief. "Legend has it that you were all blown to pieces when the great lake collapsed sending ash and steam all over the country. The old people who once inhabited this land talked of you and said you would protect them. We thought they were only trying to invent a way of protecting themselves before we put them to death."

"As you can see, I am all too real. You have forgotten the protocol. What are you called? I am Rahitan of the Atema. This human I overlight is Arthur and is not to be psychically or physically harmed in any way at any time. That goes for the two women. They are also Atema." Rahitan presented an outward calmness, but Arthur could feel every fibre of his body tensing.

Without answering, the group of intruders swept away as suddenly as they had come, bending the trees double. Strange cloud formations in the shapes of the warriors formed above. From a clear blue sky a large rainbow appeared, absorbed the clouds into itself and held its shape for several minutes before slowly dissolving. The crowd cheered and called, "Uenuku, Uenuku, our protector and friend."

"Now," said Rahitan, "let us continue."

Half an hour later the trio descended, followed by the crowd of spirit helpers, back to the parked car.

"We are to return the cloaks and enjoy the feasting," said Lynda. "Even spiritual beings enjoy sustenance." Bending down, she picked up a piece of obsidian and handed it to Arthur. "A confirmation of your gift."

Earlier, they had each been gifted with a transmitter/receiver in the shape of a golden crown bearing different stones, placed on their head by a spirit tohunga. Arthur received obsidian, Lynda lapis lazuli, the colour of the clothes she was wearing, and Judith received a pearl.

"What a day this has been," said Arthur. "Let's get back to Taupo."

On the drive back, Arthur stopped the car. "That Rahitan has been talking to me nonstop. He is explaining about some golden scrolls buried in a stone-lined room deep under the hill where we met the Atema. He says they hold the wisdom of the universe and are sorely needed to be rediscovered and read at this time. They apparently had a profound effect on him and all his people, even though they considered themselves to be enlightened. He is suggesting we dig them out, but I am trying to explain to him that it would involve a huge amount of consultation with both the Pakeha and Maori responsible for this area, and that they could never agree to this excavation, let alone believe our reason for it, especially those who don't believe that The Wall is man-made. Rahitan finds it hard to understand that we are so goverened by rules and regulations made by unenlightened people, or why we just cannot bring a few people with spades and begin to dig. He is also talking about a greenstone statue holding a golden ball, made in the likeness of Aloma and imbued with the love of all his people. He would direct the excavators to the exact spot and also read the scrolls to us, as they are written in an ancient language that perhaps few on the planet can interpret. What a coup finding that would be for New Zealand. It would undoubtedly change the history of this land. The Maori would never go for it as they have a vested interest in maintaining they were the first inhabitants. Rahitan tells me that if they could only hear the wisdom of the golden scrolls their whole history would have to re-written. Can you see that happening?"

Garlita spoke through Lynda. "Those scrolls, of which there are twelve large and twelve small ones, for identification are each wound around a rod carved from a different coloured semi-precious stone. They were very ancient even when we found them. We initially knew they existed during our first gathering together as Atema, a very long time ago, and then forgotten about them until they were rediscovered, following a dream by Thieron, our scribe, towards the end of our last incarnation. We were just beginning to live by their teachings when our village was again destroyed."

"I have an idea," said Arthur. "Or rather Rahitan has an idea. If I would allow him to use me as his physical mouthpiece, he would teach this wisdom to those who wish to listen. The vibrational energy emanating from the scrolls would be diminished, but at least the ancient teachings could be shared with the people of New Zealand, and in other lands if there is an interest. He, along with Garlita using Lynda's body, think it is urgent that this wisdom is shared with the current population, who seem much more evolved and open to spiritual teachings than in past times. He has been informed by Aloma, that as she and Kaitewha travelled with Judith prior to Time Shift, they found that there is a great thirst for true teachings here. What do you say, Lynda? Can we become spiritual teachers and share what Rahitan and Garlita want us to reveal.?"

"As I am a school teacher, that should not be a problem. And with Rahitan's presence all Arthur needs to do is stand on the stage and open his mouth. The teachings should just pour out. But how will anyone know about us. How can we publicise ourselves?" Lynda sounded aprehensive.

"Leave that to me," smiled Judith. "We will talk to Vernon at the Tauhara Centre, let him hear what Rahitan and Garlita have to say, and let him do the publicity. The Centre has a large database and their followers are always open to enlightened teachers."

"Ah, Judith," said Arthur, "I never cease to be amazed at how the universe works. I will agree to this journey if Lynda does, and suggest any profits be given to Zuvuyaland for its continuing upkeep. What do you say, old girl?"

"Sounds like the work we have been preparing to do for the past year, but didn't know what it was. Yes, 'old man', let's do this." Lynda laughed at the way things fell into place.

A deep laugh came from Arthur's throat as Rahitan said, "Just wait until we get to the scroll with the rose quartz rods. You will never be the same again after hearing that. It had a very profound affect on Garlita and I, and indeed anyone else who read it, for it has a high vibration that changes one's belief system."

Arthur started the car again and drove directly to the Tauhara Centre, where Vernon greeted them. "How lovely to see you Judith. Who have we here. I suspect they carry information that will change us all."

"How did you know, Vernon? But then I am not surprised, as you are a very intuitive man. This is Arthur and Lynda who are incarnations of Rahitan and Garlita, the High Priest and Priestess of the Atema. They have agreed to be the mouthpieces of the ancient ones, to bring their knowledge and that of the golden scrolls into the light of present day consciousness. I am overjoyed, for we are in dire need of such teachings. As an incarnation of Aloma, I know how amazing they are." Judith laughed at Vernon's expression.

"Golden scrolls? What are the golden scrolls?" he stuttered.

"Oh, just something Rahitan mentioned they used to have. But they were all blown up during the last eruption." Seeing the effect that mere mention of golden scrolls had on someone as spiritual as Vernon, Judith decided they had better not mention their existence for the time being. An image of hundreds of people with shovels digging into the hill, flashed into her mind and she knew the scrolls could be found by seekers of monetary treasure and not spiritual treasure. Gold fever was a disease without a cure. As was rumour.

Arthur picked up on Judith's disquiet. "We have had a long day, Vernon, and need to get home. We will contact you tomorrow to begin sharing Rahitan's teachings and you can judge for yourself if anyone would be interested."

As she had arranged to stay at the Tauhara Centre, Judith bid goodnight and made her exit to ponder and write on the day's events. She didn't wish Vernon to question her on her slip of the tongue.

That night Judith had a dream. She dreamed of the man with whom Kaitewha would merge. Transported to a garden filled with large, bright flowers, she wandered around before entering a tent of filmy white curtains floating in a gentle breeze. A small fountain of tinkling water played softly in the centre. Carpets and cushions covered the floor. Music and perfume wafted in the air. She was joined by a being of light who looked into her eyes, into her very essence with intense love, then moved away. They stood across the tent from each other expanding their auras in and out, touching and merging then retracting, expanding and retracting until they filled the area with their merged auric fields, moving towards each other to intertwine energies, closer and closer until they were one essence, yet separate cores, then merged cores. Total union occurred between them, consummating the essence of love between twin souls. This was essence merging into essence to become one in love and a passion, an ecstasy she had never felt with an earthly lover. As they separated, a line extended from the two merged as one into her body lying asleep in the bed and another towards a man somewhere on earth, also in a sleeping physical body. Kaitewha was calling the aspect of himself to merge with the Aloma aspect of Judith. As she woke feeling blissed out, Judith wondered if indeed she would ever meet the physical man. Was the electro-magnetic force exuding from them both strong enough to connect continents away? Unless he knew his aspect of Kaitewha, would he be able to merge with her in true intimacy?

I fervently hope so, for I am tired of being alone. I wonder if that is Aloma or me feeling such longing. The ache deep in my heart is beginning to cause a physical pain. I had a check-up recently and the doctor said nothing could be more normal, so why does my chest feel so much pain? And the area around my shoulder blades and neck is so painful at times, I can hardly move. It is worse when I lie in bed. Any ideas, Aloma?

The Aloma aspect of Judith replied, *"It is the formation of your etheric wings, Judith, and the changing vibrations on this planet that are causing pain in your body. Ever since you underwent the Twenty-one day process of learning to live on light, your body has been undergoing massive alteration. It is a process we of the Atema all experienced shortly after joining the temple. We all lived on light and prana back then. This is my influence on your being as I really do not enjoy the experience of eating. I am sorry about the pain. It will pass. And I also miss Kaitewha so much that I am influencing your thoughts regarding calling a partner. I don't know where he is."*

Judith groaned and sat up in bed. "Aloma, does the fact that I do eat small amounts of food bother you? I have eaten no meat for many years but as I am still in a human body, enjoy the sensation of eating certain foods."

Aloma responded in Judith's mind. *"Not much. I can manage, but our vibrational level is affected when you eat foods containing sugar. There are many places we do not feel comfortable in, like large cities and negatively affected areas and sugar makes it worse."*

"I'll cut out the sugar," Judith promised.

Shortly after this experience Judith met a woman called Erina who asked her to accompany her on a drive to Northland to visit an old friend of her family. He had once run a caravan park where they spent many pleasant holidays. Now he was old, his wife had died and his family of six lived in Auckland. The Major, who everyone called him, was delighted to see them and remembered Erina fondly. During their conversation he said sadly, "My family think I am too old and sick to remain living here alone. I had a woman companion looking after me since my wife died two years ago, but she has just left and I am indeed alone. I have told my children they will have to carry me out in a box, for I will not leave this piece of paradise on earth."

Judith gasped as an idear formed in her mind. "Major John, I have been tasked with writing a book on ancient New Zealand and was looking for an ideal place. Would you consider me staying here as a caregiver for you until it is finished?"

The old man adjusted his body seated in a wheel-chair and beamed. "My dear, that would be absolutely splendid. When can you start?" Even after forty years in NZ his very English accent was strong.

"Well, I have nothing planned except for a trip up to Cape Reinga with Erina, so next week would suit. I will need to collect my computer and a few clothes from Erina's mother's place. Then I will return here. Thank you, this is perfect."

"My pleasure, Judith. Now would you be so kind as to make us a cup of tea," he requested, his face beaming. She hardly noticed that he wore an artificial right lower leg; the reason for him being wheel-chair bound.

"I have a nurse who comes daily to get me out of bed and dress me, so won't need any special care. Just a bit of companionship and a few meals. I don't eat much these days, but I do enjoy the odd glass of whiskey," he confessed.

As Judith and Erina drove away they decided to spend the night in KeriKeri where Erina believed her Maori grandmother had lived.

Although she was fair and blue-eyed, Erina's family had descended from a Maori princess who once lived in the area and had married an English kauri timber cutter who had become quite wealthy. A number of European immigrants had wished to marry daughters of Maori chieftains to obtain access to land and permission to farm and log timber. Erina mentioned that her mother once told of Maori women also wanting to marry white settlers, as apparently their native seed was weakening and they needed new blood to produce strong children.

In KeriKeri they happened on the annual meeting of local Maori women who remembered Erina's grandmother, and welcomed her profusely, telling her where to find her grandmother's grave, which the two women visited before finding a B&B in which to spend the night.

The following morning they set out to drive to Cape Reinga, where, according to mythology, the spirits of the dead travel to on their journey to the afterlife to leap off the headland and climb the roots of the 800-year-old pohutukawa tree and descend to the underworld to return to their traditional homeland of Hawaiki, using the Te Ara Wairua, the 'Spirits' pathway'. En route they visited the ancient cave where the spirits of dead Chiefs were prepared to enter the underworld. A lonely and desolate place, it was a fitting spot for such a journey.

Three days later Judith bought a used car, having decided that she needed transport if she was to live in such an out-of-the-way place for the next couple of months, and settled down in the Major's home to begin writing the story of the Atema. The spirit of Aloma and the other Atema were constantly guiding her thoughts as she typed, for she was convinced that the information flowing onto the screen could not have come from her own mind. A routine developed, for each morning Judith walked along the shore of the Bay of Islands, seeing the town of Russell just over the water, shimmering in the morning sun. After a small breakfast, she wrote for several hours before taking a longer walk to a headland overlookng the magnificent Bay. In the evening she and the Major ate a meal before he retired early. Once a week she would drive into Russell for supplies and to fetch a carton of cigars, a cask of red wine and a bottle of whiskey for the Major.

It is his choice, I am not going to say anything about his habits, for it keeps him happy and he never appears intoxicated. What an interesting old man, full of war stories and of his early pioneering days in this area, starting a dairy farm and then running a caravan park. I am truly pleased to spend time in his company. His family visit occasionally and they each have a bach around his house. He has had a hard but good life.

Three months later the book was finished and Judith told the Major she had to return to Australia. He tried to convince her to stay, but her life had to continue so she made plans to leave. The next morning after he arose, the Major informed her that his wife had come to visit him last night and taken him dancing with many of their old friends, who were now deceased. He looked very happy.

Oh! He is going to die. His wife has come to get him and he is so pleased to see her again. I had better be prepared.

The following morning the house was extremely quiet. Usually the sound of the Major's deep coughing woke Judith, but she could hear nothing. Cautiously, she walked along the corridor to his room and knocked. Hearing no sound, she gently pushed the door open but could see nothing, until she saw him slumped in his wheel-chair, head forward as if asleep.

"Major John, are you awake?" she called, walking into the room.

He made no movement as she put her fingers on his neck to locate a pulse. Nothing.

THE ATEMA

Farewell dear old man. Travel free and enjoy you next adventure without that old body. I will miss you.

Going to the phone, she rang his daughter and waited in the lounge until the nurse came to verify her diagnosis. Yes, he was indeed gone. Together they laid him on his bed and waited until the local doctor came. His death was the passing of an era, as a poineer of this area and a legend to those who knew him. His funeral, held in the historic church at Russell, was attended by hundreds of people all gathered to farewell a well-known pioneer of the area. Judith left the follwing day to return to Australia. She had heard from Arthur that Vernon was amazed by the teachings Rahitan gave and swiftly organised for a gathering to hear them. Aloma stayed in Taupo with Kaitewha and the remaining Atema.

A year later, Judith returned to New Zealand to live in Nelson for several months. The spinner wheel of Lake Taupo/Tongariro had expanded so much that a hill adorned with a Tesla device in Nelson, designated as the Centre of New Zealand, had become the pivot, with the spinner wheel now covering the whole of both Islands. There was work to do, stabilising and balancing it. New Zealand was fast coming into her role as the instigator of a new model for survival in a rapidly changing earth.

One evening she turned on the television she was amazed to see a programme segment on the Wall in the Kaimanawa Forest. Judith recognised a friend whom Lynda and Arthur had recently introduced to the site, an archaeologist turned writer and storyteller. Dozens of people tramped around the area and Department of Conservation officials totally disagreed with archaeologists being interviewed, who said it was a man made structure. The DOC people insisted it was a natural formation and a heated debate raged. Judith watched in disbelief as various so-called experts gave their opinion. She knew it was not a natural structure. Even if she had not experienced the meeting with the Atema, she had visited numerous archaeological sites in several countries. The cyclopean blocks of perfectly hewn stone resembled those used to build ancient monuments in Peru, Greece, Israel and Egypt. Let the learned men show their ignorance of other dimensional worlds or a desire for truth. So what if the history of this land had to be re-written to encompass a far greater story than that of the last two waves of invaders. Was truth at any cost not more important than fixed belief systems. Obviously, Arthur had not mentioned the existence of the golden scrolls or the outcome may have been very different. There would come a time when the scrolls and the statue of the Princess could be revealed, and as Rahitan had mentioned, they were probably still in another dimension for safe-keeping and no amount of digging would expose them. For now, let the Wall lie in peace until a proper archaeological excavation could be conducted and then the scrolls may allow themselves to be found.

The truth is be revealed when the time is right, thought Judith. *This debate will come to the only conclusion possible in the fullness of time. That maverick archaeologist from America has some credibility, but he upsets the egos of the local people. It is not my role to become involved in this debate. Aloma, Kaitewha and I well get on with our part of the story. Lynda and Arthur are doing their roles extremely well, as is Barry, the storyteller. In another few years this land will be ready to stand tall and announce to the world that she is a chemical free country, producing bio-dynamic crops and animals for export to a chemically poisoned world. I hope her government and people have the courage to follow such a path. Her woman Prime Minister really has her finger on the pulse of New Zealand. It is already nuclear free and will not permit nuclear fuelled, atomic weapon carrying warships to visit her ports. The only thing likely to sabotage her future role is the growing disharmony between the two dominant races living here. The 'dangerous superiority of a once suppressed race' syndrome is beginning to emerge and may delay the process. We will have to be vigilant. However, the creator gods are watching us and will not allow the tribal consciousness to prevail at the expense of true freedom. By the 21st century New Zealand will be on track and the Divine*

Feminine once again will walk in harmony throughout the land, in equal partnership with the divinity in the male of the species. Already many inventions to assist humankind have originated in the fertile minds of her inhabitants, and there are many more to come. Now the only thing for me to achieve here is for Kaitewha to find me. Where are you Kaitewha?

How that manifests waits to be seen.

EPILOGUE

There has been a resurgence of activity at Zuvuyaland over the last few years.

In 2008, just before Vivien returned to the Hawkes Bay to live, she gifted Zuvuyaland to the Tauhara Centre in Taupo. During this time they had Woofers and local volunteers regularly doing physical work there, keeping paths open and areas like the waterfall and spiral weeded. The local man who mowed Tauhara's lawns had been mowing the entryway and spiral at Zuvuyaland for Vivien and continued for Tauhara. Vivien 'passed on' in 2011 and her remaining trustees took over liasing with Tauhara Centre. After a few years Tauhara decided to hand the role of caretaker back to the Zuvuyaland trustees. So, the then two remaining Trustees from Vivien's core group, continued to hold Zuvuyaland with great love and integrity to the vision. Since then the only physical work that was done was by a handful of locals, along with the trustees, (and sometimes their husbands) about twice a year.

Over some of that time a woman neighbour, who had developed her abilities to feel land energies with Richard James, the dowser who worked on the ley lines and pilgrimage in preparation for Time Shift, lived next to Zuvuyaland and had daily walks there. One year she and another neighbour did an enormous amount of physical work clearing big areas of a vine that was smothering many trees and blackberry which had grown rampant. The following year they ran a monthly working bee hoping to continue the work but unfortunately there was little response. Then about two years ago she moved to the Bay of Plenty. The present owner of Vivien's house has also contributed immensely with the physical care of the parkland.

Before Vivien left, she had paid for the installation of a solar powered water pump to keep the flow-form waterfall flowing. Unfortunately it frequently broke down and we found out that it was going to cost thousands of dollars to fix it, so it remained a dry fall for five years or so. Then, about two years ago a local woman, who had helped organise the annual Reiki retreat at Tauhara for about twenty-five years, visited Vernon and I and said she had someone who would like to pay for the refurbishment of the waterfall. And so it was done. She also has loved working physically on the land and has contributed enormously. Also, around the same time, another 'Zuvuyaland Earth Angel', who lives just a few properties along, made contact with us. For the several years he had lived in the area and loved Zuvuyaland and since he made contact with us he also has done an enormous amount of work there. Their enthusiasm and help has lifted the sense of 'burden' from the shoulders of the Trustees and Vernon and I, (after all, we were a very small group of ageing persons between sixty and eighty years !!) With regular working bees over the past couple of years, a tree management program in place, an updated notice board and a new website and ongoing cash donations from 'unknown' visitors to the land, Zuvuyaland is flourishing, as you can see from the photos on the website.

So, what happens at Zuvuyaland other than physical working bees?

One thing that's been a regular happening over the last ten years is that our local Steiner Kindergarten has come to Zuvuyaland for their Spring Festival and four years ago, for two years, they brought the children for a weekly visit to have a 'Bush Kindy' morning. It was lovely knowing the children's beautiful energy was there. Unfortunately the cost of transporting them out from town went up in price and they have stopped that now...but the Spring Festivals continue. Some of the families come to our working bees too.

There is a particular group who work with connecting significant land energy spots in New Zealand and around the world, with cosmic connections. Gill and James Goodison, who lead this group, had done work with Richard James a while back.

Below is the introduction of the work they do....

....."The School of Planetary and Divine Union has been in existence since 2006. It's a School without Walls, comprised of meditators in Aotearoa, who are deeply attuned to planetary matters. Those who have walked before us have made a lasting impact. We are continuing a Mystery School tradition. Our School is named Te Ranga Haurua Uenuku. "The Place where the Inner and Outer Rainbow are Woven". The name is literal. Sounds interweave and produce form. We re-build the planet through sounding rhythmically with Great Beings at the right time."

We introduced the group to Zuvuyaland about two years ago and it is now one of the important points for their work. One of the group lives in Taupo and through her, we now have a regular 'Full Moon meditation' there, in the spiral and with 'the White Lady'. 'The White Lady' is a great Earth keeper crystal, which Vivien bought for Zuvuyaland, and it is now placed beside the 'Christ Energy' site, a place not too public, so she is available to 'those who know' to visit. We are aware that there are 'others' who do esoteric work at Zuvuyaland (mostly through synchronistic meetings) and this brings joy to my heart.

So, as of March 2020, Zuvuyaland is 'singing' as it is 'held' in the hearts' of, not only, the now four trustees, but many locals and visitors from NZ and around the world. The 'Shining Ones' call us and heal us, in places such as Zuvuyaland, helping us to bring in 'the

New Age of Love and Joy' that Vivien (who is referred to as Veronica in the novel) often talked about.

We are truly blessed to be part of its Being and always feel the privilege of helping in any way we can. I love ringing our crystal singing bowl and playing my Mayan temple flute there whenever I visit. And I love telling the Spring Story to the children each year. For those who wish to visit Zuvuyaland please check the website.

https://www.zuvuyaland.org
Wishing you much Love and Many Blessings,
April Smith, Taupo, New Zealand. 2020

At the beginning of 2020, the world was awakened and changed by a virus called Covid-19, that forced humanity to rethink priorities and lifestyles, and ways of working and communicating. Collectively humanity was lifted into another dimension of Earth's radiant being and asked to regain some of the attributes of The Atema. Those who awoke to this call lived and thrived, although much hardship accompanied this transition for others, and many chose to leave their body at this time for they could not pass through the veil of awakening. After two thousand years, The Atema, and other Enlightened Ones, are again awakening and gathering in New Zealand and around the earth to assist in teaching a greater awareness of living and loving.

Archaeologists are finding evidence dotted around the Earth, of very ancient advanced civilizations that were catastrophically destroyed at the ending of the last Ice Age, around twelve thousand years ago, when a meteor slammed into North America, causing the thick ice cover to melt very quickly, and great floods to cover the earth. Many legends tell of a flood that destroyed their homelands and of enlightened beings who appeared to assist in the rebuilding of their devastated homelands.

This novel is factitious, mostly fantasy but the last chapters actually occurred in New Zealand in 1992. Those involved in Time Shift got on with our lives, but were changed in consciousness and continue to work for the upliftment of Earth and her Beings. It is up to the reader to sort out fact from fiction. New Zealand continues to thrive.

Robyn Adams
2020
http://www.auraliarose.net

Printed in the United States
By Bookmasters